CROWN

OF

SORROWS

R.E. PALMER

FrontRunner Publications

Copyright © 2024 R.E. Palmer

All rights reserved.

ISBN: 978-1-8383995-4-2
www.FrontRunnerBooks.com

Cover art by Kentaro Kanamoto
www.kentarokanamoto.com

DEDICATION

For Bern, Tim & Neve

…Pip and Smudge

ACKNOWLEDGMENTS

Another huge thanks to Erin Kahn, Amanda Brand, Gizmo Beardon and Janet Allmey who once more took on the unenviable task of wading through my first drafts.

Your feedback is most valuable. One more book in the series to go… I promise :0)

A large version of this map is available to download and print at www.frontrunnerbooks.com/map.html

THE LOST REALMS
ELESSYN SEA
KARAJAN SEA
PERRAN
PYMOOR
RHYDOR
RANMOOR
KERNRIM
PERRAN HILLS
MERYN
KRAN RIVER
KOLOSSOS MOUNTAINS
VORTIMOR
VYMARL
KRAN
TALLABAR
PYNMAR
SAPHIRR
EMRYST
EPHRIM
SALAHA
STOWE
GWELAYNOW
KIRIK
TELAMIR
KALMIR
RIVER ALYS
CASTER
VINLAYN
CAPRAY
HAMM
CASTEL DOR
NEVERDOR
FORANFAE FOREST
RAVENHILL
SEARITH
PORTLEA
RIVER LOR
TAMARAND FARRAND
RAVENSLYE
MUND
HURST
SYRIS
HOLM
CAERMUND
LOROMAR
ABERNOST
CARAMUND
WEST HAVEN
ARCHONHOLM
SINON RIVER
TRAITOR'S ISLAND
CAERWAL GATE
CAERWAL MOUNTAINS
MUNDRAKE'S ISLE
N

1. The Road to Borrund

Elodi could not take her eyes off the storm clouds looming behind the treetops of the North Forest. While they had retreated from the skies over Roth's Doom, the snowstorms had not abated in the north. She glanced to the trees, then back to the gloom above to check they had not moved, fearing they would roll back over Ormsk to avenge their master's defeat. She turned to Toryn riding beside her and noticed his attention also laid to the north. 'Scouts report much of Lunn lies beneath thick snow and the marshes of Lumreek are frozen.'

Toryn shivered. 'Then it seems the warlocks are keen to keep a Norgog presence in the region.' He nodded to the mud-clogged road. 'It may have thawed quickly, but this will soon freeze over if those icy gales resume.'

Elodi twisted to look over her shoulder. 'And if the warlocks yet maintain their hold over the elements, it suggests the Amayans have failed to avenge Amyra.' She slumped back into her saddle. 'While many in the realms will rejoice as news of our… victory travels south, you and I know this does not end here.' She glanced behind and lowered her voice. 'I'm exhausted, Toryn. My body cries out for rest, and my eyes yearn to look upon Calerdorn's towers once more.' Her jaw clenched. 'Is it too much to ask that I wake after a long, restful night's sleep and not find an aide standing beside my bed bearing bad news? I want to look those under my command in the eye and not dread them dying in their hundreds from the decisions I have to make.' She let out a long sigh. 'I want to breathe air not tainted by the stench of death. I just want to…' Elodi looked away as a tear ran down her cheek.

Toryn leaned over and took her hand. 'You, above all others have earned a rest, Elodi. Borrund is not far. And no one would deny you a few days peace and quiet.'

Elodi's eyes flashed. 'A few days! I need a whole…' Her shoulders sagged. 'I'm sorry. I did not mean to snap.'

He tried to smile. 'I can't blame you. A few days? It's me who should apologize. That may have come across as a little… insensitive.'

Elodi peered ahead, hoping to see Borrund's famed bell tower, but many leagues still lay between them and a warm bed. She yawned. 'If I had a whole month, I still don't know if I would have the strength to face the slaughter of another battle. When I opened my eyes this morning…' she stifled a sob, 'do you know what my first thought was? As I looked at the raindrops running down the roof of my tent, I wished I could've rolled over and not wake until this was all over.' Toryn went to speak, but Elodi held up her hand. 'The thought of facing another day was torture. It took all my effort to throw off my blanket and pick up my sword.' She jabbed her finger to the north. 'And look. They mock us still. They taunt us. And would death bring relief? If they command the elements, do they command the afterlife? But… no, I don't think they would grant us the release of death.' Her hands clenched the reins. 'I doubt it, Toryn. They'll have other plans for the likes of you and I, should they take us alive.'

Elodi rode on in silence but continued to observe the clouds in the north. But when she looked down at the muddy road, all she could see was Aldorman lying face down in the grime of the battle. Sadly, he was not alone. Elodi muttered to herself. 'So many dead… so many fine people lost in the mud.'

After several minutes of listening to the horses' hooves slushing through the thaw, Toryn broke the silence. 'I know how you feel, Elodi, but we cannot let our enemy get into our heads. We now have twice the number of Amayans on our side. Nyomae learns more of Draegelan's ways, and you have just halved the dark ranks able to ride against us. Surely, we can take some hope from that. Not all goes against us.'

Elodi whispered. 'I wish I had your confidence, Toryn.' She thumbed over her shoulder. 'But we don't know if the Amayans have survived, Nyomae lies in a deep sleep, and I'm certain our enemy can rebuild their armies faster than we ever could.' She eyed the North Forest as the Borrund Road turned and came within a few hundred paces of its border. The cobwebs fluttered in the breeze, blowing out like tattered curtains by an open window. She shuddered. 'I hope the Nym remain true to their word and rid that place of the spiders. I don't have the heart to send in another force to destroy the nests.'

Toryn's skin crawled at the sight of the webs still clinging to the trees. He straightened. 'Yet you wouldn't find any who'd refuse should you ask. You are held in high esteem, Elodi. You've earned their respect and trust. But I trust the Nym will keep their promise. They saw the harm the aralaks inflicted upon the forest. They won't tolerate them over-running the place.'

Elodi looked back to the line of wagons bearing the badly injured, and trailing behind them, the sorry sight of the walking wounded. 'I do hope so.' She winced. 'We're terribly exposed strung out along this road. Imagine the casualties even a dozen of those vile creatures would wreak upon us. Our lines must look very tempting to a hungry spider. To them, we're a good source of food, food that has little strength to fight back.' She patted Sea Mist's neck. 'And I doubt even Misty has the legs to outrun a ravenous aralak. Our horses are in desperate need of warm stalls and nourishment.'

Toryn nodded at Shepra trotting alongside his horse.

'The same for my faithful hound here. She's had her fair share of spiders' poison. It's a wonder she survived, but how much more of those foul fluids could she take? She's saved my life at least twice.'

'At least?'

'Amyndra told me Shepra fought bravely at Roth's Doom. I wasn't aware of her for most of the time, but she had my back. It looks as if' — Shepra whimpered — 'ah, she's limping.' Toryn slid from his saddle, lifted the dog, and placed her on his horse. He climbed up behind and lifted her paw. 'She's wounded.' He stroked her back. 'You must forgive me, lass. I hadn't noticed.'

Elodi reached across and patted Shepra. 'The poor thing has suffered in silence.' She winced as she examined the injured paw. 'She deserves the attention of a healer as much as any soldier.'

'Then I hope Borrund's healers are both plentiful and skilled.' He glanced to the wagons.

Elodi noted his concern. 'Elrik is strong. A blacksmith I believe. I'm sure he and Lorek will soon recover.'

'I do hope so. They've proved to be excellent fighters. But too many would struggle to wield a weapon any time soon. It's going to take at least—' Toryn clutched his stomach. 'Something's... changed.' He twisted in his saddle to look about them.

Elodi went for her sword. 'Are we under attack?'

'No... it's not that. It's difficult to say... this is going to sound a little strange, but I can't feel the mountains.'

'Pardon? You mean you can usually *feel* them?'

Toryn frowned. 'I suppose so... yes. It wasn't until just now that I realized I can. They've always been there. The Kolossos are the backbone of this land. Although I could barely see the top of Caranach from my village, they seemed ever-present. And even later when in Archonholm, I could still sense them.' He turned to the west. 'But just now, it felt like they had gone. I feel empty… yes, that's the word.'

Elodi reached over and placed her hand on his forehead. 'Are you… feeling alright? You could be coming down with a fever.'

'I'm as good as can be expected.' He continued to check the grasslands. 'Do you feel anything? Something odd… different perhaps?'

She let out a long sigh. 'I've felt something different for weeks. But at this moment, I'm exhausted. I'm not certain I'd notice Ormoroth if he crept up behind us.'

Toryn's hand rested on his bow. 'I hope it's not a forewarning of an attack. We're in no state to meet even a small force.'

Elodi's eyes wandered back to the forest. 'Then we'll all welcome the sight of Borrund's sturdy barricade.'

Bardon returned from his inspection of the wagons. 'Then you won't have to wait long, Elodi. We should see Borrund's solitary tower once we crest this ridge.'

Elodi sat straighter, looking like the victor at Roth's Doom as the people now perceived her. She attempted to smile. 'Aside from knowing it's the largest city in the realms constructed entirely from wood, I'm ashamed to admit my knowledge of Borrund is somewhat lacking. I'm afraid my attention waned once my tutors moved on from heroes and the great battles, and onto more mundane subjects. Although, I seem to recall Borrund wasn't always the principal city of Ormsk.'

Bardon laughed. 'Then not all your tutors' time was wasted. Centuries ago, the city of Borrusk was the home of the Ormsk Council. Borrusk was situated forty leagues to the east when the river was almost thrice the length. It now sits beneath the waters of the Borr Estuary.' He chastised Elodi with a grin. 'I'm surprised the story of the Flood of the Great Sorrow didn't get your attention, young lady. It's quite a dramatic tale.'

Elodi stroked Sea Mist. 'One to take my mind from our current woes perhaps?'

Toryn straightened. 'Oh, most certainly if it's the story I know, then yes.' He grimaced as he eyed the sludge. 'But it does involve floods.'

Bardon smirked. 'It appears the education in Toryn's backwater surpassed that of the best scholars of Calerdorn. It's a story worthy of a warm fireside, but I imagine we'll have more important issues to discuss on our arrival. I shall try to do it justice from my saddle.' He took a breath. 'Legend has it that a storm to end all storms blew for a week and a day.'

Elodi scoffed. 'Well, if only that part was true. I think the storm over Roth's Doom… and not to mention the one that struck the *Celestra* at sea, would run yours a close second.'

Bardon glared from beneath his bushy eyebrows. 'Now, Elodi. Let me finish.' He grinned. 'Now I know how your tutors must have felt. But… back to the tale. It was said the storm was so violent, it stopped the spinning of the dome, thus the night seemed never-ending. Yet that was not the worst of it. The seas rose and swallowed the lands to the east, and Borrusk with it. And, unlike our enemy, the sea holds onto its gain.'

Elodi felt her face redden. 'Now I see I should have been more attentive. Did Ormoroth raise the storm? It must have been catastrophic.'

'No one knows for sure. But some believe it was the rage of the gods as they mourned the loss of their daughters.' He chuckled. 'But the storm was a mere thousand years ago. If the gods still grieved after all those years, perhaps they should have come to their daughters' aid sooner. Other accounts talk of the land shaking due to the Evil One's efforts to free himself from his vault.

Whatever the cause, it certainly was catastrophic. The three islands of Gwend Bay were once part of the mainland and formed the coastline. Countless towns and villages lie under the waves. I believe some of their spires can still be seen at low tides.'

They reached the top of the ridge. Below, the roof of Borrund's bell tower held its head above the mist still clinging to the lowlands. Bardon raised his hand and grinned. 'Behold. The great timber city of Borrund… or at least its tower. You'll have to believe me when I say the rest of the town is quite a sight.'

Elodi felt the tension in her shoulders ease. 'And mercifully not too far.' The sun climbed as they rode down the slope, and soon the mists retreated to reveal the whole town.

Toryn used his *farsight*. 'Those walls certainly look sturdy and tall enough to keep the spiders out.'

Bardon squinted. 'Your *farsight* would be most useful to an ailing old man like me. But yes, the barricade is well-made, constructed of whole trunks from the tallest and stoutest trees in the region. It's said they're as strong as a stone wall, and will not burn thanks to a treatment prepared by the finest alchemists of Ormsk. But not even on pain of death would they reveal the ingredients of their concoction.'

But Elodi shuddered. 'That may be so, but could they resist an attack by those Reapers? By the Three, Bardon, did you ever think we'd see such terror in our lands?'

Bardon's jaw tightened. 'It was no mean feat to summon them. But if we're lucky, it would be a long time before our enemy has the strength to call back those beasts. Especially as they left empty-handed. No, I hope I never see them again in my lifetime.' He looked to Toryn. 'But I imagine those creatures may feel the same of Lady Harlyn.' He beamed. 'Riding straight at them was a sight to behold. I doubt they expected to be challenged in such a fashion.'

Toryn nodded. 'As I rode with the Amayans to the battlefield, we feared we'd be too late when we saw the Reapers rise up from the ground. Now I wish I could have sat beside you to see Elodi and Sea Mist ride against them.'

Elodi shuddered. 'Perhaps you could refrain from all this praise, gentlemen. At this time, I would rather forget the battle.'

Bardon sighed. 'I will grant you that wish. But tales of your victory travel ahead of us and will already be doing the rounds in Borrund.'

'Our victory is in the past. We must turn our minds to the present.' She pointed to the city. Please enlighten me, Bardon. I appreciate Ormsk has the best trees in the realms, but why build a large city from wood and not stone?'

'Ah, now that's due to the pragmatic nature of the people. Borrusk was made of stone and that was lost in the flood. They reasoned if the seas could rise once, they may rise again, not satisfied with its spoils, thus wreak more devastation. The builders of Borrund believed if made of wood, it could be dismantled, transported, and rebuilt farther inland if necessary. Hence the tall bell tower. A constant watch is kept. Beacons are maintained along the river and out to the coast. Should the waters rise again, the beacons will be lit, and the bells would peel. It is said every man, woman and child in the city knows what's required of them should the bell toll.'

Toryn stared. 'The whole city? Surely not.' He grinned. 'I wonder if anyone has been tempted to light the beacons to test their response.'

'Only if they wish to suffer a slow and painful death.' Bardon frowned at Toryn. 'The Borrund folk take the threat seriously. I'd say they're more concerned about a second flood than a breach of the Caerwal Gate. They're a practical, if stubborn folk.'

Elodi agreed. 'Pragmatic indeed.' She glanced up to the ridge as it stretched out to their left. 'But why not build their city on top of that? Surely, there's not enough water in the Karajan Sea to reach a town up there.'

'Ah. I'm afraid that's due to my ancestors. Lunn and Ormsk have a long history of being at each other's throats.' Bardon pointed. 'Borrund is situated by the river for easy trade with the south, and, with the added advantage of a quick evacuation if besieged. As I said, Borrundians are a practical folk, if not always the most welcoming.'

Elodi looked upon the imposing city. 'Perhaps the realms would be in a better position if more had taken such precautions. When all this is over, we should—'

'Spiders!' Elodi twisted in her saddle. A dozen aralaks scuttled over the top of the ridge. She groaned. 'The wounded. They go after our weak.' Without a thought, she turned Sea Mist. Toryn drew his bow and followed as they sped back along their lines. Luckily, a detachment of First Horse were closer, and true to their motto, they were ready. They lowered their lances and charged, skewering three spiders as they crouched, ready to spit their poison. Toryn's first arrow found the eyes of the fourth, but others pounced to claim their victims. Elodi's heart lurched as a wounded knight cried out as pincers tore into his flesh and snatched him from a wagon. She drove on Sea Mist and slashed down at the soft body as the aralak spun about and tried to escape. The Amayan blade opened its trailing abdomen. It stuttered as its legs folded beneath. Elodi leaped from her horse and severed its head. The knight rolled to the ground and groaned his thanks. Elodi turned to see Toryn and the First Horse make short work of killing the remainder. She kneeled beside the injured knight as a tired healer arrived. She caught Elodi's eye as she tended to her patient, and Elodi could see the healer also carried an injury.

A woman screamed. 'My brother!' Toryn twisted in his saddle to see a large spider had waited and then sprang as the wounded were left defenseless. The creature had snatched a young, injured soldier from a wagon, and now skurried along the road. Toryn spurred on his horse and nocked an arrow. The spider swerved and clambered up the slope. Toryn followed, but it was too steep for his tired horse to catch the aralak. He halted and took aim. But this spider was cunning. It slung the young man onto its back and held him in place with one leg. Toryn cursed. The angle meant the soldier protected the spider's head; an arrow to the abdomen would not be enough to stop it escaping with its prey. Toryn thought quickly… and came to the only conclusion. He let fly just as the spider reached the crest. He looked away, once satisfied his aim was true, saving the young man from a dreadful ordeal. Toryn closed his eyes hoping the soldier's soul would find peace in another realm.

He rode slowly back to Elodi and the agony of the soldier's sister. He shook his head as Elodi approached. 'There was nothing I could do. I had no other—'

'I know, Toryn. It can't have been an easy choice, but you saved him from an unthinkable end. And as painful as it is for his sister, she'll come to acknowledge you made the right decision.' Elodi looked on with pity as the woman slumped to the ground and sobbed. 'We live in such times. We are all touched by evil. None will be spared the burden we are forced to bear.' She dismounted and wiped her blade on the grass. 'These foul creatures cannot be allowed to breed.' She prodded a dead spider with her foot. 'These are young judging by their size. Imagine the horrors fully-grown beasts could inflict on this region.'

Bardon approached and climbed down from his horse. 'I think you'll find the people in these parts are much like those of Dorlgoth. They're tough and have endured much hardship. But yes… the last thing we need is a colony of these creatures running amok.'

Elodi turned to Borrund. 'Our first task on reaching the town must be to train those who can hold a spear on how to rid Ormsk of the threat.' She checked behind, concerned more would appear from the top of the ridge. 'We can't get to Borrund quick enough.'

Borrund seemed farther than it had first looked, and despite the dread of another attack, the pace of the exhausted soldiers and horses slowed. The sun had begun its descent down the west side of the dome before they reached the head of the Borr River. From here, the road widened as it covered the last league to the town. But Elodi could not relax as she constantly searched for signs of movement in the reed beds bordering the road. She looked longingly ahead to the solid barricade. When she spoke, she found she whispered. 'It was good of Glambul to offer the services of his healers.' On seeing Bardon struggling to hear, Elodi raised her voice while maintaining her watch. 'Nyomae appears to be comfortable, but I'll be happier once a warm bed and shelter can be found for her. And I fear Captain Gundrul's condition worsens.' She sighed. 'We've been through so much since I first met him onboard the Celestra. He was like a father to the young and inexperienced guards under his command. I dearly hope he pulls through, but the healer says she cannot prevent him from shivering. He sleeps uneasily as if troubled. And if I'm not mistaken, even Ruan's stoney face could not conceal his concern.'

Bardon glanced to Toryn. 'Then I pray his dogged strength sees him through. But I feel there is something you both should know about our host. I've learned over the years that when Glambul offers anything, it's not out of kindness. He's a wily old fox. He'll have his own reasons to throw open his gates.'

Elodi frowned. 'I note Glambul has the title of Lord Ormsk. Why is it only in Broon each ward has its own lord?'

'Ah, Elodi, you did learn a little more of the realms other than the major battles and acts of heroism and treachery. I'll do my best to explain the unique situation of Broon before we arrive. It may help to prevent a…' he looked to Toryn, 'shall we say, a diplomatic blunder.'

Toryn nodded. 'Point taken, lord.'

Bardon raised an eyebrow. 'Good. Then I shall begin.' He spoke as if reading from a book. 'Lunn and Ormsk were the last wards to be united and brought into the Seven Realms. But I'm afraid the old disputes were not easily settled. The people of the two wards were… still are, fiercely proud of their lands, so both yet retain their independence. The title of Lord Broon was established purely to satisfy Draegelan who would not tolerate division for obvious reasons. Our enemy has always been only too ready to sow their seeds of disquiet. So, to this day, both Lunn and Ormsk have their own leaders, my main responsibility as Lord Broon was to prevent minor disputes escalating to open warfare. But it's not an easy task. To succeed at the trials for lordship, required skills in diplomacy in the same measure as skill with a weapon. But that was all thrown out of the window to allow Nordryn to take my position.'

Elodi jumped as the reeds rustled. But to her relief, it was just the breeze. 'That must make for a complicated arrangement in Keld, does it not?'

'That it does. Two lords sit in the old stone city. But in Ormsk, and especially Borrund, I have little say in their matters. Fortunately, in times of trouble, the two wards usually cooperate, and the military are at least loyal to the overall leader. But I hear Nordryn imprisoned Lord Lunn when he declared his loyalty to Nordruuk.'

'Amyndra alluded to this when I first met her at Archonholm.' Elodi's nerves eased as the main gate came into view. 'I trust she arrived safely and has appraised the healers of our needs.' She turned back to Bardon. 'But I had not realized the wards remained so divided. What can you tell us of Lord Ormsk?'

Bardon rubbed his shoulders. 'He's an honourable, but difficult chap, a stickler for correct procedure. There's a saying in Lunn that sums up the man perfectly, if a little unkind. Let me see… ah yes, he's as tough as the timber of Ormsk, but not as bendable. It's something along those lines. I can't remember exactly but I'm sure you get the idea. Let's just say he's never been known to change his mind.'

Toryn scoffed. 'He'd have got on well with the Castellan.'

The old lord grinned. 'I'm sure he would have, but I doubt he's ever stepped foot outside of Ormsk. The matters of the wider world do not concern him until they arrive on his doorstep.' He held out his hands. 'As we bring him now. But it's not just him. It's a trait of the folk of the region. They say there are two types of people here. The first are those who never walk more than a day from their place of birth. The second are those who go farther, and once they've seen the world beyond their fences, never return.'

Toryn laughed. 'I heard something similar from a miner of Drunsberg. But that was about the people of Lunn. Perhaps they're not as different as they'd like to think.'

Elodi groaned. 'They certainly do sound like the people of Dorlgoth, although they tend to be of the first sort. Or rather they were until their fabled son returned and led them to the slaughter on the Dorn Plain. And I'm still unsure of what happened to the remainder, aside from that poor girl, Meloni. I hope she'll be free of Dorlan's spell with his passing. But now she lives in a city occupied by Ruuk.'

Toryn stood in his saddle. 'A rider approaches.'

Bardon peered ahead. 'I'll take your word for it, Toryn.' He looked to Elodi. 'Don't expect Glambul to be grateful for expelling the enemy from his lands. Knowing the old fox, he'll be unhappy because you chose his ward to make your stand. And he won't be best pleased to see I survived, even if that means I can unseat Nordryn.'

Elodi gasped. 'Surely, he can't prefer to see that traitor sitting in Lunn?'

'He'd prefer if neither of us held the title. He holds me responsible for the loss of the Archon's payment of gold for the timber. While it did go to Keld's vaults first, I tried to ensure it was spent for the benefit of both wards. But, as Glambul is so keen to point out, if the wagons had taken the gold to him, Nordryn would not have got his filthy hands on it.' Bardon sighed. 'As much as I look forward to eating a hot meal and sitting beside a fire, I would rather it was not in his city.'

Elodi held up her hand to greet the rider. She lowered her voice to speak to Bardon. 'I can see this may be a difficult relationship to build. But then I don't envisage staying long.' She turned to the wagons bearing the sick. 'And I hope the same can be said for Gundrul and Nyomae.'

2. Speak His Name

Nyomae dropped to her knees and wept. The driving rain stung her face and dashed her tears away. Before her, Elodi and Toryn lay half-buried in the slush of the battlefield. Not afforded a decent burial, the once noble Amayan warrior, and the brave young man of Midwyche lay where they fell. Nyomae's strength deserted her as the brutal nature of her dear friends' deaths became apparent. Elodi's mouth still gaped, filled with mud, forcing her jaws wide, freezing her face in the moment of her appalling demise. The Amayan's glassy eyes stared at the skies through dried blood and matted red hair as if pleading with the gods to save her. But they had not come. The gods had not come to save their daughters until too late; they were not about to answer the call of a mere mortal.

Nyomae's heart broke as she witnessed the final act of Elodi's short life through her eyes. The great Dorlan, knight of the Ul-dalak, servant of the Dark Verses, bore down on her. But her attempt to deflect his heavy blade failed and it had cleaved her skull. Sadly, her ordeal had not ended with her death. To her horror, the Ruuk had stripped and defiled Elodi's corpse, then left her to rot in the dank mud.

Beside Elodi's shattered body, Toryn lay with his arm outstretched in what looked like a desperate attempt to save her. Nyomae could barely watch as she saw his last moments. Aghast by the death of Elodi, his strength had deserted him, and his attack faltered. And Dorlan had made him pay. As Toryn fended off a Norgog's hammer blow, Dorlan had driven his blade deep into Toryn's back. He had staggered through the slush with blood spouting from his gaping mouth, desperate to stop the Ruuk sullying Elodi's prone body. Dorlan laughed, goading Toryn as his feet became stuck and he sank to his knees. But Dorlan stayed his hand, allowing Toryn to bear witness to Elodi's final humiliation. Only then did the dark knight stride forward and deliver the fatal blow that sent Toryn sprawling into the mire. Nyomae gasped; he had not died from Dorlan's strike — Toryn had drowned in his tears.

Nyomae lifted his cold hand and placed it into Elodi's. She wiped the hair from Elodi's face, gently closed her glassy eyes, then cleaned the mud from her mouth. She looked about the many bodies lying where they had died and found a cloak. It was not befitting for an Amayan to be seen in such a state. Nyomae placed the cloak over Elodi's nakedness, then turned to Toryn. His broken and twisted back could not be straightened in death, but she arranged his limbs out of their cruel contortions to grant the brave warrior at least a semblance of the dignity he deserved.

Nyomae stood and surveyed the battlefield. The silence belied the carnage. Thousands had fallen. But they would never be given an honorable burial. The victors would leave them to decay... along with the memory of their once free realms. Nyomae slumped. She had failed. Dorlan had led the charge and mowed down all who dared stand in his way. Bardon, Aldorman, Ruan, and Gundrul had all fallen at Roth's Doom. Such brave and gracious warriors trampled into the ground by the boots of brutal fighters who knew nothing of honor. But perhaps they were at least free from the cruel world, free to roam wherever their souls had gone.

The rain grew heavy, hammering down on the dented armor as if mocking its failure to save those they were meant to protect. But this was not a cleansing rain, or tears of sorrow for the many who had lost their lives. This was a punishing torrent of sleet, brought in from the north to pour shame on those who had failed to defend their realms. Nyomae tasted the fetid water on her lips. What poison did this rain bring? How much more punishment could the land endure?

Nyomae turned from the battlefield, but not from the horror. At the rear, a long, gray line of conquered soldiers stood chained together by their ankles. They were the unfortunate who would live to see the hurt soon to be inflicted on their beloved folk and lands. They were to be drafted into the dark ranks of the Ul-dalak. Jubilant Ruuk and Norgog taunted the vanquished. Those who dared raise their heads were beaten until their gaze dropped to their fallen comrades in the grime. Nyomae walked among the living and the dead, but no eyes of friend or foe looked upon her. Had she too departed from the mortal lands?

The puddles sparkled. Nyomae looked up to see a clear sky, but it was a cold, harsh blue that failed to ease her grief. The storm clouds had moved on to take its misery to the warm skies of the south. The enemy had gone, satisfied they had taken everything from the dead. Like the clouds, they had moved on to find fresh victims and the promised spoils of the poorly defended farms, villages, and cities of the south.

Nyomae groaned. Elodi and Toryn had gone. She could not grant them the burial they so rightly deserved. But what did the enemy want with them? Nyomae sank to her knees, appalled by their wicked ploy. They would raise Elodi and Toryn from the dead; thus, they would be forced to fight against her. Nothing could save them now. The realms were lost.

A voice echoed in her head. *Speak his name, Imaari. Speak his name and it will be done.*

3. The Restless Sea

Toryn remained to be convinced the city of Borrund could be dismantled and moved out of the way of floodwaters. Close to three thousand people lived beneath the sloping timber roofs that overhung the roads that crisscrossed the town. He was impressed by the thick pegs that held the structures in place. But who had the strength to lift mallets large enough to dislodge them? Toryn had never seen wooden buildings so sturdy and strong. It appeared to his eye that Borrund could withstand anything the elements could hurl against it, natural or not. However, as much as Toryn tried to forget as he strolled about the bustling city, he could not rid himself of the vision of his arrow plunging into the back of the young soldier. Had he not shot him, the unfortunate man would be hanging from a tree, pumped full of foul poison, waiting to be eaten alive. But still, he could not ease his guilt. The soldier had survived the battle of Roth's Doom, only to die with an arrow in his spine… shot by one of his own.

Bardon had been right about Glambul. While the folk of Borrund had welcomed the victorious army, Lord Ormsk had shown no such gratitude to those who had driven back the enemy at great cost. More than once, Toryn had to stop himself from saying something he would later regret, angered by the wily Lord's abrupt manner in his dealings with Elodi. But Elodi remained cordial, appreciating diplomacy would serve better than words of bitterness. And it already appeared to have worked. Beds had been found for Nyomae, Gundrul and the hundreds of severely injured soldiers. And for the walking wounded, many Borrundians had thrown open their doors to board hundreds more. For the remainder, tents were pitched outside the walls, and cooks prepared the first substantial hot meal many had eaten in weeks.

Yet, the immediate danger was far from over. Elodi had tasked the reserves who had not fought at the battle, to set watches along the Lunn border. She was all too aware they remained vulnerable. The realms had lost many at Roth's Doom, and it could be many weeks before a viable fighting force of note could be raised. No one knew how many Ruuk, Norgog, and other unworldly creatures the Ul-dalak commanded. And all feared an early counterstrike would render the sacrifices at Roth's Doom meaningless.

Toryn could see Elodi was eager to drive the Ruuk back over the Nordruuk border. But Lord Ormsk had chaired the first of many meetings, and as Bardon had predicted, his priority was for the safety of his own ward, and not for the greater good of the realms. Understandably, Glambul was concerned the aralaks would soon breed in numbers that could overwhelm Ormsk. Toryn had spoken of the Nym's promise to clear the forests, but Glambul appeared reluctant to either believe in the powers of the *Faerl*, as they were known in the region, or whether they could be trusted. Thus, Elodi had agreed to assign a company comprising of Archonians and Ruan's spearmen to hunt down the clusters that eluded the attention of the Nym.

Yet amid all the uncertainty, Toryn was relieved to see Gundrul had improved with treatment, but he remained concerned about Nyomae's condition. She tossed and turned as if distressed by nightmares, and more troubling, Toryn's efforts to enter her Verse were met with resistance. But as yet, he could not determine *who* resisted.

An exhausted Bardon had retired for the evening, but

Elodi could not rest. She found Toryn on one of the many balconies lining the bell tower. He jumped as she touched his shoulder. 'I see you've also abandoned the hall.'

He turned. 'You'd think with all the wood in this place, they'd have built better chimneys.'

She took a deep breath. 'The air is fresh up here. But if I'm honest, I needed a break from Glambul. He's such a tedious man. Just being in the same room drains my strength. While I appreciate the lord has offered us a place to recuperate, I believe it won't be long before he makes more demands in return for his *hospitality*.'

'I don't know how you can stay so calm. I find I'm clenching my fists just looking at him.'

Elodi smiled. 'There I have an advantage. My father saw to it that I wasn't just trained in the ways of the sword. Ah, and talking of tedious men, we're to have the honor of a visit from Lord Kernlow.'

Toryn gaped. 'He's giving up his luxurious quarters in the citadel to take to the saddle?' He looked out across the Borr River glistening under the half-moon. He chuckled. 'So, it's not just the north we need to keep an eye on. But at least we have three weeks to prepare.'

'I'm afraid it's less than that. He sent a bird, but I never had time to read the message as we prepared for Roth's Doom. I opened it this evening. He left ten days ago.' She grinned. 'Would you believe his exact words were, *I'm on my way to lend a hand.*'

'Lend a hand?' Toryn shook his head. 'Well, you've got to admire the old boy for his confidence.'

Elodi took another deep breath. 'He seems to have got it back after he appointed me to lead his armies. It must have stirred the young soldier in him. How odd that he spent all that time sitting on his backside, and now all of a sudden, he wants to help. And with the news of our victory, I dread to think what he has planned.'

Toryn leaned against the wooden rail. 'Even so, I'm surprised he's leaving after all the fuss he made over setting up his council. Why would he come all this way himself? Could he not just send reinforcements?'

Elodi sighed. 'I hope he doesn't want to take back control. I never got the opportunity to formally challenge his claim to lead the realms. I expect he feels we've saved the land for the time-being. Perhaps he's grown tired of the comforts, and talk of *glorious* victories on the battlefield has awoken the desires of his youth.' She laughed. 'But in a way, Archonholm will benefit. Kernlow has appointed Marrick as steward in his absence. And as cruel as it may sound, I believe Kernlow spending time on the road is best for us all. He will not be able to resist stopping along the way to reassure his subjects that he has everything in hand. But perhaps his presence may help to allay the fears of some.' Elodi stretched out her arms and yawned. 'But I do welcome the opportunity of speaking face-to-face with him. Written messages can easily be misinterpreted, and I want to stress the importance of preparing for what comes next. But if his warrior spirit prevails, we may have to rein in his desire to go all out in an open war.' She shook her head. 'Not so long ago I was desperate for him to act, now it seems I'll have to dampen his enthusiasm.'

Toryn grinned. 'Then we can look forward to one of the good lord's morale-raising speeches.'

She smiled back. 'Well, he'll have plenty of time on the road to prepare one.' Elodi looked up to the stars. 'On the way here, you mentioned you could no longer *feel* the mountains. Is that still the case, Toryn?'

He looked to the west. 'The hollow feeling in my gut has not gone. I know the mountains haven't just suddenly disappeared.' He tried to laugh. 'I'm sure we'd have felt the ground shake, not to mention the boom from their collapse.'

Elodi placed her hand over his on the rail. 'Now I've rested, I also have a strange sensation something has changed, but I cannot fathom what that might be.' She turned to face him. 'Would you...? No, that wouldn't be fair.'

He took her hand. 'Would I... what?'

'It's been a long day, and you must be looking forward to your bed, but... would you like to accompany me on a ride?'

Despite his tiredness, Toryn could not find it in himself to disappoint her. 'I would, but please bear in mind I'm not the accomplished rider you are.'

Elodi beamed. 'Then I will ask Misty to go slow so you can keep up.'

'Then yes, I would. Perhaps it will help to clear my head.'

'Good. Then let us ride out. Misty would welcome a free run away from battlefields and foul beasts. And I'm sure your mount from the First Horse would also appreciate the open roads and fields.'

Toryn's eyes were drawn to the east. 'How far would you say it is to the coast?'

'Perhaps twenty leagues? Certainly, no more than twenty-five if my recollection of Kernlow's most wonderful map is correct.' Elodi noticed the look on Toryn's face. 'Have you never seen the ocean?'

He shook his head. 'Before I rode with the Amayans to Roth's Doom, I had a rare moment alone while I waited for Eryn. Strange, but do you know what my main regret would have been had I fallen that day? That I've never seen the sea. I remember as a child I found it hard to believe Hamar's stories of Karajan and Elessyn. I didn't think it was possible for so much water to be in one place. The River Tam is barely more than a stream as it passes through my village, so my eyes were opened when I first saw the Great Elda and Menon. But I'm sure they can't compare with the wide oceans.'

Elodi looked up to the top of the tower and smirked. 'Well... the bell remains silent. And the beacons are not lit. Therefore, it must be safe.' She nodded. 'Then the coast it is. We'll follow the river out to the estuary. Then we'll find a suitable place up on the cliffs to give you the best view. If your horse can keep up with Misty, we'll make it in time for sunrise.' She strode towards the doorway. 'I'll leave a note for Bardon, but I'm pretty sure the way east will be free of danger, well... certainly nothing that two fine horses of the realms can't easily outrun.'

The horses appeared to enjoy the ride east as much as their riders. They had made good progress and arrived at the Borr Estuary long before dawn. Elodi led them at a trot across the wooden bridge to the south bank and up onto the cliffs. From there, she believed they would get a view not obscured by the islands that had formed the east coast before the rising of the seas. Thick clouds had blocked attempts by the moon to light their way, but as they approached the clifftops, the sea breeze had cleared the skies for what Elodi promised would be a glorious spectacle.

Despite the darkness, Toryn sensed the vast open space before them. They dismounted and stood as close to the edge as they dared. Toryn stopped as he heard something that awoke a desire deep within him: the call of the sea. Far below, the waves crashed onto the rocks as if angry for blocking their path and causing them to topple over. But between the waves, a prolonged rumble filled his ears. Tears brimmed as Toryn listened to the song of the sea, a song that had prevailed since the day the Maidens had raised them out of the chaos. The mighty Karajan Sea had ebbed and flowed through the ages, caring not for the troubles of the land. The sea had seen the Nym in their youth; and then the rise and the fall of the Elorym, to be followed by Toryn's people. But unlike their brief existence, the seas remained, advancing and retreating at the moon's beckoning, and would continue to do so until the world fractured, and the waters spilled into the lands beneath.

Elodi grasped Toryn's cold hand, anticipating his awe as the sun rose to unveil the full wonder of the ocean. 'Wait until you see it. While a sunrise over land is a sight to behold, it does not compare to this. The sea mirrors the skies above as if paying tribute to its beauty.'

Far to the east, the sky grew lighter to draw a dark line across the edge of the world. Toryn gasped. What had looked like a flat plain in the dark, now moved. He took a step back as the Karajan Sea seemed to surge towards him. For as far as he could see, the ocean swelled, creating peaks and troughs much like a plowed field. But farther out, while it appeared calm, it did not conceal its immense power. Now Toryn understood why the people of Borrund maintained a watch; surely, the sea could swallow the lands right up to the foothills of the Kolossos Mountains if it so wished. He felt Elodi squeeze his hand and knew she watched his face. But for that moment, he only had eyes for the sea. He struggled to take in the vastness of the water. What great beasts swam in its depths? Did they know of those living on the land?

Elodi whispered. 'The sun rises.' A red line divided the sky from the sea. At the center, the lip of the sun peered into their world. Its light spilled over onto the sea, laying a path to the foot of the cliffs as if offering an invitation to walk across the restless waters to greet her. The sky grew brighter. Smears of orange and yellow spread, pushing back the night as the dome revolved to take the darkness at their backs to the world beneath. But the sea was not to be outdone by the sky. As Elodi promised, the water reflected the skies above but chose to embellish its beauty as the swells brought the picture to life.

Toryn stammered. 'The sunset on Midsummer's Day was quite a sight, but this... I don't have the words. I—'

'Then don't try. Words are not necessary.' Elodi lifted his cloak and wrapped it around her shoulders as the breeze picked up. They watched in silence, listening to the sea while he imagined the wonders that lay at the edge of the ocean. Did it cascade down the dome and rise to the top and fall as rain on the other side? But if there were oceans below, why did it not rain continuously on the Five Realms? He opened his mouth, but Elodi laughed. 'Just admire the view, Toryn. There are simply too many questions that cannot be answered.'

'But the sea holds so many mysteries. I find I can't just look. I must know what lies beneath all this water.'

'Well, the old city of Borrusk sits on the seabed somewhere out there.'

Toryn's eyes strayed across the horizon. 'But what of the creatures? Surely, it's too big for just fish.'

'Ah. I know of at least one. Just before the storm struck the *Celestra*, I saw what the helmsman convinced me was Behemora.'

'One of the great whales?'

'The very same. Such a tragic tale. The lands rose and separated them many years ago. Horace told me, those who hear her calling for her mate, will never take true love for granted again.' She stared out to the horizon. 'And according to the legend, her mate is somewhere out there, calling for her, never to be heard.' Her hold on him tightened. 'Their agony must be unbearable.'

Toryn turned to her. 'Then we're lucky we don't have the breadth of the realms between us.'

Elodi clasped his hand. 'Remember when I told you on

the terrace at Archonholm that I could not…' she laughed, 'I believe my exact words were… I could not invest more time for you.' Her face reddened, but not from the rising sun. 'That must have sounded quite… cold at the time. But I hope you knew what I was trying to say. I… I didn't want you to—'

Toryn held her. 'You don't have to apologize to me, Elodi. You had far more important things on your mind.'

She stroked his cheek and looked him in the eye. 'Back then, we had no idea whether we'd live to see the autumn. Yet, facing what I thought was certain death at Roth's Doom, I appreciated life is precious and… we must live each day to the full.' She stammered. 'So, what I'm trying to say is… is…' Elodi pulled him close and kissed him. Toryn's head spun. In that moment, a precious, brief moment, the world beyond ceased to exist as even the seas no longer held his interest. It was just the two of them, and nothing else mattered.

Toryn put his hands behind his head and watched the gulls as they glided effortlessly in the air rising from the cliff. But while he took solace from the care-free display in a troubled world, he knew he could not neglect his duties for long. He turned to Elodi as she lay sleeping beside him. For the first time in months, she looked at peace. Toryn wished he could stop the dome and delay the moment he had to wake her. For a few blissful hours, the demands of the realms had seemed so far away. The open sea promised another life, a life away from the horrors, a life without responsibilities and the weight of command. Given the choice, Toryn would build a fine ship for Elodi, then sail far away from the realms to a new, untroubled life together. But, in his heart, he knew that was never going to happen. Yet, at least today, she would wake and breathe fresh air, and not find an aide standing nervously beside her bed.

Toryn let her sleep while he went to find some autumn berries and fresh water. Thankfully, the snow and ice had not reached the coast, thus the bushes were unspoiled and laden with their late fruit. He ate one, recalling the taste of the berries Hope had brought to him at the Singing Stone in the timeless wood. These did not taste as good as Hope's, but this morning he did not need a sweet berry to rejuvenate him. He returned, kneeled beside Elodi, and watched her as she slept peacefully, not once taking his eyes from her. Toryn vowed he would not forget how she looked at this moment. In the hard times he knew awaited them, he would recall her face to give him the strength and resolve to fight on in the face of darkness.

The light breeze blew her hair across her face. Toryn's heart lurched as he remembered the first time he had laid eyes upon her. He had silently declared his loyalty as she led Harlyn's force across the narrow bridge leading to the Caerwal Gate. Back then, a sense of dread had convinced him to follow her into the pass, but he could not have envisaged the dangers that lay ahead. How many more challenges could they survive?

The sun continued to climb. He could wait no longer, but as Toryn fretted whether to wake her, she stretched and opened her eyes. They exchange no words, just glances as they recalled the precious moments they had spent together. Elodi smiled as she sat and gratefully accepted the breakfast of berries. But the time passed too quickly, and the demand of the realms could not be denied.

Toryn stood and turned to the sea. 'Are we looking at the edge of our world, or do more lands exist on the other side of the water?'

Elodi placed the blanket on Sea Mist's back. 'When in Telamir, Nyomae saw Elorym ships leaving these shores.

Some answered the call when Ormoroth returned, but they were too late.' Her chest rose and fell. 'Is it too much to hope the Elorym thrive elsewhere? Would they one day come to our aid?'

Toryn placed his arm around her. 'Eryn believed a few Amayans may have left during the Age of Shadows. But where are they now?'

Elodi gazed at the dark line dividing the land and sea. 'I wonder if there's any means to contact our long-lost ancestors. What I wouldn't give to see them sailing back to our shores. Imagine if we could bring a host of Amayans back for real, and not just for the fleeting moment you achieved at the plain.'

Toryn climbed onto his horse. 'Nyomae is a powerful Imaari, but I doubt even she could enter the Verses of far-off lands.'

Elodi looked back along the coast. 'Securing the forests in Ormsk means we can resume shipbuilding at Caermund, and Kernlow assured me plans were being made for West Haven to build a fleet. It was to strengthen our hand and speed up deployment of our forces, but… if the Ul-dalak return in greater numbers, we may be forced to abandon these lands.'

Toryn's gaze went back to the sea. 'But at what risk? We'd be setting sail into the unknown.'

Elodi mounted and kicked on Sea Mist. 'That may turn out to be a gamble we have to take.'

4. A Just Reward

'Young man, it appears your faerie folk have not kept their promise.' Toryn groaned as Glambul thumped the table. 'Or if they have, they've simply cleared their own forest and forced those spiders into *my* land.'

Elodi held up her hand to Toryn, seeing his frustration. She stood and addressed the Council of Ormsk and captains of the Five Realms. 'From the accounts coming from the east of your ward, I would say we're talking about dozens, and not the hundreds that built their nests in the North Forest.' She held the gaze of the old lord. 'Believe me, Glambul, if the Nym had not kept their promise, your lands would be overrun by now. And thankfully, we've had no sightings of new aralak nests. You should be grateful for Toryn and the Archonians who endured unspeakable horrors to destroy the sacs before they had chance to hatch.'

But Glambul would not back down. 'Don't speak to me of horrors, Lady Harlyn. I served my time at the gorge. I suffered weeks of sickness dealing with those spiders. But am I to believe that this young pup you bring into my hall, should be congratulated for stamping on helpless, tiny spiders?'

Elodi's fist clenched; Toryn stiffened. Bardon spoke first. 'Lord, you appear to be unaware of Toryn of Midwyche's role in events of late. If it were not for both his and Lady Harlyn's intervention at the Caerwal Gate, we would not have had the strength to drive back the Ruuk. And I'm sure those who undertook the grim task in the forest, would take issue with your comment about *helpless* spiders.' Bardon turned to Toryn and grinned. 'And I doubt the warlock he bested in Vortimo, of all places, would view this man as a *young pup*. Toryn has looked one of these dark commanders in the eye and lived. None to my knowledge have achieved that feat in recent times.' Toryn nodded his gratitude.

Glambul scowled. 'That may be so, but if you people in the south had not been so comfortable in your safe fortress, you would have sent more guards to assist my watch on the fences. Then those hairy beasts would not be feeding off my people as we speak.'

Elodi considered her next words carefully, but Toryn spoke first. 'Lord Ormsk. No one did more than Lady Harlyn to urge Lord Kernlow to act sooner. Your ward is free of Ruuk, and your people spared from the worst because of her forces' brave stance at Roth's Doom.'

Bardon agreed. 'And as for the spiders, let us be honest, did any foresee the enemy setting them free?'

Glambul dismissed Bardon's reasoning with a wave of his hand. 'Then obviously Lady Harlyn did not try hard enough to prize the fat lord's backside out of his throne. If the south had mobilized earlier, Ormsk would not have suffered as we did. We could have held the Ruuk and Nordryn's traitors at the banks of the Kel. They would never have reached the gorge to free the spiders in the first place.' He smirked. 'But… perhaps I could expect nothing less, seeing that Kernlow chose to appoint a commander who had failed to defend her own city.'

Elodi pushed back her chair. She took a breath. 'Lord Ormsk. While I am grateful for your hospitality and offering your healers to tend our wounded, I am not prepared to listen to what are nothing more than insults.' Glambul went to stand, but Elodi raised her voice. 'Surely, you must be aware of the thousands lost at the Caerwal Gate. Yes, perhaps Lord Kernlow could have strengthened our front in the north sooner' — she glanced to Toryn, realizing she now defended Kernlow's position — 'but you cannot appreciate the shock and grief many in Archonholm suffered. And even in the south, we were not spared the attention of the enemy. A warlock had entered the city…' she paused as gasps went around the room from those hearing the news for the first time. Again, she caught Toryn's eye, deciding not to add it was a *kruul* and not a warlock in person. 'So, let us not hurl insults at each other. We are allies against a most formidable and devious foe. *Our* victory at Roth's Doom has brought us a little time, but that is all. I believe the dark arts of our enemies will aid their recovery all too soon. None in living memory have faced such a threat as we do now, save the likes of Nyomae, an Imaari who lies unconscious in your infirmary. We are all in the dark when it comes to what comes next.'

Bardon nodded. 'Lord Ormsk. Lady Harlyn is right. None could have predicted just how much our enemy had grown. We were all misled by Uluriel to believe the threat came from the south. But now we know different, we should not bicker over what has happened and who is to blame. Only our enemies will benefit from our division.' Bardon appealed to those around the table. 'Now, perhaps we should move on to what needs to be done in the weeks to come. As Lady Harlyn states, we have a breathing space, nothing more, but let us use it wisely.'

Glambul sank back into his chair and eyed the faces of his Council from beneath his knitted brow. Elodi sensed they were coming over to her side. She spoke with confidence. 'Lord Ormsk. Your aid will be vital if we are to secure this region. You are right to say we should have formed a line farther north, and I dearly wish we could have achieved that. Then let us do so now. Let us consolidate your ward first. Then we can determine our next move.' She glanced to Bardon. 'Which, of course requires your approval, and then all here to agree.'

'Then I must speak with my Council… alone.' Glambul waved his hand. 'We shall convene later this afternoon.'

'She looks troubled again.' Toryn held Nyomae's clammy hand as her eyes moved behind her closed lids.

Elodi kneeled and dabbed the sweat from Nyomae's brow. 'And I assume you've yet to enter her Verse?'

He shook his head. 'It's as if there's a wall surrounding her. But I cannot tell if she's protecting herself, protecting me, or… if another has imprisoned her.'

'Uluriel?'

'Most likely, or perhaps a warlock. But for what reason? If they've trapped her, they may attempt to discover her Maidens' Name and expel her from the realms.'

Elodi clutched the Imaari's hand. 'We cannot let that happen. Is there anything you can do to help her?'

'If I can't reach into her Verse, I can do nothing. I feel so helpless. I've tried all I know, which still isn't much, and I cannot get through to her. There's so much more I need to learn, but she's the only one who can teach me.' Toryn turned her hand over and traced the lines on her palm. 'But if Uluriel possesses her, I'm sure she could have killed her by now if she so wished. And remember, the *kruul* in Archonholm also had the opportunity.' He lifted one of her lids and looked into her eyes. 'They appear to need her alive. Uluriel has a purpose for her… but what?'

Elodi shuddered. 'Nyomae was concerned Uluriel had brought her into the Order for a reason. Once she solved Aber's last line, she assumed it would be to take the risk of invoking Ormoroth's Name.'

Toryn sat back. 'Whatever the reason, I hope she has the strength to resist. She knows the enemy's ways better than the both of us.'

Elodi stood and walked around the bed. She placed her

hand on his shoulder. 'Can you possibly try again, Toryn? We can't delay our plans regardless of her condition. Just one more attempt, please?'

Toryn closed his eyes. He recalled the time at the first Singing Stone when she had changed from the old woman into Nyomae, and then on the Menon Bridge as she had instructed him on the ways of the Song. The sounds of the room retreated. He whispered her name. But his way was obscured. A silent, swirling wall of water surrounded her Verses, akin to what had concealed the Nym at the heart of the Foranfae. He called to her. For a moment, he saw her walking across a desolate landscape. She appeared distraught; her back bent by a great burden. Toryn called again, but his voice sounded weak as a gale blew across the plain. He forced his way into the barrier and yelled. But his voice was torn to pieces by the maelstrom. Yet, Nyomae stopped and appeared to turn towards him. But just as Toryn thought he could breakthrough, another presence made itself known. The barrier darkened… Nyomae was gone.

Toryn collapsed back into his chair. 'It's useless. Something is keeping me out. I may have gone a little deeper, but I cannot penetrate the wall surrounding her. It could be a warlock's *kruul*, or Uluriel. I cannot tell. But I can see she's distressed. Her strength wanes.' He looked to Elodi. 'Perhaps the Amayans can help.'

Elodi turned to the window. 'First we need to know what's happened to them.'

'I fear this dog's fighting days are well behind her.' The healer shook her head as she examined Shepra. 'She bears more injuries than at first meets the eye.'

Toryn ran his hand along her back. Shepra's brow furrowed as she looked up to him. 'I think she understands what you're saying.' He patted her head. 'Never mind, girl.

You've done more than enough to avenge your family. And I certainly wouldn't be here if you hadn't been at my side.' He turned back to the healer. 'But she'll be able to run again?'

She nodded. 'I believe so, but not as fast or for so long.' The healer sat and stroked Shepra. 'She's got a good few years left in her yet. That's if she's looked after and doesn't have to fight.' She thought for a moment. 'I have a brother who has a farm nearby. I'm sure his children would be delighted to welcome this lass. If you're in agreement, I believe he'd be more than happy to have another working dog.' Shepra's ears pricked up.

'You see. She does understand.' Toryn laughed. 'And a farm! Just like an Archonian, Shep. You deserve it as much as any guard. And you won't have to wait to get to the plains of Evermore...' He stopped, not wishing to give away the secret of their Oath. Toryn tickled her ear. 'A life on a farm with a new family. How does that sound, lass?' Shepra jumped up. Toryn stood and shook the healer's hand. 'I think we have a deal.'

She smiled. 'I shall arrange it. Shepra will be fit and ready to leave in a day or two. I'll let you know so you can come and see her off.'

Toryn's jaw tightened. 'That I will. I've known her only a short time, but we've shared much together.' He wrapped his arm around the dog. 'And I'll come and visit you on the farm when I can, Shep. Couldn't have worked out better, eh.' Toryn walked to the door, but dared not glance back, worried he could not hide his sorrow at their inevitable parting.

'You're looking much better, Gundrul.' Elodi was relieved to see some color return to the old guard's cheeks. She laughed. 'It won't be long before your face returns to what I believe your people call the Lunn Leather.'

The captain croaked. 'Thank you, ma'am. And yes, we Lunn folk are proud to show off our wind-battered faces.' He struggled to sit. 'My recovery comes not a moment too soon.' Gundrul grinned at Ruan by his bedside. 'I was ready to depart these lands if only to save myself from yet another tall story from this big lug.'

A rare smile cracked Ruan's lips as he looked to Elodi. 'I'd barely begun, ma'am. There's plenty more tales of my fine spearmen's deeds. And I hadn't even got to the part where we drove those spiders from the plain.'

Elodi winked at Ruan. 'Then our plan has worked, Captain.' Her mirth faded. 'But I hope you feel you have avenged your brother, Ruan.'

He nodded. 'Many times over, ma'am. Those creatures will not be so keen to rush at our spear tips so readily next time.' The big man stood. 'Now, if you both will excuse me, I am to speak with Lord Broon, the true lord. I've had word from my men in Keld. They're ready to aid Lord Broon's return and drive out the imposter.'

Elodi grasped his arm. 'That is indeed good news. And, again, I cannot thank you enough for crushing our enemy's right flank at the plain.'

'Just carrying out our duty, ma'am. But...' he glanced to Gundrul, 'we were late to the battle. Had you and this brave old fool not held the center, I and my men would have served only to provide the sport following *their* victory.'

Gundrul choked as he chuckled. 'It's taken many years, but finally... praise from the big man of Breck.'

'Breck?' Elodi frowned. 'I must apologize for my ignorance. I do not know where that is.'

Gundrul smirked. 'I wouldn't worry, ma'am. Only those from Breck can find it on a map. Few would willingly choose to visit. Not quite as bleak as Flint on the bony witch's finger, but it runs it a close second.'

Ruan thrust out his chest. 'But a place that breeds fine warriors.' He held his stance for a moment, then laughed. 'But Gunny is right. It's a grim part of the realms… and I can't say I miss it.'

Elodi placed her hand on his shoulder. 'Then I shall be ever grateful to the people of Breck for their fine warriors. And I will be sure to mention it so others will come to know of its importance to our cause.'

Ruan bowed. 'I thank you, ma'am.' He straightened. 'And I swear my Breck brothers and spearmen will do all we can to put Lord Broon back in Keld before autumn is done.' He nodded to Gundrul and squeezed through the door leading to the corridor.

Elodi sat beside Gundrul. 'Now, seeing as you're back in the land of the living, we have our deciding game of *Squares* to play.' She smirked. 'I think I have just enough time to beat you before I attend this evening's meeting.' But if Elodi had wished for a trouble-free hour absorbed by their game, she was to be disappointed; a messenger came bearing news from the north.

Elodi took her seat at the table with Bardon, Glambul, and captains of both Ormsk and Elodi's forces including Ruan, Amyndra and Cubric. While Elodi was disappointed to lose the deciding game of *Squares* to Gundrul, she was encouraged to see his tactical mind was as sharp as ever. And while they had played, the old captain had shared his thoughts and how the Five Realms should proceed in the coming months.

Glambul began the meeting. 'I give thanks to the Archonians and Captain Ruan's spearmen for offering some protection against the spiders. But…' he eyed Elodi, 'dozens of my people are still lost each day, and I cannot be sure they're not building more nests in the woods where the *Faerl* have no interest.'

Elodi shifted in her seat. 'Then I shall... with your agreement, lord, assign more spears to the task.'

If Lord Ormsk was grateful, he did not show it. He looked down to the stack of papers on the table. Glambul grunted. 'And next, there is the matter of my stocks. The extra demands placed on Borrund's cooks, farriers, saddlers, and healers, has rapidly depleted my supplies that should see us through the winter.'

Again, Elodi answered. 'Then you will be reassured to know I have made arrangements for provisions to be brought here from the south.'

He glanced around the table. 'Then I am reassured, Lady Harlyn. But I trust I will not have to wait long. Winter will be upon us all too soon.'

'And all the sooner if we do not take back our lands.' Elodi took a breath. 'And this relates to another matter I need to bring to this table. This afternoon I received grave news regarding the Amanach stones. News that has helped Toryn and I understand something that has been concerning us of late.'

'Amanach?' Glambul frowned. 'Please, Lady Harlyn, you'll have to bear in mind many here are not as well-traveled... or as educated as yourself.'

'My apologies, lord. They are more commonly known as Singing Stones, set by our ancestors to keep the dark forces at bay. If the stones fail... and should we somehow survive, we will see the return of the bitterly cold winters and bleak summers from the old tales. But that would be the least of our worries.' She exchanged a glance with Bardon. 'One of the seven stones has already fallen... and others will soon follow. While relieved to have received word from the Amayans, it was a brief but troubling message. It's apparent the power of these stones fade, and that means the strength of the Amayans will also decline.' A murmur spread through the room. Elodi continued.

'This has been going on longer than we thought. The warning signs were there, but we did not see them. Harlyn's springs have been cooler in recent years leading to lower crop yields. And as the stones weaken, our enemy may discover the locations of the remainder. If they're destroyed, our enemy would grow ever stronger.' Elodi turned to Glambul. 'Thus, unless we can put pressure on the enemy, I fear we may not have the warmth of the summer sun to lift us from the misery of the bitter winter I fear will be upon us all too soon.'

Bardon spoke. 'Then I suggest we discuss how we might prevent the nightmare Lady Harlyn describes.' He stood. 'If I may, lord, I wish to speak of Keld.' Glambul waved a hand. Bardon nodded. 'I propose we consolidate the east of the mountains first. While Drunsberg and Calerdorn will need to be taken back, it is my belief Keld is the priority. If we can force Nordryn and his ilk out of Keld, it would give us a position of relative strength to mount a concerted effort to drive the Ruuk out of Lunn and over the border. The longer the Ruuk are allowed to consolidate their position here, the harder it will be to extract them. And, as Lady Harlyn states, winter will bring more than just icy winds, and I for one would rather not face the Norgog if possible.' He looked at the grim faces around the table. 'And let's not forget, Nordryn will be thinking the same. He poses an immediate threat while he sits in Keld. Therefore, I propose we take it as—'

'And just how do you propose to achieve that, Bardon?' Elodi noted Glambul never used the correct title. Glambul leaned forward. 'You and I are only too aware of Keld's thick stone walls.' He looked to Elodi. 'In years past, Borrund's forces have hurled many a rock trying to take Keld, but never succeeded.' His eyes narrowed as he held Elodi's gaze. 'We were stronger back then, Bardon. Thus, how do you propose to achieve what my ancestors failed to do… and with a lesser force?'

Ruan grunted. 'If I may speak, lord?' Glambul scowled as he realized Ruan's question was directed at Bardon.

'By all means, Captain.' Bardon's jaw clenched. 'That is if Lord Ormsk is prepared to' — his mouth curled — 'listen.' Glambul nodded. Bardon held out his hand as he sat. 'Then I yield to Captain Ruan.'

'Thank you, lord.' Ruan pushed back his chair and stood. He stiffened, and Elodi noted he looked nervous speaking to the assembly. Ruan threw back his broad shoulders. 'Nordryn commanded my spearmen to return to Keld when he became lord. But I could not leave' — he turned and gave a slight bow to Elodi — 'the good Lady Harlyn without my support after the first attack on Calerdorn. It was the true Lord Broon who commanded me to assist, and I was not going to turn my back on a city under threat. So, following the wise council of Wendel, may he be resting in peace, I sent back a small detachment to satisfy Nordryn and—'

Glambul groaned. 'Thank you for the history lesson, Ruan, but can we move this on?'

Ruan bristled. He glanced to Bardon who nodded his approval of his captain's approach. The spearman continued. 'Very well, but I believe what happened in the past should not be ignored.' Elodi could not suppress her grin. Ruan looked to Glambul. 'Borrund's forces failed to take Keld because, as you say, the city's stone walls are strong and thick. But your forces do not have the advantage that we now have.' Ruan's eyebrows raised. 'And that's my thirty men that bolster Keld's defenses.'

Elodi noticed not even Glambul could conceal his interest. Bardon took over. 'Thank you, Captain. We can be grateful Nordryn kept Ruan's spears within the walls and prevented them coming to Roth's Doom. But Nordryn is unaware Ruan is in contact with his men using the very birds he believes sends word to his masters in the north. We have much to discuss, however, this is not the place to determine the tactics, but I am confident we can take back Keld with minimal losses. But not forgetting, Nordryn lost many Ruuk at Roth's Doom. His masters demanded he commit a large part of his force with the assumption they would be victorious.' He nodded to Elodi. 'But they hadn't taken our strengths into consideration, and now Nordryn will be desperate to replenish his numbers and attack here, before we can strike at him.'

Glambul sat back and folded his arms. 'Does anyone here know how many Ruuk he commands? Or, in fact, how he intends to fill the gaps in his ranks?'

It took Elodi a moment to appreciate it was a good question, and not a taunt at Bardon. She cleared her throat. 'My experience at Tunduska led me to believe there are far more Ruuk… and Norgog over the border than we at first thought. My captains estimated they lost close to twenty thousand at the battle, but I do not know how many were held in reserve.'

Glambul nodded. 'Then perhaps it's wise to presume Nordryn may rebuild his forces faster than we can. Then I will take your word, Bardon, and will provide resources to your mission to retake Keld.' He looked to those around the table. 'Are we in agreement?' None dissented. 'Lady Harlyn? Will you partake? Will you also allocate resources?' She nodded. 'Then that is settled.' He turned to his scribe. 'Let it be recorded that Lady Harlyn and Bardon will take responsibility to unseat Nordryn and either kill, capture, or at the very least, drive the usurper out of the realms.' He clapped his hands. 'This seems like a good place to pause. I have other meetings to attend.' He smiled, and for the first time, Elodi believed it to be genuine. The lord stood. 'You'll be pleased to hear that, despite our supplies running low, my cooks have prepared a fine supper for you.'

5. Crown of the Kolossos

Nyomae choked on the acrid smoke from the fires still feasting on the ruins of Vymarl. The reserves had not stood a chance against the hordes that had poured out of Vortimo. She turned. More fires burned as the combined forces of the fortress and the victors at Roth's Doom surged south. Karrock had fallen; its tall twin towers sacked and razed to the ground. The lands to the south now lay open.

Nyomae collapsed and wept. What could she do? Their armies had failed; their strength lay trampled into the mud at Roth's Doom. *Nyomae.* She spun around. A warlock stood on the opposite bank of a river. He held out his hand. *Allow me to cross. I can help you.*

She climbed to her feet. The warlock edged back as the water flowed faster, seeming reluctant to step into the river without her consent. Nyomae stood tall. 'I deny you, warlock. I do not allow you to cross.' Its dark shape shimmered and faded. She heaved a sigh of relief. A small victory. But she needed more. The answer came to her: Telamir. Did the lake tower yet stand? If she could to anything to help the poor people of the realms, the answer would be there.

'You have to hand it to Glambul.' Bardon took a bite of a chicken leg as he sat. 'He chairs an effective meeting. It would have taken a week for Kernlow to achieve what took less than an hour.'

Elodi agreed. 'I must admit I thought it would take longer. And perhaps it's best we devise our strategy before Kernlow arrives and wants to urge caution, or,' she grinned, 'ride out with abandon if he's rediscovered the fighting spirit of his youth.'

'Ah, but let's not forget, agreeing to take Keld was the easy part. Glambul will be the beneficiary sitting here in his hall, while we take all the risk.'

Elodi sighed. 'And will he be ready to commit his forces elsewhere? As soon as Ormsk no longer forms the northern border, I imagine he'll withdraw his help. Drunsberg and Calerdorn represent much harder territory to win back. And while Nyomae remains in the infirmary, I'm reluctant to plan too far ahead. And as with Roth's Doom, I believe much rests upon Nyomae's shoulders in the battles ahead.'

Bardon pushed his plate away. 'Has Toryn made progress on determining her condition?'

'He's with her now. He tries night and day to make contact, but he's none the wiser.' She looked up. 'Ah. Captain Cubric. Would you please join us. There is a matter I wish to discuss with you.'

'It would be an honor, ma'am.' Cubric pulled up a chair and eyed the supper. 'Things certainly move a little quicker in these parts, eh. My dear Lord Kernlow would still be arranging the banquet.' He turned to Bardon and held out his hand. 'And may I say what a pleasure it is to meet a lord who can still swing a sword.'

Bardon readily shook Cubric's hand. 'And for me to meet a captain who's achieved so much in such a short time. Lady Harlyn speaks very highly of you.'

Cubric nodded his thanks to Elodi. 'Only too happy to help you rid Lunn of the traitor. How long before we're ready to ride on Keld?'

Bardon rubbed his chin. 'I would hope to ride out in two weeks at most. Ruan suggests we take the route through the hills. It will be slower going but may give us the element of surprise. But there may be another factor in our favor.'

'Something in our favor?' Elodi frowned. 'I find that hard to believe. It seems like the gods have long since abandoned us.'

'Hear me out.' His eyebrows raised. 'Ruan's spearmen report there's a Ruuk tradition of celebrating the coming of winter. I can't imagine why, but the Ruuk are an odd folk. They'll wait for the full moon which is about three weeks from now. I'm informed the drinking and debauchery will likely go on for days.' Bardon grinned. 'The timing couldn't be better. If Ruan's men can open the gates, we may catch them at unawares, and possibly not in the best condition to fight following their festivities.'

Cubric took a gulp from his glass. 'Ah, Lady Harlyn, perhaps the gods are still watching over us.' He wiped his chin. 'And what role would you like me to take?'

Elodi placed her hand on his. 'I have something else for you, Cubric. It's been on my mind for days, but I've not had chance to discuss it with anyone. But seeing as you've joined us, this seems like the right moment. I'd like to hear your opinion.' Elodi took a breath. 'I believe we should make our move on Drunsberg as soon as possible. And from what I've just learned, it would be better still if it coincides with the Ruuk celebration. And from what you told me onboard the *Celestra*, I think you would be the ideal man to lead... along with Toryn. You have served in the mines, and Toryn has the means to help you execute an effective attack.'

Bardon frowned. 'At the same time? It would place a strain on our forces to undertake two such missions.'

'That cannot be avoided at this crucial time. And that's my thinking. Time is vital, but I believe it would give our enemy a shock if we can simultaneously take both objectives. And not forgetting, the Ruuk at the mines will most likely follow the same tradition as their folk at Keld.'

Cubric nodded. 'I've seen them celebrate, ma'am, and they could run many an Archonian to a close finish in a drinking contest. And let's not forget, they'll be knocking back the good stuff from the stores at the mines, and the barrels they've filched from the rest of Dorn.'

Bardon agreed. 'Then you may have a point.'

Elodi smiled. 'I believe a small force should head for the mines as soon as possible. We cannot afford to let the ores of Drunsberg continue to be sent north. We have much re-arming to do. Our smithies have a thirst for resources the other seams cannot quench.'

Bardon scratched his chin. 'I know little of the mines, but I'm told the narrow road to the town makes it a difficult place to attack.'

Elodi held out her hand to Cubric. 'The captain knows of a disused tunnel that bypasses the road, and that's not all. He believes there're still stocks of Shreek's Rage stored deep in the mine.'

Cubric beamed and mimicked an explosion with his hands. 'We'll frighten the miserable lives out of them Ruuk, lord. It's scary enough when you know it's going to blow, especially in those tunnels. But if we can take them by surprise, they'll jump out of their thick skins.'

Elodi continued. 'The entrance is someway south of the gate. It was our intended plan to use it back in the summer, but that was before we learned of the poor souls being taken to Durran Wood.'

Bardon ran his fingers across the table as if tracking a line on a map. 'We cannot go through Lunn to the mines as we don't know the Ruuk positions. The mission is doomed before it begins if they run into a large band. And even if they could avoid the enemy, they'll have to negotiate the way around the Kolossos Crown... and that's not a place I'd readily return.' He tapped a knot in the wood. 'The only viable route to Drunsberg would take at least twelve days hard slog and means taking the Kolossos Pass. That in itself is fraught with danger if the cobtrolls decide to be a nuisance. But as you say, Elodi, the days of avoiding risks are long gone. And *not* taking Drunsberg from our enemy will lead to more strife.'

Cubric turned to Elodi. 'And what of your city, ma'am? We can't have those scoundrels living it up in such a fine place.'

Her shoulders sagged. 'While it pains me daily, I accept both Keld and Drunsberg must be brought back into our hands ahead of Calerdorn. Our borders here are effectively open while Nordyn controls large swathes of Lunn. There is little activity west of the Kolossos at present, but should this change, we will have to review our strategy. But there's another risk. When Uldrak learns of our desire to take back what is ours, he'll look to strengthen Calerdorn's already formidable defenses.'

'Or...' Bardon's fingers drummed the table as he thought. 'If we attack both Keld and the mines simultaneously, the warlocks might demand he sends forces to their aid. It could work both ways. But, as you say, Calerdorn represents a far greater challenge than Keld, and even the mines.'

Elodi nodded. 'Perhaps. But...' she turned to Cubric. 'Could you possibly take some of this fine food to Gundrul? You could also tell him what was discussed at the meeting. I did promise to keep him informed.'

Cubric grinned. 'Certainly, ma'am. I'm sure he'll be happy to see me.' He winked. 'And now you can say what you don't want me to hear.'

Elodi waited for Cubric to leave. She glanced around the table and lowered her voice. 'Cubric doesn't miss much. He's a shrewd fellow. There is something I want to speak to you about, something I've not told a living soul. And while I would trust Cubric with my life, I'm not so sure he could keep a secret after an evening of imbibing the ales he's so fond of.' She leaned over. 'As far as I'm aware, the only other person who knew what I'm about to tell you, died onboard the *Celestra* at Seransea.'

Bardon nodded. 'Wendel, I assume. Such a loss. Only a fool ignored his sage advice.'

Elodi smiled. 'Ah. Then I may have been judged a fool on the odd occasion. But I'll forever be grateful for his long service... and his wisdom. In the rush to evacuate Calerdorn, he had the foresight to retrieve a scroll. One I knew nothing about.' Again, she checked she could not be overheard. 'Taking back Calerdorn may not require a full-scale frontal assault. Whether the architects anticipated such a need, I do not know, but it's possible for us to get inside through a secret entrance beneath the cells. It can be accessed from a tunnel beneath the Calern Mountains.'

Bardon's eyes widened. 'Then what we learn taking the mines could prove useful for the assault on your city. It would be quite a feat, eh. And one that would cause concern for our enemy. I imagine they see Calerdorn as a prize possession.' He laughed. 'That would give them something to think about if we could snatch it from under their noses, and in the same month as Keld and Drunsberg.'

Elodi patted his hand. 'Well let's not get too far ahead of ourselves. But... yes, it would be quite a blow.' She looked to the ceiling. 'Yet, I dread to see what damage they have inflicted on my people and the city.'

'Ma'am.' Elodi turned to see an aide. He cleared his throat. 'Nyomae's healer has asked me to inform you of a... development.'

'Then please update me on her progress.'

'I'm afraid to report that she has... has gone missing, ma'am.'

'How can she just get up and leave without anyone seeing her?' Elodi stared at the crumpled sheets on the empty bed.

The healer rubbed her eyes. 'I… I cannot explain it, ma'am. I was sitting by her bed when she suddenly convulsed with such a force, I feared her back was about to break. But as I stood to see what I could do for her, I became dizzy and the next thing I knew, I found myself face down on the bed.'

'And outside this room? Did no one notice?'

'Now there's the strange thing, ma'am. I found them in a similar state. They seemed to have suffered the same bout of drowsiness as me.'

Toryn rushed in. 'Bardon told me. Where could she have gone?'

Elodi looked back to the healer. 'How long has she been missing?'

'It can't be more than two hours. I'd just relieved my colleague so she could get something to eat.'

'Nyomae's been bed-ridden for days and hasn't eaten since before the battle.' Elodi looked to the door. 'Surely, she can't have gone far.'

Toryn frowned. 'But why leave without…?' His shoulders dropped. 'It must be a *kruul*. She's been possessed.'

Elodi's face paled. 'Possessed? Or worse… has she been turned? That would explain the healers' drowsiness, and she made no effort to find us. If she goes to the other side, we're…' she grabbed his arm. 'Can you find her Verse, Toryn?'

He bowed his head and took a deep breath. Elodi watched as his eyes flickered behind their lids. He shook his head. 'Nothing. I can't see her.' Toryn opened his eyes. 'But something happened here, something that caused the Verses to splinter.' His jaw clenched. 'It does suggest

Nyomae is at the mercy of another force.'

Elodi rushed to the door. 'Then we send for Janae. She's the best scout we have. If she can't pick up Nyomae's tracks, no one can.'

Janae slid from her saddle. She kneeled and placed her hand on the ground. 'Yes, I'm certain, ma'am. Nyomae's heading south. She turned off the road here.'

Elodi frowned. 'South? I was certain she'd go north. If a *kruul* wished to take her to the enemy, I would've thought she'd cross the border.'

'Her tracks don't lie, ma'am. Not many go wandering barefoot in these parts at this time of year.' She pointed to the trees in the distance. 'They lead towards the forest.'

Elodi turned to Toryn. 'Can you try again with your *farsight*?'

Toryn stood in his stirrups and looked across the plain, dimly lit by the crescent moon. 'There's something still not right. I can see as far as the forest, but... it remains altered. It looks as if the present Verses are delayed. The stars are out tonight.' He sat back. 'But they're not in the Song. I must be seeing yesterday when there was heavy cloud.'

Elodi kicked on Sea Mist. 'Then surely that means we're on the right track if someone has gone to the trouble to obscure the Verses. There's no reason to—' she spun around. 'Horses!' She drew her sword. 'Nordleng?'

Toryn turned. 'I see two riders. But not Nordleng. Amayans, yet... they don't look comfortable in their saddles.' He frowned. 'And they've not seen us yet.' Toryn called out. 'Eryn?'

One of the riders held up a hand. They turned their horses and stopped. Toryn and Elodi dismounted and walked to meet them. Toryn was pleased to see Eryn, but shocked at her appearance. The light from her eyes had gone, and she stooped as if it took a great effort to stay on her horse. Beside her, Arijan looked only marginally better. They almost fell from their saddles. Toryn went to Eryn's side. She slumped against him. A faint light flickered in her eyes as she saw Elodi. She barely had the strength to speak. 'Greetings, sister. For a moment, I thought Eleni stood before us.'

Elodi stuttered. 'Eleni? She… she was my mother.'

Arijan hooked her arm under Eryn's and Toryn felt a little of her strength return. She straightened as they both held out their hands to Elodi. She stepped forward and accepted their invitation to join their circle. A faint light glowed from their joined hands and Elodi's eyes glimmered in the starlight. Toryn felt the hairs on the back of his neck stand up. Eryn managed a smile. 'You have your mother's strength, Elodi.'

Elodi held Eryn's gaze. 'I would dearly love to hear about her when we have the time.'

'There is much to tell.' Eryn exchanged a glance with Arijan. 'And we'll gladly tell it. But you also have much to share with us. Perhaps you're unaware, Eleni named you after the first Amayan to slay a warlock many centuries ago. And from what we hear, you are worthy of her name.'

'Then I hope I can do my mother, and my namesake, proud.' Elodi looked over Eryn's shoulder. 'What happened? Where are the others?'

Her head dropped. 'I trust you received our message.'

Elodi nodded. 'We did. And it did not make for good reading.'

Eryn sighed. 'We suffered a defeat. As we closed on Vordrak he was joined by another. We were confident we could still avenge Amyra, despite the Amanach's power waning, but as we gathered to attack…' she faltered.

Arijan clutched Eryn's hand. 'A shadow loomed ahead, riding a great horse of the likes we've never seen.

And we remembered him. He is Jehenum, and one of the oldest and most powerful of Ormoroth's commanders, but he seemed stronger than ever. Not even the six of us could hope to have defeated him. We chose to pursue them at a distance. If they were wary of us, we could not tell. We followed them many leagues north and came to suspect they seek the Amanach they know to be in the region.'

Elodi frowned. 'Do they not know its location?'

Eryn shook her head. 'Mercifully not. It lies at the most northerly point of the Kolossos. The Crown Stone is the second most potent after the Foundation Stone in the south.'

Toryn glanced to the forest. 'Yet Hamar and I found two. And I know other guards have stumbled across them. They were tasked to report their location to the Archon.'

Eryn explained. 'The stones are concealed from those who can do them harm.' She smiled. 'Your good-natured friend and his guards are deemed not to be a threat.' Her smile faded. 'But it's true in times past, not even an Imaari could have *stumbled across* them. Their power declines, thus they become vulnerable in the mortal world. We cannot fathom how, but even with the loss of one, the others should not be so compromised to be found so easily. Something drains them... or deprives them of their power. And as our enemy grows stronger, the whereabouts of the lesser stones will soon become known. The warlocks seek the Crown Stone, knowing if they find and destroy it... the others will quickly fall.'

Elodi glanced at Toryn. 'And are they likely to find it soon?'

Eryn shoulders dropped. 'That we cannot tell. Following our pursuit, we were too weak and had to withdraw. We dared not take sustenance from the Crown Stone for fear of disclosing its location.' She sagged against Toryn.

Arijan continued their tale. 'They have long suspected it lies within the four mountains that form the Crown. But it remains well protected. The peaks tolerate neither keshwing nor corvraak. Tunnel diggers find they go around in circles when trying to find a way through. And the pass through the mountains remains concealed to the wrong eyes. But as the warlocks' recover their old powers, it may not remain hidden for long.' Arijan locked her arm in Eryn's. 'We must be ready. But even if all of us ride against the warlocks, we cannot be certain of saving the stone.'

Toryn looked between their horses. 'Where are the others, Eryn?'

'They maintain a watch of the warlocks in the north. But we have come south to replenish our strength at the stone in the forest. Calestri has gone on ahead. Arijan and I were coming to Borrund to find you.'

'Borrund?' Elodi pointed behind them. 'You were heading in the wrong direction. The town lies to the east.'

Eryn groaned. 'Our strength fails more than we feared if we can so easily lose our way.' She looked to Toryn. 'Then it was a stroke of luck we came upon you when we did.'

Toryn grinned. 'If Nyomae was here she would chastise you. Luck? She does not believe in luck.'

'And what of Nyomae?' Eryn looked over Toryn's shoulder. 'We have been unable to sense her presence of late. We assume it's because of our ailing strength.'

Elodi caught Toryn's eye. 'There may be another reason. She has not woken since Roth's Doom. We fear a *kruul* possesses her. Or worse, the Ul-dalak may have turned her. She walked out of Borrund just hours ago. Janae has tracked her this far. We're now certain Nyomae is heading for the forest.'

'But why would she——?' Eryn looked to the south.

'Ah, she seeks the Amanach within for good or ill. If she bears a *kruul*, they will see through her eyes and discover its true location. But if the unthinkable has happened and she has turned, Nyomae could bring about the end of the stone quicker than any warlock.' She grabbed Moonbeam's rein. 'We must apprehend her.' Eryn nodded to Janae who stood transfixed by the talk of stones and warlocks. 'But I think it's best if your scout does not accompany us. What we find in the forest may… overwhelm her.'

Elodi agreed. 'Thank you, Janae. We shall continue from here with the Amayans' assistance. Please, return to Borrund and inform Bardon of our situation. I shall return as soon as we have found Nyomae.' Janae stiffened, then nodded, and reluctantly departed.

Eryn mounted. 'We push on. If Nyomae reaches the stone and… well it doesn't bear thinking about the consequences.'

6. By the Light of the Amanach

All around her, Nyomae could see nothing but death and destruction. Charred skeletons of once fine towers, halls, and houses; scorched fields, once abundant with crops, destroyed in battles fought and lost. Sadly, the losses did not end there. Knights, guards, farmers, cooks and… to her dismay, their children, lay side-by-side where they had fallen. None had been spared the horror.

Nyomae stopped. Water lapped at her feet. She looked up, elated to see Telamir rising in defiance above the desolation. While the Elorym tower stood, perhaps there was still hope for the land. A memory of a distant time flickered in her mind. She had once crossed the lake and entered the tower. And she had once believed the realms had a chance of victory. A remote chance, but a chance all the same.

Telamir shuddered. Nyomae shuffled back from the lake's edge as the tremor sent ripples across the water. Her stomach turned. Something had changed. The tower was now overshadowed by the Kolossos peaks, when in the past it had appeared taller. Her eyes wandered up its twisted structure that in days past had defied the watcher to fully take in its beauty with one glance. But now there was no enchantment. It looked ugly, built by unskilled hands with no thought for splendor. Stripped of its Elorym cloak, the tower now cast a hideous reflection in the surrounding lake, akin to that of the wooden tower of Wyke Wood.

Nyomae attempted to enter the Song, but something prevented her. Her way may have been blocked, but the cries of the Elorym as their race fell to Ormoroth, echoed across the bleak land. Nyomae clenched her hands as if trying to hold up the tower. It could not fall. Cyloris and Qaamir were lost. If Telamir collapsed, would the three elegant spires of Syris be next? And what of the fabled fifth Elorym tower far to the north? If all the Elorym structures were lost, the realms were surely doomed.

Nyomae looked back to the tower. *How did I get here?* It seemed only moments ago she had stood among the horrors of Roth's Doom. Yet, she had no memory of what would have been a four-day journey. But she had no horse, thus it should have taken two weeks on foot. Nyomae had seen no other living soul in days. Her heart sank. *Had the shadow returned?*

The ground shook. The ripples on the lake became waves that crashed over the shore. Nyomae leaped back as the water stung her feet. On the opposite bank, the air shimmered and darkened. Three tall creatures emerged from the gloom, advancing towards the tower with long strides and an unsteady gait. Nyomae knew what she faced. Reapers! A vast army followed. An army of shreeks, shrouls, and on their flanks, jittering aralaks, all keen to tear Nyomae apart and devour her flesh.

The army stopped at the lake's shore. But it was not the Reapers that sent Nyomae staggering back. A robed figure strode through the parting ranks, more terrible to behold than the horrors behind. She gaped as it lowered its hood and its glowering eyes fell upon her.

Uluriel! The Ul-dalak commander sneered as she raised her arms. Nyomae's neck stiffened. Her head was forced back to look up to the top of the tower. Uluriel swirled her arms and stirred the depths of the lake. Her fell voice rose above a squall as the water churned. It swirled violently, drawing water to the center, rising to form a funnel as if a whirlwind. Higher and higher it climbed until Telamir was surrounded. Nyomae teetered on the ledge as the yawning, dark hole of the bottom of the lake gaped wide far below. She clasped her hands to her ears against the wail of the maelstrom as it thundered around the tower.

Then silence. The wall of water shuddered to a halt, then collapsed. Nyomae was thrown back as the great weight of water crashed back into the lakebed. But not one drop escaped. The water sat as if a mirror, yet this time it did not reflect the tower. But Nyomae's hope that Telamir had withstood Uluriel's assault, was short lived; the lake's surface foretold what was about to come. The twin spires of Telamir twisted. The air boomed as the tower groaned as if in agony. Nyomae's ears burst as the Reapers blew their great, mournful horns in triumph. The tower buckled as if struck by Ormoroth's hammer, slowly toppling forward as the last of the Elorym power was torn from its bones. Nyomae cried out, throwing her arms in front of her face as the lake hissed and steamed, burning her eyes and skin.

The air cleared as the ground settled. Where the lake had once sat, fetid, green water smeared the land like an infected wound. The sludge bubbled, spewing foul gases into the air. Two bulbous eyes broke the surface and stared straight at Nyomae. The monstrous creature crawled out of the pit. She gaped in horror at an abomination of a cross between a large fish and a horse. Its gray scales, glistened in the weak sun, giving off a stench that choked Nyomae. The creature's glassy, unblinking eyes fixed on hers as it lumbered across dry land on its ungainly limbs.

Nyomae spun away in disgust. The army had gone. Uluriel did not come for her; she did not have to confront or capture her. Uluriel had drained Nyomae of all hope. She had lost her friends and allies. The powers of the ancient world had failed one-by-one. There was little else for her to do. *Speak His name. Open the gateway.*

Nyomae bowed her head. She went deep into her

Verse to a place she had locked away. She shuddered as she retrieved the word. Her lips moved, then froze. *No! I will not utter it.* Nyomae clenched her jaw and thrust the Name from her head.

But deeper still, another voice pleaded. *There is another way.*

The thin slit of the moon and the clear, starry skies had provided enough light for Elodi, Toryn and the Amayans to find their way to the forest. But once under its canopy, their pace had slowed, as they led their horses over the uneven ground, guided only by the dull light of Arijan's sword.

Toryn walked alongside Eryn having locked his arm under hers as her strength failed. Tall dark figures seemed to accompany them as the ghostly light of Arijan's blade shed distorted shadows out from the twisted trunks. The emptiness spread from Toryn's stomach into his chest. He turned to Eryn. 'I feel what ails you. Something has changed, but you say no stone has fallen since the one at Wend Gap. Can you be certain the Crown Stone stands?'

Eryn sighed. 'It stands, but how much longer it can evade the warlocks' eyes, I cannot tell.'

'And what of the Foundation Stone? If that is the most powerful, can that remain hidden from our enemy?'

'The stone is still strong. It lies deep in a cavern at the foot of the Kolossos and mercifully appears beyond the reach of the warlocks. But as each stone fails, so too will its ability to cloak itself from the mortal world.'

Toryn felt the tension ease a little from his shoulders. 'When we were in the tunnels, I sensed a surge of power from a river deep beneath our feet. Could that be connected to the Foundation Stone?'

Eryn shrugged. 'We had no memory of this river until you spoke of it. But as the shadows retreat, we have recovered much of what was hidden. The river beneath the mountains does indeed serve the Amanach. It is the same source of power that Ormoroth sought to corrupt with his pillar of iron, the Angorlith.'

'Has it run dry? That would explain the sense of loss we're feeling.'

Eryn sagged against him as she stumbled in the dark. 'Had it gone, the Amanach would have failed. It yet flows, but… there appears to be another force at play.'

Toryn helped the Amayan over a fallen branch. 'Can we continue to fight if we lose another stone?'

Eryn's voice weakened. 'It will strengthen the warlocks' hand. They draw their power from the Angorlith, as we do from the Amanach. The stones counter the influence of Ormoroth's vile pillar. With the loss of another, the emboldened warlocks will make their move against the remainder. As each fall, the stones become weaker, the Angorlith more potent.'

Toryn stared ahead, desperate to see Nyomae. 'And how long before a second stone could be lost?'

Arijan took Eryn's other arm. 'It took years to destroy the first. A concerted attack on a second could perhaps lead to its fall within a month or two. I imagine the third would be a matter of weeks if we cannot protect it. And if that is lost, perhaps only days for the remainder.'

Toryn dared to ask. 'And you believe the Crown Stone is next?'

Eryn's voice was now barely a whisper. 'Possibly. The Foundation Stone eludes them and will continue to do so until the others fail. While they get closer to discovering the one that sits in this forest, and the second, the Elda Stone in the hills south of the river, it's the Crown that they most desire.'

Elodi counted on her fingers. 'You have mentioned six stones, where is the seventh?'

Eryn bowed her head. 'Where we laid Amyra to rest in the woods on the hill outside Hadrin. There is an orchard nearby. The locals believe their apples are the finest in the realms due to the soil and favorable weather. But it's the hidden stone on the hill that lengthens the growing season and sweetens their fruit.' She mumbled. 'We must not let their apples fail. What would the people...?' She slumped.

Arijan steadied her sister. 'While the locals may treasure their crop, Eryn, our priority lies elsewhere. Amyra suffered greatly at the hands of Vordrak, we cannot allow her peace to be disturbed, and another stone to fail.'

Eryn straightened. 'Yes... yes, of course. I tire. My thoughts are... muddled.'

Arijan lifted Eryn with ease. 'Let Moonbeam take you from here.' She placed her on his back and caught Toryn's eye. 'She'll recover once we reach the stone.' Her jaw tightened. 'But we have little time. The warlocks will not rest. We suspect seven are active in the realms at present. The three we tracked, strive to assail the stones. The others we assume work with Uluriel, perhaps to prepare the way for Ormoroth's return. If only there were more of us, we could—' Arijan looked to Eryn. 'Ah! That reminds me. You may help us solve a mystery, Toryn. Perhaps you can help us with something that has baffled us since Roth's Doom.'

Eryn appeared to recover a little. 'Baffled indeed. It relates to when you brought the Amayan host to the battle.'

Elodi smiled as she recalled the moment. 'At first, I thought the sun had come down to the plain. That was an impressive feat to bring a vision of their charge as they rode to Draegelan's aid. It broke the Ruuk lines and saved our right flank.'

A glimmer appeared in Eryn's eyes. 'But it was more than just a vision. We saw the front riders of Toryn's *apparitions* strike down dozens of Ruuk.'

Toryn gasped. 'But… surely that's not possible. I didn't even get the chance to fetch an apple under Nyomae's guidance. To bring Amayans back in the flesh would be well beyond my ability.'

Arijan beamed. 'It appeared the strength we gave to you on that day, greatly enhanced your powers. Not all the host were present, but it looked to me as if the front ranks had physical form.'

Elodi patted Moonbeam. 'Then I am encouraged. To bring back even a dozen Amayans would considerably strengthen our hand.'

Toryn remained unconvinced. 'But remember, that only works if we face our foes where the Amayans have ridden in the past. I imagine our enemy are only too aware of our shared history. If I commanded their forces, I'd take that into consideration.'

But Elodi was not to be deterred. 'Then we must dictate from now on where we face them. The crucial points in the realms have not changed. The battles to come will likely be fought in the same places.' She peered into the darkness. 'But first, we find Nyomae. Can you *see* her?'

Toryn tried the *farsight* but could see little. 'The stone must stand a little farther ahead. Either it doesn't permit my *farsight* to see it, or another hinders my vision. But I believe Nyomae is here. I sense a… ripple in my Verse.'

There is another way.

So cold. Nyomae had never experienced such cold. With her head bowed down against the driving snow, she shuffled on into the face of a gale. *Another step… one more step.* She had to keep moving. The last remaining hope for the realms lay a little farther ahead. She could not fail. *One more step… keep moving.* To her left, the sheer drop into oblivion awaited her. The ice beneath her feet promised the void her deliverance. But not to be outdone, the wind hurtled down the chasm, crying out in glee as it sought to topple the Imaari. The snow thickened; the gale strengthened, each vying to satisfy the gaping maw's desire to drag Nyomae into the underworld. But it was the cold that Nyomae feared would bring about her end. Its groping fingers probed deep, tightening its grip to wring every last trace of warmth from her aching body. Her lips, fixed into a grimace on her frozen face, cracked as she tried to utter words that would bring strength. But her way to her Verse was shut; others had joined the fray.

Voices merged with the howls of the wind. At first, they gave Nyomae hope as their chorus calmed the gales. But as the wind ceased, their song changed. The harmonies conflicted; the lilting voices became shrieks. Nyomae clasped her hands to her ears but could find no peace. But she knew them. The Three Maidens screamed, pleading for her to release them from their icy cell and end their torment. *Speak his name! Speak his Name and let us be free.*

Nyomae yelled against their wails. 'I cannot. I dare not speak his Name!' As their voices faded, their desperate cries echoed down the chasm to be heard by the odd traveler, foolish enough to be out on such a night. The snow eased. Nyomae stopped. Ahead, the sheer face of a gigantic mountain rose sharply, thrusting its peak beyond the skies to pierce the Great Dome. No longer able to spin, it would be forever night, forever winter in the mortal lands. Nothing could grow without the light of the Maidens' Day and the warmth of summer. The dying trees would bow their heads in despair at Ormoroth's return; the seas would cease to ebb and flow, frozen in horror as the darkness assumed its rule.

The blood in Nyomae's veins froze. Her stomach roiled. Low at first, a throb pulsed as if a hammer pounded at the very foundations of the land. The mountain before her wavered. The rocks faded. Deep within the mountain, the black pillar stood. More solid than the mountain itself, its presence violated the Maidens' creation. It bent the power of the land to its will. It was the source of Ormoroth's strength — and Nyomae felt its power grow as the Amanach diminished. It had to be destroyed.

Toryn's face tingled. He looked up to see a glimmering light between the old, gnarled trunks. A bright lamp appeared to move behind them. Long shadows shifted across the forest floor as if trying to bewilder unwelcome visitors. He squinted into the light but could not see Nyomae. Yet he no longer felt the need to hurry. He moved as if in a dream without a care. Ahead, Elodi and the Amayans strolled towards the light but cast no shadow. He stared, enthralled by the change. The light from the Amanach shone through the Amayans. Eryn and Arijan wore long, flowing cloaks of blue silk that shimmered as if stars reflected off a still lake. On their heads, bands of silver glistened like crowns. Toryn knew he looked back into the distant past when the Amayans were young and their power undiminished by the evils of time. Yet Elodi appeared different. The light dimmed as it passed through her, and she wore no cloak or crown. But that did not diminish her. Elodi appeared as if a queen of the old days in Toryn's eyes, walking tall and with ease to inspire confidence in all who followed.

'He's got that look on his face again, Eryn.' Arijan's voice echoed. Her mouth moved slower than her words. Her eyes glowed as she smiled at Toryn.

He held up his hand against the dazzling light. 'You look different. You've all changed.'

Eryn laughed; it seemed like music to Toryn's ears. 'Ah. Then we shall excuse you on this occasion. We are passing into the time of the stone. Things may appear a little altered for a while. This stone retains much of its old power. But...' she glanced back towards the light's source. 'Your Imaari heritage must be strong. Few can see our true likeness, even in the light of the Amanach.'

Toryn bowed his head. 'Then I'm honored. You are truly... magnificent.'

Arijan tilted her head. 'The stone has also changed you.'

Eryn agreed. 'You bear more the likeness of your father, but... there's something else. While I see Finromir, there's another presence. Yet, I cannot fathom who... or what.' She turned. 'We are nearly through. Don't be deceived, Toryn. Keep moving, don't stop or you may be lost.'

Toryn gaped. The trees had gone. Behind the Amayans, the air shimmered with a brilliant blue light. One moment it seemed a wall of flame stood in their way: another, as if a powerful waterfall. He did as told and walked through. A blinding light took his vision. But he did not need his eyes. 'She's here. I can feel her.' Toryn clutched his stomach. 'But... there's another. A *kruul*. And I'm certain it's that of Uluriel.'

Nyomae stood before the iron gates of Ormoroth's stronghold of the north. Greater than Vortimo, no Imaari had ever laid eyes upon the ice fortress of Vorkirik. Its thick walls encased the mountain that bore the citadel that crowned its peak. Nyomae quailed in its presence. But how had she crossed the treacherous lands of the far north, and then eluded the dark creatures guarding the narrow bridge?

The vast gate swung silently open. An eerie green haze lit her way along the stone slabs, inviting her to enter. But for what purpose? Nyomae stiffened, wishing to turn and flee, but she knew she had no other way open to her. She drew upon her last reserves of strength, passed beneath the arch and entered Vorkirik.

The Amanach stood upon a knoll beside a pool of glistening, blue water, surrounded by a circle of young trees. Toryn and the Amayans were now in a different time and place. At his back, morning had broken in the South Forest, yet above him a clear night sky, burst with vibrant stars. For a moment, Toryn could believe all was well and the power of the Elorym prevailed. But the Imaari blood in his veins knew otherwise. The stone pulsed, but it seemed not with an ancient and timeless power. It appeared labored, strained by the dark forces determined to bring about its demise. The edges of the Amanach wavered as if a great source of heat sat behind.

Calestri strolled to meet them. 'Nyomae is here. But not the Imaari we know. Another possesses her.' She led them around the stone. Nyomae stood with her head bowed and her arms outstretched. Unlike the Amayans, Nyomae cast a shadow… but a shadow of another. Toryn gazed in horror at a bent figure of a woman wearing a crown of twisted spikes. Her long fingers reached out, groping at the air towards the stone. Nyomae spoke, but not with her voice. Her words pained Toryn's ears. The stone emitted a low squeal.

Eryn held her finger to her lips. 'We must not awaken her. To do so now could cause grievous harm.' She placed her hand on the stone's dark surface. Beneath her fingers it rippled as if she touched water. 'We have time… but must not delay. We shall attempt to draw out the *kruul.* We must be ready for what may surface.'

The Amayans and Elodi joined hands and formed a ring around Nyomae. Eryn turned to Toryn. 'Please, join us. Your Imaari blood will strengthen our circle.' He gladly accepted and took the hands of Elodi and Calestri. Eryn continued. 'We'll call upon the Amanach and direct its power at the darkness in Nyomae's heart.'

The Amayans began to sing. Toryn's head swam as their voices evoked a deep memory that he knew he shared with his ancestors. It awoke an ache in his heart to be somewhere else, akin to what he had felt at the coast watching the sun rise over the restless sea. Elodi clutched his hand; she too sensed her connection to the past.

The stone glowed brighter. Toryn's body tingled.

High above Nyomae, the vaulted ceiling flickered red, but if the light came from a fire, its heat could not penetrate her chilled bones. The throbbing shook her teeth, assaulted her ears, and forced her heart to beat to its harmful rhythm. She should turn and flee, but still her feet took her towards the source of her pain. Nyomae found herself at the edge of a deep pit... and the source of the light. Her toes clenched as she looked down. The walls glimmered. First red, then lower down through orange to yellow. Nyomae looked down the shaft the Norgog had mined many centuries ago. Sunk so deep, it pierced the veins of the land and bled its power. Between the dull thud of the Angorlith's pulse, Nyomae could hear the roar of the furnaces beneath her, fed by the magma from the shaft. But what new devices of evil did the slaves forge? And who toiled in the heat to work the vast engines?

But she had not endured the long journey to destroy the forges. On the opposite side of the pit, a tall and narrow arch led to the very heart of Vorkirik... and the vault that suffered the Angorlith. That was where she must go. She circled the shaft, enduring the pain of every step. Nyomae passed beneath the arch and into the darkness. Inside, blacker still, stood the Angorlith. It devoured the warmth and light of the world to feed its insatiable hunger. A green light flickered beneath its slimy surface that seemed to ooze dark blood that pooled at her feet. It sickened Nyomae to the core, but she forced her aching body towards Ormoroth's vile iron pillar.

Nyomae hesitated. *I cannot do this. I am too weak.* But the voice that had brought her this far, spoke. *Draw upon my powers. Together we can destroy it.* She let the energy from below flow through her. Nyomae raised her hands and spoke with the voice from deep within.

The Amayan voices rose. The stone blazed but Toryn found he could endure its light. Nyomae writhed as she grasped at the stone. But now the light shone through her to reveal a dark presence at her core. Like dye in water, its fingers reached out, seeking to infect her body and soul. The blot quivered… then rose through Nyomae's throat. She threw back her head. Her mouth gaped as if pleading for her life. Eryn yelled. 'Begone! Leave this soul!'

Nyomae shuddered, then vomited forth a dark fluid that dispelled like smoke in the Amanach's light.

The walls of the vault collapsed. A scream tore from Nyomae's throat, but she made no sound. Sunlight filled the gloom. The light revealed not a gigantic iron pillar, but a smooth, black stone. Her legs buckled. Strong arms caught her.

Toryn held Nyomae. 'She's free.' He lowered her to the floor beside the stone as the Amayans dropped to their knees and gave thanks to the Three. Nyomae shivered. Her wide eyes beheld Toryn, but she seemed not to see him. He spoke softly. 'Nyomae. Do you know me?'

Her hand went to his face as she whispered. 'I know you, Toryn…' she looked passed him, 'and my sisters. You're here.' A tear trickled down her cheek. 'I thought you were all dead, and…' Nyomae frowned as she looked to the trees. 'And… I was at Vorkirik. And this stone was the Angorlith.'

Toryn helped her to sit. 'You are in the South Forest… and the Amayans have rid you of the Uluriel's *kruul*.'

'For that I am grateful, but… I cannot fully return just yet.' Her body warmed as she regained some of her strength. 'Now I am free, I see what must be done. Please… allow me to return to the Song. I must not delay. My time runs out.' Nyomae closed her eyes and sagged against Toryn.

He looked up. 'Her time runs out? What does she mean by that?'

Eryn stood. 'I trust Nyomae knows her mind.' She turned to her sisters. 'We must go. I shall ride to Hadrin to ensure the stone is safe, and Amyra's soul is at peace. Arijan and Calestri will rejoin Igrayne on her watch at the Crown.' Then to Toryn. 'Nyomae is free of the *kruul*. I suggest you take her back to Borrund and allow her the time she needs to recover.'

Elodi kept her eyes on Nyomae. 'Is there anything more we can do to assist her?'

Eryn strolled back to the horses, calling over her shoulder. 'Let the healers care for her. I doubt there's much else you can do… except wait.'

Toryn lifted Nyomae and followed Elodi. He placed her on his saddle and climbed up behind her. 'I know little of the Crown, only that it's the name of the first mountains in the Kolossos.'

Eryn patted Moonbeam's flank. 'The first… or the last, according where you live. I cannot tell you who gave it that name, but if you approach from the north, there are four peaks that form what could… with a stretch of your imagination, look like a crown.' She mounted. 'The entrance was once guarded by a fortress. It was built by the Elorym in the early years of strife with Ormoroth. It was their most northerly defense against the forces pouring out of Vorkirik.' Eryn turned Moonbeam away from the stone. 'I imagine in its day it was quite a feat, even for the Elorym. It sits upon a great rock shelf in the shadow of the Crown, reached only by a narrow ravine through a cliff face. The wall looks as if a giant wave is about to break on the Nordruuk Plains.'

Arijan drew her horse next to Eryn. They exchanged a glance. 'We fought a battle many years ago in that place.' She turned to Elodi. 'It is where your mother was mortally wounded… and Tanis fell.' She patted Calestri's hand. 'And where poor Cali bore the brunt of a shreek's attack.'

Elodi shuddered. 'It sounds a cursed place.'

Calestri whispered. 'Cursed indeed.'

Eryn approached the shimmering wall surrounding the stone. 'The fortress still stands, but much is in ruins and is not a place that is easily defended. The lookout towers of the mountain sides have fared little better. However, it no longer has the feel of an Elorym structure. The fortress has changed hands numerous times over the years. Too many lives have been lost defending or attempting to recapture it. Atrocities that should not be spoken have been committed beneath the shadow of the Crown. And alas, thanks to the attention of the warlocks since Draegelan's day, what remained of the Elorym's power has long since diminished. Sadly, the warlocks now see it as their own.'

Toryn ducked as they passed through the Amanach's shroud. Outside, the late afternoon bathed the dreary trees with a dull, gray light, but he could not tell if it was the same day. He turned back to see the Amayans no longer shone. He frowned. 'The Crown Stone lies nearby, yet the warlocks have not found it?'

Eryn kicked on Moonbeam. 'It's half a league south. Yet it remains hidden. They must believe the fortress was for defense against Ormoroth alone, and not to guard the precious stone beyond. The Amanach nestles between the peaks of the Crown. It can only be reached via a hidden way that scales the side of Gorgonach, the mountain that forms the crest at its front.' Eryn turned her horse. 'Now we go. We will send word of our progress.'

Elodi opened her mouth to wish them luck, but they were gone.

7. Sword of the Realms

The aralak activity in and around Borrund had all but ceased. The patrols had quickly learned to spot the signs of a likely presence of the spiders. And with guidance from Cubric, they had devised tactics to deal effectively with the beasts while reducing casualties. But Lord Ormsk still appeared ungrateful. A week had passed since Elodi's forces had arrived, and preparations for the missions to Keld and Drunsberg were well underway. But while Elodi was pleased with the recovery of Captain Gundrul, and many of the wounded, Nyomae remained in a deep sleep despite her time in the presence of an Amanach.

Elodi walked with Bardon through the temporary camp set up outside Borrund's barricade. The sounds of swords clashing and captains bellowing their commands, greeted them as they approached the camp's center. From his bedside, Gundrul had issued a command to restart daily weapons training, and Elodi was pleased to see the drills resumed.

Elodi watched the guards rest as a flask of water was passed around. She was reminded of the young reserves training at the port of Seransea shortly after Calerdorn's fall. While her hastily arranged speech had helped to raise their spirits, she had feared for their lives once faced with the battle-hardened Ruuk. Mercifully, the enemy had stayed mainly in Dorn, but she wondered how many would have gone north to bolster the defenses on the border. Had their training prepared them for the demands of the front?

Bardon cleared his throat. Elodi turned to him, realizing he had been speaking. Her expression gave away her guilt. Bardon winked. 'Forgiven. Thankfully, you're more attentive where it counts, eh, on the battlefield.' He gestured to the guards. 'Cubric, Gundrul and I have discussed tactics for Keld. We'll take a force comprised of those loyal to Broon led by Captain Amyndra, plus Ruan's spearmen, ably supported by Cubric and a company of Archonians. We believe a total of eight hundred in all should suffice. Then we'll aim to drive the Ruuk back over the borders.'

Elodi nodded. 'Good. Those in Lunn caught in the middle will be more at ease if it's Broon's own soldiers leading the mission.'

He straightened. 'But I believe you, Elodi, should take overall command of the mission.'

She stiffened. 'With respect, Bardon, I disagree. It should be you. I wouldn't deem to impose on matters concerning your realm. While Kernlow gave me command of the Five Realms' forces, it should be the true Lord Broon who marches on Keld.' Elodi attempted to smile. 'In fact, as commander, I command you to lead.'

'Then I accept your decision. And… thank you for your faith. But I trust you will still ride with us, Elodi?'

'I… I hadn't intended to.' Her stomach knotted. 'I didn't think my presence would be necessary.'

Bardon stopped and turned to her. 'If you need longer to recover from Roth's Doom, please just say so. No one can blame you. You've faced terrors few could expect to withstand.'

Elodi paused as the guards restarted their training. 'But many who fought and were injured will march on Keld. I cannot stay here while others fight. But…'

'But nothing, Elodi. There is much work to be done away from the battlefield. You'd be just as valuable here planning for the Drunsberg and Calerdorn campaigns.' He rested his hand on her shoulder. 'You have my full support if you wish to sit this one out.'

Elodi jumped as swords clattered onto a shield wall. She straightened. 'No. I *shall* ride with you, Bardon. We have a saying in Calerdorn. If you fall off your horse, you get straight back on it. To delay...' she took a breath, 'to delay makes it harder to resume.' Elodi looked back to the guards as one side prevailed, pushing the shield wall back to the delight of their commander. 'I admit my nerves were frayed in the aftermath of the battle. During the fighting, I didn't have the time to think, it was about surviving one blow to face the next. But afterwards... the death, the suffering, the cries of the wounded, shook me to the core.'

Bardon let out a long sigh. 'You have seen so much in your short but eventful life, more than many who've lived thrice your years. It's no surprise you now have doubts.'

The guards laughed as those retreating slipped and fell onto their backs into the mud. Elodi watched them as they tried to regain their feet, only to fall back into the mire. 'It's good to hear their mirth. I dearly hope we will one day be able to sing our songs and enjoy life once more.' Her hand clutched her sword. 'This is why we fight, Bardon.' Her jaw clenched. 'It's my destiny. I must do all I can to secure the realms. I will get back onto my horse and ride with you to Keld.'

'That is good to hear, and trust me, Nordryn will shudder when he sees your plume at the head of our ranks.'

Elodi strode on. 'And knights, Bardon? You see no need for them taking part?'

'An unnecessary luxury. They'd serve no real benefit. The terrain does not suit, or warrant, a mounted attack. And once inside the city, should hand-to-hand fighting ensue, the narrow streets would present a problem.' He groaned as he stretched out his back. 'I hope to be back on a soft bed before long. The dispatches smuggled out from Ruan's men inside the city, report the heavy losses suffered at Roth's Doom have severely depleted Nordryn's forces. Morale is low and I'm hopeful the Ruuk stationed in Keld will not defend it with the same enthusiasm as they would their own land.' His bushy eyebrows raised. 'If we're lucky, many may choose to turn tail and run when they see us coming.'

Elodi pointed to the benches. 'Let's sit. You need to conserve your strength.' Bardon gratefully accepted. She nodded to the young reserves who beamed as they approached. 'And what of Nordryn? Do you believe he's keen to hold out?'

Bardon slowly lowered himself to the bench. 'He's a difficult man to read. I knew a little about him before he took my position. But I must admit, I never had him down to be a traitor. His ancestors came south almost four hundred years ago and had, until now, been loyal to the Lords of Broon. I imagine whether he defends Keld or not, depends on the demands of his new commanders, be it Uluriel or the warlocks.'

'Then I would assume he'll fight. I can't think our enemy would wish to concede such a strategic position as Keld. While we've protected the forests, we don't know if they've sourced inferior timber elsewhere to build a fleet. If they have, then the city's port is vital.'

Bardon shuddered. 'Indeed. The seas to the north are not for the faint-hearted sailor. I for one would not relish sailing those unpredictable waters.' His face paled. 'Or for that matter, I would not willingly set foot on a boat even if it sat on a flat pond.'

'And none would blame you after your last ordeal at sea.' Elodi patted his leg. 'So, let us prepare for a fight on land for Keld. And I would hope the inhabitants will rise to support you once you ride through the gates.'

A young man approached wearing the colors of Lord Ormsk. He stopped a few paces short and stuttered. 'Ma'am. Lord. Apologies for interrupting your... your meeting, but... Captain Toryn asked me to inform you he believes Lady Nyomae is about to wake.'

Elodi entered the infirmary to find Toryn clutching the Imaari's hand. He glanced up but did not speak. He nodded to the chair on the opposite side of the bed, then bowed his head. Elodi sat, noting the color had returned to Nyomae's face. Toryn muttered under his breath. He paused as if listening for an answer, then opened his eyes and smiled at Elodi. 'She's waking... but I cannot tell what state she'll be in.'

Nyomae's eyelids flickered. Her breath quickened, then she gasped and sat bolt upright. Her gaze darted about the room, but she soon calmed as she recognized their faces. Nyomae relaxed and lay back against the headboard. When she spoke, her voice was quiet but steady. 'It is good to be back.'

Elodi exhaled. 'You are most welcome.'

Toryn beamed. 'You cannot imagine just how relieved we are.'

'I have much to tell.' Nyomae smiled. 'But first, seeing as we're all here, I assume we were victorious at Roth's Doom.'

Elodi glanced to Toryn. 'Yes... but at great cost. But had you not freed Dorlan from Uleva's grip, I think we'd have seen an entirely different outcome.'

Nyomae sighed. 'And was I right about Dorlan's fate?'

'He lived long enough to turn the battle in our favor.' Elodi's scalp prickled. 'I rode with him. We charged down the enemy and turned the tide. Dorlan slayed Uleva and many more. Toryn and I had the honor to be with him at his death.' Elodi held Nyomae's hand. 'You released

Dorlan from a most terrible ordeal. And you were correct. Deep down, Dorlan was aware of the vile deeds Uleva forced him to commit.'

Toryn clasped Nyomae's other hand. 'Before he died, I believe Elodi helped to ease his guilt. She told him his actions swung the battle, and perhaps helped to right some of the wrongs done in his name.'

Nyomae tipped back her head and closed her eyes. 'That is good to hear. The poor man had endured many years of pain and humiliation.'

Elodi leaned forward. 'And what of your ordeals of late? You also seemed to suffer.'

'Suffer? Yes, I suppose I did, but nothing compared to Dorlan.' Nyomae looked at both their faces. 'I apologize for my abrupt manner when I woke at the Amanach. I had much I wanted to learn before Uluriel shut me out of the Verses I sought.'

'You have no need to apologize to us.' Toryn laughed. 'But you will if you don't tell us what you've learned.'

Nyomae nodded. 'Then I shall proceed as best I can recall.' She took a breath. 'When I found Dorlan on the Nordruuk ice plains, it was Uluriel who commanded him back then. She came as soon as she sensed my presence in his Verse. I was not aware at the time, but while I fought to free Dorlan, the Uluriel from the present entered my Verse at the battlefield. I believe she foresaw the defeat at Roth's Doom, thus took steps to hinder my recovery.' Her head dropped. 'She drove me to despair, leading me to believe we were defeated,' she gripped their hands, 'and you were both dead, and the undefended realms sacked and burned.' Nyomae looked up. 'Uluriel did this to force my hand, to convince me there was no other way than to... I came to the brink of invoking Ormoroth's Name.'

Elodi's blood froze. 'And in your despair, Uluriel would have exploited your weakness to open the gateway?'

'Thankfully, not directly. In my dream state, speaking the Name would serve only to reveal it to Uluriel, but it would not have opened the gateway. Of course, had she learned of it, she could invoke it herself. But those who utter the Name of one so powerful as Ormoroth, will leave themself exposed. There are many dangers when breaching the barrier between the mortal lands and those beyond, many unknown to both I and Uluriel.'

Toryn frowned. 'Then can we assume Uluriel doesn't know Ormoroth's Name?'

'That is correct. Thus, I know the Nym did not grant Uluriel access to Telamir when in the guise of the Archon. Hence, she did not solve the Maidens' Cypher and discover what she desired. But Uluriel has underestimated me. Even in my state of despair, she could not wrest the Name from my mind. For my own sake, I took the precaution to bury it deep, placing it beyond easy reach, even for myself. It is only in the direst of circumstances would I choose to retrieve that word.'

Elodi glanced to Toryn. 'And the stone? Was that Uluriel's doing?'

'When she failed to retrieve the Name, she used me to attack the Amanach.' Nyomae winced. 'I thought I stood before the Angorlith. Can you imagine, I actually believed I could destroy it.'

Toryn thought for a moment. 'Thus, Uluriel still needs you to speak Ormoroth's Name. Therefore, she cannot kill you, or expel you from this realm.'

'That is both a blessing and a curse. While I live, I can either save or condemn the people of this land.' Nyomae coughed. Her hand went to her throat. 'I'm parched. I have much more to tell, but I fear my voice will be lost.'

Elodi gasped. 'Ah, we must apologize. How thoughtless.'

Toryn stood, found a glass, and filled it with water.

He handed it to Nyomae and grinned sheepishly. 'We were so relieved to see you back, we did not think.'

Nyomae drained the glass. 'Thank you. I'm sure you have much that occupies your minds.' She smiled. 'So… you are forgiven.' The smile faded as her gaze went to the small window. 'Uluriel may not have got from me what she desired, but I believe she seeks other means to bring back Ormoroth.'

Toryn stiffened. 'Is that possible? I thought the only way was to invoke the Name and open the gateway.'

'Uluriel is well versed in the ways of the Song, more so than any living Imaari. She may have failed to find Aber's last line, but she has ventured deeper into the Song than any since Draegelan. But she has been absent for much of the past year.' Her brow creased. 'Uluriel is up to something, something that eludes me. While she wishes to discover Ormoroth's Name, I'm certain she knows of another way to bring him back.'

Elodi took a deep breath. 'Then how can she be stopped? It's beyond our ability to find her, let alone challenge her.'

'Not all is yet lost. Her failure has set her back. If there are other means to open the way for her Master, I imagine it will take time… and much of her strength. And I am stronger than she suspected.' Nyomae's eyes narrowed. 'And… Uluriel has made a mistake. By entering my Verse as she did, she has weakened the bonds. Thus, I can now enter Verses previously closed to me. But that does leave me vulnerable to being separated from my own.' Nyomae looked to Toryn. 'And I now realize you tried to help me while in my stupor. Yet, you appeared as a warlock, that is why I repelled your attempts. But that may have been for the best. You would have been exposed to Uluriel too soon, and… she would not have spared you. Or perhaps worse, she would use you against Finromir.'

She patted his hand. 'He still lives, Toryn. But she keeps him alive for some foul purpose.' Her jaw tightened. 'I'm certain now he figures in her plans for Ormoroth's return.'

Toryn's fists clenched. 'We must be ready. She'll surely make an appearance sooner or later.'

Nyomae sighed. 'I can find no presence of her in the Song, despite my new powers. Uluriel is plotting. And like the Ruuk, I fear her most when I cannot see her. Therefore, I am not safe. Uluriel will not rest until she has Ormoroth's Name, or forces me to invoke it. But I don't suspect she'll come for me directly.'

'Nordleng?' Elodi gripped the edge of her chair. 'Those swine are her preferred weapon for stealth. I shall ensure the guard is doubled. We cannot—'

'That won't be necessary.' Nyomae looked to the door. 'I don't envisage being here long.'

Toryn looked to Elodi. 'Is it wise to leave Borrund?'

'In my sleep, Uluriel showed me many terrible events, and took me to dark places.' Nyomae folded her arms. 'But in my travels, I came across Idraman.'

Elodi gasped. 'Your predecessor lives?'

'As I had suspected, but he's close to death. Idraman has spent the last three hundred years in Elmarand's dungeons. I cannot imagine how he has survived all this time while sustaining his Word of Forbidding at the gate.'

Toryn frowned. 'But he saved them by sealing the pass. How did he end up in a dungeon? And what of the Lost Realms? Can they help us?'

Nyomae shook her head. 'There is much I cannot tell within the mists that cloud the many Verses that lead to the south. But I perceive the Lost Realms are weak and have not recovered from the losses inflicted at Gormadon Plain. And unfortunately, both Idraman's and my actions in that battle contributed to their current state.' She held up her hand at Toryn's protest. 'The powers in the south must have blamed Idraman for the devastation.'

Elodi grimaced. 'But it's been three hundred years. The poor man must have served his time by now.'

'Perhaps the rulers in the south remain wary of Idraman's powers, and despite his advanced years, they still see him as a threat.' Nyomae pulled back her sheets. 'I have been in my slumber too long. There is much to be done.'

Elodi placed her hand on Nyomae's shoulder. 'You have been through a most terrible ordeal. You must rest, surely, it can wait a day or two longer.'

But Nyomae stood. 'I must meet with Idraman... in person.'

Toryn gaped at her. 'But he's in the south, and not to mention the small matter of the Caerwal Gate being closed.'

Nyomae grasped Toryn's arm to steady her balance. 'I need to place my hands in his to learn what he knows. I believe he is also in possession of Ormoroth's Name. But why has he not invoked it? Yes, there are dangers, but Idraman is an Imaari of great strength. While his mortal body weakens, he is still a formidable presence in the Song. Idraman briefly connected with the Maidens at the Caerwal Pass. He went deep into the Song, perhaps as far as Draegelan. He bonded with the old powers beneath the Caerwals to speak *my* Name. If he knew Ormoroth's, why did he not use it in his moment of despair? Does he know something I do not? He is a most honorable man. He would have taken the risk of being dragged into the Void along with Ormoroth, if it meant he saved the realms.' Nyomae picked up her scarf beside the bed. 'I shall go to Archonholm.'

Toryn wrapped it around Nyomae's neck. 'That is at best a three-week journey, even on the fastest horse. And then how far to Elmarand? You could be gone months.'

'We need you here, Nyomae.' Elodi sided with Toryn. 'We cannot fight this battle alone. A horse is too slow. There are no ships capable of negotiating the treacherous seas of the east coast.' She paced the room. 'To reach the port of Calerdorn to take the *Celestra*, would add weeks. And even then, the old lady is vulnerable to rough seas.'

Nyomae smiled. 'I do not intend to go by sea... or road' — she glanced to Toryn — 'or by tunnel, or river.'

Elodi threw up her hands. 'Then how? That leaves only... no, surely not.'

Nyomae beamed. 'I found it, just before I woke. The corvraak lies injured in a wood near Gwend. It knows death approaches. I will seek to locate and heal it.'

Now Toryn became exasperated. 'But a corvraak?' He exchanged a glance with Elodi. 'It pains me to suggest this, but are you certain you're fully in command of your mind? Can you be sure Uluriel does not influence your thoughts?'

Nyomae laughed, suddenly resembling the powerful Imaari again. 'More than ever. In an odd way, Uluriel's intervention has opened my eyes. I have always seen things based upon the morals of my upbringing. But seeing into Uluriel's mind has made me a little more... devious, yes, that's the word. I can appreciate a little better what motivates our enemy. And I wonder if our chances of survival will improve if we deploy some of their methods against them.' She held out her arms as if a bird. 'If Uleva can fly, then why not I?'

Elodi listened. 'That may be so. If we can understand more of our enemy, perhaps we could anticipate their next move. But Toryn still has a point. Would a corvraak willingly allow you to ride it?'

Nyomae looked to the sky outside. 'I admit it's a risk. It may attempt to rip me limb from limb, but I believe deep in its dark heart, I can find the spirit of the noble raven from which it is spawned. The bird still yearns to dominate the skies. I can offer it a final flight… or hopefully two so I can return. If I can appeal to the raven within, it may welcome the chance to fly once more. Uleva is dead, and Uluriel appears to have no use of its service at present. If successful, I could make the journey to Archonholm in two days.'

Elodi straightened. 'Could it fly over the gate?'

'That I will not attempt on the corvraak close to the end of its life. There are larger flying beasts from Ormoroth's reign that may yet live among the snowy peaks of Nordruuk. They could possibly make the journey, but I doubt they would suffer my presence.'

Elodi shuddered, remembering the claws of the dark raven. 'There are flying beasts larger than a corvraak?'

'Ormoroth found ways to corrupt much of the Maidens' creations. Sadly, the eagles of the north could not evade his attention. Some were captured, spoiled, and then used to spawn the keshwing, foul creatures capable of inflicting great harm. Most were destroyed by Draegelan's elite knights and archers, but some may have fled north and survive to this day.' Nyomae walked to the window and looked up to the sky. 'Keshwing can fly higher and possibly cross the Caerwals. But I would not wish to seek and disturb them.' She yawned and stretched. 'The corvraak will suffice. There's more to those mountains than meets the eye. An old power resides within, one that Idraman briefly called upon to aid us at Gormadon. Those powers would most likely resist an attempt by one of Ormoroth's abominations to fly over them, even under my influence. I would not want to be on its back in full flight should the bird fall. Besides, I doubt a corvraak could tolerate the heat of the south. It may even struggle with the warmth of Archonholm, but I hope the autumn has driven the heat away by now. And, if I'm right about the people of the south, the sight of a *wyke* riding a monstrous raven, would do little to convince them to allow me access to Idraman.'

Toryn recalled the blank space beyond the Caerwals on Hamar's map. 'How far is Elmarand from the pass?'

'No more than four days on a swift horse. The roads are lined with canals and trees that offer shade and water aplenty for the long ride.'

Elodi joined them at the window. 'Then you will open the gate?'

'There's no other way. The way south by sea remains closed. The waters still churn which leads me to suspect Uluriel doesn't want me to find Idraman.'

But Elodi remained to be persuaded . 'Or... some plot she's hatching that she doesn't want us to discover yet.'

'That is a risk. But one I will have to take if I'm to consult with Idraman.'

Elodi's lips pursed. 'What if our enemy's dark arts conceal what truly lies on the other side of the gate? Could Uluriel have an army waiting for it to open?'

Toryn ran his finger down the damp windowpane. 'Dravic and his builders must have finished Kernlow's Tower by now. You could see for yourself what's on the other side.'

'That would be a wise precaution. I cannot be certain of what I've seen of the south is real or one of Uluriel's deceptions.'

Elodi watched the farmers' carts trundle along the cobbles to bring their produce to the market. She turned back to Nyomae. 'But if those in the south see us as a threat... we may find we have another front to defend.'

Nyomae sighed. 'That is true, but I desperately need to speak with Idraman.'

Elodi accepted Nyomae's reasoning. 'Then once through the pass, you will need an escort. We cannot risk losing you in an attack by superstitious locals.'

'No, I think it's best I go alone. A company of riders will attract more attention. I can avoid most eyes, or I could appear to them as…' she winked at Toryn, 'a certain bent old lady you once met.'

Toryn laughed. 'Surely no one will see *her* as a threat.'

Nyomae chuckled. 'Ah, the bliss of ignorance. But those days are gone. I cannot predict how I will be greeted by those in Elmarand, but I don't anticipate a warm welcome.'

Toryn turned back to the room. 'It will be a hazardous journey, but I agree, it's one that must be taken. I wish I could come with you. Even if we were denied entry, to see the city where my father once lived would be worth the journey.'

Nyomae took his arm. 'Perhaps one day we can make that journey together, Toryn. But alas, I fear it may not be the city it once was. While its towers and walls must still stand, I doubt its people do it justice. Idraman would not be incarcerated if they were like those I knew during my time of study.'

Elodi walked to the door. 'Then we must get a message to Lord Kernlow. Only he has the authority to open the gate. I shall have to word it carefully to give him no choice but to agree. He must be only a few days from the Ormsk border by now. But I cannot risk such a message of importance falling into the hands of our enemy. Ah, yes. I know just the horse and rider. Tempest and Lena. They have proven most trustworthy. It was Lena who rode to Tunduska Gap to tell Ruan of Calerdorn's fall.' She exhaled. 'This mission will surely be less dangerous. I couldn't shake the thought back then that I had sent horse and rider to their deaths across Dorn Plain teeming with Ruuk.'

Nyomae retrieved her cloak from the bedside and

threw it around her shoulders. 'Then let us not delay. My strength returns. I am twice the Imaari I was before the battle. I shall leave first thing in the morning to find our coarse-feathered friend.'

Elodi and Toryn accompanied Nyomae to the main gate and said their farewells in the gray light of the new day. They watched as her horse galloped towards the snow-covered hills of Lunn. They both knew the risks Nyomae faced but had accepted her mission was essential. Every part of her journey would come with its own dangers. Even the first stretch involved crossing country that could be occupied by rogue bands of Ruuk, or worse, Nordleng. Once at the outskirts of the forest, Nyomae would set the horse free to return to Borrund; neither horse nor corvraak would welcome the sight of the other. Then, she had to locate the bird in a forest likely infested with the spiders escaping Borrund's patrols. Nyomae was confident she could deal with that threat, but she then had to tame and heal the corvraak. And if successful, the flight south would not be easy in the thin air. But the real challenges would begin once she reached Archonholm. Could the gate be easily opened after three hundred years? And then came the journey into the unknown to reach Elmarand.

Elodi clutched Toryn's hand. 'I know she's stronger now, but so much relies on her success. And by the Three, Toryn, what if we lose her?'

They turned to walk back to the main gate. Toryn glanced to the road as a dozen carts trundled in. 'But if she discovers what Idraman knows, and perhaps brings him back… that would strengthen our hand somewhat.'

'Ma'am?' An aide approached. She held out her hand. 'A message from Eldamouth.'

Elodi accepted the envelope and slid her finger along

the seal. She read the few lines and placed it in her breast pocket. She thanked the aide then turned to Toryn. 'It's best we discuss this in my room.' They walked through the streets, already crowded with morning traders setting up their stalls. Elodi nodded towards them. 'It's good to see some semblance of normality. At least the roads are open to the south. Winter rapidly approaches, so I hope Glambul is filling the stores. It doesn't bear thinking of the consequences if the supply routes close.'

Elodi led Toryn up the stairs to her quarters. Frost clung to the inside of the windows, and Toryn was sure it felt colder in the room than it had outside. Elodi shivered. 'I'd feel guilty burning precious firewood just to heat the room for myself. Besides, quite soon we'll be riding out into the winter.' She pulled out a chair for Toryn. 'Perhaps it's best if I prepare for the cold.'

Toryn noticed her room was as sparse as the one he shared with a dozen guards. 'Even so, Elodi, surely you can allow yourself some comfort.'

'I dare not get soft, not now. And you'll be off all too soon.' Elodi took out the message. 'This confirms a company of Archonians will meet you on the road just south of the Dorn Border. They've left Seransea and will await your arrival. They say the border has been quiet since the battle, so let's hope it stays that way for the last leg to Drunsberg.'

Suddenly, the importance of his mission dawned on Toryn. 'And the miners? If we're successful we'll want to start extracting ore as soon as possible. Jedrul reckons it shouldn't be difficult to resume, seeing as the Ruuk have been keen to keep the seams active.'

Elodi stood by the window overlooking Borrund's main square. 'I'm reluctant to send out a request for miners just yet. The fewer people who know of our plan, the better.' She turned back to Toryn and frowned.

'Something troubles you.' She sat opposite. 'But this isn't about Nyomae, or your mission to the mines.'

'Is my face so easy to read?'

Elodi grinned. 'For me, yes. But I hope it's harder for our enemy.'

Toryn leaned forward and clasped her hands. 'You're right. I'll tell you, but only if you promise not to… laugh.'

'Laugh, what could possibly make me…? Ah, of course. This is about Shepra, your dog.'

Toryn felt his face redden. 'She left for the farm this morning. I can't explain it, but it hurts to be parted from her. I've lost many a good friend in recent months, but this… this seemed to be the hardest to deal with. I never thought I could become so attached to an animal. We had dogs on the farm, but with Shepra… it was like we have this bond.' He stared out of the window. 'I seem to know her thoughts, and she knows mine.'

Elodi turned his face to look him in the eye. She smiled. 'It's the same for me and Misty. Perhaps in this world of pain, we clutch onto any comfort we can, and from whatever source. I believe it's what separates us from our enemies. And I believe it is what will help us to prevail. While we have a love for all living things, we will fight for them. Our enemy has no such cause. They fight to fulfil their dark desires.' She glanced back to the town square outside. 'If the gods still care for this world, surely, they will not allow the dark to prevail.'

Toryn watched a mother lift her crying child to comfort him. 'Then I hope you're right. I can't bear the thought we'll be parted for good.'

Elodi spun away and strode to a large trunk at the foot of her bed. 'Your mission to Drunsberg will be fraught with danger. You must have a sword.'

Toryn's hand went to his belt. 'I'm not certain the sword is the weapon for me. My first broke at Drunsberg, and my second was lost at Roth's Doom. A blade has not served me well in the past.'

Elodi opened the trunk and rummaged inside. 'Ah, here it is. Kernlow was so distracted by his new role of speechmaker, he totally forgot about' — she removed the cloth and beamed — 'the Sword of the Realms.' Elodi drew the weapon and wheeled it over her head.

Toryn stepped back. 'I'm happy with my Amayan bow and Nordleng dagger.' He pulled out the short blade from his belt. 'I would have been a tasty morsel for a fat spider, had I not had this little fellow handy.'

'Nonsense. Your skills have improved tenfold since I've known you.' She smirked at the dagger. 'You must have a real sword. If you find yourself in another bloodbath, which sadly is more likely than not, you cannot fight armed with just a bow and that… toy.' Elodi held out the weapon and looked along the blade. 'This is a fine weapon. I have my mother's Amayan sword, Nyomae has no need for it, and Bardon has his own trusty weapon. So, as leader of the armies of the Five Realms…' she grinned as she kneeled and held out the handle to Toryn, 'I bequeath the Sword of the Realms to you, Toryn of Midwyche.'

He bowed. 'Then as my leader, I cannot refuse your most precious gift.' Toryn reached out. His hand tingled as he wrapped his palm around the handle. It warmed. The blade flickered as if it were a candle in a breeze.

Elodi gaped as it glimmered with a silvery light like the moon. 'What the…?' Her eyes shone blue in the blade's light. 'There's more to this weapon than at first seems.'

The warmth from the sword spread through Toryn's body and down to his feet. 'I can feel its power. What do you know of it?'

Elodi stood in awe. 'Not much. Just that it's the

weapon passed down through the line of Archons. I don't know when it was forged, or how many Archons it has served. I was not aware it was anything more than just a relic.' She ran her hand over the blade. 'It's a shame Nyomae cannot enlighten us. But perhaps she is also unaware of its past.'

Toryn bowed his head and entered the Song. 'Its Verse goes back many years. But much is hidden by the mist of the ages. I shall attempt to find out more on my way to Drunsberg.' He opened his eyes. 'We may have discovered a new weapon to strengthen our hand.' The room dulled as he sheathed the blade.

Elodi groaned. 'If only I had given it to you earlier. It may have led to a quicker victory at Roth's Doom.'

'But if we'd found out about it earlier, it may have changed our plans and led to a defeat. We cannot know.' Toryn placed the sword on the table. 'And just because it glows in my hand, doesn't mean I can use it. Like our other skills, I imagine it will take time to master… time we don't have.' He looked down at the weapon. 'Nyomae believes things happen at the right time, and for reasons not known to us. According to her, luck and coincidence don't figure in our fate. Perhaps it was meant to be that it's only now we've discovered some hidden power.'

Elodi ran her fingers across the handle. 'Then let us hope that is so. If anyone can use its power, I trust it will be you.' She stroked his face and looked into his eyes. 'This is so hard. It seems we're destined to spend our time apart.' Elodi turned away. 'Now you must go and prepare.' She spoke as she looked out onto the crowds outside. 'Your company must be made aware of the dangers of this mission. I don't want any to volunteer unless they know of the challenges ahead.' She laughed, but her voice wavered. 'But on the other hand, they won't have to deal with Lord Kernlow. He's due to arrive in three days, and if you're really lucky, you'll have entered the pass before his entourage gets onto the Borrund Road.' Tears brimmed as her jaw clenched. Toryn wrapped his arms around Elodi and drew her close.

He spoke into her fragrant hair. 'If Nyomae is right, it won't be down to luck if we're to meet again. But I do know this…' he held her tight, trying to keep the pain from his voice. 'When I first saw you, I knew our fates were entwined. And I'm not going to let any warlock, dark beast, or Ruuk keep us apart.'

8. Heart of a Raven

Nyomae dismounted under the first boughs of the ancient wood. Her journey had been uneventful but challenging as her horse struggled with the deep snow on the hills. The old fence on Lunn's border was barely visible, sagging under the weight of snow and ice threatening to bring it down. Nyomae hoped it was a sign of the end of Uluriel's reign. While in possession of the Archon, she had decreed the building of long fences to isolate the wards, thus slowing their emergence from the so-called, Age of Shadows. But thankfully, Lunn's border fence now appeared as a relic, incapable of preventing even a fox from crossing. The few frozen Archonians at the gate, stamped their feet and warmed their hands over a brazier and failed to see her approach. Nyomae did not wish to make her presence known in case others watched the border. Bands of Nordleng had been sighted in the region and would see a lone rider as easy prey. And if her identity was discovered, they would be eager to claim a reward. But she had felt sorry for the guards stuck out in the middle of nowhere in the cold. So, Nyomae had used a simple trick to ensure entry without question. They stood gaping as the likeness of the legend, Gildorul of Keld, rode his great stallion through the gate. Perhaps she could have chosen another disguise, but the story of Gildorul's ghost coming to their aid, would soon spread and help to raise morale.

Nyomae patted her horse as he ate the last of his rations that should see him home. She thanked him, then sent him on his way to Borrund. The last of the daylight dwindled, yet night had long fallen among the tall, dark firs. Their branches drooped under the weight of snow, and Nyomae hoped it would make it easier to spot any webs in the gloom. But if the spiders had any sense, they would avoid the corvraak; even a sick raven would be more than a match for them. She watched the horse gallop safely over the ridge, then turned and walked into the trees.

Only a thin layer of snow lay on the woodland floor, but it had frozen, and the ice crunched under her feet. Nyomae found a spot she felt to be free of predators, entered the Song, and located the corvraak. As a creature of Ormoroth's making, the raven possessed no Verse of its own, but the suffering of the tree forced to tolerate its presence, echoed through the Song. It clung to a branch at the center of the wood, acutely aware an Imaari approached. Nyomae winced as she felt its pain. But not all its pain was of the flesh. Something else troubled the beast.

Nyomae stayed in the Song, wishing to learn more of the corvraak before confronting the ancient beast. It would require time to pass through each Verse of the people and places upon which the raven had inflicted its pain. But it would be worth the delay — understanding its dark mind would surely improve her chances of recruiting it to her cause. She quickly found her way to Elodi's confrontation with the corvraak. While Elodi's sword had failed to find its dark heart, it had opened an old wound. The creature had sustained many injuries over its long life, but had never before encountered an Amayan blade. And this was to be its undoing. In the weeks following Elodi's strike, the raven would finally succumb to the ravages of time. But it would suffer a slow and painful death, sustained by Ormoroth's cruel gift of a near immortal life regardless of its injuries.

Nyomae moved with caution through the Verses.

Many had ridden on its back. Warlocks, Uluriel, and most recently, Uleva. It had once flown with hundreds of its kind, turning the sky black as if a storm cloud descended upon its enemies. Its talons had torn flesh from Dorlan's arm as he had driven his great blade at its chest. Its beak had plucked out the eyes of many an injured knight as they lay helpless on the battlefields of old. Yet, among the many atrocities, Nyomae found something she could use — the corvraak loathed its commanders.

The branches creaked overhead. Nyomae departed the Song and looked up. There was no breeze. A dark shape moved through the tree. A thud. Something landed heavily to her left. She spun around to see eight glistening eyes glowering back at her. Another landed behind, followed by two more. In the silence, Nyomae could hear the drool dripping from their mouths, splatter on the frozen ground, and the ice hiss as it melted. She raised her arms, circled them over her head, and entrapped herself and the spiders within a dome. The creatures stopped, but too late did they appreciate the danger. They could not escape the Imaari's attack. Nyomae brought her hands together to warm the air, then threw out her arms and hurled a hot blast at the spiders. They stood no chance. The burst ripped them to pieces, slinging their body parts into the branches behind. Nyomae wiped her hands as if cleansing herself of their dark blood. But others came as their lust for her sweet meat overwhelmed their fear.

Nyomae waited, grinning as a dozen or more scuttled towards her. She entered the spiders' Verses and listened to their dark thoughts as they formed a circle. Predictably, they devised a plan to overpower the defiant Imaari. But Nyomae noted, no consideration was given to how they would share the spoils. She contemplated stirring up a debate, and then watch them rip each other to pieces to claim the prize. But she had seen enough death of late.

Nyomae smiled. No. She had a better idea. Unlike the corvraak, the lesser aralak had a presence in the Song. Ormoroth had merely tampered with the humble spider to breed the larger, vicious beasts to serve his purpose. With her newly acquired powers, Nyomae quickly found the corrupted lines. The aralaks edged slowly closer, now wary of the Imaari that appeared as a bright light in their dark eyes.

Nyomae searched the trees. Nearby, a tiny spider sat on its web, slumbering in the early winter, waiting patiently for the spring. It would be oblivious to the monstrosities its distant ancestors had help to seed, but now it would play its part in their downfall. Nyomae borrowed a line from the tiny, fly-eating fellow, then replaced the curse within the aralaks. She departed the Song and could not prevent laughing out loud. The large shadows had gone. At her feet, the aralaks would wonder how their prey had suddenly grown so tall, and why they found themselves surrounded by ridges of ice. Nyomae walked on, careful not to squash them as they scuttled away to find something else to eat.

Ahead, the corvraak had not moved. It knew she came, and Nyomae sensed it now welcomed her approach; but she could not determine why. She drew upon her Verse and brought some light into the gloom beneath the trees. To the creatures nestling in the branches, she appeared as if the moon had come down to walk among them. But Nyomae cared not for who or what saw her. She had nothing to fear in this place; not even the corvraak.

The wood thinned as she reached its heart. The trees had spent years vying for the scant nourishment to be had from the soil, barely covering the rocks beneath. But the victorious had grown tall and strong over the centuries, strengthened by the hardship, much as Nyomae. The clouds cleared, and the sliver of the crescent moon shed a little more light into the canopy high above… and onto the corvraak. She looked up to see its beady eyes watching her from the tree.

Nyomae spoke. 'I wish to speak with you. I can climb this tree, or you can come down.' It tilted its head, appearing to consider her offer. She continued. 'You are hurt. I can ease your suffering quicker if you come to me.' Its mournful cry of pain carried far through the woods as it opened its wings and stepped off the branch. The stench of death arrived just before the bird landed heavily, unable to slow its descent. But the corvraak was still a proud beast. It endured the agony to straighten and stand twice Nyomae's height. Its head twitched one way, then the other as it observed her, still unsure if to treat her as a friend or a foe.

Nyomae stood in awe. While an abomination, it had retained some of the beauty of the sleek, noble bird from which it was created. She reached out and gently placed her hand on the side of the bird's enormous, curved beak. It flinched at her touch, but Nyomae soothed the beast, softly singing a song about a raven she had learned as a child. The corvraak's glowering eyes softened and it lowered its head to rest in her hand.

Satisfied the creature had accepted her presence, Nyomae resumed her journey through the Verses tarnished by the corvraak's acts. It had lived more than a thousand years. The bird was female, and had herself spawned many offspring. Nyomae's heart went out to the beast. Despite Ormoroth's art, the corvraak had retained some of the spirit of the valiant raven. Ormoroth had not named her, but the bird had chosen one for herself: Ashala — *queen of the sky* in the old tongue. Had she named herself to gain the attention of the Maidens?

Nyomae stroked the coarse feathers of her neck. 'You

are a fine bird, Ashala. You have chosen a beautiful name, a name I'm sure the Maidens would have given you.' The corvraak's head dropped. 'But you have been badly treated. You know of the Maidens' love for the raven. Your dark masters have no such love for you. They exploit your nature of which you have no control. They have made you what you are, and forced you to commit vile acts for their gain. You did not choose this life, Ashala. You were created for the sole purpose to serve their evil desires.' She held the bird's gaze. 'Do you wish to know of the Maidens' Love?'

Ashala blinked. Did a tear form in her eye? She did not move, but she listened. Nyomae continued. 'Then I can help. I can heal you, Ashala. You can fly again, to fly and atone for the acts your masters compelled you to perform. But if I take this pain from you, I will ask for your service in return. I will not command you. This is *your* choice. I do not ask you to kill or maim. I wish you to bear me to Archonholm in the south, and then wait for my return. You will fly high over the mountains once more. I will protect you, thus the sun will not scorch your feathers. You will be free of your creator's hatred to experience the joy of flight.' Nyomae stood back. 'Will you accept my offer, Ashala?'

The corvraak had not the gift of speech, for it was by their actions that the beasts of Ormoroth spread their terror. But Ashala had lived long after the last of her kind had departed the realms. And in those years, she had developed a mind of her own, beyond what Ormoroth had intended. She had listened and discovered the Dark Verses that bound her to him. Thus, Ashala had learned words that gave form to her thoughts. She had observed the world from above, looking down on the lands of the free... and those of the oppressed. Thus, Ashala had grown to despise her masters, and longed for a life free of tyranny. But she could not break free from her bond and had sought the only path to freedom open to her: death. Yet, swords and spears could not pierce her tough hide deep enough to bring about a swift end.

Ashala led Nyomae to her memory of the encounter with Elodi. She knew she faced an Amayan. The warrior's blade had gone deeper than any before, but as she had gripped the weapon to drag it into her heart, Uleva had hauled her back to deny her wish.

Nyomae stroked the raven's neck and assured her. 'You may speak, Ashala. You and I are alone within this Verse. No others will hear.'

Ashala's head lowered and nestled Nyomae. She spoke for the first time. *I wish to atone for my deeds. I will serve you, Imaari. Then I desire to depart this world and be free.*

Nyomae hugged the bird. 'Then I grant you this chance. And when you have completed this task, I shall assist you on your way.' She looked deep into the corvraak's wise eyes. 'And by your last deeds you shall earn the Maidens' Love.'

9. OF SWORDS & WATCHTOWERS

Elodi touched Toryn's face. 'Yet again we find ourselves in the same predicament. You go one way, while I go the other. We both face unknown dangers, unsure if we'll…' she turned away.

Toryn placed his hand on her shoulder. 'We are both stronger than when we last said our farewells in Archonholm. You're an Amayan, Elodi, and I for one would not want to face you in battle.' He patted the sword at his side. 'And now I have this, perhaps the balance tips in our favor… once I've learned of its secrets.'

Elodi turned back to face him. 'That may be so, but our enemy have defeated both Imaari and Amayan before us. They too learn from each encounter, and I fear their confidence grows as the Amanach weaken.'

'But our position will improve if we can take back Keld and Drunsberg.'

She sighed. 'Neither are a given. And you'll have to negotiate the Kolossos Pass before you even reach the mines. The cobtrolls may have been reluctant to trouble Ruan and Aldorman owing to their numbers, but they may be tempted to take on a smaller force.'

Toryn tried to calm her fears. 'I made it through the valley to Vortimo. I can't think the Kolossos could be worse.'

'Then I hope you're right, Toryn.' She held him and whispered into his ear. 'I pray to the Three we can be together again soon.' She let go. 'Then we can take back Calerdorn side by side, and perhaps one day emerge from this dark shadow that looms over us.'

Many of the volunteers for the Drunsberg mission, had ridden with Toryn to free the Amayans from Vortimo. To his relief, Elrik and Lorek had reported fit for duty and had readily joined him. Janae was an obvious choice as a scout, and both Roold and Jedrul were keen to return to the mines. Their knowledge of the tunnels and caverns would be invaluable if they were to mount a successful attack. Then, if victorious, Jedrul would oversee production to ensure the supply of valuable metals resumed as quickly as possible.

Toryn pulled his horse to one side and rode back down the line. Janae had gone on ahead to find a suitable place to camp, and Toryn wanted the company to know his plans. It had been three days since departing Borrund, and Toryn was eager to reach the Kolossos Pass the following day. The first part of their journey had been mostly uneventful. They had spotted a small cluster of aralaks close to the South Forest, but they had scuttled away as they approached.

Toryn had spent the first evening alone, exploring the Verse of his new sword. He had gone back to the time of Gormadon, and witnessed the battle through Mordram's eyes as he fought beside Hadrul, the warrior Archon. Hadrul preferred his mace to the sword, thus it was Mordram who held the Sword of the Realms as depicted on the tapestry in Archonholm. Even through the mist of the Verse, Toryn had thrown up his hands as the three drayloks had loomed over Mordram. Their fiery whips tore into his flesh as he desperately tried to fend them off. Toryn noticed the sword did not glow as it had in his hand, and Mordram was eventually overpowered and possessed by Uluriel. Yet the blade had concealed its power, appearing as a common weapon, thus Uluriel did not perceive it to be a sword of power. Toryn withdrew from the plain before Nyomae invoked the Verse of

Unmaking. But as he had tried to go deeper into the sword's past, a thick fog obscured the Verses, and he could find no way through.

On the dawn of the second day, Toryn had risen early and was relieved to see the peaks of the Kolossos Mountains in the distance. He knew the mighty mounts could not have fallen, but somehow, they seemed different. Toryn could not explain it, but they did not appear to emanate the power he had always sensed came from them.

At midday they reached the part of the road where the enemy had crossed on their way to Roth's Doom. Most of the cobbles were damaged, and the ground on both sides bore the scars of thousands of boots and hooves. And while much work had been done to clear the plain, many Ruuk still lay dead where they had been pursued and cut down as they retreated. Elodi had vowed to plant a new forest to rid the land of the scars, but perhaps it would take the Nym to fully heal the hurt of past and present battles. Lorek had ridden with him for much of the afternoon, speaking of his brothers and his life in Tamforth by the sea. Toryn had appreciated the distraction, but the tales did not have a happy ending for Porek and Dorek.

Toryn looked up as Janae returned. The company were relieved to hear she had found a sheltered place a little farther ahead. The camp was soon established, and the fires lit to cook a nourishing hot meal. Cubric chuckled as he chewed on his roasted rabbit. 'That must be Lord Kernlow's camp.'

Toryn followed his gaze. About a league south from their position, the low clouds glowed orange. He laughed. 'Looks like he's brought half of Archonholm with him judging by their campfires.'

Cubric chuckled. 'No doubt enjoying a banquet. He'll

fill Roth's Doom with all the left-over bones come morning.' He stood and stretched. 'I don't envy Lady Harlyn having to deal with him.'

Toryn yawned. 'Well at least we'll have a few more swords for the coming battles.' He turned to find his blanket. 'I need to sleep. We'll make an early start. I'd rather not bump into Kernlow. But then again, I doubt he'll hit the road until he's had a hearty breakfast.'

Toryn woke in the dead of a silent night. The flickering flames of the watchfires cast grotesque shadows across the grasslands, appearing as if hands reached out to claim his sword. He threw back his blanket and drew the weapon. As before, it glowed with a silvery light. His hand warmed as he entered its Verse. The fog he had encountered at his last attempt had retreated to reveal the sword in Malendra's hand. She was known as a fine warrior and had become Archon following Draegelan's death. Yet, the blade remained lifeless as it had at Gormadon to deceive Uluriel. Toryn attempted to go deeper into its past. The sword's Verses stretched out before him like a long corridor in Archonholm's crypt. In the shimmering air, Toryn thought he saw Draegelan hold the blade aloft on the battlefield. But when he tried to enter the Verse, he was pulled back as if the sword itself denied entry.

Toryn opened his eyes to find it glowed brighter, throwing long shadows away from the campsite. He stood and swung the blade, sending its light far across the plain. But it was not the brilliance of its glow that awoke the company. The blade sang as it swished through the air, leading his companions to believe they dreamed of the Maidens returning in their time of need.

Unbeknown to Toryn, the warlocks spread far and wide across the north, quailed at the sword's reawakening.

They knew it to be the *Elorsil*, a mighty blade that had separated many a warlock's head from their necks. The weapon welcomed the hand that grasped it, a hand of an adversary, Ormoroth's commanders would treat as their equal. But it would take time to master the sword's power. The weapon and hand had to be parted. Two warlocks abandoned their foul schemes, called for their horses, and sped south.

The Kolossos peaks glimmered pink as they rose to meet a rare sunbeam, peering through a gap in the clouds smothering Ormsk. Toryn shivered in the chill of the autumn morning, but it was not from the cold. In a few hours they would enter the Kolossos Pass. Hamar had told him stories of the cobtrolls coming out from the mountains to raid nearby villages, but they were more of a nuisance than a threat. But the pass was their territory, and they did not tolerate trespassers. Yet, Toryn looked forward to seeing one of the old wonders of the Seven Realms. Hamar had made the journey three times while serving with the Archonian Guard, and each time had endured the attention of the trolls. *Keep a shield handy*, he had advised. *Always ready to hurl a rock at passers-by.* Toryn could hear his old friend's voice as if he stood at his side. *But you'll rarely see the blighters. It's like they blend into the mountainside.* A glint caught Toryn's eye. He looked up to see the sunlight reflecting off the conical roof of the East Watchtower. It glistened beneath the mighty peaks, but did not look overawed by the towering mountain wall.

'It will be my fourth time.' Toryn turned to see Roold. 'But still can't say I'm looking forward to it.'

'Hamar told me it takes around three days. Is that your experience?'

'Depends. Sometimes the cobs had caused a landslide that would take time to clear. Or if they're feeling upset over something, they might harass us all the way. They won't come out in the day, yet still manage to toss the odd rock from caves high over the road.'

Jedrul joined them. 'It's the nights when they become a real threat.' He pointed to his mouth. 'Lost one of my front teeth when a stone hit me square in the face.'

Roold sighed. 'Delays can cost you dear. More so than one of Jed's teeth. I've known the crossing to take three days, a week, or even ten days, as one of the old miners once told me.' He stretched out his back. 'We won't know until we make it to the other side.'

Toryn watched the sunlight descending the tower. 'Unless the trolls have been busy since you came through with Ruan, I'm hoping it's still clear. We've got a few days grace to time our attack at the mine. But if we're late, the Ruuk's heads would have cleared from their celebrations.'

Cubric strode towards them, nodding down the road. 'Best be making tracks, folks. Can't risk Kernlow has broken a habit of a lifetime and skipped breakfast.'

The tower still bore the wounds inflicted by the spiders, much like the lines of horror etched on the faces of the guards. Captain Waldryn greeted them at the outer gate. 'It's been quiet down there since the spearmen's passage.' He looked up to the slopes towering behind the inner wall. 'But that don't mean nothing to be honest, so I don't want to be getting your hopes up.'

Cubric addressed the captain. 'Have the forts been restocked?' He turned to Toryn. 'We only stopped briefly on our way to the battle, but I'm afraid we had to fill our bellies. Can't be asked to fight on an empty stomach, eh.'

Waldryn nodded. 'We sent down a wagon the day before yesterday. And I gather the west tower will have done the same.' He explained to Toryn. 'There're two garrisons along the route. They were built when the pass was formed, so they're as secure as Archonholm. They're set at the distance of roughly a day's march. Just remember to travel by day, then rest at night in the forts.' He folded his arms. 'Couldn't be simpler, eh. But you'll have an escort. He's an experienced old hand. He knows the ways of the little blighters. But then things don't always go to plan… which explains why the supply wagon hasn't returned yet.'

Toryn peered through the inner gate to the winding road leading into the pass. 'Is that normal? Could it have been waylaid?'

'It does happen. But it's more likely they've lost a wheel or the like. The cobs don't like our food, so they don't pinch it.' Waldryn grimaced. 'But while our cooked meats aren't to their taste, I'm afraid they're partial to our raw flesh. So, it's not the contents of the wagon that concerns me. Only thankful they don't come out here more often.' The captain rubbed his chin. 'But who knows what's going on under our feet. We used to send the odd expedition down to find out. But it ain't pleasant work, we'd lose the odd man, and can't say we ever learned anything to justify the losses.'

Cubric patted Toryn's shoulder. 'This brave fellow here has quite a few tales about the world below, but' — he raised an eyebrow — 'I don't suppose we have the time to hear them over a hearty meal.'

Toryn laughed. 'Perhaps on our return, eh.'

'Ah, thought so.' Cubric looked back to the captain. 'So, what do you reckon? Will our lads get a quiet passage?'

Waldryn glanced to Toryn's company taking their rest. 'Being a small party can work both ways. You might sneak through without catching their attention, or they might see you as an easy… meal. But they also hanker after shiny treasures such as our swords and armor. Can't think why seeing that they dislike the sun so much, and they've never been known to use any of our weapons. Rocks and their long fingers are their favored tools.' He nodded to the sky. 'But at least you'll have the sun for the next day or two, so that'll help. They may come out under heavy cloud, if hungry enough, but at night... well, they're a different beast altogether.' Waldryn grinned. 'That's what the forts are for, eh, Cub.'

Toryn could not take his eyes from the road. 'I hope you're right. If all goes well, we'll be coming back this way within the month.'

Waldryn frowned. 'So, can I take it the rumors are true? You're on your way to the mines?'

Toryn lowered his voice. 'That we are, but I'd ask you to keep that to yourself. While I trust your guards, we know our enemy may have ears where we least expect them.'

The captain nodded. 'Noted. Not a word of this will pass my lips, but others are saying the same. But as soon as you head north on the other side, I reckon your intentions will become clear to any who see you. And once you get close to the Dorn border, you're in land held by the Ruuk.'

Toryn sighed. 'We won't be able to keep it secret for long. We're to be met by a company of Archonians in Noor. We'll travel by night, but then we're dealing with the unknown.' He looked to Cubric. 'Just getting to Drunsberg will be an achievement. And then we have the small matter of clearing the mines and town of the Ruuk.'

Waldryn turned as a guard approached. 'Here comes your guide. He'll get you through in good time. We'll send a bird to inform the west side you're on your way.'

Toryn squinted up to the top of the tower. 'You have a beacon up there? Would that be quicker?'

'You have good eyes. It's a beacon, but the bird can cross in a matter of hours. That's quick enough. The west will soon send one back if you're not through in a week.'

Toryn's stomach clenched. 'Is that when you light the beacon?'

Waldryn rubbed the back of his neck. 'Sorry, that's for emergencies. I know it will seem like one for you and your lads, but it still don't warrant sending a force down the pass. You're more or less on your own once you're in.' He scratched his chin. 'We've learned from our mistakes in the past. Lost too many chasing after others who were already dead. I'm afraid that's how it is out here.'

The guide held out a hand to Toryn. He grinned. 'Amrul's the name, getting you through to the other side is my game, Cappy.'

The captain scowled. 'Cappy? Let's keep this formal, eh, Amrul. *Captain* Toryn is one of Lady Harlyn's top commanders.'

Toryn's face reddened. 'Honestly, I don't mind informal.' He nodded to his company. 'You'll find the rest of us on familiar terms, Captain.'

'Well, that's your decision. You know best for your own people.' He turned to Amrul. 'But don't forget I'm still *your* captain.' Waldryn sighed. 'And… just be sure not to lose any this time.'

Amrul protested. 'I can hardly be responsible if a fool decides he wants to get a better look at a cob's cave.' He turned to Toryn. 'We block them up when we get the chance. Don't let on, but we maintain our own supplies of Shreek's Rage. But as quick as we can blast them out, they open another. Busy little fellows these cobs.' He shuddered. 'The poor sod's feet didn't touch the ground once the cob got his hands around his throat. Disappeared down that hole faster than a guard into an alehouse after a long, hot day on watch. But if he thought I'd go in after—'

'Your *guide* has the key to open both forts.' Waldryn glared at Amrul. 'And perhaps it's best that you keep some of your stories to yourself until you get to the other side.'

He wrapped an arm around Toryn's shoulder and led him away from the others. Waldryn lowered his voice. 'Make sure you don't lose Amrul. To be honest, it's the key he carries that's more valuable. Sadly, our locksmiths have never been able to cut one as good as those back in the day. We've few left that will open the forts, so that makes a key one of the most valued treasures in these parts.' He patted Toryn's back. 'Well, good luck to you all. Hopefully, I'll see you on your way back, eh.' The captain turned. Toryn wondered how many travelers Waldryn had seen go down the pass… but not return.

The Kolossos Pass had a very different feel to the one that led to the Caerwal Gate. The mountains here rose almost twice as high, and even in full sunshine, Toryn felt as if there was a roof over their heads. But thankfully, he had yet to experience the sense of dread he had felt in the valley leading to Vortimo. However, he noticed his shoulders hunched and his head dipped. He wore a helmet, and had a shield at his side, but he doubted if either would save him from a rock dropped from a great height. He kept a close eye on the mountain walls, seeing dozens of gaps that could be an opening to a tunnel or cave. Toryn shivered as he recalled the cavern in the Wend Gap where he had sheltered with Hamar. That night, his old friend had told him of the horrors of Wyke Wood. Back then, tales of cobtrolls, ghouls, and wykes had helped to pass the time. And back then, Toryn had dismissed them as nothing more than myths.

The road climbed shortly after entering the pass before levelling out. At times it hugged the north side of the Kolossos, and others, a bridge spanned a gorge to take them to the south. Despite his trepidation, Toryn was in awe of the work of his predecessors. The bridges were wide and looked as if they would stand until the mountains themselves crumbled to dust. He tried to imagine what the range looked like before the pass was built. It must have been an immense task. Where would one begin? Did a single mason with a mallet and chisel make the first notch in the side of a mountain? And had another started the same day on the opposite end? Aside from the crossings, the road was mainly straight, but at times it had no option but to wind its way around what must have been particularly stubborn slabs of rock jutting out from the slopes. But in spite of Amrul's assurances, Janae insisted she go on ahead and check their path. And not for the first time, Toryn was impressed by her bravery and devotion to duty.

Few spoke as even a whisper echoed a long way down the pass, and more to the point, up the near-vertical slopes. Toryn noted Cubric, the most talkative person he had met since Hamar, also seemed reluctant to speak. Travelling in silence gave Toryn the chance to contemplate his plan for Drunsberg. Cubric had briefed him on the location of the Shreek's Rage as best he could. Jedrul had worked out the route to get as close to the main hall without detection. He also suggested where to ignite the black powder for maximum impact without trapping themselves inside. But the miner had to admit, much could have changed since they had lost Drunsberg, and their plans may have to change. A nagging doubt had gnawed at Toryn's gut; what if the Ruuk had bolstered the defenses both inside and out? There were so many things that could go wrong, yet each played a vital role in their success.

The Archonian Guard who would accompany them across the Dorn border, were to position themselves out of sight on the road. They were to wait for signs of a skirmish, then rush the main gate. But as Toryn recalled, the road was narrow, the crevice deep, and a few well-aimed ballistae bolts would soon thin them out, sending many tumbling to their death.

Amrul nodded ahead. 'Not too far to the fort now, sir.' He glanced up. 'And not a moment too soon. It'll be dark in just over an hour. And believe me, even when the full moon's out, you'd struggle to see your hand in front of your face, unless it's directly overhead… which it rarely is.'

Toryn looked to the slopes in the west, already turning red. 'Then let's pick up the pace a little. I'm sure the horses won't mind getting off this road and a chance to rest. And… Amrul. You don't have to call me sir. If I'm honest, it makes me feel uneasy.'

'Sorry, but old Waldryn's right, although I didn't want to admit it in front of him. And you obviously have the respect of your company… so it sort of seems right.'

Toryn grinned. 'Well, if it makes you comfortable, but again, it's not necessary.'

Amrul saluted, then grinned. 'Aye, aye, sir.' He checked over Toryn's shoulder and muttered under his breath. 'Joking aside, I don't want to cause alarm, but I thought we'd have met the supply wagon coming back this way by now.'

'Ah, I've been so distracted I'd forgotten about them.' Toryn peered ahead. 'Could they have stayed over at the fort? Waldryn said they may have lost a wheel, perhaps they've repairing it.'

Amrul's hand rested on his sword. 'That would be the most reassuring explanation, but nothing can be taken for granted in this place.'

'I guess we'll soon find out.' Toryn leaned forward and kicked on his horse who seemed to anticipate his desire to get to the shelter. The air quickly chilled as the day approached its end, and Toryn found his hand clenched the handle on his shield tighter.

The fort appeared on the south side of the pass as they rounded a bend. The last of the sunlight reflected off the peaks on the north side and down onto its high walls and single tower. It stood clear of the slopes on a plateau that must have taken much work to carve out of the mountain. Amrul explained. 'I'm told they didn't want to risk the cobs tunnelling through the back walls, that's why it stands alone. And the foundations are made of granite with a thick iron plate on top. Wouldn't want the sneaky fellows coming up from under your bed.' He grinned. 'Perhaps one of the safest places in the realms. Though not in the most pleasant of spots.'

Toryn glanced up to the darkening slopes. 'Pleased to hear it.'

'But I must warn you, it ain't built for comfort.' Amrul pointed. 'No windows, not even at the top. And that overhang on the parapet makes you wonder just how high those blighters can climb.'

Toryn kept his eyes on the fort, re-assured it would offer a secure place to spend the night. The company crossed the bridge as darkness suddenly descended on the pass as if the gods had drawn a curtain. In the gloom, the sound of the horses clattering over the bridge, echoed far down the pass. Toryn hunched in his saddle, certain any creature within two leagues would learn of their arrival.

Amrul led them to the small gate. He dismounted, reached into his tunic, and pulled out a brass key hanging on a chain around his neck. He kissed it, then carefully placed it in the hole while muttering to himself. He turned the key and a loud clunk announced the lock acknowledged its master. Amrul turned and sighed. 'Got into the habit of holding my breath doing this. One of these days I worry it won't open. The cobs sometimes try to stuff rubble into the locks, but have yet to keep us out. They may be sly, but mercifully they're not too bright, and rarely work together.'

Amrul placed his fingertips on the gate, and with

barely a push, it swung silently open. He noted Toryn's surprise and grinned. 'Marvelous skills our ancestors had, eh. You'd never know it's stood here for over a thousand years. Doesn't even make a creak or a squeak.'

The company wasted no time in getting off the road and into the safety of the fort. But if Toryn felt he could relax, he was wrong — they found no sign of the wagon, its horses, or its guards. Cubric returned from his visit to the stores. He grimaced. 'Judging by the low stocks, I'd say they never made it this far. It can only mean the cobs tipped it off the road, and the guards… well, that don't bear thinking about, not with night coming.'

Toryn shivered. He turned to Amrul. 'Does that happen often?'

Amrul shook his head. 'Can't say I've heard of many cases. There are a few tales doing the rounds, but, as I'm sure you're aware, us guards are guilty of making them more… interesting.'

Toryn patted his horse, but more to settle his own nerves. 'Perhaps Waldryn will send another, better guarded wagon down when they don't return tomorrow.'

Cubric lifted a torch from the wall and lit it. 'We can't be worrying about what's behind us now. I suggest we eat what's left, then get our heads down so we're ready to be on our way at first light.'

The company sat at one of the long tables in the hall and ate a lighter supper than they would have wished. Toryn's anxiety had eased a little as he looked to the familiar faces around him. They had already proven their courage beyond doubt at Vortimo, then during the ghastly ordeal at the spiders' nest, and later at Roth's Doom. Toryn hoped Drunsberg would not turn out to be a step too far.

Jedrul amused Lorek and Roold with tales of how he had lost each of his teeth. Toryn suspected Roold had heard them many times before, but he laughed along with Lorek, helping to keep their spirits high. Elrik sat opposite, but Toryn noticed his usual cheery face had gained a few more lines that looked deeper in the candlelight.

Elrik glanced down the table. 'Takes you back, eh.' Toryn frowned. His dear friend rolled his eyes. 'You can't have forgotten the night we greeted the knights to our humble hall of Midwyche.'

Toryn smiled. 'That seems a very long time ago.' His smile faded. 'But we were just boys back then, knowing little about the wide world beyond our rickety fences.'

Elrik tutted. 'And to think I actually looked forward to becoming a hero of the realms.'

Toryn patted Elrik's hand. 'Well, you've certainly fulfilled that ambition. Hamar would be proud.'

'Me the hero?' Elrik beamed at him. 'Who'd have thought the scrawny lad who didn't want to get his feet wet, would end up leading a mission to take back Drunsberg. And it's not even your first.'

Toryn drained his cup. 'I guess this means that lazy day we've promised ourselves back in Midwyche, isn't going to happen any time soon. That's if we ever get back home.'

Cubric squeezed in beside Toryn. 'Room for a small one? Sorry to break up your talk of home and the like, but I've been thinking about the cob tunnel that's going to get us into the mines.' He nodded to Elrik. 'The big fellow here may find it a bit tight. It was a struggle for me, and I'm only a tad taller than your average cob.'

Elrik scoffed. 'Don't you worry about me. I'll find a way through, even if I have to widen it myself.'

Toryn turned to Cubric. 'That he will. And I pity the Ruuk who come up against him in a confined space.' He lowered his voice. 'We all know how dangerous this mission is. But what if the Ruuk have discovered this tunnel? There must be at least four hundred of the brutes at the mines, and I imagine they've brought in more heavy weapons. They know of its importance to both sides and will not give it up lightly. It will be difficult for the Archonians to attack the south gate as I remember it, and if they've strengthened it… well, it could take them ages to come to our aid.'

Cubric leaned forward. 'I'd be surprised if they know about it. It's well out of the way of the main tunnels, more of a passage really. We only found it when we went looking for the black powder. I reckon it was made long before the mines opened.' He patted his tunic. 'The fair Lady Harlyn gave me Wendel's map of the place… just in case my memory fails me. The passage will take us to the seams that have long since been exhausted of any useful ores. They were closed over a century ago, so I doubt these Ruuk fellows would have any reason to go down there. Unless…' his brow creased, 'unless that is, they've got bored and somehow learned of the black stuff.'

Toryn glanced to Elrik. 'Then let's hope their masters have kept them busy. Are you certain you can locate these barrels, Cub? I don't give us any chance of taking the mines without them.'

'I'm not going to lie. It'll be a challenge. Once down there, the tunnels and caverns all sort of look the same.' He grinned. 'But I guess the walls will still be blackened by the small pile we let off. If I can find that, then I can find the powder.' Cubric stood. 'Well, I don't know about you, but these bones are ready for my bed.' He looked along the table. 'I'll arrange the watch for tonight. Just two hours apiece, I reckon. These fellows will need their sleep.'

Toryn pushed back his chair. 'I'll take first watch.'

'No need. You're in charge of this mission, that brings some privileges, and a full night's rest is… ah, perhaps the only one, now I come to think of it.'

Toryn did not argue and gratefully found a bunk. But before he settled, he took out the sword. It glowed, warming his hand, heart, and spirit. He entered its Verse. The corridor leading back through its long history appeared. He felt as if the sword led him through the ages, passed Gormadon, beyond the days Malendra served as Archon, and back to the time of Draegelan. The haze cleared. Toryn beheld the great man circling the sword as he rode at the head of an immense army. They charged into a blizzard of such force the sword was dimmed by the shards of ice hurled against them. But it could not stop Draegelan leading his force across the frozen borders of Nordruuk. Draegelan sought Dorlan, racing to fight at his side, aware the knight faced Ormoroth at Talaghir. The storm worsened. But just as it seemed it would halt Draegelan's advance, he raised the Sword of the Realms. Toryn watched aghast as the Archon called upon the Amanach. The stones lay many leagues to the south, but the sword connected with their lines of power. Draegelan yelled into the wind and unleashed a searing bolt, blasting the hail, diminishing the storm's violence. The Verse shattered. A dark shape lingered at the edges of Toryn's vision: a warlock had followed him into the Song.

Toryn withdrew, gasping for air. Draegelan had called out the name of the sword to draw upon the Amanach. But he had failed to hear his words above the din. Or had the warlock obscured Draegelan's voice to prevent him discovering its name? Toryn placed it beneath his bed. His head sank into the pillow, but his mind would not rest. He must learn of the sword's name if he was to use its power. But it seemed the warlocks knew he possessed it and looked to block his path through its Verses. Toryn was exhausted. Another way would have to be found on another day. Now, he needed to sleep. He looked up at the smooth, stone ceiling and pondered how many who had slept in the same bunk, had lived to see the other side of the pass.

'Toryn.' He awoke to find Lorek at his bedside. He thumbed over his shoulder. 'We've got company… outside.'

10. An Amayan Remembers

The people of Borrund stared in awe as Eryn rode through their narrow streets. While the tales of the Amayans' role at Roth's Doom were now commonplace, few beyond the battlefield had ever set eyes upon the warriors. Her time at the Amanach in Hadrin had rejuvenated Eryn, and to mortal eyes she appeared to glow.

Elodi ran down the alley to meet her at the stables. She stopped as Eryn approached. While an Amayan herself, Elodi still felt an outsider and somewhat inferior, not yet counting herself as an equal. She stood back and held the gate open for Eryn to bring Moonbeam into the stall. 'I hadn't expected to see you so soon. I assumed you'd be riding north after you'd checked the stone in Hadrin.'

Eryn passed the reins to the stable boy. 'I was on my way. The stone remains strong, and Amyra is at peace. But…' she lowered her voice. 'I've come to warn Toryn. He's in danger.'

Elodi's face paled. 'He's not here. Toryn left for Drunsberg three days ago.'

Eryn groaned. 'Ah, that explains why I cannot locate him. He must have entered the pass.'

'You say he's in danger?'

'The *Elorsil* has awoken from its long slumber.'

'*Elorsil?* You must refer to the Sword of the Realms. It glowed at his touch. But surely that's a blessing? He said it gave him strength.'

'That it will, undoubtedly.' Eryn rubbed down Moonbeam. 'But the blade burst back to life last night. It sang for the first time in a thousand years. However, its awakening will also have come to the warlocks' attention.'

Elodi's stomach clenched. 'Then he is in danger. Toryn and just twenty riders are on the open road. They're on their own until they meet the guards on the Dorn border.'

'Ah, that is not good news.' Eryn paused while the stable boy brought in fodder. She thanked him, then continued. 'The warlocks know only too well of its power. In Draegelan's hand it killed dozens of their kind. But they'll know it will take time for Toryn to learn of its ways. Thus, I believe our enemy look to take it from him before he does.'

Elodi gaped at Eryn. 'And if they do?'

Eryn pumped fresh water into the trough. 'Two warlocks are coming south. I fear Toryn would not survive such an encounter if that is their purpose. Yet three more now ride to attack the Elda Stone in Darrow. They've abandoned their search for the Crown Stone, but we are stretched thin. They lead us this way and that, leaving us to guess their strategy. Ah! What to do?'

'Which would be the greater loss?' Elodi held out her hands. 'The stone or the sword? But... if Toryn is lost in the process...' her shoulders bunched. 'Our enemy appears to know exactly how to drain us of hope.'

Eryn leaned against the stable door. 'If they take possession of the *Elorsil*, they may bend it to serve their will. It would indeed be a loss to us, but if they destroy a second Amanach... that would have a greater impact.'

Elodi held her gaze. 'Then it sounds as if the stone has priority. But... could Toryn yet use this sword to some effect?'

'Only if he's uncovered some of its many secrets. He's had little time, but then he has not failed in the face of adversity yet. And he did prevail in Vortimo, where many would have feared to enter.'

'Then as difficult a choice it is to make, I believe you must go to the aid of your sisters in Darrow to protect the stone. But... should I ride to the pass?'

Eryn stroked Moonbeam's neck. 'It is not for me to say. But I believe you may better serve your realms by avoiding the Kolossos. I have no choice but to take that way to Darrow. But the warlocks will learn of Toryn's whereabouts each time he handles the sword. And now they know of his path, my guess is they'll strike while on the treacherous road through the pass. He'll be vulnerable as there are few ways to escape. If I can aid him along my way, I will do so. But my priority has to be the Elda Stone.'

Elodi tried to recall Kernlow's map. 'How long before the warlocks can reach the pass?'

'They'll take the tunnels. Their mighty steeds can cover that distance in little time. They may already be there. No, Elodi. I believe it is too great a risk for both of you to be in that place. Our enemy would achieve a far greater victory if they defeat you both.'

Elodi stared into Moonbeam's dark eyes. 'Alas, we knew it would come to this. But you're right. We cannot offer our enemy an easy win. I will have to trust Toryn's judgement and skill. But you must take nourishment while your fine horse takes his. Come, join me for supper.' She led Eryn from the stables. 'I know little of this sword. Only that it was handed down from Draegelan through the Archons' line.'

Eryn linked her arm in Elodi's. 'The sword had gone from our memory until it awoke in Toryn's grasp. Draegelan was the last bearer who engaged its powers. It was forged by the Elorym, as you may have determined from its name. There were three in total. Their forging took many years to complete. More would have been made had the war not gone so badly. They were formed by gifted smithies for the mightiest of Elorym warriors.' Eryn withdrew her sword and looked along its blade. 'Ours were made in the same manner, yet not from the same rare metal, said to be sourced from deep beneath the Caerwals. Two of the three were lost in the bitter conflict against the warlocks of the day. One is believed to be at the bottom of the lake at Telamir, but the waters jealously protect their treasure, thus I doubt it will ever be retrieved. The other was lost in the tunnels beneath the Kolossos. The warrior and sword were buried when the warlocks brought down the ceiling to aid Ormoroth's retreat from Vortimo.' Eryn stopped outside the dining hall. 'The *Elorsil* was kept safe by the Amayans after the fall of the Elorym. Centuries later, they bestowed it to Draegelan, following his victory over Ormoroth at Roth's Doom.'

Elodi gasped. 'A fine gift indeed.'

Eryn nodded. 'And one that shows how much the Amayans admired him. And their decision was justified. The sword responded to his hand as if an Elorym warrior.'

Elodi grasped Eryn's arm. 'And now also to Toryn's touch. This is both good and bad tidings, I had thought—' An aide rushed towards her with papers in each hand. She groaned. Aides never ran when they brought good news. She took the messages and found an empty table away from the crowds. Elodi slumped as she read them both. 'Oh, the poor man. He should have stayed put in Archonholm and enjoyed his last days in comfort.' The first dispatch had come from one of Kernlow's birds. In his nonchalant way, he had simply reported they were being followed and anticipated an attack. Thus, his arrival might be a *tad delayed*. The second, was from an Ormsk captain who had come across the dreadful aftermath. None had survived. Elodi stared at the words, reluctant to believe them. The captain had found two dozen charred remains of both horses and riders, the lord's three aides, three cooks, and lastly Lord Kernlow.

Elodi could barely read the description of the manner of Kernlow's death. The captain had found him tied to a stake and undoubtedly had been tortured for the amusement of the attackers. Had Nordryn sent them? It would seem a sensible tactic to delay his enemies riding on Keld.

Elodi blinked back a tear as she handed the second dispatch to Eryn. The Amayan read quickly. She sighed. 'I did not know this man. But this is a most dreadful deed. To not allow the man to face death with a sword in his hand is most cruel.' Eryn stood. 'But perhaps it signals the next stages of this interminable war. I shall ride west this night. I ask much of Moonbeam, but this cannot wait. I and my sisters must deliver a blow before the warlocks locate the Elda Stone.' She turned to Elodi. 'Please be wary. There's more afoot than perhaps what first appears. It is not my place to say, but whoever attacked Lord Kernlow must not be allowed to roam these parts uncontested. And remember, the Ul-dalak may have learned of the location of the stone in the South Forest. Uluriel's attempt to destroy it may have failed, but she was inside Nyomae's head when she found it.'

Elodi groaned. 'I will step up patrols around the forest. Regrettably, the enemy forces our hand once again.'

Eryn placed her hand on Elodi's. 'There is another reason I came to Borrund. There is something we must do before I leave.' She glanced behind. 'But not here. It may unsettle the simple folk. Is there somewhere we could be alone?'

'There's my room. But what could possibly—?'

'An Amayan ritual. I have discussed this matter with the others. We believe it's time to bring you fully into the sisterhood.'

11. The Company Rides Out

Toryn leaned over the parapet. For a moment, he was reminded of the ledge over the main entrance at Drunsberg. 'I can't see a thing down there... but I can hear them.' He shivered as the patter of feet on stone reminded him of scuttling aralaks.

'Here you go, Cappy.' Cubric held a torch over the ledge and let it drop. 'This will give them a nasty surprise.' Its light flickered against the wall as it fell.

'By the Three! And a surprise for us all.' Toryn gasped as dozens of cobtrolls scampered away on their spindly arms and legs as the torch landed. They squatted, lifting their big heads to look up at the fort. Toryn stepped back as pairs of large, dark eyes, glistening in the torchlight, stared straight at him. One raised its hands, splayed its long fingers, then snatched them back as if clasped around his neck. Toryn's hand went to his throat. While they seemed no bigger than children, even the toughest guard dreaded the thought of a cobtroll's fingers closing around their windpipe.

The torch dimmed. Three cobs rushed forward and stamped out the flames with their over-sized hands and feet. 'The little blighters!' Cubric scoffed. 'I'll go and get some more. We'll need to keep an eye on them.'

Toryn turned to Amrul. 'Has the fort ever been breached?'

'Never.' Amrul patted the stone. 'As strong as the mountains themselves. The cobs make the odd strike, but they never get inside.'

Toryn looked up to the tower and the dark mountain looming behind. 'And they can't reach us from above?'

Amrul flapped his arms. 'Not unless they've worked out how to fly. It's too wide a gap for them to leap across. And no one has ever seen them use rope... well, not yet.'

Toryn grimaced. 'Then I hope they don't have the service of a corvraak.'

Amrul frowned. 'I thought they'd all gone.'

'I can assure you they have not. I've met one. At night, on the edge of the Foranfae. And I dearly hope it's the last of them.'

'Well, who'd have thought it.' Amrul's nose wrinkled. 'But then... there's plenty of other nasty creatures showing their faces we'd once thought long gone.'

Toryn warmed his hands over the brazier. 'How many years have you been at the pass, Amrul?'

'On and off over the last twenty... no, it's more than that. Must be twenty-five years now.'

'And what's your experience of the cobtrolls?'

Amrul rubbed his chin. 'I had this very same conversation with an Amayan a while back. She'd had more run-ins with the little fellows, and I wondered if she knew how many years they'd been in these parts.'

Toryn straightened. 'Amayans are given passage through the pass?'

'Ah, well, not officially. We have a sort of... agreement with the west side. We don't keep a record of them passing either way. Makes life a little easier, like.' Amrul winked. 'You won't find a guard who can say no to an Amayan.'

Toryn recalled the first time he saw Eryn's face. 'I can imagine. But as for the cobs, I've heard they're descended from larger trolls from Draegelan's day.'

Amrul's brow creased. 'I've heard similar. I guess that makes us lucky. The fellows cause enough trouble now considering their size. Getting through the pass back then must have been quite a trial if they were bigger.' He looked up to the dark sky. 'The Amayan reckoned they've been here long before any of us. Perhaps one of the gods themselves made 'em. But thank the Three the same god didn't create anything else.'

Cubric strolled back along the flagstones with an armful of torches. 'Here we go, gentlemen. Should keep us going for a while.' He dropped them at his feet and held one out to the brazier. Once lit, he handed it to Amrul.

The guide tossed it over the parapet. 'Well… would you look at that. The bridge is full of them.' He scratched his head. 'Now this ain't normal, sir. Not seen this many in one place for some time… or if ever if I'm being honest.'

Cubric tightened the buckle on his breastplate. 'And the gate will hold, Ammy?'

'Don't you go worrying about the gate. It's solid oak, bolstered by iron. I'm sure bigger fellows have tried and failed over the years.' Amrul nodded towards the tower. 'And we've got the means to thin them out should they threaten to put as much as a scratch on it.'

'Then what do they expect to achieve?' Toryn looked down the pass but could see nothing in the dark.

Amrul groaned. 'They want to stop us getting a good night's sleep with all this commotion. They've been known to slap the walls before. And with hands like shovels, they can make quite a racket. They'll certainly achieve that.' He pointed. 'Would you look at that. More are pouring over the bridge. There's enough of 'em to surround the whole fort.'

Cubric chuckled. 'Now if there was any mud around here, we could fill our ears.' He tapped his head. 'Worked for me a Wyke Wood. Although Lady Harlyn chose not to take my advice. Can't think why.'

Despite Cubric's humor, Toryn's unease grew. 'I don't mind losing a night's sleep, even if they try the same trick at the next fort. But… part of me suspects there's something else going on here. I'll take a look down the pass.' He relaxed and let the *farsight* come. He heard Cubric explain his ability to Amrul as he entered the pass. The darkness became a thick fog. Shapes moved along the road from the direction the company had come. Behind them, Toryn saw more cobs emerge from a cave above the road, and clamber down the rocky slope with ease. As the fog in his vision cleared, he could see they all carried a rock. He withdrew and looked to Cubric and Amrul. 'I don't think we need worry about loss of sleep, but our next meal might be a problem.' A rock hitting the gate echoed up the mountain sides.

Amrul shrugged. 'They can throw a thousand, it won't matter because...' his hand went to his face, 'ah, I see. They don't want to break in, they want to stop us getting out.' He pointed to the tower. 'We've got some ballast we can drop on their heads. That should slow them down.'

'Wait.' Toryn held up his hand. 'It won't work. Even if you've got enough for the hundred or so already down there, it will only add to the rubble we'll have to clear before we can get out.' He slapped the parapet. 'Don't you have birds, Amrul?'

The guide shrugged. 'Never had the need really. If we don't reach the watchtower in three days, they'll signal the other.'

Toryn held back his frustration. 'But from what I gather from Waldryn, they won't send anyone. Even if they decided to help, they won't know what they'll face.'

Amrul grunted. 'Cobtrolls. That's what they'd face. It's what we've always had to deal with. But every guard accepts you're on your own once you enter the pass. No sense in putting more guards at risk to save others.' He glanced over the edge. 'Even if they sent a hundred, they'll struggle against this many now they're working together.'

Toryn slumped against the parapet. 'But what if...?' He held his words not wishing to worry the rest of the company. 'Let me see if there's something I can do.' He closed his eyes and searched the Verses for signs of Ruan's company as they had come to Roth's Doom. He sighed. 'That's not going to work either. Every army that's marched through here in the last few centuries, would have been during the day. The time is wrong. I can't scare the cobs away.'

'Then we have to use our archers.' Cubric whistled to Lorek. 'Bows to the wall.' He looked to Toryn. 'We can retrieve the arrows in the morning. We don't have to kill them all, just frighten the blighters off… or at least slow them down stacking their rocks.' He dropped another torch over the wall. 'Ha. They don't seem to realize the gate opens inwards. The twenty of us could easily clear a pathway come morning, no problem. I shouldn't think it would take longer than an hour. If they think they can prevent us riding out, they need to think again. Even if they keep going 'til dawn' — he glanced up — 'which is an hour or two at most away, it won't delay us long.'

Toryn nodded. 'Agreed. Good thinking, Cub.' He turned to the rest. 'Let's see what a few arrows raining down on their heads will do. Then come morning we'll soon be out of here.'

The company did enough to slow the trolls below. Unlike the Ruuk, they did not seem keen to sacrifice themselves in battle, believing greater rewards awaited them in the next world. A few well-aimed arrows, and the odd rock, made them wary of getting too close. Above, the sky grew lighter, and the cobs began to thin out. Cubric peered over the parapet. 'Hardworking little fellows, I'll give them that. It's quite a pile they've built. Would've been handy at the Caerwal Pass. They'd have soon cleared all that rubble.'

Toryn regarded the pile. 'Shouldn't take too long to clear.' He stretched out his back. 'But they've achieved part of their objective. I hope we can get some sleep at the next fort.'

Amrul grumbled. 'If they try the same trick tomorrow, we'll take it in turns to sleep. I reckon ten of us should be enough to keep them under control.' The guide's breath drifted like a ghost over the wall. He shivered and rubbed his hands. 'That's odd. It's getting colder, yet dawn comes.' Amrul held up his torch. 'Would you look at that. Ice. Ice on the stone, and we're not halfway through autumn.'

Toryn's stomach clenched. 'Cubric, ready the company. We must clear our way and ride out now. We can't stay here a moment longer.' He glanced to the bridge. 'There'll be bigger fellows to deal with before long.'

Cubric had a good eye. It took Toryn's company just under the hour to clear a path from the gate. But as the air had cooled, Toryn's unease had grown. To Amrul's surprise, the cobtrolls had re-appeared on the other side of the bridge and had thrown rocks. Thus, four men were taken off removing the rubble to form a line of shields to deflect the stones. But it was not the cobs that troubled Toryn. He kept a close watch on the pass in both directions in the growing light. Did the Norgog come? Even a small band would be a threat. The road was narrow; they could not possibly ride through a solid line of Norgog without losing half of the company. And if they came from both east and west... they could be trapped inside the fort. Amrul had confidence in the fort's gate, but once the supplies had gone, the strength of the gate meant nothing. And it was not just the Norgog that concerned Toryn. The pass was noticeably colder than even in the dead of night. Of their many enemies, only the warlocks had the ability to change the weather.

Toryn felt the heat from the sword seep through his body. As soon as the company had gone back inside to ready their mounts, the cobtrolls had advanced on the gate. Toryn knew it was not by choice. Something must be keeping them from their caves so close to dawn. The overcast sky would dim the rising sun, but to the large eyes of the cobs who shunned the day, it would be enough to cause them pain. Norgog… or worse had to be near, but they still needed the cobs to delay their departure.

Toryn looked to the company lined up and ready to burst through the gate. Each carried a flaming torch, but much relied on him to set his sword ablaze to startle the cobtrolls. But just as important, he would have to light the way for the horses to negotiate the road in the gloom. He held up the glowing sword. 'Ready?' Amrul nodded. He turned the key, threw back the bolts, and opened the gate. Toryn leveled his blade and kicked on.

Hooves clattered across the flagstones, proclaiming their departure to all within a league. But they had no choice. Speed was vital if they were to make it to the next fort before nightfall. Outside, the cobtrolls hissed and clasped their hands over their eyes against the glare of Toryn's sword. His horse stumbled but kept his balance as the cobs scattered. Some fled back towards the bridge, others down the road leading west. Toryn wheeled the weapon, scything the pass with its blinding light. The company formed a column three horses abreast and waited for Amrul to secure the fort. Toryn checked the way ahead. The road looked clear, but Toryn feared the cobs had found places to hide, and would assail them as they rode through. But the bridge to the east was still packed, and Toryn could see why. He had been right. Behind the dazed trolls, a thick grey wall of Norgog advanced, driving those before them back towards the fort. The cobs were caught in the middle, fearful of facing Toryn's light, but risked being crushed by the Norgog if they tried to hold their ground.

Toryn called out. 'Hammerskulls! On the bridge. Ride.' The horses soon gained speed, confident of finding their way in the sword's silvery light. He glanced over his shoulder. Many of the cobs had been flung over the bridge by impatient Norgog, but even their punishing pace could not keep up with the frightened horses. The gap between them widened, but Toryn kept up the pace. More trolls gathered on a ledge a short way ahead. He cried out. 'Shields!' The company rode into a hail of stones. They clattered off shields and horses. A few stumbled but recovered to clear the danger. Yet Toryn chose not to ease their mad dash. He kept his eyes fixed on the winding road. Each bend possibly concealing a dreaded band of Norgog; each bend possibly spelling the end of their mission. But on they galloped.

The sun climbed at their backs, finally bringing daylight to the pass. The air warmed. Satisfied they were out of immediate peril, Toryn held up his hand to slow the company. While he would have been happier to put more leagues between them and the Norgog, tired horses could slip, and on the narrow road there was little room for error. And like the company, the horses would have had little rest with all the disturbance outside of the fort.

Amrul drew level with Toryn. He pointed. 'The straightest stretch of the pass is about two hours ahead. There's an overhang of solid rock, so we won't have to worry about stones raining down on our heads. It's a good place to catch our breath as we can see a good distance in both directions.'

Toryn stroked his horse. 'Then we'll maintain this easy pace and take our rest there. And how far to the fort from that place?'

Amrul brushed rock dust from his shoulders. 'As long as the road is clear, it's another two to three hours, and hopefully we'll find the west tower has restocked it.' He frowned as he observed the thin strip of sky overhead. 'Ahh, wasn't expecting clouds today. It can get a bit treacherous in a storm. This road can quickly turn into a river.' Amrul studied the clouds once more. 'If there's any rain to come, I reckon it won't be until this evening. If we're lucky, it will unleash its worst while we're asleep under a roof and in warm beds.'

Toryn tried to envisage Hamar's map. He had a plan, but wished to think it over before he put it to the rest of the company. He nodded. 'Then let's press on.'

Amrul turned out to be a good judge of the weather, and Toryn was pleased the rain held off. The occasional gust, funneled by the steep sides of the pass, battered into them, threatening to topple them into the ravine. But to the relief of all, the skies remained free of the dark storm clouds they feared. The company reached the resting place in good time, and Toryn had finalized his strategy. Now he had to convince the others. He waited until the horses had been fed, rubbed down, and watered, and their riders had eaten a light meal.

Toryn stood and used his *farsight* to check the road to the east and west. Confident both directions were clear, he spoke to the company. 'I'm sure you could all do with a good rest, but…' he looked to their dust-caked faces and took a breath, 'it's likely we'll face the same problems at the next fort as we did last night. And, I also believe we may have attracted the attention of something other than just the Hammerskulls. I reckon a warlock may be on our tail.' The dust cracked on their brows. Toryn waited for the murmurs to die. 'Only they have the power to freeze the air, command the Norgog, and organize the cobs in the numbers we've seen.'

Amrul agreed. 'Has to be something at their backs. Them cobs don't willingly come out of their caves with dawn approaching.' He eyed Toryn. 'But what would a warlock be doing down here?'

'Ah, that'll be… because of me.' He tapped his hip. 'It may be my sword. Perhaps they can sense its power. Or… they don't want us to get to Drunsberg and have been watching all the routes we could take. But for whatever reason, I'm certain a warlock is here, and we need to reach the other side. So, that means we may have to…'

Elrik laughed. 'Just say it, Toryn.' He looked to the others. 'I think we all know we can't take the risk of being walled up in the next fort.'

Lorek stood. 'And if there's a warlock on our tail, it makes sense to ride through the night and get across as quick as we can.'

Toryn heaved a sigh. 'Yes, that's my plan.' He turned to their guide. 'Your thoughts, Amrul?'

'Well… it goes against my usual advice, but what we saw last night was a little odd. Perhaps we've made it too easy for the cobs by sticking to the same routine all these years.' Amrul looked back over his shoulder. 'But a warlock? That's a new one for me. Yet cobs are still a danger in the dead of night whether we're riding or not. If they've blocked the road, we're stuck out in the open and vulnerable… night or day.' He rubbed a bit of grit from his eye. 'But I guess our chances of getting out of here are better if we keep moving.'

'Thank you, Amrul.' Toryn glanced around the company. 'But, you should know, if a warlock leads the Norgog, it will likely bring them through the tunnels. It's possible they could overtake and come at us from the west.'

Cubric lowered his flask. 'Now don't we find ourselves in a pickle.' He looked to the others. 'But who here hasn't been in a worse position? From the gruesome stories I've heard about the spiders' nest, I think I'd rather be here and face a warlock. And Roth's Doom was no stroll in a summer meadow.' He placed his hands on his hips. 'We're fighting for Lady Harlyn, and I can't think of a better leader to serve. No one said it would be easy.' Cubric patted Toryn's shoulder. 'And this man here has looked a warlock in the eye and lived to tell the tale.'

Elrik laughed. 'And who can stand in his way now he has his fancy new sword.' The company cheered.

Toryn could not keep the grin from spreading across his face. 'Well let's not make it any easier for them to find us with all this hollering. But, if they find us, it's me they're after, so don't let yourselves get caught up in my battles. I'll hold them up while you get away as quick as you can.' He turned to Cubric. 'And if anything happens to me, Cub knows the plan for Drunsberg. That is the priority.'

Amrul pointed to the sky. 'But please be wary, lads. There's rain coming, I can feel it in my bones. And when it rains here, it comes down in buckets. Our torches will soon be doused.' He thumbed over the ledge. 'And if you go too fast in the dark, the only place you'll get to in a hurry is the bottom.'

Toryn held out his sword. 'Then I'll attempt to light our way again. It will alert the enemy of our position, but as I see it, I don't think there's another way.' He looked at the company in turn. 'That's my plan. It's a race to the west with our foe. If any of you have a better idea, I'm happy to hear it.' None spoke. 'Then, are we in agreement?' But while Toryn was relieved to see all approved his plan, he was unsure whether he had the strength to keep his sword aglow for the whole night. And what if they met a warlock on the narrow road? He had bettered the one at Vortimo, but back then the warlock had droogs to command, and Amayans to constrain. Here in the pass, Toryn would contend with the full might of one of Ormoroth's commanders, and one that had likely faced Draegelan on the battlefield.

12. A Sisters' Bond

'Perhaps it's best you sit.' Eryn led Elodi to the armchair. 'You may feel a little faint at first.'

Elodi took her advice. 'Does it make a difference I'm only half Amayan?'

'That I cannot tell. I have no memory of my childhood. I do not know my parents, or how the Elorym intended us to replace our fallen. You're the first new sister any of us have encountered.'

Elodi made herself comfortable but could not prevent the butterflies in her stomach. 'How far back can you remember?'

Eryn sat opposite. 'Until the lifting of the shadow, not very far at all.' Her gaze went to the wall behind Elodi. 'But I now recall I fought at the first battle of Roth's Doom. That was many, many years ago, but I cannot tell you my age, or how many generations of Amayans have lived.' She looked back to Elodi. 'But I imagine those of us who remain have, like you, mortal fathers.'

'Could there be more you don't know about? You weren't aware of me until recently.'

Eryn thought for a moment. 'If the Fire awakes them, then we would instantly know. Our numbers have dwindled over the years. Thus, it's likely you're the last.'

'Have you...' Elodi looked down to her hands, 'have you tried to... have your own?'

Eryn took Elodi's hands. 'Your mother is the only Amayan I've known to carry a child. Perhaps with time, as the Amanach weaken, we've become barren.'

Elodi thought back to Wendel requesting she produce an heir. 'Then it's imperative we defeat our enemies before the Amayan line is lost.'

'Then let us proceed, and do not be concerned. We have all passed through this ritual… and so will you.' Eryn grinned. 'For one who has proved herself beyond doubt in the face of terror, you do look a little anxious.'

Elodi tried to settle. 'When you insisted we retire to my room so as not to disturb the locals, then yes, forgive me for being a little anxious.'

'That's for their sake. There may be the odd glimmer of light, or the air may crackle, which they may find disconcerting. It's better we do this alone.'

Elodi sat at the edge of her chair. 'Now I'm intrigued. But what does it mean to bring me into the sisterhood?'

Eryn straightened. 'We are connected. We have ways to communicate… after a fashion, over distance. We believe we use the lines of power that emanate from the Amanach. While at times you could sense our presence, as with Amyra's suffering, you yet remain outside. The Amayan Fire was kindled by your encounter with the *kruul* in Archonholm. But as yet, you are unfettered, and therefore not fully coupled with us. But… before I proceed you must be aware the gift comes with a great burden.'

Elodi sighed. 'Alas, my shoulders have grown accustomed to carrying the weight of responsibility.'

Eryn patted Elodi's leg. 'Then I trust they can bear a little more. But it is only fair to inform you of what this entails. At times you will endure the pain of the land as it suffers the evil inflicted upon it. You'll hear the Amanach scream when under attack… and worse, you may come to sense the relentless heartbeat of the Angorlith, when all is quiet.' She held Elodi's gaze. 'So… with your consent, I shall complete the bond with your rightful sisters.'

'It's a burden I'm willing to bear.' Elodi took a breath. 'Then you have my consent.'

Eryn smiled. 'I expected nothing less from you, Elodi. I

don't know what visions may be visited upon you. I have no recollection of my initiation, but what you see must never be shared. Each Amayan's journey is different. It may be the Elorym foresaw the strife to come after their time. Thus, what is revealed to each new warrior is determined by the needs of the day. Or they keep the full truth of our powers hidden to protect the sisterhood if one is turned by the Ul-dalak.'

Elodi nodded. 'I am ready.'

Eryn placed her fingers on Elodi's temples. 'You need do nothing. As I said, you may feel lightheaded. Now… please close your eyes.'

Elodi did as asked. Her temples warmed; all sounds outside ceased, and the room descended into silence. Then, in the distance, she heard water. A trickle at first as if a spring bubbled up from the ground. It grew louder as a vision formed. Elodi saw rivers surging from a source deep beneath the mountains. Her head spun as she suddenly rose high over the snowy peaks of the Kolossos range. Yet the rivers remained visible, glistening as they flowed through tunnels and caverns to eventually surface at the sites of the Amanach.

The vision faded. Elodi stood alone surrounded by fog. A clash of steel rang through the gloom, followed by mournful cries of pain. She spun around as the fog cleared. All about her, a battle raged. At its center, a tall Amayan fought. Elodi knew her: it was her mother, and she stood on Gormadon Plain. Despite her strength and immense skill, Eleni was driven back. But while others fell, Eleni yet resisted the unworldly creatures of Ormoroth's dark pits. Elodi yearned to rush to her side, but the battlefield darkened, Eleni was lost in the shadow, and silence descended.

A vase appeared in the darkness. An empty, glass vase sat upon a table. It glistened in the sunlight streaming through a narrow, arched window, bathing a white wall behind in the colors of the rainbow. But as the sun set, the rainbow slid down the wall to form a pool of dark blood. The ceiling cracked; a hole opened. A black fluid poured forth and trickled into the vase. Once filled to the brim, the vessel melted, and its contents oozed onto the table. Dark fingers spread across the wood, spilled over the edge, across the floor, then up the wall and out of the window. Outside, a storm raged; the ground shook; the walls crumbled.

'It is complete. You are at one with your sisters, Elodi.' She opened her eyes. Eryn sat before her, glowing as she had at the Amanach. Her eyes glimmered, and Elodi knew hers also shone. She looked about the room, unsure of her surroundings. Eryn smiled. 'Your senses are heightened, and for a while the mortal world will look a little… jaded. It will change back shortly. But be wary. Use your new senses with caution. For the most part, you will know of your sisters' whereabouts anywhere within the realms, but so may the warlocks. Only look for us when in need.'

Elodi waited for the dizziness to pass. 'This will take some adjustment on my behalf. But…' she gasped, 'I can feel them. Yes… my sisters. And they are with me.' Elodi looked at Eryn. 'But you said for the most part. What determines the strength of this bond?'

The light in Eryn's eyes began to fade. 'There are places where the Amanach's power cannot reach, or it's weakened by the Angorlith. If you cannot find us, it often means we are in a dark place.' Eryn held her gaze. 'Take care, my sister. With time, the bond will grow stronger, but for now, be both wary and patient with its use. I dearly wish we could spend more time together. We have many stories to share, but alas they will have to wait for better times.' Eryn stood and led Elodi to the door. 'But for now, we have separate paths to take.' She stopped with her hand on the latch. 'Yet we seek the same destination. May we meet again, my sister.' With that, she opened the door and strode down the corridor as Gundrul and Bardon approached. Elodi watched her go as the two men gaped open-mouthed as she glided past.

Bardon stared at Elodi. 'You… look different.'

Elodi frowned. 'And you also.' She had not noticed before, but the pain from his ordeal on Mundrake's Isle was etched on Bardon's face, and it troubled him still. Elodi turned to Gundrul, who had just remembered to close his mouth. The captain's knowing eyes concealed his desire to hang up his sword and shield. He was drained by his life of service, and longed to return to his family farm in Lunn to tend his sheep. She looked away, suddenly overwhelmed by the doubts and fears the two men had buried deep. Yet, still they served, guided by the sense of duty and loyalty to the realms.

Elodi invited them into her room. 'Eryn has performed my initiation. I am bonded with the Amayans.' As she spoke, the significance of the words dawned on her. She would never be the same, and the world would never look the same.

Bardon sighed. 'It could not have come at a better time. I hear events have taken a darker turn.'

Elodi handed over the messages from her table. 'A sad end for a man who, regardless of what we thought of him, served for many years, and devoted his life to the good of the realms… in his own manner.'

Bardon read and passed the notes to Gundrul. He sat. 'I see the captain suspects it's Nordleng.'

Gundrul groaned as he finished reading. 'Everything burned, soldiers tortured.' He dropped the papers on the table. 'That is their way. Could be no other. But why the horses? In days passed they would have taken and sold them.'

Elodi spat. 'Cowards! Every last one of them. This is the first such attack since the battle. Are we about to see more?'

Bardon sat and reread the messages. 'It was a planned attack on Kernlow. It has to be. The Nordleng aren't known for their bravery, as we're only too aware. I doubt they would attack a detachment of Archonian Knights willingly, whether they slept or not.'

Elodi shook her head. 'Did Kernlow not set a watch? Perhaps being so far from the northern border, he assumed he was safe. But… surely, not even Kernlow would be so careless.' She clenched her fists. 'The Ormsk scout reckoned close to thirty attacked the camp. But Kernlow must have had more than enough skilled fighters to see off the Nordleng. Such a loss… and a preventable one at that. I cannot imagine the pain Kernlow must have suffered at the hands of those fiends.' She slapped the table. 'Nordryn must be laughing at us.'

Gundrul picked up the second note. His eyes moved slowly across the lines. 'But if Nordryn had sent them, ma'am, why not capture the lord? He could have used him to bargain with, or demand a large ransom.'

Elodi frowned. 'That would have been a clever move, and it certainly would have put us in a quandary. Do they believe Kernlow still commands our forces? That's the only reason I could see why they would kill him.'

Bardon nodded. 'Perhaps it was Nordryn's intention to abduct him. But these Nordleng rascals are a law unto themselves. My concern now is there's a band of them with a taste for tormenting good folk and plundering villages. We saw few at Roth's Doom. They'll fight for who has the biggest purse. With our enemies licking their wounds, they may take it upon themselves to raid at will across Ormsk.'

Elodi exhaled. 'And we can guess who Glambul will blame for this.' She turned to the captain. 'Gundrul, how many of the First Horse are fit for duty?'

He straightened. 'Easily fifty, ma'am. More recover daily. We'll soon see their numbers approaching eighty.'

Elodi stood. 'Then I shall lead a company of thirty to match the Nordleng one on one. Let us see how they fare against us. The Nordleng tend to leave a trail of destruction, so it shouldn't be too difficult to find them.'

Bardon looked up. 'Ma'am? Is that...?' he sighed. 'Yes, that's a sound plan. We cannot have these scoundrels terrorizing Ormsk. And the people must see them punished for what they did to Kernlow... and for the atrocities I fear they'll commit before they're found.'

Elodi picked up her sword belt. 'Eryn advised me there may be more going on in these parts than at first meets the eye. Perhaps this band of raiders have another purpose to serve.' She looked to the window. 'We have six days before we depart for Keld. Gundrul, I want to see you fully fit for the saddle when I return. Bardon, you, Amyndra, Ruan and the good captain can put the finishing touches to the tactics. I don't foresee I'll be gone more than five days. If I and thirty First Horse can't track and kill these rogues, then we may as well surrender to our enemy now.' She took a breath. 'I shall make them pay for what they did to Lord Kernlow and his camp. He was a lord of the realms. His ghastly death cannot go unpunished. Word has been sent to Marrick in Archonholm. His body has been recovered and arrangements will have to be made for his burial in the crypt at Kirik. Then, as is the way of Kernlow, his son will become lord.'

Bardon cleared his throat as he glanced to Gundrul. 'Ma'am. And if you don't succeed in five days?'

'Five will be ample, Bardon.' Elodi's hand clenched her sword. 'I am stronger than when I last had the pleasure of

Nordleng company. I've faced far worse.' She looked to the dying fire in the hearth. 'No. Five days, that is all. They'll pay for this atrocity, and for the many more they've no doubt committed during their miserable time in our lands. But if, for some reason, I am delayed, do not wait for me. You must take back Keld, regardless.'

13. Riders in the Dark

The light from Toryn's sword burned bright as he led the company along the narrow road. An eagle passing overhead could be mistaken for thinking the moon had plunged from the sky and hurried to reach the west before dawn. But while the glow allowed the horses to gallop with confidence, a little way beyond its light, the way was black as if an impenetrable wall spanned the pass. Toryn kept his eyes fixed ahead, ready to bring the company to a halt should the road be blocked by rubble, Norgog ... or a warlock. They had made good progress, reaching the second fort before dusk. Inside, they had found ample supplies, and after a brief rest and meal, the company had set off into the night and resumed their dash for the west. Toryn had been hopeful they would see the watchtower at sunrise, but he had grown uneasy as the air had begun to cool and the wind had picked up.

Thankfully, the cobs had stayed out of sight, and Toryn had pressed on well past midnight before stopping. But the conditions worsened. The cold rain blowing into their faces, had turned to hail. Toryn found a shallow inlet that offered some respite from the weather, but he knew they could not afford to stay for long. But Amrul was not so sure. He called out above the gusts. 'If this gets any worse, we'll have to wait. Look.'

Toryn held out his sword and groaned. Ahead, the road glistened as the hail had turned to ice. He bellowed. 'Is there anywhere nearby we can shelter until this blows over?' But as he asked, Toryn knew in his gut this was not a natural storm — it would not stop until they were trapped.

'There'll be a few caves we've not walled up. But they'll likely have tunnels at their rear.' His brow furrowed. 'And we both know what that means.'

The hail turned to thick snow. Toryn blinked as the flakes melted in his eyes. 'This weather forces our hand. We don't have a choice. I'd rather take my chances with a sword in my hand than risk our horses skidding into the chasm.' He glanced over his shoulder and groaned; his sword was not the only source of light in the pass. Not more than half a league behind them, the mountain walls flickered blue.

Janae brought her horse next to Toryn. She had also seen the lights. 'We call it Cold Fire. That means Norgog. Their flames don't go out in wind or rain, but it still burns the skin.'

Toryn lowered his blade. He peered as best he could into the blizzard, but could see nothing to the west. 'We have to assume they'll come from both directions and trap us in between.' A sudden gale slammed into them. He tensed as he felt his feet slip. Toryn looked to Amrul's fraught face in the dull glow of his sword. 'Have they chosen this spot? If we find shelter, do the cobs await us inside?'

Amrul looked back to the flickering light behind them. He stuttered. 'I… I couldn't say, sir. I've never seen anything like this.'

Janae pointed. 'There's a cave down there. See.' She waved her hands. 'The snow swirls as if the wind has found somewhere else to go.'

Cubric yelled against the squall. 'I'd rather fight in a cave than in this ledge.'

Toryn agreed. 'We must get out of this storm. We'll head for that cave and take our chances there.' The horses at the rear screamed. A dark mass of Norgog rounded the bend brandishing their cruel hammers. Others held torches of Cold Fire, burning bright, and as Janae had said, were untroubled by the wind howling through the pass. Toryn grasped the reins as his horse stumbled, struggling to find a grip on the ice as it looked to bolt. 'To the caves!' They set off, hugging the mountain wall, desperate to avoid the sheer drop to their left.

Toryn heaved a sigh of relief as once again, Janae was proven right. He turned his horse and waited at the entrance as the company led their nervous animals into the cave. He dismounted and handed the reins to Cubric. His voice echoed. 'Organize the defense inside, Captain. I'll see what I can do to thin out the Norgog.'

Cubric glanced down the pass. 'Don't wait too long out here. I didn't think it possible, but this wind is getting stronger.'

Toryn stepped back out onto the road. He set his stance and braced against the gale at his back. The Norgog had picked up their pace, untroubled by the storm and icy road. He glanced up to the slope above them. Toryn knew the sword had power; he had seen bolts of lightning shoot from the point within its Verse. But Draegelan had called out the sword's name to channel the power of the Amanach… and that was yet unknown to him. The ground trembled with the Norgog approach. He had to try.

Toryn tightened his grip. He directed the point towards an overhang of rock, a little way ahead of their ranks. He took a deep breath, braced, and sought the paths of power connecting to the Amanach. The blade glowed… then blazed, lighting up the pass as if day had come. But that was all. No bolt shot from the sword; no rocks cascaded down onto Norgog heads. Toryn stared at the weapon in his hand. He cried out into the wind. 'What is your name?' The gales answered, but they carried not its name, only howls of scorn. Raindrops hissed as they fell on the hot blade. But that would not stop the enemy. Did he only have the strength to make it glow? Toryn gaped back at the Norgog. The front rank faltered as they shielded their tiny eyes. But all he had achieved was to slow their pace with a dazzling light — it was not enough.

Toryn stumbled into the cave, appalled by his failure. Inside, the company had formed a barrier up to waist height with loose rocks. Cubric held out his hand to pull Toryn over. 'Not much I know, but it might keep their hammers at bay for a while.' Toryn clambered over. Roold and Jedrul had managed to light some of the damp torches and had wedged them into cracks in the rock. Cubric continued. 'We're almost ready. The horses are at the rear but are a bit jittery. Elrik is trying to settle them.'

Toryn had to think fast. Their survival depended on shield and weapon if he could not call upon the power of the sword. He glanced to the back of the cave. 'Is there a tunnel?'

'As Amrul expected. Janae said it starts to descend a hundred paces in. Got to admire her bravery, eh. I wouldn't be keen on going down there alone.' Cubric turned and nodded to the entrance. 'But we've had a stroke of luck. The opening is wide enough for the horses, but also narrow enough to defend.'

Toryn looked around the cavern. 'That may be so, but I'm sure it's no coincidence we find ourselves here. This is planned. We'll have both front and rear to defend all too soon.' He turned and eyed the dark opening to their rear. 'It wouldn't be my first choice, but we may have to take our chances down that tunnel if the Norgog get inside.'

The company readied for the attack. Lots had been drawn to determine their positions. Elrik and Jedrul took their place at the front of the shield wall. Three guards could stand abreast in the opening and lock their shields. And to their advantage, perhaps only two broad-shouldered Norgog could form their front. The shields were four rows deep, but all were aware the first two would be vulnerable under the hammer blows. Cubric was reluctant to waste arrows on the Norgogs' tough hides, and it would be close to impossible to rotate their lines in the tight space. Thus, much rested on the shoulders of those at the front.

At their rear, they set a line of four across the tunnel, leaving only four in reserve, ready to take their place where needed. Cubric stood at the mouth of the tunnel with Amrul and Roold. Toryn paced in between the two defensive positions with Janae, feeling guilty that he had been spared a place in the lines. But Cubric remained convinced Toryn could save the day with his sword. But unless blinding them with a brilliant light would suffice, they had a tough fight on their hands.

Toryn looked up from his dull sword and called over to Elrik. 'Any sign of the storm easing?' But he knew the answer. And that could mean only one thing — a warlock… possibly two. He bowed his head and entered the Song, desperate to find something within the Verses to aid them. His vision blurred as time slowed and the company faded from sight. However, to his regret, the cave was formed only a few decades ago by cobs, hence he had little to work with.

Toryn heard Elrik yell. 'They come!' He turned to the entrance and watched through the shimmering veil of the Verses stretching back to the present. But Toryn found nothing to repel the attack. The blue flames of Norgog torches burned ominously slow in the Verse, shedding a revealing light upon their flat faces. Toryn shuddered as he saw why the guards named them Hammerskulls. Their skulls did indeed resemble the head of their weapon of choice. Small black eyes glowered from under hooded lids, and their wide nostrils flared as they prepared to attack.

They wore no armor — they had no need. A Norgog's thick, gray hide could blunt many a weapon, and only a carefully aimed strike with a keen blade could bring them down. But it would not be easy to be so accurate in a tight space. Perhaps luck would play its part after all.

As the company's shield wall braced, Toryn had an idea. He may not have the means to use his sword, but perhaps there was one trick up his sleeve. As he expected, the Norgog launched their torches of Cold Fire over the rock wall, looking to set the shields ablaze. A dozen blue arcs slowly rose from their ranks, poised to rain down onto the defenders. Toryn acted. He circled his hands, isolating the Verse above the shields to ensnare the torches. Clutching his hands, he snatched them from the present, then sent them back in time to land harmlessly in an empty cave.

Exhausted by his efforts, Toryn stumbled back and into Janae. The Norgog paused, bewildered by the vanishing fire. But it mattered not to them. They bellowed their challenge and charged the rock wall. Elrik led the defenders, driving his sword through the shields at anything within reach. Those at the back, hurled stones over their heads, but seemed not to trouble the thick Norgog skulls. One attacker fell, but another stepped on him, using his comrade to gain height and swing his hammer. Yet, Elrik and Jedrul stood defiant. They lunged at the dark eyes and slit mouths of the Norgog. Toryn recovered a little of his strength and climbed onto a rock to get a better view. At least six Norgog lay dead or injured. Elrik and Jedrul fought on, but they would soon tire.

The Norgog roared anew, heaving the dead and injured ahead of them into the makeshift barrier. Rocks began to shift; the Norgog edged forward. Toryn peered over their heads. How many more waited outside?

Cubric yelled from the rear of the cave. 'Cobtrolls!' Janae and the two reserves rushed to their aid as the cobs' long fingers grappled with the shields looking to break their wall. But the line held… for now. But Toryn saw the problem. The cobs were small, but if only a few clambered over the line, they would soon be at the throats of those facing the Norgog.

The horses reared. Toryn feared they could bolt in either direction, thus slam into the backs of the defenders. They were trapped, but Toryn knew which of the two assailants he would rather face. The rock wall collapsed; the Norgog surged forward. More hammers crashed onto the shields at the front. Toryn saw two of his company go down under the blows. The storm outside raged. His mind was made up. The road was no longer open to them. It would have to be the tunnels.

Toryn cried out over the melee. 'Retreat!' But as the shields edged back, a tall, dark shadow loomed at the entrance. His stomach churned: a warlock. The commander's arm swirled. A shimmering, green sphere formed between his palms. Toryn clenched his sword, but knew he could do little against the dark arts. The warlock raised his hands; the air churned; a deafening screech thundered through the cave. But the blow did not come. The warlock twisted and hurled his attack towards the road. The air burst. A brilliant, white light blinded Toryn. But he rejoiced. Amayan Fire!

The Norgog attack faltered. The warlock rallied the rear ranks towards the Amayan outside. Eryn's voice spoke calmly inside Toryn's head. *I cannot defeat them all. Bring down the ceiling.* His body warmed a little as Eryn's Fire gave him strength. Then she spoke the words he most wanted to hear. *It is the Elorsil. Speak its name. The Amanach will answer.*

Toryn raised the sword and called out its name. The Amanach to the west in the Vale of Caran, answered. He felt its heat at his back and instinctively knew what must be done. Toryn directed the heat up his arm and into the sword. He waited for the shields to clear the entrance… then unleashed its power. The sword blazed and shot a bolt of light at the ceiling. Toryn staggered back as the rock splintered. Great slabs crashed down onto the Norgog. Dust billowed in his face, but he could see the entrance was sealed.

Toryn coughed and spat, struggling to breathe. The few torches still burning, shed a yellow hue in the thick dust clogging the cave. The *Elorsil* felt heavy at his side, and he struggled to lift and place it back in its scabbard. The last of his strength abandoned him. Toryn collapsed, slid down the wall, and slumped to the floor. His ears rang but could not shut out the moans of the wounded, and the screams of the frightened horses. Jedrul tried to calm the beasts, while others tended to the injured. But two Archonians lay dead. Toryn could only watch as Elrik and Roold lifted their shattered bodies and secured them to their horses. There would be no time to bury them where they had fallen, even if they could dig into the rock. Toryn was aware the warlock would not give up so easily. All too soon the surviving Norgog outside the cave, would clear the rubble and pursue them down into the tunnels.

A shadow limped towards him. Cubric sat at Toryn's side. He spluttered. 'That blast soon scared off the cobs. Janae has gone on ahead to—' Cubric stopped and stared. 'By the Three, you look… no, it must be my eyes.' Toryn could not find his voice and could only shrug. Cubric patted his arm. 'Sorry, didn't mean to give you a fright, Cappy. With all these flashes and bangs, for a moment, your eyes seemed to be alight. Burning a bit like Cold Fire… but not so scary.'

Another approached. Janae kneeled beside them. She fought for breath in the thick air. 'No sign of the cobs.

The tunnel is level. It's straight for the first part, then bends to the left and drops sharply.'

Cubric clutched her shoulder. 'Good work. The cappy is a bit out of sorts at the moment.' He turned back to Toryn. 'Just nod if you agree. I reckon we best get going. I'll put those who can still walk at the front and rear. You and the injured should ride, but there's a risk some of them may bolt.' Toryn nodded.

Elrik came to his aid and took his arm. 'Let's get you on your horse.' As Elrik led him across the cave, he felt some of his strength return. He whispered. 'Thank you, my friend.'

Elrik held out his hands so Toryn could mount. 'Was that an Amayan outside?'

'Eryn. And without her, I don't think we'd have lasted long.'

'Not a moment too soon, eh. Did she escape?'

Toryn took the reins. 'I believe she did. She's heading west.'

Elrik sighed. 'Then it must be urgent if she's taking the pass all by herself.' He chuckled. 'But what's not urgent these days.'

Cubric gave the orders, and the company set off. As they approached the first bend, they readied for an ambush, but thankfully their way remained clear. However, their relief was quickly dispelled as their horses struggled with the steep tunnel floor. Down was not good. The deeper they went, the farther they found themselves from the light… and none knew what awaited them below. Two had already lost their lives. How many would live to reach Drunsberg?

The *Elorsil* shuddered against Toryn's leg. He glanced behind, but it was not something in the tunnel, or even the mountain range. He could not know where or how, but with dread, he sensed the enemy had struck a blow.

14. A Splinter in Time

Nyomae clung onto Ashala's feathers as she soared through the snow-capped peaks of the Kolossos. The cold night air seeped deep into her chest, and it hurt to breathe. But speed was of utmost importance, and Ashala chose to glide on the currents rising over the mountains to hasten their way. But despite their haste, the sight of the world below, rekindled the curiosity she had felt as a young girl. The Kolossos Pass appeared as a deep wound across the range. The faint moonlight glinted off the tops of the two watchtowers, looking like the spear tips of soldiers guarding the way through the mountains. To the west, the summit of the mighty Caranach towered over them, appearing tall even in the presence of her two imposing sisters, Kinderach and Lugnach. A bright, pinprick of light flickered like a star as it sped through the pass. It stirred something within Nyomae, but she had no time to investigate: her path lay south.

Ashala flew on, never tiring, exulting in the freedom from those who had enslaved her for centuries. Nyomae spoke to the corvraak, assuring her the Maidens would rejoice at her change of heart. To the east, the sky turned pink. Nyomae used the *farsight* to see the twin towers of Karrock casting their long shadows across Amman. Behind, the restless Karajan Sea swelled, frustrated by the string of islands that hampered her efforts to lay claim to the land.

Ashala soared higher as the air suddenly churned beneath her wings. Nyomae knew its cause. Far below, not even the pure light of dawn could cleanse Vortimo. The hard, cruel walls of the fortress jutted out from the mountains that suffered its intrusion. But their patience would one day be rewarded. The brief time of those who fought their petty wars, would one day end. Thus, Vortimo would eventually succumb to the elements and crumble into the valley to free the land of its stain.

Ashala sped on. At times she climbed, rising on a current of warmer air, then rest her wings and spread them wide to descend as if sliding down a hill. The sun rose until directly in line with the southern Kolossos peaks, shedding its light into dark valleys where no mortal had set foot.

Farther south, Nyomae felt their presence before she saw them. The twin pinnacles of Telamir seemed but a few feet beneath Ashala's belly. They appeared to rise above the mountains and reach towards them as if to urge them on their way. Nyomae recalled the dread of seeing the Elorym's spire collapse in Uluriel's vision. Now she took encouragement; the great tower yet stood, tall and valiant in the face of the shadow.

The range began to taper as they approached its end. Ashala descended as the vast green canopy of the Foranfae Forest came into view. Below, the Menon River sparkled in the bright sunlight, flowing strong in its youth as she fought her way out from beneath the Kolossos. Nyomae traced its winding path to the edge of the forest, where it disappeared until it emerged in the south. Her stomach clenched as Ashala flew over the Foranfae's heart: the bare, tainted plain where the finest fighters of the Seven Realms had fallen. But Nyomae drew hope. The poisoned ground had surely shrunk. The trees appeared to have advanced, slowly healing the devastation caused by her invocation of the Verse of Unmaking. Nyomae's heart swelled. Had the Nym grown stronger?

Another presence made itself known. Ahead, the glistening, white wall of the Caerwals rose over the horizon. And before them, the towers of Archonholm.

The blue banner appeared is if a tiny butterfly's wing, fluttering in the breeze, vying for attention against the immense mountain wall behind. The Menon River emerged between the thinning trees, leading the way to Archonholm. It seemed an age ago when Toryn had steered their boat through the forest as Nyomae lay in her slumber. Back then, she had been confident of gaining the Archon's support, oblivious to Uluriel's presence, unaware of the disaster awaiting them at the Caerwal Gate. But had their predicament improved?

Ashala dipped a wing as she circled and descended. She would land short of the citadel, not wishing to attract the attention of the vigilant archers posted on the North Terrace. But it had not escaped Nyomae's attention that the warm air of the south now troubled Ashala.

The raven landed. Nyomae slid from her back, happy to feel the solid ground beneath her feet. She stroked Ashala's neck. 'You have done well, my beauty. It has been an honor to witness you in full flight.' The bird's head bowed. Nyomae stepped away. 'Please. I ask you to wait for me in the mountains away from the heat. I will call for you on my return.'

Ashala sprang up and gladly flew north. Nyomae watched until the distance gave her the appearance of a natural raven. She turned back. Archonholm's new defensive wall had progressed, now rising tall on the opposite bank of the Menon River. But another sight caught her eye. Beneath the shadow of the wall, the lush green fields between the river and the wall, bristled with headstones. At first glance, they appeared as if a crop ready for harvest, but those beneath the fields would rise no more. And this was just one of many fields set aside to bury the dead from the Caerwal Pass.

Nyomae bowed her head, gave thanks for their sacrifice, then turned and walked towards the bridge. With

Marrick in charge of the city, Nyomae hoped entry would be granted without delay. She took a breath and approached the bridge, trusting she would not have to use the same trick as she had on her previous visit.

'Kernlow is dead?' Nyomae stared at Marrick. 'Do we know the details?'

'Lady Harlyn suspects a band of Nordleng. She is to lead a company of First Horse to track them down.'

Nyomae sat on a bench on the South Terrace as the sun set for the day. She spoke to herself. 'It appears the pause after our *victory* was brief indeed.' Her eyes wondered across the steep slopes of the Caerwals, suddenly wary of entering the Lost Realms. Nyomae gathered her thoughts and turned to Marrick. 'And Lady Harlyn has informed you of my requirements?'

Marrick nodded. 'Yes, ma'am. It took me a while to interpret as it was a little… cryptic, to avoid prying eyes I imagine. However, I'm afraid the wooden tower at the gate remains incomplete.'

'It's not finished? Surely, it should have been done by now.'

'That it would have been, but Lord Kernlow's last act before departing, was to divert all workers to the outer wall. He gave that priority over all other projects.'

Nyomae sighed. 'How cruel he met his end so far beyond his new defenses. But I cannot delay. I must meet with Idraman. I shall attempt to determine what lies on the other side of the gate by other means. But unless the very demons of the Underworld stand poised to attack, it will have to be opened.'

Marrick nodded. 'As directed, the engineers have been at work assessing the task, ma'am. They estimate it will take several hours to move it far enough on its runners to allow a horse to pass through.' He rubbed his hands together. 'But they stress that is just a guess. And it could take just as long to close it if we find a threat on the other side. But I would hope we can successfully defend such a small gap if needed.'

Nyomae stood. 'Then I request we open it tomorrow.'

'Will you require an escort, ma'am? May I suggest the First Horse?'

She walked to the railing and peered over the edge. 'That won't be necessary. I must go alone. It will be easier to conceal my presence. I do not want to attract attention.'

'So be it. I shall speak with the engineers to ensure the gate will be ready to open.'

Nyomae glanced back to the pass. 'Thank you. I must rest a short while. Then I shall spend the night in the pass to prepare.'

Nyomae shuddered as she walked through the Lower Gate. She glanced up, expecting to see the spirits of those still trapped beneath the rocks, waiting patiently to be freed and laid to rest. The wooden walkway creaked as she strode through the night towards the gate. It seemed a different age when she had last walked the entirety of the Caerwal Pass. Back then it was seen as a marvel, a success of the Seven Realms, and an honor and pleasure to traverse. But for the last three hundred years it had been a threat, a gap in the defenses, and a drain on the realms' limited resources. And now, forever a place of tragedy to be spoken of in the same breath as Gormadon Plain.

Nyomae approached the ruins of the Archon's Tower with trepidation. But the Angorsil set by Uluriel, had lost all but a remnant of its power, and now emanated just a sense of ill will towards those who came too close. She nodded to the dozen or so guards who sat outside their hut warming their hands over a brazier. Its flames flickered a short way up the gate in the predawn gloom, seeming unaware it would soon open.

Nyomae looked up to the sliver of sky overhead. Was the hour before dawn truly the darkest? In the case of the realms, it certainly was the darkest of times — did better days lay ahead?

'Need any help, ma'am?' An Archonian approached. 'I'm told you're to be left alone, but I don't want to seem rude by not offering.'

She nodded to the guard who looked too young to be in service. 'Thank you for your consideration, but I do need to be alone for what I'm about to attempt.'

'Oh… I see, ma'am. Apologies for the interruption.'

'None needed. But…' she glanced to the brazier, 'a cup of something hot when I'm done would be most welcome.'

The guard grinned. 'I'm sure we can manage that, ma'am. I'll leave you in peace. Just come over when you're done, and we'll have it ready.' He strolled back to the hut. Nyomae watched him join his companions and wished Elodi and Toryn could be at her side. But they had their duties in the north, and Nyomae had work to do in the south.

She walked to the gate. Only the first few slabs and iron rails were visible in the light of the guard's fire. But the overpowering presence of the immense structure, rising hundreds of feet up, could not be denied. Nyomae placed her hand on one the gigantic bolts in the lattice ironwork holding the huge slabs in place. It was cool to the touch. The stones were the depth of a tall man, but she sensed a hint of warmth from Idraman's Word of Forbidding on the other side. She bowed her head and ventured into the Verse of the gate, but Idraman's barrier concealed everything behind.

Nyomae learned of its nature. Idraman had created a curtain of air outside of time. While just the thickness of a silk veil, nothing could exist within it, thus nothing could pass through. She had to find another way to penetrate the void. Nyomae doubted she could create a gap in the barrier without Idraman's help. But if she failed, opening the gate would be pointless. Nothing existed in the Song within a Word of Forbidding, so she would have to use the Verses governing the air over the gate... or the rock beneath. Fortunately, with the power of Uluriel's stone waning, the way through the ground was open. Nyomae entered the Verse and descended into the bedrock. She winced as the tainted ground yet endured the corruption that had foiled Idraman's attempt to raise the rock and seal the pass. Her pain grew worse as she ventured back in time towards the time of Gormadon.

Nyomae emerged on the opposite side. She gasped as she witnessed the moment Idraman had closed the gap. The Imaari blazed with the Maidens' power as he had called upon the foundations of the Caerwals in his time of need. But Nyomae could find no way into Idraman's mind to open the barrier. Yet while he sustained it, she could perhaps connect with the Verse of his cell in Elmarand. Her lips moved as she repeated his spell.

The Verses of the south opened to her, and the unmistakable presence of Idraman made itself known across the distance. But Nyomae noticed his Verse had dulled. And although she could not see the man, she felt his suffering. Yet, he clung onto life, striving to keep the pass closed after all these years.

Nyomae spoke. *Idraman?* His Verse recoiled. It shimmered as if a pebble had dropped into a pond. She tried again. *Idraman. It is Nyomae. Do you remember?* Now his Verse hardened, appearing as if a shell. Nyomae withdrew and waited. He had not the strength to shield himself for long. But he was weak, and she was strong. It would devastate the man to remove the sole purpose of his existence, and she did not want him to give up hope. She would have to find the means he maintained the barrier and try another approach.

Nyomae listened to his command that sealed the pass, words that he had repeated over and over since the defeat at Gormadon. With care, Nyomae planted a word into his faltering mind, and he unknowingly obliged. It merged with his invocation. And it was enough to open a splinter at the center of the veil — just wide enough for a horse and rider to pass through.

The Word of Forbidding was overcome. Now it was down to Archonholm's engineers to shift a gigantic gate just a few feet... but a gate that had been shut fast for three hundred years.

15. Trail of Destruction

Elodi had risen before the sun. For a moment, she struggled to make sense of her surroundings in the dark. But the rustling trees of the South Forest, and the damp clothes sticking to her cold skin, soon reminded her of the grim nature of her task. A dull throb had pervaded her troubled dreams, but it did not stop when she woke. Was it the heartbeat of the Angorlith?

The two riders on watch nodded as she led Sea Mist to the nearby stream. But as she bent to splash her face, her stomach knotted. Elodi pitched forward and threw out a hand to steady herself. The pain increased as if a dagger thrust into her gut. But this was not her pain alone to bear. Her sisters also suffered, and she knew its source. A second Amanach was under attack; a second stone had been found. The other stones responded to aid their stricken companion. The pain eased a little, and Elodi felt her strength return. But how long could the stone survive against a determined attack?

'Ma'am. A rider approaches.' Elodi looked up to see the captain of the First Horse, Lindell, had also risen. She shook the water from her hands and strolled out of the trees. She turned to the sound of hooves, and immediately recognized the gait of Tempest at full gallop.

Elodi let out a long sigh, thankful her rider had not been among the victims at Kernlow's camp. 'That is my messenger, Lena. Perhaps she has news of our quarry.'

'She rides well.' Lindell nodded his approval. The captain reminded Elodi of Aldorman, carrying himself with the same confidence, or at least before Aldorman's encounter with Uleva on the edge of Durran Wood.

'One of our finest… and fastest.' Elodi left Sea Mist to drink and walked to greet her messenger. Tempest slowed and Lena slid from his back and strode toward Elodi without breaking step.

Lena recovered her breath. 'I trust you've had word of Lord Kernlow's end, ma'am?'

'It's a tragedy, and an act that we are here to avenge. Did you have the opportunity to… assess the scene?'

Lena's head bowed. 'I did, ma'am. I've seen some sights these last months, but what happened at that camp sickened me to the core.'

Elodi nodded to the stream. 'Please, you both must drink first.' She followed Lena to the brook. Sea Mist looked up and whinnied on seeing Tempest. He trotted over and rubbed noses with his friend. Elodi managed a smile. 'I imagine they have much to share since they last met. It's reassuring to see there is still room for friendship in these dark times.' Elodi waited for Lena to quench her thirst. 'I know you're familiar with the Nordlengs' ways. Are you certain this was their… handiwork?'

'No doubt about it, ma'am. But…' she frowned, 'this was possibly worse than anything I've previously seen of their *work*.'

Elodi's heart sank. 'Dare I ask how?'

Lena's mouth curled. 'The Nordleng like their sport, but this time it went far beyond cruel. It's their custom to select the unfortunate few, and either make them fight to the death, or give the injured a head start, and then track them down.' She shook her head. 'But this time they went to great lengths to prolong their suffering.'

Elodi groaned. 'Had Kernlow set a watch? I find it difficult to believe a band of Nordleng could so easily overwhelmed two dozen of his finest knights.'

'It was difficult to tell. The whole area was burned. If a watch was set, evidence of their fires would have been lost among the scorched grass. But as you say, ma'am, surely Kernlow's company should not have been so easily overrun. There was no sign of Nordleng dead, and they're well known for leaving both their dead and wounded where they fall. They have no compassion for their own, believing those who die or are injured, deserve what they get.'

Elodi stroked Tempest's nose. 'How do these men become so brutal? It seems their only reason to live is to cause pain and suffering.' She recalled waking on the Dorn Plain after Uleva had tortured one of her archers. 'How did those poor souls die? Could they all have been killed as they slept?'

'I'm afraid that would have been better for them. But... aside from Lord Kernlow, it looks like the others were bound and then... burned.' She swallowed. 'And judging by their positions, I would say most were still alive when set alight.'

Elodi closed her eyes, trying but failing, not to see the carnage. 'And I presume Lord Kernlow was forced to witness that, having the time to contemplate the manner of his own death.'

Lena whispered. 'That is how I saw it. And... the horses, ma'am. Why destroy those fine animals? They're among the best in the land. In the past they would have taken and sold them.'

Elodi jaw tightened. 'How did the horses not escape? I believe the Archonian Knights rarely tether their loyal mounts. Why did they not bolt? Did they try to defend their riders?'

'I found them... also bound together. Can you,' Lena stifled a sob, 'can you imagine their screams? And knowing the Nordleng, they would have forced their riders to watch as their beloved beasts burned.'

Elodi shuddered. 'It doesn't bear thinking about. But I cannot fathom how even thirty Nordleng could overwhelm the camp. Kernlow had time to send a bird to Borrund informing us he suspected an attack. Surely, if he knew one was coming, he should have been ready.' She sighed. 'I suspect there was some dark art at play that aided the Nordleng. And now, we must deal with the same threat.'

Lena scooped up a handful of water and poured it over her neck. She stood and pointed. 'I'd say they're heading for the settlements south of this forest. They'll know our attention is elsewhere. I can't think there'll be much plunder for them, so it's probably just for… pleasure.'

Elodi took Sea Mist's rein and led him up the riverbank. 'And to resume their reign of terror.' She looked up as the sun appeared from behind a cloud. 'But I suspect we have more than just these hoodlums to worry about.'

Elodi's scalp prickled as they sped across the grasslands, scarred by the aralaks as they had gathered to attack Omstrad. She hoped with the autumn rains softening the ground, the grass would grow back come the spring and heal the hurt. She glanced back to her company, worried the horses might stumble on the churned ground. But the mounts of the First Horse were among the finest in the realms and galloped with ease despite the terrain. And their riders were well-trained and had fought with bravery and great skill at Roth's Doom. Formed by the warrior Archon, Malendra, the First Horse brought both speed and deadly force to the troubled parts of the realms. More agile than the knights, and faster than the guards, they were a proud regiment with a proud tradition. While lacking the powers of the Amayans, they were not to be taken lightly. And Elodi was pleased Lena had asked to accompany them. Aside from being a rider of repute with a keen eye and deep knowledge of the land, Lena was also skilled with both bow and sword.

Elodi wished she could have stopped at Omstrad for a short visit. The town had done so much to quell the threat of the spiders, and she would have liked to have shown her gratitude. But a promise had been made to Bardon to end the Nordleng threat within five days, and midday approached on the second. Perhaps she had been rash to make such a promise, but the Nordleng could kill and torture many in such a short time.

Elodi's heart sank as they rounded the edge of the forest. A pall of smoke hung over the foothills where she had stood with Nyomae on the night the Amayans had fought Cymori. Elodi groaned. More folk of Ormsk will have met with an unfortunate end, and more tales of Nordleng raids and cruelty would soon be spreading across the region. She rose in her saddle and wheeled her sword, driving the company on to hopefully quash the perpetrators before more died at their hands.

Sadly, the sight awaiting them was all too predictable. But they could not stop and give the farmer and his family a decent burial. The Nordleng had not long left, judging by the fires that still burned, and Elodi was keen to engage them. She choked. 'How many of those brutes would you say were here?'

The tracker walked besides the churned grass. 'Easily thirty. It looks like they've stayed together.'

Elodi searched for signs of their horses. 'In a way that makes it easier. Which direction did they take?'

'They're heading for the trees, ma'am. Perhaps they believe they'll have the advantage once inside.'

Elodi spoke more to herself. 'There may be another reason.'

'Ma'am?' The tracker frowned.

Elodi used her *farsight* but could see nothing passed the hills. But her Amayan instinct told her it was not just Nordleng they pursued. She turned to her tracker. 'Another leads them, of that I'm certain.' Elodi's mind raced. Could it be Uldrak? Or something far worse? Eryn believed the warlocks had come south. But Elodi had yet to look a warlock in the eye. A *kruul* in Archonholm had almost broken her; how would she fare against one in the flesh? Should she lead her riders against him? She had yet another difficult decision to make. Many of her riders would surely perish against a warlock. But it was likely the Ul-dalak had discovered the way to the Amanach in the South Forest through Nyomae's eyes. And if another stone was destroyed, the source of both Amayan and Imaari power would diminish yet further. Elodi clutched her sword. She had to act. She was an Amayan; Elodi could not allow another stone to be attacked.

Elodi called the company to her. 'I'm afraid we may be up against more than just a band of Nordleng.' She looked at their taut faces, disgusted by the carnage at the farm. 'It's my belief they are led by a warlock.'

Lindell stiffened. 'A warlock, ma'am?' He glanced to his company. 'That makes it a different challenge altogether.'

She turned to the captain. 'But one, I'm afraid, we have no choice but to accept.'

He pushed back his shoulders. 'Perhaps you misunderstood, ma'am. It's a challenge we'll gladly accept. None here have faced a warlock. Yes, we know of the legends, and many of our predecessors have fallen by their foul hands. Yet all here would willingly take the test to meet one of our most powerful adversaries. It's our purpose, ma'am. That is why we volunteer to undergo the trials and train for the First Horse.'

'Ah, then I apologize. It was perhaps my own trepidation that clouded my judgment.' Elodi clasped Lindell's shoulder and looked to his company. 'The bravery of the First Horse is not in question. We shall ride together and give whoever leads the Nordleng a reason to fear us.'

The company cheered. Lindell beamed. 'And we are honored to be led by such a fine warrior, ma'am. Alone, you'd give that dark fiend cause for concern.'

Elodi looked to the horses. 'Then let us make ready. If my assumption is right, they look to desecrate the Amanach… a Singing Stone situated in the forest.' But her stomach clenched. Nyomae had warned of the powers of Ormoroth's commanders of old. They were once Elorym captains, great and strong. Could she and her company be victorious? And still there were the Nordleng, skilled and ruthless in their own right. She looked to the young riders as they eagerly mounted their horses. How many would live to see the end of the day?

The Nordleng were heading for the forest as the tracker predicted. The band had stopped and made a campfire, no doubt feasting off the spoils of the farm. Elodi hoped they had taken their time, and thus there was a chance she could encounter them before they took cover among the trees. She glanced up. The sun had begun its descent; the daylight would be gone in a matter of hours. The stallions favored by the Nordleng were bred in the harsh terrain of the Nordruuk borders. While known for their loyalty to their riders, they also appeared to possess the same cunning as their masters. But Elodi had faith in the mounts of the First Horse, believing they could match those of the Nordleng.

The company crested a ridge to spy a dark formation moving across the grasslands less than half a league ahead, and still twice that distance to the forest. Lindell called over. 'Do we engage now, ma'am?'

Elodi spurred on Sea Mist. 'Without delay, Captain. We cannot allow them to get among the trees.' The horses raced down the slope as if determined to avenge the cruel death of their own at Kernlow's camp. They reached the flat and made up half the distance before the Nordleng saw them. They kicked on, obviously keen to gain the cover of the trees. Elodi peered, trying to see if a warlock was with them, but could see no obvious sign.

The horses sped on. Tempest and Sea Mist led the way, competing to better those of the First Horse. Elodi guessed they would catch the Nordleng just as they reached the trees. Her anxiety of facing the warlock faded as her spirits rose along with Sea Mist's back. Now they were close enough to see the Nordleng glancing over their shoulders.

Lindell cried out. 'Bows at the ready! Take them down.' It was a rare skill to use a bow at full gallop, but one the First Horse had mastered. Arrows flew and found the odd target. Elodi saw three tumble from their horses as they neared the tree line. Five more dropped as they slowed their pace and their dark, cloaked forms disappeared between the trunks.

Elodi cried out as she slowed Sea Mist. 'Be wary. They may be lying in wait.' She recalled the Nordleng were not known for their use of archers, but she kept a close eye on the trees as they drew near. But no ambush came. They trotted past the fallen Nordleng. Two groaned from their wounds. One struggled to his feet and drew a sword — but no quarter was granted.

Elodi ducked under the boughs and into the shade. The rays from the sun at their backs shone deep between the trunks, but Elodi could see nothing but shadows. The light soon faded as they rode deeper into the forest. But just as she thought they had lost their prey, Elodi sensed movement a short way ahead. She motioned to Lindell and whispered. 'Over there. See?' If the Singing Stone was their objective, she believed they had at least a league to go. They had to strike now before the trees thickened and darkness fell. Elodi drew her sword and wheeled it over her head. 'Onward! Show no mercy.'

The Nordleng turned as the company closed the gap. A flash blinded Elodi, turning twilight into day. The ground shook. Sea Mist stumbled. Elodi was thrown from his back.

16. Return to the Lost Realms

The Chief Engineer at the gate raised his flag. There was to be no grand ceremony to mark the opening of the gate. No speeches, no waving of banners, or fanfares. Many of the soldiers present, had stood in the same spot to listen to the Archon's address before he had brought down the mountains onto their heads. Thus, none had an appetite for speeches and platitudes.

Marrick glanced to Nyomae, then asked his aide to acknowledge and give the command to start proceedings. She stood behind ranks of Archonian Guards, mounted knights, and archers ready to meet any possible threat. While Nyomae was confident there was nothing to fear, her stomach refused to comply as a nagging doubt gnawed at her insides.

She jumped as a trumpet blared. Shouts went up as a hundred horses and dozens of oxen took the strain. Six gigantic chains, with links as thick as a man's body, rose from the ground. The great hinges creaked. Nyomae held her breath, along with every other soul in the pass. Three hundred years of debris was dislodged from the iron rails as the gates jolted… yet refused to move. But the proud horses and oxen would not be bettered by a stubborn gate. Their heads dropped, they snorted as they set their hooves and hauled. The wheels budged, turning barely a quarter along the runners, but enough to gain the upper hand.

The gates suddenly shifted. Clouds of dust billowed; a boom rolled down the pass. The ground shook and all in the pass felt their bones vibrate as the wheels gained traction. Nyomae blinked to peer through the slither of a gap, but the air was thick with sand. The wheels screeched, and the hinges shuddered as rusted iron grated against more rusted iron — but the resistance was broken, and the gate opened.

Nyomae gasped as a breath of air from the south blew through the slit in Idraman's barrier, sending the hanging dust into their faces. The gap widened. Some took a step forward, desperate to see what lay beyond, but more shuffled back, unsure of what awaited them. Nyomae and Marrick were among those curious to see into the south. And they were rewarded. The gap was now wide enough to reveal a little of what sat behind the great gates.

Nyomae heaved a sigh. It was as Toryn had seen: an empty pass. She walked forward, squeezing between the ranks of bewildered soldiers. Marrick followed. They stopped short of the opening to wait for the Chief Engineer's confirmation the gate was secure. Large spikes were hammered into the links to fasten the chains in place and allow the beasts to rest. The engineer nodded with a solemn gesture that reminded Nyomae of the Archon.

Marrick stared through the gate. 'I wish you'd take at least a small escort. Who knows what lies between here and Elmarand.'

Nyomae turned and smiled. 'I've journeyed far and wide, and for many of those years I didn't know my own mind.' She patted the horse chosen to accompany her. 'I travel best alone. If there's a threat to me, it would most likely be fatal to any who ride with me. Now, I must be on my way.' She took the reins and led her horse towards the gate. Nyomae ducked and drew in her body as she walked through Idraman's barrier. If any part of her touched it, it would immediately cease to exist, taken out of time, never to return.

Nyomae stepped into the Lost Realms. She took a dozen paces forward and turned. She had been right. The immense Caerwal Gate had gone. The barrier showed the pass as it had been on the day it had been sealed by Idraman. Those on the other side would look upon an empty valley; no gate, no knights standing guard, and no tower. But why was the pass abandoned in the south? It may look deserted with no sign of a threat, but surely, they would believe the supposed enemy from the north could come pouring through any moment.

Nyomae led her horse to the memorial a few hundred paces from the gate. She pulled aside the creepers clinging to the stone and read the faded words carved on its base. It commemorated the ten thousand who had died on the Gormadon Plain, defending the way to allow Idraman to close the pass. Nyomae's jaw clenched. While she knew she had little choice but to invoke the Verse of Unmaking, the guilt still sat heavily on her shoulders. She looked up to the top of the structure, fashioned as a sword pointing to the sky. Cracks had opened, and fragments had fallen from it and lay strewn at its foot. How long had it been neglected? The words meant nothing if no one repaired the stonework. But she had not come to admire the memorial. Nyomae mounted her horse and rode through the remainder of the pass. It appeared much like the road on the north side, yet it had been poorly maintained… if at all.

As Nyomae neared the opposite end of the pass, another gate came into view. But as with the road and memorial, it had fallen into disrepair. The stone wall had collapsed in many places, and little remained of the wooden gate. Most of the timber had dried and crumbled, leaving the iron hinges with little to support above the height of a man. The structure had once stood thirty feet tall, but if they feared the dark forces in the north would attack, even in good order, the gate would have presented little resistance. She stopped. Did it serve only to prevent entry to the pass from the south? The footings of three small buildings beside the wall, could have served as barracks, but they had obviously been abandoned for many years.

Nyomae slid from her saddle and approached the gate. The dry, splintered wood at the base spoke of decades of the blistering sun beating down upon it. She nudged the gate with her foot. At first, it refused to move as if remembering its reason to exist. Through the cracks, Nyomae noticed a beam holding the gate fast. It would be a simple task to enter the Song and find the moment it was installed, then remove it. But to her amusement, the last of its strength failed and it fell away as if dust. The hinges squeaked, perhaps reluctant to act after years of idleness, but like its big sister a little to the north, the gate yielded and swung open.

Nyomae passed through the relic and entered Talamaris. Named in the old tongue, Land of the Sun, Talamaris was the Second Realm of the Seven. At its prime, it was the richest and most powerful of all the realms — but those days were long gone. Nyomae stared in wonder at the flat, sandy plain. No living soul from the north had looked upon these lands for centuries: the mountains separated two very different worlds. Before the formation of the Caerwal Pass, the only way to bypass the mountains was by sea. The south had been spared the ravages of the war between Ormoroth's forces and the Elorym. For reasons unknown to Nyomae, the Elorym preferred to sail afar to distant lands, mostly snubbing the sunbaked plains of the south. Or had the gods raised the Caerwals to prevent entry? Or perhaps, the Elorym cared not for the dusty wide lands of the south, preferring the vast green forests, meadows, and the fast-flowing rivers in the north.

Yet, the ancestors of the people living in the north today, had come from these lands. The First and Second

Realms had flourished when they had built the waterways and irrigated the plains. Nyomae had once studied the people who first appeared a thousand years ago, following the demise of the Elorym. But despite a decade of searching, she had found little evidence of their origins in the archives. The transformation of the south had been sudden, leading Nyomae to suspect they were descendants of the Elorym returning to the land. Could they have been the children of the once great race who had ventured far and wide before the dark days? It would, she deemed, explain their resourcefulness and foresight.

Nyomae surveyed the land before her. After spending many years walking the Five Realms with its many forests and wide grasslands, the expanse of the sparse, ochre desert stretching in all directions, looked hostile. The odd hill rose in places where villages once clung to the life-giving rivers crisscrossing the plain. But what had happened? Many leagues of viaducts, canals and waterways had brought water from the pure Caerwal springs. The roads had been lined with trees to grant travelers respite from the hot sun in their shade. But the gullies running the length of the route were dry and had crumbled away in many places. And only sunbaked stumps remained of the once tall and leafy trees. Nyomae's heart sank. She had suspected the so-called Lost Realms had grown weak following the loss of the north, but she had clung onto the hope that some of its strength would remain from its glory days.

Nyomae cried out. For a moment, she feared an arrow had struck her in the gut. But the reality was worse. Far to the north, the warlocks had discovered a second stone. She could not determine which one, or how long it could withstand an attack, but she could do nothing but push on. 'On we go, boy. Time is against us.' He galloped across the dry ground, bringing a little relief from the heat with a breeze. But Nyomae was wary of pushing him too far in the harsh conditions.

She slowed his pace as they approached a bridge. Nyomae remembered it from her last journey north. She and her Order had sped to the aide of Sylvena, believing her to be in mortal danger. But Uluriel had fooled them all, and it was they who had ridden into a trap, signaling the start of their current woes. The bridge was wide and long, and its buttresses had been carved to resemble the bows of great sailing ships, facing upstream to meet the strong current. It spanned a wide canal whose name she could not recall, but to her dismay, neither the bridge nor the waterway had fared well. Parts of the parapets had collapsed, but the stones lay where they had fallen as the once fast-flowing water was now barely a trickle. Nyomae guided her horse down the canal bank and across the cracked riverbed. He gratefully drank while she filled her flasks with the brown water.

Nyomae stood and looked downstream. How could the people of the villages dependent on the river survive? What state would she find the once grand city of Elmarand? The journey would be difficult if a supply of water could not be guaranteed. But she had to make it. She stroked her horse's nose. If they were in danger of dying from thirst, she could attempt to enter the Song and bring back part of a river when it had flowed strong. But water was a challenge. It was not as simple as fetching a solid object such as the small boat she had found in the Foranfae. It would drain her strength and slow their progress, but in the heat of the sun, death came quickly to those whose thirsts were not quenched. She mounted and continued the perilous journey, thankful she had come alone.

The farther Nyomae rode south, the more her heart

sank. The last time she had made the journey from Elmarand to the Caerwal Pass, the roads had been flanked with abundant fields growing crops for the large cities of Talamaris. But now it had returned to the bare, dusty landscape it had once been, long before Elmarand was founded. As in the region close to the mountains, the canals that once brought water to the fields were dry, and the aqueducts in a sorry state of repair. But worse, few settlements were visible from the road. Once, the route had passed dozens of villages and farms. Travelers had many inns and hostelries vying for their trade with well-furnished rooms, soft beds, and local delicacies to tempt the hungry visitor. But aside from a cart that had crossed her path the previous day, Nyomae had not seen a soul. And the man driving his half-starved horse had not even looked her way. Instead, he had chosen to keep his eyes to the front and hide under the large, brimmed hat shielding him from the searing sun.

Nyomae's eyes watered as she tried to swallow. Her tongue had swollen in her parched mouth. She had replenished her flask from a shallow pond the day before, but it seemed longer. But her horse had drunk most of it; he had to take priority. If he died, she would quickly follow. Nyomae had not envisaged the south being in such a bad state. She scanned the horizon for any sign of a well or settlement, but if the crops had failed, it was unlikely many could survive in these parts. Progress was slower than she had hoped. Following the punishing heat of the first day, she had decided to travel at night, and find refuge beneath the bridges to sleep during the sun's reign. But the days were still long in these parts and thus limited the hours she could ride. Nyomae looked south; she would be lucky to make the journey in six days.

Late the day before, lights had flashed in the skies to the east. At first, Nyomae feared it was a battle, but if the enemy had landed at the port of Umnavarek, who fought back? But as a light breeze brought fresher air to the plain, she realized it was a storm and hoped it would bring its rain to the plains. The storm had continued long into the night, but only the odd rumble rolled over their heads. But if enough rain had fallen, perhaps some might find its way into the canals.

Nyomae rose in her saddle and let the *farsight* take her south. She sped many leagues across the plains, expecting any moment to see the reassuring sight of Elmarand's tall towers. But a sandstorm billowed to the south and she could not penetrate the giant wall of dust. She withdrew, wearied by her efforts, and with her spirits failing.

Disheartened, she patted her horse. 'Time to rest, Orlo.' With the hurried preparations, Nyomae had neglected to ask the name of her horse. But he did not deserve to remain nameless as they suffered together. So, she had chosen a new one for him; her father's name, hoping he would prove to be as dependable in times of need. She led him beneath another dilapidated bridge as the sun peered over the horizon with a promise of yet another blistering day. Nyomae dismounted and to her relief, heard the pleasant sound of water. It could barely be called a stream, but mercifully, enough rain must have fallen in the east to make it this far along the dry riverbed. And better still, it looked clearer than any water she had come across to date.

Orlo dipped his head and readily drank while Nyomae emptied the dregs of her flasks to refill with the fresh water. She looked east. Perhaps some of the canals still functioned. Had the people abandoned the parched plains and moved to the higher ground where water was available? But wherever they had gone, it was obvious the population had greatly decreased; now she understood why the Caerwal Pass was left unguarded. But how bad did it have to be to abandon their gate? Yet, if they believed the north had fallen to the Ul-dalak, surely they would still maintain a watch, no matter how depleted their resources.

With their thirsts quenched, they retreated to the shade under the bridge. After a night of shivering under the clear, starlit skies, Nyomae would soon be struggling to sleep in the cloying heat, despite the shelter. But at least they now had water for the next day, and if lucky, the storm would also have filled the canals farther south. Luck? The Imaari smiled. She had gently chided Toryn for using the word. But perhaps on this occasion it was just a matter of how far the winds had blown the clouds. Or did other unknown forces influence the skies above. The warlocks had driven a ferocious hailstorm into their faces at Roth's Doom. In her youth, she had known what the weather would bring the next day, and even as far as a week ahead. Yet strangely, as her abilities grew with her studies, her weather forecasts had become less reliable. But she had no idea why that had happened.

Nyomae tethered Orlo and curled into a ball close to the pier. As much as she had developed her powers, there was still much in this world she could not comprehend. But, then... perhaps that was best if she desired untroubled sleep.

'Elodi!' Nyomae sprang up. She had been in a deep sleep trying to converse with Toryn via her dream, but it was a scream that woke her. Elodi was in danger. She sat and entered the Song. While Nyomae's abilities had grown of late, the distance would still be a challenge. She sought Elodi far to the north, skimming through the Verses of Farrand and onto the adjoining lands. She found her and stared aghast through the mist of her Verse. Elodi was vulnerable, and now powerless in the face of a dire threat.

17. A Promise Remade

The Nordleng yelled with glee as they fell upon them. Elodi clambered to her feet, still giddy and dazed from the blast. Lindell staggered beside her, drawing his sword to meet the attack. Two of her unhorsed company went down under swift blows. Others fought to control their mounts as they reared up. A black, robed figure came for Elodi, raising a long, curved blade, poised to remove her head. Her sword blazed as she sprang aside, swinging at the stunned Nordleng. He fell without a sound. Lindell took down another with a deft strike and strode to meet the next attacker, but the rest of the Nordleng had withdrawn. Elodi turned to see them disappear between the trees and head deeper into the forest.

The horses recovered from the shock, but four of their riders had met their end, and six more lay injured. Elodi looked upon them with pity. She addressed Lindell. 'Leave one to tend to the wounded. But we cannot delay. We will return this way to care for the fallen, but now we must pursue the enemy. Dark will be upon us all too soon, and I would rather engage them before they reach the stone.' Lindell gave the command to saddle up. Sea Mist nudged Elodi. She leaped onto his back and led the charge. 'Ride on! They must not get away.' She ducked and dodged under the low branches as Sea Mist surged ahead. The speed of the First Horse was renown, and soon Elodi spied the Nordleng as their horses struggled to negotiate a path through the thickening forest.

Elodi cried out. 'There! Ride them down.' The Nordleng turned their mounts, peeling off on both sides, then merging to meet them head on. Arrows flew from the

First Horse, but now the trees prevented many finding their targets. Elodi leveled her sword. A bolt shot forth, knocking three from their saddles; dead before they hit the ground. Horses whinnied, and riders shouted their challenges as they clashed. Her company claimed four more, but two of Elodi's riders were lost as another flash blinded them.

Lindell called over. 'What is this devilry?'

Elodi blinked, then swerved as more dark figures rode at them. 'It has to be a warlock.'

Her captain lunged and took down another. 'But I don't see him.'

'He must have armed the Nordleng with his dark devices, while he pushes onto his objective.' Elodi's vision blurred as she grew dizzy. A mist formed ahead. She yelled. 'Another trap. That can't be natural.' A fog rose quickly as if smoke from a fire. Then suddenly, it was upon them.

Elodi choked. 'We must be nearing the forest's heart.' Her insides clenched. 'Yes. The warlock is—' She gaped. Lindell and the remainder of the company had gone, as had the fog. Elodi drew Sea Mist to a halt. She was alone… and night had fallen. An eerie silence surrounded her. She heard no sounds of horses or the skirmish.

A faint light in the distance shed long shadows across the forest floor.

Elodi turned towards the source of the light and saw the Amanach. Ahead, a lone figure stood. The warlock had discovered the stone and found a way through its defensive veil. Elodi had no choice. She had to confront the dark commander. She was a Sister of the Stones — it was her duty to protect them.

Elodi drove Sea Mist through the shimmering air. She dismounted and strode towards the warlock. But as she was about to challenge him, she suddenly stopped. In the light of the stone, she saw not the creature she had expected, but a tall and noble Elorym warrior. Elodi stared in awe at the majestic form, imagining an army of such fighters at the height of their powers. How could any force have defeated the Elorym? What horrors did Ormoroth set upon this once mighty race?

The figure turned and walked towards her. Elodi took a step back. She could not afford to be swayed by such an illusion. As he drew near, the light of the Amanach revealed his true semblance. Elodi recoiled. Three thousand years of service to his evil master had torn any last vestige of his Elorym heritage from his face. Moist, dark eyes glowered from sunken sockets behind a bony nose, jutting out over a thin, cruel mouth. His long, dark hair was pulled back but failed to cover his large, misshapen skull. But despite his advanced age, his powerful frame moved with the grace and confidence of an agile fighter. Beneath his cloak, intricate engravings adorned light but impenetrable black armor, well beyond the skills of even Draegelan's smithies. Elodi raised her sword and sought the Fire within. 'Do not come any closer, warlock.' The shadow continued. Elodi took a breath. 'I am an Amayan and will…'

The warlock held up a hand as if greeting her to his hall. His deep voice echoed through the forest and shook the leaves from the trees. 'Lady Harlyn. So pleased you could accept my invitation to this most sacred of places.'

Elodi frowned. This was not how a warlock was meant to act. She kept her sword pointing at his throat as he stopped a dozen paces from her. Elodi stiffened. 'These are not your lands, warlock. I command you to leave and never—'

'On the contrary, *Lady* Harlyn. I…' he blinked, appearing to remember his past, 'I walked among these trees when it was one glorious forest.' His voice softened, surprising Elodi with his mellow tone. 'I climbed these trees in my youth. I remember a time when—' His eyes narrowed. He scowled. 'I lived here long before the fools who now claim this place were born. And you...' he cackled as he took another step. 'Have the gall to demand *I* leave?'

Elodi stood her ground, determined to meet his gaze. 'I am an Amayan.' Her jaw tightened. 'I will not let you harm the Amanach.'

'*Half* Amayan.' His thin lips cracked into a grin. 'Yes, Elodi. I know of your lineage. You have no right to—'

'You betrayed your people to serve Ormoroth.' Elodi bristled. 'And now you seek to corrupt and destroy the Maidens' creation. It is you that have no right to make—'

The warlock hissed. He surged forward, coming so close, his breath froze Elodi's face. She gagged; it stank of sour milk, like that of a shroul. He spat out his words. 'I serve the lord who did not abandon us. I serve Lord Ormoroth who promises eternal life. I owe nothing to the weak daughters of hapless gods who had not the wit to finish their work.'

Elodi could not move. She spoke through clenched teeth. 'Yet my ancestors remained true. It was you that abandoned all that is right and good.'

The warlock snarled. 'Right and good? You have been fooled.' Elodi gasped. With dread, she knew she had seen his face before... in Archonholm. It was the *kruul* that had possessed the Castellan. His dark eyes flashed. 'Yes, Elodi, we have met before. But I did not have the chance to introduce myself.' He held out his hands and bowed low. 'I am Shokresh. Our first meeting was brought to an abrupt end. And if that wretched Imaari had not intervened,' he placed his hand over his heart, 'be honest with yourself, *Elodi*, you would have gratefully accepted my offer.' Shokresh stepped back and turned to look about them. 'I see you are alone today. That hag is not here to come to your aid, and your riders are engaged elsewhere.' He tilted his head. 'It is just you and I, Elodi.' He reached out and stroked her cheek. 'Ah. I see your *sisters* have accepted you into their merry band.' The warlock's eyebrow raised. 'But the bond is yet weak, and not yet fully formed.' He splayed his fingers in front of her face. 'This may hurt, but perhaps your pride more than your flesh.' Elodi winced as Shokresh raised his elbow and closed his hand into a fist. He pressed his other hand against her shoulder and slowly withdrew his fist.

Elodi cried out as a sharp pain seared between her eyes. She clenched her jaw, desperate to resist, but Shokresh easily won the tug-of-war. A bright light, not unlike her blade, bulged out of her forehead and into the warlock's grasp. He snatched back his arm. She cried out as the light flared, then scattered as if starwings caught in a breeze. Elodi collapsed, panting for air as the force holding her up had gone.

Shokresh grinned. 'And now I have severed that bond.'

'No!' Elodi screamed with her remaining strength. Shokresh had wrenched the Amayan gift from her. The bond from which she had taken solace, was no more. She felt alone, isolated, and vulnerable.

The warlock sneered. 'You value their bond too highly. It was weak and ultimately means little.' He smirked. 'I could have broken it with a snap of my fingers. But I thought you would appreciate something a little more... dramatic.' He turned and looked to the trees. 'I'm afraid your sisters will have felt your pain and will believe you to be dead. And now all of your company are dead. No one knows you're here. No one will look for you. You are alone, Elodi. Totally alone.' She stifled a sob. Shokresh smiled. 'But this is not the time for sorrow. I can offer you something far superior to your *sisterhood*.' He held out his hands as if to take hers. 'Will you accept, my lady?' He caressed her face, stinging her cheek as if icy water poured over her skin; but she could not pull away.

Shokresh leaned closer. 'I promise you a life you could not dream of living as a mere *lady* of Harlyn. You know of what I speak. You would no longer have to justify your existence to fat, ageing lords who care not for your ideas.' He dismissed them with a flick of his wrist. 'They know nothing of the real world, and have little time for you, Elodi. You could achieve so much more at my side.' His voice rose. 'I would grant you freedom to do as you see fit to serve the true lord.' His dark eyes held her gaze. They appeared dry and cracked, but age had not diminished their potency, as he seemed to probe deep into her very soul. His voice deepened. 'I know of your desires, Elodi. Let me show you what you could become.'

Elodi tried to refuse, but her jaw locked. Her vision blurred as Shokresh revealed the life awaiting her if she chose to join him. No longer a lady of a realm — she would be a queen of all the known lands. Elodi saw herself upon a throne beside him in Vorkirik, the ice fortress in the north. She wore a crown of tall, twisted spikes, and a cloak of black silk that shimmered with the light of a thousand stars. The people of the realms worshipped her beauty, a beauty that would never fade through the ages.

The warlock's words lulled her. 'And this is just the beginning, Elodi. When our master returns, we shall rule the lands beyond these realms. None will stand against us. We will undo the hideous mistakes of the Maidens to restore these lands to the brutality of chaos. My race lacked imagination. We made this place docile, too comfortable, it numbed our minds, and stunted our ambition. But when Ormoroth challenged the Elorym, I finally saw the error of our ways. He opened my eyes to the wonder of disorder. I came to crave a world of chaos in place of the staid, predictability of order. People should not live in comfort. Life is a gift, Elodi, but a gift that can all too soon be taken for granted if we do not suffer. Pain and hardship sharpen our senses and heighten our desires. That is what we seek to impose.'

And Elodi understood. The years before her father's death had been too easy. Despite her training, she acknowledged she had led a sheltered and privileged life. Shokresh was right. She had never felt more alive when riding into battle to kill and maim. As much as she had tried to deny it, the thrill of combat and fighting for her life had given her a purpose. And if she was honest with herself, she enjoyed the admiration that came with her hard-earned status as a victorious warrior.

The warlock's foul breath chilled her face. 'I grow impatient, Elodi. I offer you great power and immortality. And all I ask in return is the location of the Amanach in the north. You know the lesser stones will soon fall. You have no reason to protect it.' Shokresh grinned. 'You can give it to me now… or I can break you, and then discover what I desire to know.'

No! A voice. Her voice. It came from deep within. *Do not listen.* The vision of glory shattered. *You do not want this.* Elodi recalled the faces of Toryn, Nyomae, and then Sea Mist. She saw the banners fluttering from the tops of Calerdorn's towers. And her heart swelled to hear the birds greet the dawn with their lilting chorus. The warlock's world had no place for love, beauty, and loyalty. But Shokresh had her trapped. Her body cried out as his will penetrated her thoughts, seeking to possess every part of her. Inside, she screamed, but not even a whimper escaped her lips.

Shokresh clicked his fingers. 'You may speak.'

Elodi spluttered. 'Never.' She took comfort knowing the Crown Stone yet eluded the warlocks. She met his gaze. 'And you will not break me.'

An eyebrow raised on his lined brow. 'I would not be so sure of yourself. But I accept your challenge. And I shall enjoy proving you wrong.' He stroked her neck, then stepped back to admire her. 'While it would be desirable to enjoy the obvious pleasures of your flesh, I can find others who would readily give themselves to me. Perhaps not such a fine form as you, my lady, but that can be… overcome. But it is only fair to tell you, if you resist, you will not be my queen… you will be my slave.' He smirked. 'That would be a most unpleasant and miserable existence.' Elodi now saw herself naked, half-starved, chained to a dungeon wall deep beneath Vorkirik.

Elodi stretched out her fingers to her sword. But it felt wrong. It did not warm to her touch — it cooled. Shokresh looked down. 'Ah yes, your sword.' He made a mock apologetic face. 'You may recall our time together in that hovel you call Archonholm.' Elodi groaned. He continued. 'The Castellan proved a most useful vessel. I doubt you would have readily given your sword to him, but the Palace Guards handed it over at my request.' He reached down and drew it from her scabbard. A sob escaped Elodi's lips as the warlock held it in his cruel hand. He turned the blade over. 'A fine sword. I was acquainted with the smithies who forged these weapons.' His eyes flickered as he appeared to hark back to his previous life. But they quickly hardened as his jaw clenched. 'I had a similar one once.' He spat. 'Before that preening knight, Dorlan shattered it.'

At the mention of his name, another vision forced its way into her head. Elodi fought back, desperately trying to hold onto the faces of her loved ones. But they looked different. No longer her friends, they schemed behind her back, waiting for her to fail so they could take her place. And now Elodi saw Dorlan in a new light. Vain, selfish, concerned only for the stories of his glory spreading across the land. And Draegelan was no better. Both cared not for the people, seeing them as servants to carry out their will for their own purposes.

The warlock swung Elodi's sword. To her horror, it glowed a sickly green. He sneered. 'You see, Elodi. The short time I had this in my possession, I persuaded it to recognize my hand, thus you can no longer use it against me. As a *kruul*, I could not resist it.' He held out his arms and bowed. 'But against my true form… you will find it utterly useless.'

Shokresh straightened and lowered the point to Elodi's throat. She winced as it stung her skin. 'Your mother was a fine Amayan.' She stiffened. He withdrew the blade. 'I commanded the shrouls that fatally wounded her. She was remarkably strong, even for a *sister* of the stones. But carrying you in her belly weakened poor Eleni. I'm afraid you were the cause of her death, my dear.'

Elodi stared at him, clenching her jaw, determined not to let him see how deep his words struck. She whispered. 'I don't believe you. My mother had the strength to ride back to Calerdorn.'

But she could not fool the warlock. He continued with relish. 'I think the right words would be, she fled back to Calerdorn. But that was somewhat unfortunate. I would have enjoyed discovering the secrets of her fine form had she not left so soon.' His eyes narrowed. 'But I shall gladly accept her daughter. You are very much like her, Elodi.' He sighed. 'Not as powerful obviously. You are only half an Amayan. Your father's feeble blood has diluted that of your mother.'

Elodi tried to turn away, but her body froze. Now only her eyes could move. She glanced over his shoulder, imploring the Amanach for aid. The warlock followed her gaze. 'Ah yes, the Amanach, a valiant, but ultimately futile attempt to resist the power of the Angorlith.' He looked back to Elodi. 'You'll be aware, one by one, they will fail. And this one will shortly crumble to dust.' Shokresh stepped away. 'I shall grant you the honor of witnessing its demise. Come.' He walked to the stone, forcing Elodi's legs to follow him to his huge, black horse standing patiently beside the stone. The warlock took something from his saddlebag. He held out three shards of a dark material for her to observe. Her insides convulsed, and the bile rose in her throat merely at the sight. 'I believe the inept Imaari has given you a rudimentary lesson on the work of Lord Ormoroth.' He appeared to take pleasure from Elodi's pain. 'In your heart you know what I hold. Yes, Elodi, these are Angorsil, hewn from the Angorlith, my lord's greatest work.'

Shokresh paced around the stone, placing the shards at an equal distance. Immediately, they glowed the same nauseating green Elodi had seen at Tunduska. The air pulsed as the Amanach recoiled from the dull heartbeat emanating from the Angorsil. The warlock continued. 'It will not resist long. The loss of the first has already weakened it.' He spun around. 'Do you finally understand, Elodi? It is pointless to resist. I know you try. You may see the faces of your pathetic friends and your skinny nag. Or hear the birds twitter their incessant, tuneless din. But they are fleeting. They will be gone soon. Your resistance only prolongs the day when we will be victorious.' He held out his hands. 'Why delay the inevitable? Why sacrifice more lives when you could live under our glorious rule?'

If Elodi had not been held by the warlock's will, she would have collapsed. He was right. Why did she think they could fight the might of the Ul-dalak. They had come close to defeating Draegelan and Dorlan, commanding many times her current strength. How could the much-depleted realms resist?

But why resist? Shokresh promised her eternal life, a life of power and pleasure. Only a few were worthy of his gift, and after all the pain she had endured of late, did she not deserve it? Let the weak lead an existence of fear and strife; let the weak be grateful for what little they had. Elodi's head swam with visions of what the warlock had promised. She should renounce her ancestors, starting with her name. He would give her a new one, a name not tainted by those who rejected the way of Ormoroth.

The Angorsil glowed, but this time it did not turn her stomach; it offered hope. From their base, green veins stretched out towards the Amanach. The ground glimmered like a lily pond and Elodi could see the roots of the stone reaching deep into the earth. She sensed it drew power from a river beneath the Kolossos via the many streams that flowed out from the mountains. But now she saw the water as a source of corruption, staining the lands far and wide. She willed the warlock's shards to drain the stone until it collapsed and signal the end of the resistance to Ormoroth's return.

Elodi let the green light seep into her limbs. She allowed Shokresh to caress her, aiding her transformation to his queen. She would surrender to his… The Amanach flickered, turning from a silvery light to blue. Her core warmed. She had not realized how cold she had become until it retreated.

Elodi. The voice was familiar. But not hers. This was someone from her past; someone she had cared for, and someone who had cared for her. Nyomae! Elodi remembered. Toryn's face came back to her. *Resist.* A bird sang, whether in the forest, or in her head, she could not tell. Its song chased the cold from her limbs. The melody formed words, repeating over and over. *Call upon the stone,*

Elodi. The warlock may have broken her bond with the Amayans, but she felt the power of the stone reach out to her.

Shokresh pushed Elodi's sword into the ground as if a stake to tether his horse. He turned back, angered by the change in the Amanach. 'My offer expires once the sword fades. Speak now. Make your choice!'

Elodi faced the warlock and whispered. 'I reject you.' Her voice recovered. Elodi bellowed. 'I am Elodi. I am an Amayan, a Sister of the Stones!' She snatched her sword from the ground and thrust it at the warlock. 'Begone!'

The Amanach blazed. Shokresh cried out and lurched as if stabbed in the back. The light from the stone shot a beam to her blade. Her body ignited as the light burst from her sword and blasted the warlock. She yelled. 'My sword may be useless against you, but the Amanach sees your dark heart.'

Shokresh staggered back. The light faded. Elodi gasped for air, blinking in the dark, searching for the warlock. She heard him muttering but could not make out his words. Elodi sank to her knees. Behind, Sea Mist squealed. His hooves stamped at the ground. She reeled as someone stabbed her in the back. Elodi collapsed onto her face. A dark shape loomed over her. Its warm breath moistened her neck.

18. In the Heart of the Mountain

'Will this tunnel ever come back to the surface?' The torchlight lit up Jedrul's lined face. 'We'll be in the Underworld if it goes any deeper, and I'm in no hurry to meet them Reapers again.' The company had descended for many hours, and now the walls seemed to close in as if trying to swallow them whole. The snorts of the horses echoed, and their damp breath clung to Toryn's clothes.

Cubric lifted his torch. 'At least we can be thankful the cobs have stayed away.'

Elrik scoffed. 'Probably for good reason.' He turned to Toryn. 'Are we walking into a trap?'

Toryn had been deep in thought. For the last hour he had considered turning back. But back to what? To certain death? He had brought down the ceiling of the cave, and even if they could clear it, did the warlock and Norgog await? But if they had gone, how long would it take to dig their way out? He began to regret collapsing the cave. Perhaps they should have fought their way out back to the road.

Janae returned. 'It levels out around the next bend. Then after a few hundred paces it begins to climb.'

Toryn's shoulder relaxed. 'Up?' He glanced to Elrik. 'That has to be good, eh.'

Janae shrugged. 'Perhaps. I believe we've walked beneath the ravine and are now on the south side. But…' she glanced over her shoulder. 'If we find a way out, would we be on the same side as the road? The cobs have no use for it. We could find we're faced with a mountain to climb. The horses won't cope, and we'd be exposed and vulnerable to an attack.'

Cubric groaned. 'Then how deep are we? It was a long drop off the edge of the road, and I don't welcome the thought of clinging to a mountainside one bit.'

Amrul tried to offer hope. 'The road crosses the ravine at least half a dozen times as it nears the west. Some of the tallest peaks of the range are within a few leagues of the watchtower.' He looked at Toryn. 'If we're in luck, we might find ourselves close to the road.'

Toryn stared ahead to the edge of their torches' light. But it was no more than a few paces as the darkness seemed keen to smother the intrusion. He had recovered from his earlier use of the sword but was reluctant to use it for any other reason than defending against an attack. 'We have no choice. We keep going.' He turned to his horse. The flaming torches reflected in its wide black eyes as it suppressed its fear. Toryn rubbed its nose. 'Brave, boy. Not long now.' But what if there was no road? They would have to abandon them to suffer a long, drawn-out death. Or… put them out of their misery by sword. Toryn looked away, reluctant to have to make that choice. He eyed the tunnel as the light reflected off its smooth sides.

Toryn looked up. 'Wait. This is big enough for horses to pass through. Would the cobs go to the trouble of digging one this size?' He ran his hand along the wall. 'This has been dug by either our ancestors or our enemy. Whoever did would surely connect it to either a way out of the mountains or to a road.'

Cubric nodded. 'That makes sense, Cappy. But it's going to be quite a climb.'

Elrik grabbed the reins of his horse. 'As long as it's up, that's fine by me.'

It was a steep ascent, seeming to take even longer than the way down. The tunnel turned almost back on itself at every hundred paces as it climbed, reminding Toryn of the road leading to Vortimo. Their food ran out on the third stop, but thankfully, numerous underground streams trickled along the route to quench their thirst and cool their sweating brows. Spirits had risen as the tunnel had widened and finally leveled. 'Shush.' Janae held up a hand. She turned and whispered to Toryn. 'I hear something.' He strained his ears. A faint patter echoed through the tunnel.

'Feet?'

Janae frowned. 'Doesn't sound like cobs' feet slapping on rock. It could be boots, but they're some way ahead.'

Toryn turned to the company. 'Draw swords. Archers, ready your bows.' Then to Janae. 'We'll wait here a moment. Then we'll have a better idea if the sound is getting closer.' They held their breath.

After what seemed like an hour, Janae shook her head. 'Whatever's making that sound isn't moving.'

Toryn looked back to the company. 'Then we'll move towards it.' Making as little sound as possible, they advanced, then stopped again to listen.

Janae tilted her head. 'That's not feet. Sounds like tapping. Tools perhaps?'

Jedrul agreed. 'Hammers on chisels, or I'm not a miner. I'd say they're chipping away at the rock.'

Toryn sighed. 'That rules out cobs then. They don't use tools. But who is it?'

Janae raised her torch. 'Only one way to find out.'

'Then I'm coming with you.' Toryn turned to Cubric. 'Wait here. We'll go on ahead.'

Elrik took Toryn's arm. 'Want to make that three?' He patted his sword. 'Might not hurt to have an extra blade.'

Toryn was happy to accept. 'So long as you can keep your big feet from alerting them.' The three edged forward. Before long, the light began to grow. Toryn whispered. 'That looks like daylight. Are they making windows?'

Janae shrugged. 'But who? It can't be our folk. Amrul would know of any such work.' She crouched. 'Let me check the last stretch alone. I can go unseen. If I need help, you'll soon hear from me.'

Toryn glanced at Elrik. He nodded. 'Victory would be certain if all our forces were as brave as you, Janae.'

'It's what I do, Captain.' With that she turned and disappeared around the bend.

They leaned against the wall. Elrik smirked. 'Did she blush just then? She's one of the boldest people I've met, but flattery seems to unsettle her.'

Toryn grinned. 'Then let's hope the enemy don't discover her weakness. Although I can't imagine they use compliments often. I think she'll be safe… for now.' They sat in silence, assured Janae had not been seen as the tapping of hammers continued. Toryn jumped as she re-appeared unheard.

Janae frowned. 'I'm not sure what to make of it. It is natural light. Small slits have been carved out of the walls. From what I could see, there're at least two dozen laborers, looking much like our folk. They work the stone with hammers, rods, and chisels. But they're chained at the ankles… while Ruuk stand guard over them.'

Toryn gripped his sword. 'Slaves!' He lowered his voice. 'This far south? What are they building?'

'This tunnel opens out into a hall. They've set thick posts at the entrance but have yet to hang a door. They're obviously not expecting company beyond their own kind.'

Toryn's jaw clenched. 'Then let's give them a surprise they won't forget.' He stood. 'How many Ruuk? Could there be more elsewhere?'

'No more than six in the hall. But there's another entrance at the rear. We can't rule out they'll be more.'

Toryn thought for a moment. 'Our archers could soon take out six without raising the alarm.'

Janae grinned. 'They stand on wooden platforms overlooking the work. That makes them easy targets.'

'Good. If we take the hall and free the workers, perhaps we'll have the numbers to deal with the rest. They'll be keen to make better use of their hammers if they've been held here long.'

Toryn sent Elrik to bring up the rest of the company. Janae whispered. 'But why are they here? Are they building a fortress?'

'It would make a useful base if large enough. And with the tunnels, the enemy could move their forces unseen to anywhere in the realms.' He peered down the passage. 'You believe we're south of the pass, but we won't know for sure until we can take a look out of those windows.'

Janae shivered. 'I look forward to seeing the open sky again. These tunnels are no place for us.'

'I know what you mean. I'd prefer to admire the mountains from outside, rather than from beneath.' He turned as the approaching torches flickered along the rock. 'We'll leave these to the cobs, eh.'

Cubric led the company to Toryn. Eight had their bows at hand, while the remainder stayed at the back to calm the horses. Toryn expressed the need to avoid a sword fight as it would surely bring the rest of the Ruuk to the hall. He took his Amayan bow from his horse and joined Janae and the archers. A short way ahead, the tunnel widened.

The clinking stopped. Toryn froze. Had they been seen? A Ruuk voice echoed through the passageway. 'Drink your fill, then get back to work!'

Toryn sighed. 'That'll help. If there are more Ruuk beyond the hall, they won't be suspicious if the work stops when we attack.' Janae moved silently to the entrance. She turned back and indicated the Ruuk positions. As stated, there were six. Toryn assigned an archer to each guard with two free to take down those the first volley missed. They nocked their arrows and edged forward. On Toryn's signal, they sprang into the hall and let loose. Five fell with the first round, the last with Toryn's arrow in his chest. The workers leaped up. Toryn held his finger to his lips and thankfully they understood and remained silent. The archers rushed to the other entrance and stood guard.

A young worker grasped Toryn's hand as others greeted the company. His voice croaked. 'Well, you're a welcome sight.' He finished his water, then kneeled and used his rod to lever open the crudely made band around his ankle.

Toryn looked around the hall. 'Where are you all from? How long have you been here?'

'Greendell. My name is Jorim. Our village was attacked——'

'In the spring.' Toryn gaped. 'I arrived at Greendell shortly afterwards.'

Jorim struggled to hold back his tears. 'Did… did any survive? All the young were herded out in chains. What happened to the elders?'

Toryn's jaw clenched. 'I'm afraid we found them…' He placed his hand on Jorim's shoulder. 'I'm sorry to have to tell you, but I don't think any escaped. We came up from the Wend Gap and encountered none coming our way. But what happened? We saw no sign of a struggle at the stockade.'

Jorim's hand went to his face. 'It was so sudden. A rare traveler had entered the day before. He seemed friendly enough. Said he was on his way to Drunsberg. But as I was getting ready for a day in the field, I saw him raise his arms and… the sky turned black… then a bolt of lightning from nowhere struck and threw me off my feet.' Jorim shook as he recalled the fateful day. 'Then this demon… no other word for it, rose from the ground. And as our folk rushed to defend ourselves, the traveler used some dark art to stop us in our tracks. The whole village could only watch as a dozen Ruuk strolled in and burned it to the ground.'

Toryn clasped Jorim's arm. 'And the demon? Where did it go?'

He shook his head. 'I don't reckon it was real. It disappeared as quickly as it had come. But it had us all stricken with fear. Before we knew it, we were chained and being led to the mountains.'

'Captain?' Toryn turned to Janae. 'Sorry to interrupt, but I've checked ahead. It's empty.'

Jorim nodded. 'They've taken the others down below. There's a larger hall being constructed beneath us. But we also suspect there's something going on deeper still. We've seen Norgog pass through. And sometimes at night, we can hear the echo of their hammers and picks, and the odd rumble. We reckon they're using the black powder down there.'

'What are they doing so far down? Are they mining, Jorim?'

'I'm afraid I wouldn't know. I'm... was a farmer. I know nothing of rocks, mountains, and the like. We don't know what's going on. And I'm not sure if the Ruuk know either. They're not allowed anywhere near the Norgog.'

Toryn glanced around the hall. 'Then what is this place? Where exactly are we?'

Jorim gestured to a large platform hewn from the rock. 'Let me show you.' He led Toryn to the far side and climbed up onto the stone slab. He picked up a rope attached to a heavy canvas sheet hanging on the wall. 'Steady yourself, it's a bit of a drop.' He pulled the covering free. Toryn gasped as a cool breeze blew in through a wide opening. Many hundreds of feet below, the top of the West Watchtower emerged between the clouds. He staggered back. 'We're inside Caranach?'

Jorim nodded. 'That's what we reckon. Quite a sight, eh.'

Cubric joined him on the platform. He peered through the gap and tapped his foot on the stone. 'Now we know what this is for.' He described an arc with his finger and whistled. 'A heavy weapon up here could land some heavy blows on the tower, gate and wall.' He sighed. 'The poor fellows below wouldn't have a chance to strike back, not in a month of full moons. They couldn't take the East Watchtower with an army of them spiders, but imagine the damage they could inflict from up here.'

'I remember now.' Toryn peered through the clouds to the land west of the watchtower. 'I saw this place. I was on my way north back in the spring.' He pointed. 'I stood on the edge of that wood, just beyond the crossroads. I was with Hamar on my way to Greendell. I saw a flash, then smoke drifting through the pass. It must have come from here.'

Elrik shuffled towards the edge. 'Then it's one heck of a stroke of luck that we stumbled across it before they'd finished and fortified it.' He looked around. 'But what now? I doubt we can hold it, even if we didn't have Drunsberg to take.'

Toryn drew the *Elorsil*. 'Perhaps I can set back the work a few months. That would give us time.'

Cubric laughed. 'Shame. It's quite a view from up here. I wouldn't—'

'Toryn.' Janae called over. 'This one's still alive.' He strode over to the Ruuk he had shot. Elrik followed. He flicked the arrow with his foot. 'It's stuck in his strap. Can't have gone deep enough into his dark heart.' The guard glared back as he coughed up blood.

Toryn kneeled. 'Well would you believe it.' He looked the wounded Ruuk in the eye. 'Do you recognize me, Grebb?' He turned back to Elrik. 'This is one of the fiends who murdered Hamar… and threw an injured guard onto a fire at Wyke Wood.' His jaw clenched. 'Well? Do you remember me now?' Grebb's eyes widened. Toryn nodded. 'I see that you do. Yes, I'm the *boy* your *lady* wanted to meet. You must have heard Uleva is dead, by the hand of the one you knew as Dohl.' Grebb stared aghast. Toryn continued. 'And the others will soon share the same fate.'

Grebb spluttered. 'It won't make a difference. You'll either all be dead or slaves before long. You don't stand a chance against the warlocks. You'll never—'

'I made a vow I would avenge the death of my friend.' Toryn glared. 'And I imagine there's many more here who have made the same pledge, judging by your treatment of these fine folk.'

Jorim spat at the guard. 'This one's been particularly cruel. Many have died at his hands. Good people at that. He liked to make them walk along the ledge after he'd plied them with their foul drink.' His jaw bunched. 'He'd wager how long it would take for them to fall.' He grasped Toryn's shoulder. 'You may have first claim, Captain, but we too have suffered by his hands.'

Toryn noted the clenched fists of the workers as they surrounded the Ruuk. He addressed Grebb. 'It seems you've made many enemies.' He stood back. 'My vow will be honored by handing you over to these good people to—' Something caught Toryn's eye. He crouched and took hold of the chain around Grebb's neck. 'Well, I'll be…' He yanked and held up Hamar's service medal. Toryn placed it over his head. 'You snatched this from a dead hero. Now I'm claiming it back on his behalf.' Grebb's hand moved to his pocket. Toryn grabbed it.

'Something else you wish to keep?' He pulled out Hamar's old map and laughed. 'It seems to be a day for justice. You stole this from me at Drunsberg.' He looked down at the old parchment. 'At least you appear to have taken care of it.'

Grebb snarled. 'It's useless to you now, unless you want to see the lands you'll lose before the year's out.'

'I wouldn't be so sure. We're not finished yet.' Toryn glanced to the prisoners as he tucked the map inside his tunic. 'My friends here will deal with you as they see fit. It'll be nothing less than you deserve. Therefore, I doubt we'll meet again.'

19. To Appease the Gods

Nyomae sank back onto the dry earth. Elodi was safe, as was the Amanach… for now. Elodi had called upon the stone, and it had responded. Nyomae had lost sight of her the moment the Amanach had ignited, therefore did not know who or what assailed her. But she assumed Elodi had survived. She drank and went to refill the flasks from the stream. Her body ached from sleeping on the hard ground, and her efforts to aid Elodi exhausted her. But Nyomae could not afford to rest. The sun was already setting; they must be on their way. She stumbled as she hauled the saddle on Orlo's back. 'Another day, my beauty. But with each day, Elmarand gets a little closer.' She fastened the straps. 'They love their horses there, or at least they did when I was last in the city. I cannot think that has changed, so you'll be well looked after, my boy.'

Nyomae turned to look back to the north. The peaks of the Caerwals had long since sunk beneath the horizon. She struggled to lift her bags, dreading the thought of another cold night in the saddle. The return journey would be just as punishing… unless the current leader in Elmarand offered to help. But Nyomae had no guarantee they would. She also had no guarantee they would allow her to leave… or live. Nyomae climbed upon Orlo.

The sudden appearance of three riders startled her. Had she not been drained, she would have sensed their approach, and now she had no strength to resist. They wore white robes, dirty from the blown sand. Their drawn swords beckoned her to dismount. Nyomae did so without a word. One slid from his saddle with the ease of an experienced rider. He motioned for her to hold out her hands with her palms up. His eyes widened as he saw the wavy lines of a wyke. He grasped her shoulders and spun her around. Nyomae's wrists were bound tight. Her head was pulled back, and a gag and blindfold secured. She groaned. As in the north, the people of the south remained wary of her kind.

The campfire revealed three faces of men who had lived a hard life. Not unlike the Nordleng, but Nyomae sensed they were not of the same cruel nature. Perhaps the harsh, unforgiving conditions of the plain had shaped them into what they had become. Aside from binding her, they had treated her well, and Orlo better: Nyomae had been right about their love of horses. The rising half-moon had been bright enough to penetrate her blindfold. They had left the road and ridden east for several hours, then turned south before taking their rest. Were they heading for Elmarand? At first, Nyomae believed they were from the city, but if they served the realm, why divert from the main route leading to the city?

The youngest rider had removed her blindfold as they had made camp, but the gag and binding remained. Nyomae wondered if the blindfold was to prevent her from seeing the way they took. Perhaps they had a secret hideaway. But she remained puzzled by their motive. If they feared her, why not kill her?

Nyomae watched the youngest prepare a meal over the fire while the others attended to the horses. They treated Orlo well, but perhaps it was purely because they intended to take him from her. None spoke to her directly, and they talked in hushed voices among themselves. She recognized the odd word of a language used by the people of the plains, but could determine little of what was said.

When the meal was ready, the cook gently guided Nyomae to the fireside. He removed her gag to feed her, then replaced it between each bite. The stew tasted like rabbit, seasoned with herbs that took her back to her childhood. She nodded her approval, hoping to assure the men she was not a threat. But Nyomae could not allow them to detain her for long. If they were taking her to Elmarand, she would readily ride with them and take her chances. But if they had other plans, she would have to find a way to escape.

The herbs gave her strength. The hunters believed her bound wrists would prevent her working a spell upon them, but she easily entered the Verse of the young man beside her. His name was Kirol. He was an honest man but lived in difficult times. And his guilt weighed heavy on his mind. Nyomae braced, horrified by what she learned.

Nyomae fought to control her dread. They were aware she was an Imaari, but now she knew why they had cared for her. The past of the young man revealed what they had in mind. As in the north, they were wary of wykes, but here in the south they served another purpose. Nyomae was to be taken to a sacred place in the desert... and sacrificed. Her warm, Imaari blood would be poured onto the sand to appease the dark gods.

She looked to her captors and found she pitied them. They were not evil, they were terrified. They had been brought up to fear what lay to the north, much like Toryn's people were led to be terrified of the south. But the folk of the once powerful southern realms must have required a more convincing story. Nyomae went back through the Verses of Kirol's family line. She soon found what she sought. Eight generations back, on his father's side, one had served in the guard at Elmarand. Stretching across the Verses of so many would soon drain her strength, but Nyomae had to know what she faced.

Through the eyes of Kirol's distant relative, she

witnessed the fear following the loss of so many fine soldiers at Gormadon. The devasting defeat had shaken the belief of the southern realms to the core. How had thousands of their valiant warriors been so utterly defeated? Idraman had initially been praised for saving the south. But rumors quickly spread. The whispers blamed him for the defeat, and even colluding with the enemy. Those who believed Idraman had prevented an invasion were told they were misled. He had closed the pass to trap their armies in the north, thus condemning their heroes to death. But the rumors had continued. To explain Idraman's betrayal, he was said to be a descendant of the dark gods.

Nyomae's vision wavered as she began to tire. She withdrew with many questions left unanswered. How had the great leaders of the south failed so miserably? And who had spread the malicious lies of Idraman's treachery?

Nyomae slumped against the young man. The most recent lines of his Verse ran through her mind. The hunters had come across the man on the cart she had seen the previous day. Nyomae had removed the concealment to save her strength, but now she realized with few travelers about, a single rider must have looked suspicious. The man had then reported the sighting. She sighed. Her oversight had cost her time, but if she could not escape, it would cost far more.

Nyomae watched them clean their plates and pots. It would be difficult to reason with the men if they were petrified of what lay beyond the Caerwals. Her words to convince them otherwise would be viewed as an attempt to place a curse upon them. And now she understood why Idraman was kept alive. If the people believed him to be a descendant of the gods, his execution would enrage them. But why would those spreading the lies want Idraman alive?

Nyomae looked down to her bound hands. Her palms bore the same lines as Idraman. But she and her kind must be considered lesser servants. Dozens of those destined to become Imaari would have suffered her intended fate. Yet they would not have known what the sudden appearance of the lines represented. Nyomae's awakening at a young age had attracted the attention of Sylvena, and thus set her on the path towards the Order of Echoes. But following the defeat at Gormadon, those with Imaari blood were feared by the people — their path led only to death.

Nyomae turned back to Kirol. These people did not enjoy the sacrifices, but as they saw it, they had little choice. No dark forces had come south, hence the people reasoned they served their purpose. Yet the Imaari line had dwindled, and the sacrifices had become a rare occurrence. But the gods would still demand blood. Who would be next when Nyomae's kind had gone?

The riders put out the fire and prepared to leave. Nyomae did not know where the grim ceremony would take place. The Verses of previous sacrifices had revealed many in attendance. Thus, she figured word of her capture would be sent to nearby settlements. Did that give her more time to recover? Her plan to escape required more strength. Perhaps two or three more meals with the same herbs her father had used, would suffice... but did she have enough time?

As the sun approached the top of the sky, the riders made their way to what had once been a fine stone building. The strong sunlight rendered her blindfold useless, and she could see much of its roof had collapsed. But enough remained to offer welcome respite from the heat of the day. They ate a meal of dried fruit, and then two settled down to sleep, leaving Kirol to watch over Nyomae. She had to escape now. If she delayed any longer, more people could soon be joining them and make her task all the more difficult.

Nyomae entered the Verse of the young man. He was anxious. Kirol had not long reached manhood and taken on the responsibility of a hunter. The other two men were twice his age and trained him in the ways of the desert. Their settlement struggled to feed even its small population. Animals rarely fattened up to their full size, thus they were forced to roam the plains and catch the odd beast to supplement their limited supplies. There had been little rain in the past months and now their trees produced barely any fruit.

Nyomae spoke to him in his Verse, using his native tongue. *Kirol.* He jumped, staring wide-eyed at her. *Please remove my gag and blindfold.* Nyomae waited. She chose not to ask for her wrists to be untied just yet. *Kirol. You're a good man. I know you don't wish to hurt me. Please. Let us speak.*

He glanced to his sleeping companions. 'But I... I mustn't. I am tasked to keep watch. You must not be allowed to speak.'

Nyomae increased the strength of her command. *You have no choice. I demand you let me speak.* Thankfully, he relented so she did not have to push the young man harder. Kirol checked behind, then untied the gag and removed the blindfold.

Kirol sat back and held his finger to his lips. 'But please. Don't place a curse upon us... and don't wake my masters. I will be flogged if they find out.'

Nyomae blinked in the harsh light and wiped her mouth. She whispered. 'I know what you intend to do with me. But it will serve no purpose. I have come from the north.' Kirol shuffled back. She held up her bound hands. 'I am not to be feared. There are people in the north just like you, but they are afraid of the south.'

He frowned. 'They're afraid of *us*? But aren't they our

enemy?'

'We're of the same people, Kirol. We fight the same enemy. Yes, there is a dark force beyond the mountains, but they are far, far to the north. And we stand between them and you.' Nyomae re-entered Kirol's Verse and, to her relief, saw he accepted her explanation. Perhaps he would respond, wanting to avoid her needless sacrifice. But if the others woke... She withdrew and leaned forward. 'I must get to Elmarand. I have to speak—'

'No!' He lowered his voice as one of the sleeping men stirred. 'We're not allowed to go there. It is forbidden. But I don't know why. Their men raid our villages and take our women.' His head dropped. 'They took my sister. She was only thirteen.' Kirol turned to the south. 'That was three years ago. I don't know whether she yet lives.'

Nyomae gaped. 'To what purpose?'

'It is said they build an army. But they don't want the men from this region.' Kirol pushed out his chest. 'They know we're strong willed and would not bow to their demands and follow their orders. But our women...' his jaw clenched. 'We believe they are taken to entertain the soldiers.' He groaned. 'We would ride to free them, but... we are weak, and the lands between us and Elmarand are cursed. Great mages protect their own forces from a plague that kills without mercy.' Kirol slumped. 'Every autumn they come and take the pick of our wives, daughters, and sisters. We try to hide them, but they're always found, and they punish us for doing so.'

Nyomae patted his leg. 'If you let me go, I will try to help.' But she knew she made an empty promise. Perhaps if successful in the north, she may be able to assist later, but if the Ul-dalak succeeded and Ormoroth returned, all would suffer the fate of Kirol's sister. She continued. 'I seek an ally in Elmarand who will help us defeat our common enemy.'

Kirol stammered. 'But... I cannot let you go.' He looked to the other men. 'They would discipline me for just letting you speak. And if I let you escape... they would kill me. Our village will receive much praise and reward for your... sacrifice. Others in the region will pay us a tribute for our service.'

'I understand your predicament, Kirol. Yet, my death would not appease the dark gods. But if I live, I could help you, your sister, and your people.' She sat back. 'I appreciate you cannot just let me go. I do not wish to be responsible for your death.' Nyomae glanced to his companions. 'But if I can overpower them to escape, they cannot blame you.'

'You would kill them?'

'No.' Nyomae sighed. 'There has been enough death. I do not wish to see more. Allow me a moment and I will construct a plan.' She entered the building's Verse and quickly found a time prior to the armies marching north to Gormadon. A division had rested their horses and spent the night at the spot when it had been an inn with many stables. Her heart broke. They were such fine soldiers, heading north with the belief they would win the day and protect their loved ones back home. But Nyomae knew they had but a few days to live. And those not trampled into Gormadon's dirt by Uluriel's beasts, were torn apart by Nyomae's words.

She retreated and bowed her head. Nyomae had no time for remorse, but she could yet atone. She nodded to her ankles and wrists. 'If you untie me, I will make it look as if an army comes this way... an army of soldiers I doubt your friends will have seen before. You will assist me in the illusion, then I will make my escape in the panic.'

He stared, looking like a young boy hearing a story of wonder. 'You can do that?'

'It will be brief, but long enough to achieve my

purpose.'

Kirol readily removed the bonds. Nyomae rubbed her sore skin and stood. She walked towards Orlo, happy to see him well rested. She turned back to Kirol. 'On my word, you will shout a warning and point south along the road.' She nodded to his companions. 'They will either rush to defend this place or flee. I do not know their minds, but whichever way they run, I shall ride the other.'

Kirol scampered after her. 'But they are good riders. They know this region well. Once they realize what's happened, they will find you.'

Nyomae stopped and smiled. 'I can assure you they will not. They will see the plain as it was yesterday. In fact, they may be confused for a while as they won't even see the tracks we made on our arrival. You will have to play along with their fear. They'll think they've been outwitted by dark magic.' She placed her hand on his shoulder. 'I may have coerced you into taking action initially, but I can see you're a good man, Kirol.'

He grabbed her arm. 'Please…. take me with you. I can help you cross—'

'I'm afraid I cannot. I appreciate your offer, but I must travel alone.' Nyomae noted his disappointment. 'And I cannot guarantee your safety.'

'But I wish to find my sister. I care not for my safety.'

'It's not possible. While your skills of surviving the desert are admirable, you would still slow my progress, and time is vital.' Nyomae turned to the desert. 'Your life here has been difficult, but I hope to return one day with more people and restore this region to its former glory.'

Kirol took her hands and looked at her palms. 'Then I shall await that day.'

Nyomae smiled. 'Then I hope you won't have to wait long.' She entered the Song. 'Now, let us execute our plan and bring that day closer.

20. Strange Company

Elodi's head bounced up and down. Her cheeks stung as if nettles brushed her skin. She lay face down with her arms and legs bound around a cold, hard shell… of an animal. It moved at speed, but this was no horse. The creature hissed and snorted from its efforts to keep up the pace. Elodi gagged as the stench of rotten meat swept over her. Her stomach clenched — would she be its next meal?

She opened her eyes, not needing to see the evidence to know what beast she rode. Four black, hairy legs on each side moved with surprising speed and agility. She was strapped to the back of a monstrous aralak, almost the size of Sea Mist. A wave of nausea flooded through her; no doubt the spider's poison still coursed through her veins. Ahead, a horse galloped — a large horse judging by the thud of its hooves. It had to be the warlock. But where was he taking her? Elodi tried to lift her head to see farther afield, but had little strength to fight against the spider's scuttling motion. Out of the corner of her eyes she could see long grass in the moonlight. It was night, but was it the same night she had first encountered Shokresh? What had happened to Lindell and the First Horse? And Sea Mist? Elodi's heart lurched. Had the spider attacked him? Sea Mist was not familiar with aralaks. Had he tried to defend her, or had he bolted? She dearly hoped he had galloped to freedom. But what would Bardon think if he had returned riderless to Borrund? Would he delay his attack on Keld if he thought she was lost? It had not occurred to Elodi that she might not return.

Despite her muzzy head, she tried to think of the consequences of recent events. She believed the Amanach to be safe. The stone had responded to her call and stunned the warlock, who perhaps abandoned his assault. Had Shokresh lied about her company? The First Horse had killed at least half the Nordleng before she was taken. She was certain Lindell, Lena, and the rest of the riders would have dealt with the last of the Nordleng. But where was her sword? Her leg felt exposed in its absence. Shokresh must have it. His *kruul* had rendered it useless against him, but could he now bend it to his command?

Again, Elodi tried to force her head up… but failed. She needed two things to contemplate an escape: her sword and her strength. Yet she had neither while the warlock possessed her weapon, and the spider's poison numbed her senses. She would have to be patient and choose her time. But how long before the nausea lifted? Elodi sagged onto the aralak's shell. She was being naïve. If she was in the warlock's position, she would not let her captive recover to attempt an escape. With dread, she realized she would have to grow accustomed to the spider's venom.

Claws clattered on cobbles. Elodi looked up. It had to be the Borrund Road. To her left, the peaks of the Kolossos glimmered in the moonlight. To her right, she could just make out the trees of what had to be the North Forest. Elodi struggled to remember the map of the region as her head spun. She closed her eyes and reluctantly pressed her head against the hard shell to gather her thoughts. The elaborate stitching of Kernlow's map came to mind. Briefly, she wondered what would come of his beloved tapestry following his death. But that was not her concern. The warlock was taking her north and west. Elodi could not conceal her dread. Her hairy mount picked up its pace… towards Aralak Gorge.

Elodi woke, retched, then vomited a foul-tasting liquid down the spider's back. But it helped to clear her head. She looked up to see the Kolossos mountains towering over them, turning pink as the sun rose at their backs. The aralak had stopped. It snorted as its fangs tore into a bundle swathed in cobweb. Elodi's stomach convulsed. Was it Sea Mist? Did this beast feed off her dear horse? She twisted away and swallowed hard. No. It could not be. Sea Mist would not have allowed a spider to get the better of him.

Beside her, the towering figure of Shokresh stood in his stirrups. He surveyed the Great Northeast Road a short distance ahead. The rising sun shone into the gap between two large peaks and the damaged fences of Aralak Gorge. Broken and snagged chains hung from iron posts ending in curved spikes. Glistening with morning dew, the railings now resembled the very webs of the creatures they had once confined.

Satisfied the road was clear, Shokresh kicked on; the spider duly followed. Elodi pulled against her bonds, but despite some of her strength returning, they held tight. The warlock led the way down the valley and crossed the road. The huts housing the watch on the gorge were deserted. For centuries, the realms had successfully contained the spiders. But many had died carrying out the grim duty. Elodi recalled Ruan's tragic account of the death of his brother, but now the spiders had escaped, few could argue it had once been a price worth paying.

The aralak crawled through the breach and Elodi shivered in the dank, cool air of the ravine. She turned to look at the warlock. Why did he bring her here of all places? The last ray of light glinted on her sword. Elodi glared. Shokresh wore it next to his own as if a trophy. Her hand itched to snatch it back and remove his head, but she could not even lift her arm.

The warlock glanced down. 'Ah, I see you wake.' His grating voice echoed down the gorge. He grinned. 'I trust you will enjoy our trek through the place of your nightmares.' He looked back to the gap in the fence. 'It was no mean feat of Draegelan to trap our fine beasts here… and for so long. But I always knew we would free them one day.' Shokresh held out his hand towards the aralak. 'Surely, you cannot fail to be impressed by their beauty, not to mention their selfish and malicious nature.'

Elodi's voice croaked. 'I wonder if you'd be so impressed if you were pumped full of their poison.' She spat. 'Which I dearly hope you will experience one day soon.'

He laughed, gesturing to the stain on the spider's back. 'I see it's not to your liking, Elodi, so perhaps I shall forgo that pleasure. It is a concoction of the most potent ingredients.' Shokresh nodded. 'But I commend you, my lady. You do well to function at all, so soon after imbibing our friend's juice.' He looked up. 'I see we have company.' If Elodi had thought the gorge was empty, she was mistaken. At first glance, the ancient, gnarled trees looked heavy with blossom. But there was no beauty to be had in the gloomy gorge — the trees were clogged by tattered webs. To Elodi's dread, she saw the blossoms would not bring forth buds… they were egg sacs wriggling with tiny legs, ready to burst out.

A ragged, old aralak, crawled down from a tree. Between its drooling jaws, a newly hatched spider squirmed. Elodi winced as it burst, unsure whether to feel pity for the tiny creature, or be grateful it would not make it out of the gorge. The feeding aralak dropped to the ground with a thud. It scuttled towards them, perhaps drawn to the odor of Elodi's flesh. It stopped ten paces short and rose onto its back legs. It spat out its meagre morsel and twitched its pincers. Her stomach churned as it dribbled and hissed. But it was half the size of the spider bearing Elodi. Shokresh raised his hand. The old beast shuddered, then squealed as its legs splayed. He flicked out his fingers. The aralak shattered, spraying its dark blood and legs in all directions. Yet its fate did not deter the others.

The trees creaked and groaned as dozens more scampered across their boughs, and down their trunks to the ground. Shokresh sighed. 'Magnificent they may be, but intelligent they are not.' For once, Elodi was pleased to have a warlock for company. He bowed his head, then threw out his hands. The air shimmered, then rapidly expanded, blasting as a gust into their visitors. As with the first, the aralaks were torn apart, along with the brittle trees. Elodi closed her eyes, wanting to be spared the gruesome spectacle. But the sound of splattering blood, and body parts breaking against tree trunks, denied her that wish.

Shokresh uttered a command. The spider rose and scuttled on, encased by a sphere that rippled like water. Ahead, the gorge narrowed as the slopes climbed higher. Elodi noted the aralaks now remained in their lairs but kept their beady eyes on the trespassers; perhaps they were not as reckless as the warlock had assumed.

After an hour, they stopped. The warlock waved a hand over his head. The protective dome disintegrated to reveal what looked like a dead end where the two rock walls met. Shokresh wriggled his fingers and a narrow entrance to a tunnel appeared. The spider tucked in its legs and squeezed through the gap, scratching Elodi's face with its stiff hairs. Shokresh followed and drew his sword. Like an Amayan blade, it glowed, but with the sickening green light she had come to despise. Its light exposed a passage that dropped steeply a short way ahead.

Elodi shuddered in the cool air, but perhaps more with dread following Toryn's account of his time beneath the mountains. The spider led, casting a large, hideous shadow on the tunnel walls as if a puppet. But despite her worsening situation, Elodi's spirits rose a little. It must have been a full day since the aralak had poisoned her, and now she felt the strength begin to return to her limbs. Perhaps an opportunity to escape would present itself on the next stop. Shokresh had brought her this far. If he was going to kill her, he would have done so in the forest when the aralak had felled her. It was now obvious Shokresh wanted her alive, for whatever foul purpose. So surely, he would have to feed her.

Elodi's mind began to race. Did warlocks sleep? Could she overpower the spider? She assumed he would untie her at some point, but if Shokresh had nulled the power of her sword against him, what could she do? She clenched her hands into fists. Would a few well-aimed blows to his head stun him so she could take back her sword? Its Amayan powers may be useless against him, but perhaps its cold steel could still pierce his heart. Elodi relaxed as much as was possible and tried to think as her head continued to clear. Of one thing she was certain — she had to escape before the warlock took her to the place he had in mind. Did more of his brothers await?

Elodi woke. The aralak had stopped. The gentle rocking movement as it negotiated the tunnels must have lulled her to sleep. They sat in a cave thrice the width of the passageway. Its walls had been carved to fashion seats surrounding a shallow pit at the center. Briefly, she wondered what function the cave served, but decided it was best not to speculate. Her bonds loosened and dropped away from her ankles and wrists. She slipped from the spider's back, opening more cuts as she slid across the hard shell. Elodi flexed her hands and stretched out her limbs, relieved to be off the foul creature.

Shokresh hoisted her to her feet, dragged her across the cave, and sat her on one of the stone seats. He opened his fingers as if warming them over a fire. But there was no comfort to be had in the cave. Elodi's body stiffened as the warlock's spell fastened her to the rock. She watched, suddenly drained of hope as the spider crawled into the pit, folded in its legs, and crouched as if waiting to be tucked in for the night.

Shokresh led his horse to a rockpool at the opposite end of the cave. Elodi noticed her sword was now strapped to the saddle and pondered whether the beast would resist if she tried to snatch it. Her thoughts went back to Sea Mist. He must have escaped. She was in no doubt, Shokresh would have taunted her had the aralak killed her beloved horse.

Elodi's face chilled. She looked up to find Shokresh watched her. He leaned forward and clasped his hands. 'You're wondering what happened to that emaciated creature you call a horse.' Elodi winced as his booming voice echoed through the cavern. He scoffed. 'It was all skin and bone. It barely filled my hungry aralak's gut.'

She cried out. 'You lie!'

'The deluded beast thought he could protect you.' Shokresh kneeled beside the pit and stroked the spider's bony head. 'But I'm afraid it was no match for this beauty.' Elodi tried to shut her pained ears to the tale, but the warlock persisted. 'A blinded, frightened horse will easily bolt and collide with a tree. Broke its scrawny neck, but it lived long enough for its warm blood to satisfy the aralak… for a little while at least.'

Elodi clenched her jaw, but the tears flowed. 'That is not true. I would know if he was… lost.' She could not bring herself to say *dead*: it would be too final, and she could not accept that was Sea Mist's fate.

'Then you deceive yourself, Elodi. Believe what you wish.' Shokresh retrieved a small vial from his saddle bag and emptied its contents beside the pit. 'But it matters not. You have no need for a horse now.' He waved his hand over the dark puddle. It bubbled, then thickened, emitting a stench that turned Elodi's stomach. The spider quivered, raised its head, opened its ragged mouth and guzzled down the jelly. But despite her disgust, she could not take her eyes from the monstrosity. She had only faced them in battle and had not had the chance to observe them in detail. The aralak's skull was the same size of a human and, along with its shell, was the only part of its body not coated with short, spiky hairs. Its pale face was dominated by six beady, glistening eyes that must surely sense every tiny movement within its range of sight. But of all its features, it was its mouth that most repulsed Elodi. She did not know what a common spider's mouth looked like, but Elodi was certain it did not resemble that of an aralak. A flap of moist skin hung over its maw, but from beneath, protruded two black fangs that could easily pierce all but the finest armor. The skin rippled as it sucked, sounding much like a child sipping soup from a spoon too big for its mouth.

Yet, as she watched the spider devour its meal, it dawned upon Elodi the abomination may be her only chance to escape. She recalled Toryn's tale of his encounter with the warlock in Vortimo. Vordrak had controlled droogs and kept the Amayans at bay. On two occasions, Toryn had overwhelmed the warlock's power by resisting its will, forcing Vordrak to release its hold over his underlings. The large aralak was obviously under Shokresh's influence. Could she wrest control away from the warlock and command the spider? But how? Perhaps her sword held the answer. But she would have little time to solve that puzzle once she had made her move.

Elodi flinched. She turned to the source of her unease to find the aralak's eyes upon her. Her skin crawled. It desired her flesh. Its secretions would plump her up and heighten its pleasure. Elodi groaned; it was Shokresh's control over the beast that kept her alive. It was obvious if she could by some means break the warlock's hold, the creature would eagerly pounce on her and take its prize.

Elodi looked back to the way they had come. She had slept so had no clue how far they were under the mountains. But even if she managed to escape and find her way out, she would still have to negotiate the gorge with its ghastly occupants. Elodi turned to the other side of the cave. What lay ahead? Would she be better facing the unknown?

Shokresh retrieved another web-strewn bundle from his saddle bag. Elodi grimaced; the stomach-churning show was not yet done. The warlock tossed it in front of the spider. 'You are wondering whether this' — he nudged the bundle with his foot — 'is part of your horse.' She looked away. He laughed. 'But which part? Its flank? A leg perhaps?'

The spider sank its fangs into the meat. Elodi choked, trying to hold down the scarce contents of her stomach, determined not to show her revulsion. Shokresh sneered. 'Not hungry, Elodi?' He reached into his cloak. 'Perhaps I have something a little more to your liking.' He held out his hand to reveal what looked like a chunk of bread. Elodi had no choice — she had to eat if she was to escape. Shokresh touched her arm. 'You can move it now. Take it.' She reluctantly accepted his offering, but to her surprise, it tasted like sweet fruit.

Shokresh sat opposite. 'We don't all eat raw, rotting meat. We are not the fiends you assume us to be. It will sustain you.'

Elodi looked up. 'Sustain me for what purpose?'

'You will discover soon enough.'

She held his gaze, enduring the pain of his glare. 'Then where are you taking me? Will you at least share that?'

'You may know of it. But I'm afraid it will not be to your liking. The very name sends many into shock. Unless, that is, you submit to me. Then the prison would become your palace.'

Elodi noticed he said little. It was in his nature to goad her, but he did not disclose what he had in store for her. Her jaw tightened. 'I will never submit to you.'

Shokresh stood. 'Alas, then a prison it will be.' Elodi felt his hold over her limbs release. She clenched her fists and readied to snatch her blade from his horse. But before she could move, he snapped his fingers. The spider clambered out of the pit. It turned to Elodi and rose. A wet, black barb protruded from its rear. She had no time to open her mouth to protest as it sprang. Its long legs grasped her tight, forcing the air from her lungs. Elodi saw her pained face in its dark orbs. She retched, shutting her eyes as its hot breath, laced with saliva, stinking of blood-soaked mud and the rotting flesh of a battlefield, spurted into her face. She fought to free her arms, but it held her fast. She cried out as its spike drove deep into her stomach. Her ears rang; her mouth filled with bile as the poison penetrated every inch of her body. Her vision faded as the warlock strode over, picked her up, then slung her onto the aralak's shell.

21. At the Crossroads

It was indeed a stroke of luck to stumble upon the Caranach fortress, but whether it was the intervention of the gods as Nyomae claimed, or a very useful coincidence, the fortress proved a blessing in more ways than one. After Toryn had brought down the hall and blocked the tunnels, the company, aided by the freed workers, had easily overcome the rest of the Ruuk. And thanks to sketches drawn by the Ul-dalak, they had found a route leading down to the road, hence even the horses could escape from the dark, dank tunnels.

Toryn stopped and turned back to face Caranach. The vast mountain loomed as if ready to topple and crush any who had the gall to look upon it. The sheer rockface of the upper peak reminded him of Vortimo. But this mountain stood many times taller, towering over the other peaks of the Kolossos. Toryn thought back to the times he had scrambled up the trees of Midwyche to gaze upon Caranach. Using Hamar's map, he had planned for the momentous day he would make the journey and scale its lofty peak. He grinned to himself. Hamar was right. It was an impossible task. But while he may never climb it, he had stood within its mighty heart, and had even left his mark with the power of his sword.

'Makes you realize how small we are.' Jedrul patted Toryn's back. 'Been here since the gods entombed that evil fellow. And I guess it will still be standing until the seas reclaim the land. Unless, that is, that fiend below breaks out.'

Toryn stepped back and craned his neck. 'If he can shift something this size, surely not even the gods could restrain him.'

'Then let's hope the story is tosh. Well, the part about his tomb, not the Maidens, eh. That has to be true.' Jedrul winked. 'And I reckon the Amayans alone sort of prove it.'

The company made their way along the remainder of the road without incident. At times, Toryn thought he heard the patter of cobtrolls' feet, but was grateful they chose to keep their distance. The guards at the watchtower were stunned when Toryn, his company, and close to one hundred workers from the mountain trudged out of the pass. Fires were lit, food was cooked, and the healers called, but the company could not stay for long. To exploit the Ruuk celebrations, the attack had to happen in five days — yet it would take at least four to reach the mines, even without delays. Toryn handed the Ruuk plans to the commander, and advised he send word to the East Watchtower to search for signs of a similar construction.

Toryn bade farewell to Jorim. The man intended to return to Greendell once the Ruuk had been driven out of Noor. But he and his surviving villagers would face a huge challenge to rebuild... and the heart-breaking task to finally lay the dead to rest.

Outside the gate, Toryn paused at the crossroads. His eyes wandered to the ridge where he had stood with Hamar to look upon Caranach as the moon had risen. The road west would take him all the way to the coast at Eldamouth. He longed for the day he and Elodi could watch the sun set over the Elessyn Sea from the clifftops. And perhaps if the gods granted him that wish, they may even hear Behemora calling for her mate. Toryn turned away and looked to the road heading south. Not since he had walked through Darrow with Nyomae, had he been so close to home. He wondered what Miram and Andryn were doing, feeling a pang of guilt for not returning to see the folks who had brought him in from the forest. Perhaps the chance to return to Midwyche would present itself come spring, but first they had to survive winter.

Toryn turned his back on the south and kicked on his horse towards Drunsberg.

22. A Warlock's Tale

Elodi woke as she coughed and spluttered a dark fluid down the spider's shell. Her head throbbed as Shokresh laughed. 'Ah, the Amayan in you still resists, but the weaker half undermines your resolve. Thus, I am afraid you will continue to suffer.'

Elodi wiped her mouth and struggled to find the warlock in the dim light. 'Yet you feel the need to keep me in this stupor. Is just *half* an Amayan enough to concern you?'

He hissed. 'Don't flatter yourself, Elodi. I could snap you in two with a click of my fingers if I so wished. I keep you sedated to avoid such inane conversation. Besides,' he nodded to the spider, 'she must have her pleasure. I won't let her eat you… yet. She needs something to placate her. Pumping you full of her essence brings her pleasure.'

Elodi swallowed the bile rising in her throat. 'And plunging my sword into both your cruel hearts would please me.'

'Then you will be disappointed.' Shokresh untied her as he spoke to the spider. 'Take your rest, my beauty. You carry this burden without complaint. You will receive your just reward before long.' Elodi slid from its back, scratching her arm on its leg as she fell like a limp doll to the ground. Her wrist burned as the warlock dragged her to the cave wall and sat her on a rock. Her body froze with a wave of his hand.

Shokresh bent and stared her in the face. But Elodi held his gaze, determined not to look away. His voice croaked as he whispered. 'You are mine to do with as I desire, Elodi. You cannot escape. You resist now, but I *will* break you.' He caressed her cheek. 'You will give yourself to me before we reach our destination.'

Elodi gritted her teeth. 'Now you flatter yourself.' The thin skin on his temples creased. She raised an eyebrow. 'You say I have no chance of escape, yet you neither reveal our destination… nor why you need me to yield to you. If I am totally at your mercy, why the secrecy?' She tensed. 'And why have you not taken your… pleasure? Does Uluriel insist I am to be untouched? It must be difficult for one so great as you, to follow orders.' With a small degree of satisfaction, she noted the corners of his mouth tighten.

Shokresh bristled. 'That is not your concern. But you'll have your answers soon enough.' He stood back, seeming eager to change the subject. 'I have a question for you, Elodi. There is something that intrigues me about your people.'

Elodi gaped. 'Then you can stay *intrigued*. Why should I help you?' She frowned. 'But what could possibly be of interest to you about my people?'

The warlock laughed. 'Yet you are now *intrigued* to know what puzzles me.' His eyes gleamed in the green light. 'Then I shall satisfy your curiosity by asking my question. Tell me, Elodi, why do your people fight when you must know you cannot possibly win? Why not spare the death and agony by surrendering now?' His finger tapped on his arm as he waited impatiently for his answer.

Elodi was astounded — he really did not know. She decided to put him straight. 'I doubt you will understand, but I will tell you. We fight because we have something worth fighting for. We will never accept defeat… that is not our way. And I believe you're aware the *Elorsil* is back in the hand of one that has awoken its power.'

He scoffed. 'In the hands of a young pretender. And, before you place too much faith in this plow pusher and his new toy, know this. Such a weapon is more of a threat to one who wields it without knowledge.' Shokresh turned away. 'We will do him a great favor by taking it from him.' But Elodi sensed the mention of the sword troubled him and the conversation was finished.

The warlock fed the spider in silence, then gave Elodi a morsel of food. She ate, but as her eyes adjusted, she noticed a dark line a dozen paces from where she sat: the slight breeze against her numb face suggested a deep crevasse. Elodi felt herself drawn to its dark lip. If she could move, she only had a few paces to salvation. She could throw herself into the depths of the Kolossos and be free of her captor.

Elodi shook her head. Her mother would be bitterly disappointed if she chose the easy way out. And her father would berate her for not using her skills to at least attempt an escape. She watched Shokresh lead his horse to an inlet a little way down the cavern. The aralak finished its supper. The warlock sat and closed his eyes, seeming to take his rest. In the silence, Elodi heard flowing water. But it came from far below, perhaps echoing up through the chasm. Toryn suspected a river ran deep beneath the Kolossos. It had given him strength, allowing him to challenge Vordrak. This had to be the same river. Could she call upon its power?

Shokresh opened his eyes. 'You hear it, but no, it will not answer your plea. An Imaari of repute may use its power, but not your kind. The Elorym were too cautious. They made their gravest error when they denied the warrior,' he smirked, '*maidens* access to the oldest source of power in the land. No, Elodi.' He sighed as if it was a chore to deliver his lecture. 'They deemed you worthy of its power only when tempered by the stones. And yet, they burdened you to protect them from greater forces... for eternity. You were given the most onerous of tasks without the proper means to do so.' Shokresh leaned forward and held out his hands. 'Don't you see? The Elorym did not trust your kind. They condemned the Amayans to a life of servitude… until you fail, and the stones fall.' He sneered. 'And you have the gall to accuse my kind of seeking to *enslave* your people.'

Elodi remembered Nyomae's words. 'The Elorym had their reasons. They knew the dangers of placing too much power in the hands of the few.'

Shokresh threw back his head and roared with laughter until the cave shook. 'Dangers? Do you not understand your dire situation is because of your masters' timidity.' He stood and walked around the slumbering spider. He sat beside Elodi and patted her knee as if she were a child. But he spoke as if full of regret. 'The Amayans could have been a most formidable fighting force had the Elorym not been so wary.' He leaned back against the wall and sighed. 'But if you become my queen, Elodi, you will have power beyond your dreams. Ormoroth is both a wise and generous lord.'

'Is? But your precious lord is imprisoned in the Great Void.'

The warlock turned. His eyebrows raised, stretching the skin around his sunken eyes. 'He rests, waiting for the day he will return. And that day will come. You would be wise to swear your allegiance now.'

For a moment, Elodi thought she saw another behind his eyes. 'You speak of Ormoroth with reverence, but you were once Elorym. Did he not torture you to gain your allegiance?'

Shokresh stiffened. 'That is a lie!' But Elodi could see her words opened a deep wound. He stood and calmed. Now when he spoke, he seemed to reminisce. 'Ormoroth did not need to coerce those who chose to follow him. He revealed the true beauty of this land. Raw, unbridled energy once coursed through its veins, shooting forth from volcanoes that shook you to the core. You have not lived until you have seen such force and destruction. It is a wonder to behold, Elodi. Yet the Maidens took it upon themselves to tame the very force that filled our hearts with desire.'

Elodi clenched her jaw. She watched as the warlock gazed to the far side of the cave. 'Describe it to me. What do I not appreciate about Ormoroth's vision of beauty?'

'Describe?' He reached out. 'I can show you.'

'No.' She held up a hand. 'I would rather hear of such wonders in your own words. You are a fine storyteller.'

Shokresh nodded. 'Ah, finally we have something on which we can agree. I am more than just a slayer of those who wish to spoil these lands. I have learned and witnessed much during my long and illustrious life.' He closed his eyes and began his tale. 'Ormoroth once ruled lands far beyond these shores. I and my brothers have traveled far and wide. You have led a deprived existence if you have not seen the force of the land's lifeblood gushing forth and flowing down a mountain. I have felt the ground shudder as gigantic waves of restless, untamed seas broke upon cliffs the height of Caranach. I have fought for my life as a maelstrom ripped mighty trees up by their roots as if mere weeds. And I had the honor of seeing Ormoroth split the bedrock to open a rift that makes Roth's Doom look like a scratch. That feat alone brought a race as mighty as the Elorym to their knees.' The warlock opened his eyes and whispered. 'Everything must fight to survive, Elodi, nothing is safe, no creature should take the gift of life for granted. The strongest forces vie for supremacy in the eternal struggle. The powerful must replace the weak. But they must never rest. The powerful must always strive for dominance against others wishing to supplant them. This is the doctrine of Ormoroth. This is what must prevail.'

Elodi saw an opening into the warlock's mind. 'You speak much truth, Shokresh. Your words alone open my eyes to the brutal, yet magnificent nature of chaos. And I admit, I am beginning to appreciate the beauty of the world before the Maidens dulled its power.'

'That is good to hear.' The warlock stood. 'But enough. We have spent too long in this place.' He snapped his fingers at the aralak. It sprang up and scuttled towards them.

Inside, Elodi groaned, but she held her nerve. 'No!' She softened her voice. 'That is not necessary. I wish to hear more of your stories. Why not tell me as we walk.' She gestured to the pathway along the chasm. 'As you have said, I have no means of escape. Allow me to walk and spare the legs of your magnificent spider.'

Shokresh held up his hand. The spider stopped. He eyed Elodi, and she felt him probe her thoughts. She held fast, and to her relief, he agreed. 'Very well. I have much to tell. But...' he gestured to the aralak, 'she is watchful and will pounce the instant you defy me.'

Elodi let out a silent breath. 'Then she'll have no reason. Why would I try to escape? I want to hear more of your wondrous stories.'

The warlock did not disappoint. Elodi could not tell if any of them were true, but his tales were indeed worthy of a storyteller of old, more astounding than any she had ever heard. And Shokresh delighted in the telling, and of Elodi's appreciation. At times, he would stop, shout and wave his arms to make his point. At others his voice would become barely a whisper as he spoke of his childhood. Shokresh told of the coming of Ormoroth into the world; the early struggles against the Nym; the terrible wars in the days of the Elorym; and to Elodi's amazement, the Battle of Talaghir. He had wept, unashamed of his sorrow as he relived the moment Ormoroth commanded his warlocks to leave the plain to spare them the devastation. Yet while he knew what his lord was about to unleash against Dorlan, Shokresh had offered to stay by Ormoroth's side. But his lord did not demand a senseless sacrifice, knowing if his warlocks survived, the path back to the mortal lands remained open.

At times, Elodi became so captivated by his tales, she almost forgot her predicament. But always the aralak watched her, poised to spring and tear out her throat. And just like the spider, Elodi kept her eyes on the warlock and the edge of the ravine, hatching her plot. His attention wavered, as his mind obviously was in the past as he told his stories. She reasoned if she lunged, perhaps her momentum would be sufficient to knock him off balance. If caught by surprise, she might tip him far enough to send his large frame toppling over the edge.

But what of the aralak? She would have just moments to reset her stance. But how could she better the eight legs of a large spider? And then there was the matter of the warlock's horse. Was it also a loyal beast? Or was it under his command? No matter how much she tried to plan, she had three possible adversaries to overcome — she was only one, and one without a sword.

Shokresh stopped. He had been speaking of the Angorlith, but something had drawn his attention. And now Elodi felt it. Her spirits rose.

23. Of Southern Spires

Nyomae's plan had worked. Kirol's older companions had reacted as if the very hosts of the old gods had risen. Nyomae had sustained the image of the Immortals of Elmarand marching north, just long enough for her captors to realize the futility of fighting, then turn tail and flee. Kirol had briefly caught her eye as they ran. She noted his wonder as he saw the might of the army that had once served his realm. Nyomae had untied her horse and headed south. Despite the heat, Orlo had maintained a brisk pace and put a good distance between them. And if Nyomae was concerned she would use up her valuable strength to deceive the hunters, a breeze had picked up and blown the sand to erase their tracks. She smiled to herself — perhaps the gods had taken her side for once.

She slowed Orlo as they approached another bridge spanning a dry canal. Nyomae knew they had to shelter from the unforgiving sun, but her encounter with the hunters had made her determined to reach Elmarand all the sooner. The situation in the south was worse than she could have imagined. But the main threat still came from the Ul-dalak in the north. If the Five Realms failed, the fall of the south would be inevitable.

Nyomae reluctantly led Orlo into the shade. She had taken only one of the hunters' flasks as she did not wish to condemn them to a slow death in the desert. But she would have to find more water the next day. She sat, dearly wishing to enter the Song and locate Toryn and Elodi, but she could not afford to deplete her strength passing through the many Verses to reach them. She closed her eyes and lay back. Elmarand was perhaps a day and a half away. In that time, she would have to decide whether to enter the city by stealth, or confront the guards and demand an audience with the city's leader. Both approaches were fraught with difficulties. To conceal her presence would take more of her strength, strength she needed to enter Idraman's fading mind. But she would also be taking a risk to make herself known to whoever held the city. Nyomae knew nothing of the current state of Elmarand beyond what Kirol had told her — and that was not encouraging. If she presented herself at the gate, she would put herself at the mercy of the leader. Did they hold the same beliefs as the hunters? She could not overwhelm a whole city if they chose to sacrifice her to appease the gods. Kirol had spoken of Elmarand building a great army. Did they have plans to invade the north? Or were their eyes on the fertile lands of the south? The fall of the north appeared to have divided the age-old allies of Talamaris and Armanoor. But surely neither could win, and the conflict would lead only to the demise of the once great and powerful realms. Nyomae's heart sank. Did Ul-dalak agents operate in the south?

Nyomae woke, relieved to find no swords pointing at her throat. She turned as Orlo nuzzled her neck. 'Not long now, my loyal friend.' The first stars twinkled in the south. Before long, she would have to find a suitable place to leave him. While she could hide herself from prying eyes, it would drain her powers to conceal them both. But she had no idea where he would be safe, and how long before she could return. And although they had spent but a few days together, Nyomae knew their parting would be difficult.

She fed and watered Orlo, drank sparingly herself, then mounted. The hunters had cost her one day but come dawn, she hoped the tall towers of the once most magnificent city of the Seven Realms, would be visible above the flat horizon. But how would it look now?

The clear sky and waxing moon lit their way. Orlo appeared to know they had almost completed the first half of their mission. But this was the easy part. So much depended on events beyond Nyomae's control, and of course, she had no way of knowing how Idraman would respond. She heaved a sigh of relief as the sky grew lighter, and to the south, the tallest of Elmarand's many spires, the Sun Tower, rose to meet the new day. She had not taken it for granted the city had survived all these years intact. But if the supreme symbol of its grandeur still stood, perhaps all was not lost.

Nyomae urged Orlo on, guessing the city lay a little more than ten leagues ahead. She hoped to find somewhere to shelter before mid-morning, and then take time to go over her strategy. Nyomae stopped, seeing something she had not expected. A thin streak stretched across the land between her and Elmarand. She stood in her stirrups. Could it be a canal? Did they farm the lands closer to the city? She stroked Orlo's mane. 'Let us go and see, boy. Perhaps we'll find more water.' But as they neared the line, it became apparent it was no waterway.

The rising sun revealed a wall, a wall that extended from east to west as far as Nyomae could see. And it was tall, being farther away than she first thought, standing close to one hundred feet high. She stared at the colossal structure. The task of transporting the stones many leagues across the plain would have been a huge undertaking in itself. And that was before the construction could begin. It must have taken decades. But who had built it? Had the rulers of Elmarand sacrificed their own people in the desert to protect themselves? Yet, if they feared an invasion from the north, why had they not fortified the Caerwal Pass with more than just a wooden gate?

Nyomae spurred on Orlo. She had come this far through the most challenging terrain in the Seven Realms — she was not about to let a menacing wall deny her a meeting with Idraman.

24. Guards on the Border

Despite having time for only a brief rest at the watchtower, Toryn's company made swift progress up the Great Northwest Road. They had crossed the Great Elda in good time, and now approached the old bridge that spanned the River Wend. Toryn checked Hamar's map. The ruins of Greendell sat just a few leagues to the west. He spat as he recalled the acrid taste the burned village had left in his mouth. Many months had passed since he and Hamar had stumbled upon the grisly aftermath. Toryn hoped Jorim and the survivors from the mountain could one day rebuild their remote settlement.

'I see their camp.' Cubric pointed. 'I'd say there's at least fifty judging by the number of tents.'

Toryn glanced across the bridge. 'Good. If we can open the gates, the more we have to storm Drunsberg, the better.' His shoulders relaxed. He had spent the last week worrying whether the Archonians would be there to meet them. If they had been delayed, or worse, waylaid, their whole plan was in jeopardy. Toryn entered the *farsight* to survey the land to the north. They would cross into Dorn the next day and enter territory held by the enemy. If they were seen, it would be obvious the company marched on Drunsberg. Toryn hoped the Ruuk along the borders would also be occupied with their revelries and be too drunk to notice. But he also had to keep another eye over his shoulder. He was certain the warlock and his band of Norgog from the pass would not readily give up their pursuit.

Relieved to see no sign of enemy forces, Toryn turned his attention to the Kolossos range now a full league to their right. How many concealed tunnels surfaced along the route? The road offered few places to form a shield wall where they would not be surrounded. But the Norgog hammers would be the least of their worries if the warlock came after them. His stomach clenched. Surely, the warlock knew they were heading for the mines. The only other reason for them to be on the road would be Calerdorn. But one look at the small band of soldiers would make it obvious that was not their destination. Toryn's hand went to his sword. It seemed a confrontation with a warlock in the confined tunnels of Drunsberg was inevitable.

The Archonian captain greeted them on the north side of the bridge. 'Good afternoon, gentlemen.' He held out a hand to Toryn as he dismounted. 'The name's Captain Drondel, and I assume you're Toryn of Midwyche.' He looked passed him. 'And if I'm not mistaken, that's my old friend and skinny scoundrel, Cub, riding with you.'

'That's Captain Cub to you, mate.' Cubric strode over, hugged Drondel and laughed. 'Dronk! It must be… ten years at least now, eh.' He turned to Toryn. 'We trained together and served in the same company on the Nordruuk borders for years. Saved my life on more than one occasion.' Cubric patted the captain's shoulder. 'And on more than one occasion since, he's come to regret it.'

Drondel beamed. 'But at least I no longer live in dread of seeing your ugly mug again. You're here now, things can't possibly get any worse.' His smile faded. 'But… we've more important matters to discuss. We'll have to bore your new friends with tales of our exploits another day.' He led them to a derelict hut beside the road. 'However, we do have time for some food and drink before we head north. But there're a few things you need to know first.' Drondel called over to one of his men. 'See the others and their horses get some grub. We'll need a full stomach for the journey north.'

Toryn and Cubric followed the captain into the hut. He held out his hands. 'Welcome to my new quarters. Not the finest you'll see but at least we can get out of the cold.' They sat. Drondel folded his arms. 'We were beginning to fear you had not made it through the pass.'

Toryn pulled up a chair. 'We very nearly didn't. But before you appraise us of the situation here, you should know we may have a warlock and a band of Norgog on our tail.'

'Ah. Then you'll not want to hear what other surprises may be in stall on the way.' Drondel clasped his hands. 'But I suppose in such times we can't expect an easy ride.'

Toryn exchanged a glance with Cubric. 'So, what can we expect over the border? Are there many Ruuk?'

'Not just Ruuk, I'm afraid. I assume you're planning the attack at the end of their festivities.' He grimaced. 'Although they're not what we'd call a celebration. The more they drink, the more they fight among themselves. We'd have nothing to worry about if it went on for another week… there'd be none left. But Uldrak has taken control of the mines from his seat at Calerdorn. He was wise not to close the inns. That would cause a mutiny. But he did take the precaution of limiting their supply of ale.'

Toryn groaned. 'Ah, that would make our task a little harder.'

Drondel laughed. 'Don't you worry. Uldrak may have played into your hands. The Ruuk have an uncanny knack of brewing head-splitting booze from almost anything. They're likely to be in a worse shape than if Uldrak had done nothing. You wouldn't believe what they can… ah, yes, that's a tale for another day. But… apart from the mines, Uldrak has recruited more Nordleng than I've ever had the pleasure of seeing in one place. We reckon he's emptied the coffers at Calerdorn to pay them. But that's not all.' He wriggled his fingers. 'Spiders, lots of them hairy monsters. Not sure how he got them here, but these aralaks are big fellows. Bigger than those I'd seen behind the fences at the gorge.' His face paled. 'They must have found some unfortunate souls to feast on along the way.'

Toryn sighed. 'They'll have come through the tunnels. Perhaps they're feeding off the cobs. They can't make much of a meal, but there's plenty of them… as we found out.'

Cubric scoffed. 'Fodder. Both for our arrows and their spiders. Starting to feel sorry for the little chaps. All they want is not to be disturbed, yet they find themselves stuck in the middle of our war.'

Drondel sat back. 'Cobs are perhaps the only creatures we don't see around these parts. But back to business. I may have a plan to avoid the attention of those who want to cave in our skulls, enslave us… or eat us.'

Toryn leaned forward. 'I'm open to any suggestions, but time is vital. We must hit the mines in four days at the latest.'

Drondel rubbed his chin. 'Four days? It would be possible in peace time, but getting anywhere near Drunsberg in the current situation would be some challenge. But we may have another route. I have a scout, born and bred in this region. He's told me of an old trail. Well… when I say trail, I hear it's mostly overgrown. It was once used by local traders to avoid our patrols at the fences and on the roads. I guess they were keen to smuggle their goods when the Archon's restrictions were in place.'

Toryn smiled to himself, remembering Hamar's tale of sneaking ale into Midwyche. He brought out his map. 'And where can we find this trail?'

'No more than a league to the west.' The captain leaned over. 'But I doubt it's on any map. My scout tells me it can be reached…' he ran his finger along the road and tapped a spot near the Dorn border, 'yes, I'd say probably about here. The trail runs almost parallel to the highway, with the odd diversion. My scout has walked it a few times. It passes through hills, woodlands, and some pretty unpleasant ditches. There might be a few places we'll have to hack our way through… which will delay us. But easier than hacking our way through Norgog and aralaks, eh.'

Cubric grinned. 'Well would you believe it. Those restrictions imposed by the Archon, or that wretch inside his head, turn out to be a boon. If it was good enough to avoid our patrols, then perhaps it'll let us sneak beneath the noses of our enemy.'

Drondel pointed to an expanse of water on the map. 'It goes as far as Findale Lake. Then we can turn east and make a run for the mountains.'

Toryn examined the route. He pointed. 'The cob tunnel lies here. On my one and only visit, I recall seeing a rickety, old bridge that's out of sight of the mine. Does it still stand?'

Drondel nodded. 'As far as I know, it was still there a few weeks back. There's an old mountain pathway the miners used as a shortcut to visit the lake town at Findale. It's a few days trek, but anything must be an improvement on the taverns at Drunsberg. I reckon the Ruuk also use it, although I doubt their commanders are aware. The path is narrow, probably the work of cobs back in the day. Can't think it was easy for the miners returning if a little unsteady on their feet.' He glanced to the window. 'But… the trail and mountain path are no place for your horses. We'll have to do it on foot.'

Toryn agreed. 'Probably best we do. We'll have no use for the horses at the mines. Perhaps a couple of your guards could escort them back to the pass for our return journey. We can't risk leaving them so close to the border.'

Drondel looked back to the map. 'Well let's worry about getting there first, eh. But it does make sense to get the horses back to the watchtower.' His brow furrowed. 'They'll come in handy for other folk... if we won't be needing them again.

25. Her Father's Gift

The Nym! Elodi's scalped tingled. Had the warlock's presence stirred them? Nyomae had spoken of the Nym of the mountains, but unlike those of the trees, they had long abandoned the surface to take sanctuary in the foundations of the Kolossos. But Shokresh also sensed the spirits.

He threw back his cloak and drew an Angorsil from his belt. The aralak backed away and crouched beside the rock wall. Yet the horse stood unperturbed by his master's side. The Nym came no closer, but Shokresh remained wary, staring down into the abyss. Did he fear them? He held the shard aloft and bowed his head. It glimmered and then burned bright.

But Elodi was free! His attention was focused on the Nym. She sprang, hurtling into him, thinking fast to measure her force so he fell, while she did not. She struck what felt like solid rock, but it was enough. Shokresh teetered on the lip. He twisted towards Elodi, aghast by her action. His eyes widened; his cloak flapped as his arms spun. But he could not defy the pull of the land. Slowly, he tilted. The aralak sprang to aid her master, knocking Elodi onto her face. But the spider succeeded only to accelerate the warlock's fall. Both tumbled over the edge.

Elodi peered into the crevice. The spider had wisely secured a line before it had jumped. Its legs wrapped around the warlock, swinging on its thread. It released her front legs and grappled for a hold. Elodi rushed to the horse, snatched up her sword, then delivered a blow to the strand of web. Her Amayan blade easily sliced through, and the warlock and spider bounced off the sides as they fell. Elodi leaned over as far as she dared. The blazing

Angorsil lit up the ravine as they plunged. The aralak's legs frantically twitched as it sought to find a hold on the sheer sides. To Elodi's dismay, the pinprick of light stopped… then began to grow larger. Shokresh bellowed a curse as the spider clambered back towards her.

Elodi spun away. The stallion snorted but made no move against her as she held up her hand and approached. Had the warlock's hold over the creature also gone when it addressed the Nym? She had no time to deliberate. She spoke softly. 'Shush, steady, boy. I mean you no harm.' Her words sounded hollow to a beast of such size, but she edged forward, keen to get away as the warlock roared anew. To her relief, the horse lowered its head. Elodi reached out and rubbed his neck. It stood a good six hands taller than Sea Mist, but thankfully it remained a horse at heart.

Elodi leaped onto its broad back and stroked its thick neck. 'Good, boy.' She looked up. Behind, the tunnel continued its path along the side of the ravine. A short way ahead, it forked. The passage to the left followed the crevasse and dipped downward. The one to the right climbed steeply, then appeared to turn east. Elodi was reluctant to turn around and end up back in Aralak Gorge. Then surely up was better than down.

Below, the warlock raged, getting ever closer. That settled her mind. Up it would be. Elodi turned the horse and raised her sword. To her relief, it responded and glowed. She urged the giant stallion to follow the light, and thankfully he obliged. With long, sure strides he gained speed, quickly reaching a full gallop, appearing just as keen as Elodi to put distance between the warlock and his hideous companion. She cried out in victory, certain their speed would outrun an exhausted aralak and bruised warlock.

Elodi laughed as they sped along the tunnel. Shokresh had mocked her for being half-Amayan, claiming her father's blood diluted her powers. But it was not her Amayan side that enabled her escape. Wendel had said her father could talk a bird down from her nest in a storm. Elodi had convinced a warlock she was considering his offer. All it took was a little flattery to distract him. Ha! She laughed again. How his pride must be wounded. A spider had to save him, then haul him up from the depths of the mountains like a lump of meat.

Elodi glanced over her shoulder. She had to remain level-headed. She was not out of danger yet. But perhaps the Nym would slow the warlock's pursuit. They had come, but had they risen from their long isolation to save her? Or would they look upon a warlock and an Amayan with equal distain.

The horse continued tirelessly as the passageway continued to climb. Elodi's euphoria passed and now had time to think. She had fallen too easily into the trap set by the warlock. Had he intended purely to destroy the Amanach, he could have entered the forest without detection. Now it was obvious, the murder of Lord Kernlow, and the ensuing sacking of the villages on route to the forest, were intended to tempt Elodi out of Borrund. And she had fallen for it. She hoped Lindell and his company had not died from her rash decision. But why had Shokresh not killed her? She was at his mercy. But he chose to take her north. But even then, he had not harmed her, aside from the poisoning. The Ul-dalak wanted her alive... and mostly unhurt. Uleva had spared her life on the Dorn Plain but had tortured and killed one of her archers. Why had Uleva not abducted her then? It was obvious the enemy had a plan for her... and she had played along. Elodi clenched the reins. She would not allow them to take her again. Whatever purpose demanded she be alive and unhurt was not going to be pleasant. And now her head had cleared, she did not believe Shokresh wanted her as his queen. Surely, Uluriel would not tolerate an Amayan among her commanders.

A sliver of light caught her attention. A clash of swords rang out. Her hand went to her own at her side once more. A fight meant friends and foes awaited. She kicked on, hoping she had not come all this way to find herself on the defeated side.

26. The Reluctant Host

Nyomae had been fortunate to find an old, derelict building to spend the day. It sat within a league of Elmarand's city wall in what may have once been a vineyard. On entering, she was reminded of the old farmhouse in Darrow where she and Toryn had encountered the shroul. It was also the moment her memory had begun to return. She recalled Toryn's face when she had remembered his name, and then his elation when she had spoken of Finromir. But that seemed a long time ago, even for a woman who had lived many centuries.

Nyomae rose in the dying light of early evening to take a closer look at the wall. And in the still air, she found its presence offended her. Protruding from the sandy plain like a bone through flesh, it violated everything that Elmarand had once represented. The city had offered hope, learning, and shelter to all who came, but now it appeared none were welcome.

Nyomae stared aghast at the scar across the landscape. Had another race raided the shores to exploit the realm in its decline? She had to know more. She sat beside the crumbling wall and sought the Verses of its origin. Construction had begun shortly after the defeat at Gormadon and had taken two decades to complete. At the time, Elmarand's leaders still allowed free entry to all who wished to benefit from their protection. Many of the old roads passed through numerous gates. But as Nyomae withdrew back to the present Verse, she witnessed all save the main gateway disappear. And now she must find her way through the single, heavily guarded entrance.

Nyomae returned inside and found Orlo had finished his rations. She spoke as she gathered their belongings. 'This is the last part, my friend. I hope to find a good stable for you to rest.' She glanced out of the window. 'I fear our return journey may be a little more… frantic.' But if he understood, he did not appear concerned.

She led Orlo outside and mounted. If any eyes from the wall saw them, they raised no alarm. But she could see no windows or watchtowers along the wall. Either the defenders did not set a watch, or they had other means to oversee their perimeter.

Under the cover of darkness, Nyomae rode west towards the main gate. To her left, the wall loomed, and at times, she was convinced it curved over as if ready to entrap them. Nyomae stopped allowing Orlo time to drink. She whispered. 'Wait here, boy. I'm going to take a closer look.' She had thought the wall was no more than twenty paces, but it turned out to be thrice the distance. Nyomae stared up at the stonework. Despite the decline of Talamaris, the masons had built a magnificent structure, worthy of their ancestors. She could see no joints, or even blemishes. Its smooth surface shone in the moonlight, reflecting a faint glow that sketched her silhouette on the sand. Nyomae reached out and placed her hand on the cool stone. She had expected it to feel wrong, but now she felt nothing as if it had no history.

Nyomae returned to her horse with more questions from her inspection. She climbed back into the saddle and clicked her tongue. Orlo set off at a brisk pace, kicking up the softer sand of a shallow ridge. They reached the top to see the flickering light of torches on the road a league ahead. Nyomae turned and rode north as the sun rose to her right, then joined the road once beyond the line of torches. She dismounted and let her *farsight* take her to the gate. The low archway looked insignificant compared to the wall. The gates were closed, but a doorway sat open at its base. Just two sentries stood guard, but she guessed many more were stationed inside.

They walked a little farther along the road up to the first of the torches. Nyomae entered the gate's Verse — it could not have worked out better. Just after dawn on the previous day, their commanding officer had returned from an inspection of an outpost. She grinned to herself waiting for the right moment, noting the mischievous child inside still enjoyed the deception.

When the time came, she confidently rode up to the gate. The guards were shocked to see their commander approach, but asked no questions and allowed her entry. Once inside, Nyomae saw Elmarand for the first time in over three hundred years. While it stood some distance away, the sight of its many white towers rising to greet the first light of dawn, kindled hope in her heart. All soared higher than any in the northern realms bar Telamir and Syris. And like Archonholm, one rose hundreds of feet above the others: the Sun Tower. Unlike the rest of the city, the tower was built from rock quarried from the Caerwal range, believed to retain the power of the gods. A small room sat at the pinnacle of the slim, spiraling tower, and had later become known as the Seat of Draegelan. Here he would survey the land for many leagues while pondering the issues of the day. Following his death, none but the Archon of the south was granted entry. Thus, Nyomae had never set foot inside, hearing only rumors of what lay behind the small, wooden door at the top of the long, winding staircase.

The rising sun found the tops of the many lesser towers. Inside the old walls, Elmarand stretched five leagues from north to south, and east to west. Nyomae had almost forgotten the scale of the vast city; Archonholm could easily be lost within even its smallest district. She turned back to the new defenses to determine the outer wall's length. She repeated her calculation, disbelieving her first answer. But she came to the same conclusion: the wall spanned at least twenty-five leagues. Had they destroyed an entire mountain to build it?

Nyomae stopped as she heard water. It had been just six days since she had come south, but it seemed weeks since she had heard life-giving water flowing in abundance. She dismounted and led Orlo to the waterway. The canal was full to the brim. He drank while Nyomae replenished her flasks. But why did the region to the north go without, when there appeared to be plenty here? She stood as the sun rose over the wall to bring daylight to the land behind. Nyomae gaped at the fields of wheat and barley, swaying in the breeze as if the gods stroked the back of a large beast. It was as if she had returned to the realm she knew. But why only here? Why did the once thriving region to the north now suffer? Nyomae had a new dilemma. If all seemed ordered, did she have to enter Elmarand in secret? Had Kirol been misled? Surely, he had no knowledge of the giant wall, otherwise he would have told her.

Nyomae jumped as a horn blew in the distance. But its harsh blare did not welcome the new day. It did not gently wake the farmers, blacksmiths, cooks, and builders to call them to their business — it demanded they report for duty. Nyomae had no choice. She would have to use precious energy to enter the Verses and discover what lay behind the apparent order.

Kirol was right, and it was Nyomae who had been misled. The rising sun may have shed more light on what looked like the land she had known, but its recent past revealed the truth concealed by the veneer of order.

The horns woke slaves from their uneasy slumber. She shuddered. Slaves! What had become of Talamaris, the once beautiful and prosperous realm? These plains had teemed with prosperous folk, happy to trade with each other, free to come and go as they pleased. Yet now, thousands lived in what could only be described as hovels, working long, back-breaking hours for little reward other than water, just enough food to keep them working, and cramped accommodation.

Nyomae rode on, appalled at the plight of the poor folk who barely raised their heads as she rode by. She resisted the urge to speak with the workers, fearful it would attract the attention of the few guards that watched over them. Nyomae passed hundreds of slaves with hunched shoulders as they trudged towards another punishing day of toil in fields and smithies. But as much as she felt their pain, she could do nothing for them at present. Her priority was to consult with Idraman and hurry back north. Nyomae did not make promises lightly. She had made one to Kirol and pledged she would honor it, no matter how long it would take to fulfil.

She looked up to the city. The glistening, white towers that had briefly raised her spirits, now appeared to boast of its dominance over those in its thrall. She winced at its show of wealth while thousands strived in its shadow. Nyomae made up her mind. She chose to enter Elmarand under a cloak of concealment.

The towers loomed ever higher as she drew near. Ramshackle huts huddled together, close to the base of the old wall, seeming grateful for the shelter from the blistering sun for at least some part of the day. Nyomae delayed for as long as she dared before she entered the Song to obscure herself in the previous day's Verse. But she took a risk. If any of her kind other than Idraman were in Elmarand, they would likely sense her entry. The city gates shimmered through her cloaked Verse. She searched for signs of a powerful presence. To her relief, she found only one solid outline among the wavy lines of the Verse inside the walls: it had to be Idraman. And as she had expected, he was held deep beneath the citadel at its center.

Nyomae resorted to the guise of the commander and entered Elmarand unchallenged. The streets were quiet compared to better times, and she quickly found a stable. But this time she took no delight in tricking the hard-working stable hands that Orlo was the horse of a revered warrior. They had avoided eye contact as they rushed to find a suitable stall for such a fine animal. After assuring them she was satisfied, she returned to the main street that led to the citadel. As she walked, Nyomae recalled her first time in the city as she prepared to be initiated into the Order. Draegelan yet lived, and the legacy of the victory over Ormoroth had begun to bear fruit. The city had teemed with new scholars and students, but now the few people hurrying through the streets, were either guards or city officials; Nyomae wondered if any of the centers of learning remained open.

Lost in her thoughts, she was suddenly surprised to find she stood at the Citadel's steps. Part of her wished she could turn on her heels, take Orlo, and ride out, never to return. But far to the north, she knew Elodi and Toryn faced their trials — she could not abandon hers. Reluctantly, Nyomae took a deep breath and began the steep climb. The steps were designed to challenge those wishing to view the citadel's grandeur, and in the mid-morning heat, they achieved their purpose.

By the time Nyomae reached the top, sweat trickled down her back. But the reward was worth the effort. Inside, the cool air and fountains of clear water, quickly eased her discomfort. She looked up to the high ceiling and ornate stone carvings that made those of Archonholm seem crude in comparison. But while the hall looked as she remembered it, its character had changed. Gone were the throngs of people engaged in conversation, sharing their knowledge, and enjoying each other's company. The few that stood beside the great pillars, spoke in hushed voices, constantly glancing over their shoulders obviously wary of being overheard.

Nyomae stopped beneath an arch and entered the Song. The stairs she sought were at the rear of the citadel, and two guarded doors stood between her and Idraman's cell. But the warrior whose semblance she had borrowed had not visited the dungeons. She needed to find another suitable candidate to gain entry. The previous day, a bent, old man wearing fine clothes and a laurel of gilded leaves, had approached the doorway. From the reaction of the guards, it was apparent he held high office in Elmarand. They had bowed low, keeping their eyes to the floor as if to look upon his face was forbidden.

Nyomae ventured a little farther into the old man's Verse. His name was Ingollo, and now the action of the guards was understandable. He was the Varsil of Talamaris, a dictator wielding absolute power. The Varsil was infallible. His word could never be challenged. And any who showed even the slightest disrespect would soon find themselves in a cell... or at the end of a rope.

In Nyomae's time, the realm was ruled by the Council of Seven. The arrangement had served well for centuries, yet now six wise minds had been lost, replaced by just one of questionable judgement. Ingollo had been Varsil for almost one hundred years. Nyomae went deeper into the man's Verse. Ingollo had succeeded another dictator, a woman, who had seized control of Elmarand, shortly after the Battle of Gormadon. Her name was known to Nyomae: Demelia. But a sense of dread pervaded. The air shimmered about the woman. Something was wrong. Demelia had been a member of the Council when Nyomae had gone north to search for Sylvena. But in the Verses following the closing of the Caerwal Gate, Nyomae witnessed a change. Her suspicions were proven correct.

Uluriel had possessed Demelia.

While the Archon slept in Archonholm, Uluriel's *kruul* had come south to sow seeds of corruption in the south. And events unfolded as she had seen in Kirol's Verse. Through Demelia, Uluriel had spread tales of Idraman's treachery. Then, one by one, Demelia had disposed of the Council, accusing them of scheming with Idraman to bring down the south. Predictably, Uluriel's lies were readily believed by the frightened people of Elmarand. Thus, Idraman was imprisoned, allowing Uluriel to impose her will unchallenged.

Yet many had refused to believe Idraman was a traitor. Debate had turned into heated arguments. The argument had descended into violence, and soon the conflict divided the whole of the south. The civil war had led to the collapse of the systems that fed and watered the settlements across the arid plains. Crops had failed and many died in the resulting famine. What little grain and cattle remained, became a source of power.

Those remaining loyal to the old ways had fled south to Armanoor. Yet even the vast fertile plains of the First Realm had struggled to feed the tens of thousands seeking sanctuary. But Uluriel's lie had also crossed the border, and like a highly infectious disease, it rapidly spread throughout Armanoor. And once satisfied her plans had borne rotten fruit, Uluriel returned to Mordram and began her scheming in the north.

Dismayed, Nyomae retreated to Ingollo's Verse. Uluriel had done much to bring about the end of the realms, and now Ingollo, indoctrinated in Demelia's ways, continued to implement Uluriel's will. Somehow, Nyomae had to find a way to rid the south of the rot. But first she had to speak with Idraman. But would a man who had spent three centuries isolated in a cell be in control of his mind?

Nyomae assumed the guise of Ingollo and walked towards the guards. They backed away and lowered their gaze as she approached. Without a word, they opened the door. Inside, she found a second guard posted a little way down the corridor, but like the first, he presented no obstacle. Nyomae descended a spiral staircase and finally came upon a small cell. The last guard situated himself behind the door as he had pulled it open, then carefully closed it behind.

Nyomae's heart thundered in her ears as she peered into the gloom. But she could see nothing in the little light coming through the small grate in the door. She dropped Ingollo's likeness... and gagged on the stench. Idraman was afforded no luxuries, not even the basics. Her eyes grew accustomed to the dim light. Then she saw him. Nyomae clasped her hand to her mouth, desperately trying to stifle her sobs to prevent alerting the guard outside.

Idraman's naked and painfully thin frame slumped against the back wall. Choking back her dismay, she kneeled at his side. Nyomae whispered. 'Idraman?'

The prisoner raised his head. 'Nyomae?' He squinted. 'Is it truly you?'

Tears filled her eyes. 'You remember me?'

'Of course.' His voice deepened. 'And you've come all this way from the north?'

Nyomae reached forward and placed her hand on his shoulder. She recoiled. It was not Idraman.

The prisoner sneered. 'Ah. I was wrong to think I could fool the great Imaari for long.' His wrinkled hand waved over the cell floor. The rubble cleared as a smooth, marble slab slid silently aside. Nyomae clutched her stomach as the familiar green glow of an Angorsil pervaded the cell. Yet... it was not the shard alone that filled Nyomae with dread. The prisoner's black eyes glistened: a *kruul* within stared back. He grinned as the door burst open and three Nordleng rushed in. Her head was pulled back, her mouth gagged, and her hands chained behind her back.

The bony fingers of the *kruul's* host pointed to the floor. The Nordleng forced her face down into the grime of the dungeon. 'Welcome back to Elmarand, *Nyomae.*' His grating laugh pained her ears. 'I trust you like the changes we have made.' Rough hands yanked her back and onto her knees to face him. Skin cracked as the *kruul* forced the old man's lip to grin. 'You will not recognize me with this face. But you will know my name.' It paused and raised the gray, bushy eyebrows of his host. 'I am Mosholuk.' Nyomae groaned. The *kruul* cackled. 'Ah. I see you remember.' The host shuddered. 'But I must leave before this bag of bones fails.' The prisoner's arm lifted as if a puppet to point at Nyomae. 'But please don't be disappointed. We shall meet again, my friend. Very soon.'

The host's eye lids shriveled and dropped from his face to reveal the horror of the warlock glowering within. His body shuddered, then sagged as he died. Freed from the mortal bounds of the flesh, the shadow of the *kruul* hovered briefly over Nyomae, taking pleasure in her humiliation before it departed. The Nordleng twisted Nyomae towards the door as another entered; the man whose guise she had borrowed. But the Angorsil's power overwhelmed her, and she sagged to the floor before Ingollo could speak.

27. The Unbreakable Bond

The warlock's horse thundered out from beneath the Kolossos. Elodi recoiled from the blinding light after days in darkness. It was a rising sun; she had emerged on the east side of the mountains. A short way ahead, dozens fought in what appeared to be a one-sided battle as ten Archonians fought a large band of Ruuk. Elodi drew her sword and entered the fray. The Ruuk turned, stunned by the sudden appearance of an Amayan hurtling towards them on the back of a warlock's horse.

Elodi cried out a challenge as they wisely chose to turn and flee. She slowed her mount as the guards, also baffled by the great beast, had formed a shield wall. Elodi called out. 'Fear not. I am Lady Harlyn.' She patted the horse's neck. 'Do not be fooled by this fellow.' With obvious relief, they raised their weapons and cheered.

The captain lowered his shield and stepped forward. 'You're a most welcome sight, my lady.' He frowned. 'But we had thought you lost. Word of your fall has spread quickly. And a bitter blow to morale if ever there was.' He bowed his head. 'But forgive us, ma'am. We did not recognize you. We've heard the tales of your red hair blazing as a flame as you rode into battle. And… well, I imagine you've been in the thick of it of late, ma'am.'

Elodi dismounted. Her hand went to the lank strands clinging to her head. 'That I have, Captain. Then I give thanks your mounted archers were occupied by the Ruuk.'

The captain clasped her hand. 'The name's Bryok, ma'am. And may I say it is an honor to meet you… at such a crucial time.' He glanced behind her. 'But how did you come to be this far north?'

'That is a long story, which I shall tell when we have time, but first,' she noticed a river a little way down the slope, 'can you tell me exactly how far north I am?'

Bryok followed her gaze. 'You look upon the Kel in its youth, ma'am.'

'The Kel? Then I am deep into Lunn.' She looked to the captain's face. 'Bryok? I know that name. And you have the look of—' her hand went to her mouth. 'Would you be one of Tombold's sons? Once in the Castellan's service at Archonholm?'

He grinned. 'That I am, ma'am! His youngest. He spoke most highly… and often of you. He'd be thrilled to hear you remember him.'

Elodi beamed. 'Well, of course I do. He's a fine man. And how is Tombold? I heard he was *retired* by the Castellan.'

'Ah yes, an unfortunate end to his long service. But he's happy now he's back at the vineyard.' Bryok laughed. 'He sees it as his duty to supply as much wine as he can for those defending the realms.'

'That is good to hear.' Elodi sighed. 'But I'm afraid it was my fault the Castellan saw fit to remove him from Archonholm.'

'My father would not hold you responsible, ma'am. He could not have lived with the guilt had he not spoken of your father's last days.' He smiled. 'But I hear we no longer need worry about the Castellan. I can't say I was sorry to hear of his death, but not the manner of his end.'

'Captain?' A guard approached. 'We must be making tracks if we're to reach Torm by nightfall.'

Bryok nodded. 'That we will.' He turned to Elodi. 'Would you grant us the honor of your company, ma'am?'

She traced the line of the Kel making its way across the plain. 'Yes. I will accept your kind invitation.'

'We're to help bolster the defenses of the south bank.

We were on our way when we spied a band of Ruuk and pursued them up this valley.' His face reddened. 'But we walked into a trap. Had it not been for you… well, I can't say what would have happened. I admit I have yet to adjust to my new duty.'

'I wouldn't be too hard on yourself, Captain. I have walked into enough traps in my time.' She turned to the warlock's horse. It snorted, backing away from those he would have viewed as a threat not long ago. Elodi walked up to him. She stroked his nose and whispered. 'You wish to be free. I will not hold sway over you. You deserve your freedom.' She unbuckled the warlock's ornate saddle and ran her hand along his broad and powerful flank. 'Then go, my beauty. Perhaps you will find others of your breed, but I know not where.' The beast's large black eyes held Elodi's. In that moment, she felt its relief of being free of the warlock. It turned. The path shuddered as he galloped, free to determine its own fate. Elodi watched it head north, hoping it would find peace after a long life of servitude to a most demanding master.

Bryok joined her. 'That was some animal. You were not tempted to keep it?'

'It would have been cruel. He may have been bred by our enemy, but regardless of his origins, perhaps the Maidens' gift of life still burns within. Like us, he doesn't deserve a life of thraldom.' She turned. 'Now. Appraise me of recent events as we make our way to Torm.' She glanced at the guards. 'On foot.'

Bryok had been drafted into the Archonian Guard following the disaster at the Caerwal Gate. He had served as a knight, but with the loss of so many horses, he had volunteered to transfer. Bryok had fought at Roth's Doom in the front ranks and had met the Norgog onslaught full on. But sadly, his older brother, Edwald, had died in the battle. Bryok spoke of many skirmishes fought along the banks of the Kel, but as yet, they were little more than raids, most likely to harass the defenders and steal livestock.

Late afternoon, Bryok brought the company to a halt to rest their legs and prepare a light meal. Elodi strolled up to a nearby ridge and looked down onto the plain. She would accompany the guards to Torm, and then find a way to Keld. If Bardon's plan to reclaim his city was underway, he would be marching north, ready to attack in three days' time. Perhaps, she could meet his force along the way. But she had no horse, and she doubted any could be spared in Torm. She thought of Sea Mist. He must yet live. Amayans had a strong bond with their horses and could summon them at will. But following Shokresh's spiteful act, Elodi could no longer sense her sisters. If Sea Mist lived, would he hear her call?

Elodi let her eyes wander across the grassy plains and let the *farsight* come. The trees of the forests swaying in the afternoon breeze, came into view, but all else appeared blurred. She imagined Sea Mist racing across the grasslands with his billowing mane. Elodi spoke his name. She felt his warm breath on her face. He lived! Of that, she was certain. She whispered. 'Come to me, Misty. I need you now, more than ever, my friend.' Her spine tingled. Had he heard?

'Ma'am?' Bryok strode up the hill. He nodded to the sun. 'It will be below the mountains in an hour, and we've still five leagues to cover. So… if you're in agreement, ma'am, I suggest we make a move.'

Elodi reluctantly turned her back on the grasslands. 'You're in charge here, Captain. No need to ask for my agreement.'

'But… ma'am, you command the armies of the Five Realms, I wouldn't be so bold to—'

'Lead on. I shall follow.' She sighed. 'And if I'm honest, Bryok, I welcome taking orders for a change. All too soon I shall be dishing them out again… and watching others suffer from the consequences.'

Bryok smiled. 'Ah, I appreciate your predicament, ma'am, and I only have a dozen under my command.'

Elodi followed him back to the road and found the company ready to depart. She noted both young and old among them, and was reminded of the two guards she had spoken with outside Vymarl. She let out a long sigh. 'Perhaps one day, we'll no longer have to give orders that lead to the loss of life. But I fear that day lies far ahead of us.'

The town of Torm had yet to recover from the recent troubles. Following Nordryn's treachery, it had become the front line of Broon's loyal forces. And if it had not suffered enough, the mass army marching to Roth's Doom had all but razed its wooden buildings that had stood for centuries. A few, hardy townsfolk had returned to start anew, but the majority of its current occupants were Archonians and reserves. The town held a strategic position between the banks of the Kel and the main road. But Elodi suspected the guards held onto it by their fingernails. Little of the old stockade remained; one determined attack by even a moderate force could easily take it.

The spirits of its defenders had risen when Lady Harlyn had strolled in with Bryok. Many gathered around to greet her. Elodi tried to find the words to encourage them, few came to mind, but few were needed: just her presence was enough. Yet, their elation served to place the weight of responsibility back onto her shoulders. As dusk fell, her spine tingled, spreading up to her scalp.

And Elodi understood.

She ran through the burned-out shells lining the main street, then out of the remains of the gate. Above, a few stars twinkled as the clouds parted to reveal the waxing moon. In the silence, Elodi heard water, yet no stream was nearby. Her body warmed as if gentle hands held her. And in a way, they did. A tear ran down her cheek as she felt Eryn, and her sisters reach out to her. Shokresh could not break the bond! And now she had escaped his grip, it had recovered. Elodi sensed the joy of the warriors as they found her: she was no longer alone.

Elodi opened her eyes and breathed in the cool, fresh air. Beyond the road, something moved across the grasslands, shimmering in the moonlight. More tears flowed as a familiar whinny echoed across the plain.

She strode out to greet Sea Mist. He tossed his mane and kicked out his legs. His hooves clattered on the flagstones as they met in the middle. Sea Mist lowered his head and rubbed against her. Elodi clung onto his neck and whispered in his ear. 'I knew you'd come. I've missed you, boy. Never. Never again shall we be parted. I'm not whole without you.' She drew him close and felt his hot breath down her back. 'I promise you, Misty. One day we'll be free of this shadow. We'll ride again across the Dorn Plain under a starry sky without a worry in the world. You and I, alone. Just like the old days, eh.'

Elodi stood back and looked him in the eye. 'But alas, that is not today. We have other matters to face. But together. Nothing will come between us again. And together, our enemies will cower before us. And—' Sea Mist's head bobbed. 'Ah yes. Of course, you're hungry and have come a long way.' Elodi laughed. 'Let's get you something to eat. I'm afraid we cannot rest for long, but at least we'll be back on the open road again.'

Elodi led him into Torm. Sea Mist drew many an admiring glance from the guards who had served as knights, appreciating a fine stallion when they saw one. She found him a place alongside the few horses in the town, and he gladly ate and drank with them.

Bryok came to see what the commotion was about. 'I've heard many stories of fearless Sea Mist.' He ran his hand along the horse's neck. 'A fine beast fitting of an Amayan and lady of the realm.' His voice softened. 'I'm ashamed to say I failed to see you both confront the Reapers. When you rode out, I was flat on my face, unable to bear the gaze of those dreadful creatures.'

Elodi placed her hand on his shoulder. 'You need not be ashamed, Bryok. Those beings were not meant for mortal lands. Every fiber of my body urged me to retreat, but thankfully Misty knew his duty.' She stroked his mane. 'Had he bolted, I doubt I would have had the strength to turn him back.'

'All the same, ma'am, together you challenged those dark creatures while many recoiled. But every soul at your back took courage from that remarkable act of bravery.' Bryok looked back to the campfires. 'And still, that deed alone stiffens our resolve against our dark foes.'

Elodi looked up to the clear sky. 'And for that I am most grateful. We fight against the odds, but I hope to strike back and turn the tide before the dead of winter.' She rubbed down Sea Mist. 'But that means I must ride east this night.'

'To Keld, ma'am? We've heard rumors the true Lord Broon seeks to take back his seat.'

She nodded. 'Once we drive out Nordryn, we seek to push on through Lunn and up to the Lind River.'

Bryok stood a little taller. 'That is good to hear, ma'am. We will remain ready to assist. Many of my guards hail from Dunmor and are keen to reclaim their homes, well… what's left of them.'

'Word shall be sent when Keld is back in our hands.

The quicker we can drive the Ruuk over the border, the sooner we'll have the foundation to reclaim Harlyn and Calerdorn.'

Bryok nodded. 'That would be the greatest prize of all, ma'am. While I have never set eyes upon your fine city, I feel as if I know the place well from the stories of its long history.'

Elodi sprang onto Sea Mist's back. 'That is my intention. Please, pass on my praise to your forces. If time permitted, I would have liked to address them myself. But much has happened since my… kidnapping. I must get back to where I'm needed.'

'Then ride true, ma'am. And I shall pass word along the line that Lady Harlyn is back in command.'

Sea Mist neighed his own farewell as he shot through the gates. Bryok called after them. 'Our enemy will not sleep easy on hearing of your return!'

28. OF FLIES & HORNRASPS

Drondel's scout soon located the trail. But while it may have gone undiscovered by Uldrak's forces, every winged creature in the region appeared to know of its existence. Flies, midges, moths and, to Toryn's dread, hornrasps, thrived in the damp, overgrown ditches. Progress was slow as they trudged through bogs, across streams, squeezed through rocky outcrops, thistles, and brambles. And the nights were worse. Toryn dared not light even a candle in case it alerted the watchful eyes of the enemy… and more insects of their presence. They ate cold meals with one hand, while fighting off flies with the other. But the hornrasps were not to be denied so easily, and several had suffered from their nasty stings, including Lorek.

On the second morning since taking the trail, Toryn was rudely awoken by a large insect taking a bite out of his arm. He cuffed the winged beast, leaving a dark smear on his skin. Cubric looked up. 'Beginning to wish we'd taken our chances on the road, eh? At least the Ruuk are big enough to hit with a sword.' His nose wrinkled. 'Although that thing on your arm would've taken a couple of blows to finish off.' He took Toryn's arm. 'Swelling up nicely. That's going to leave a scar.'

Toryn grimaced at the ensuing rash. 'And yet another to add to my collection.'

Cubric slapped his hand back. 'Remember what your mother used to say? It'll only get worse if you itch it.'

Toryn's arm prickled. 'Is there any truth to that? Anyway… my mother isn't here.' He scratched and grinned at Cubric. 'You're not going to deny me the only pleasure to be had in this place.' He looked down to the *Elorsil*. His skin and clothes were caked in mud, but the scabbard was as clean as the day Elodi had given it to him.

Cubric noticed it glisten. 'How cruel. You have what's likely the most powerful weapon in the realms… yet you can't use it against these ruddy creepy-crawlies and bugs.'

Toryn ducked as another large insect buzzed passed his ear. He clutched the sword. 'Even if it means alerting the warlocks, I'm almost willing to take that risk.'

Drondel waded through the murky water towards them. He kneeled beside Toryn. His eyebrows raised as he noticed the squashed remains of Toryn's predator. The captain laughed. 'Ha! Biggest one yet. Could almost make a meal out of that one.'

Toryn itched. 'Well, I would have been its breakfast had I not squashed it.'

Drondel pulled out his map. 'We won't have to suffer too much longer. I reckon we'll make the lake by midday. My scout tells me the trail widens a little farther ahead.' He slapped his neck. 'Then we'll be free of these flesh-eating pests.' Drondel held out his hand to Toryn. 'Would you look at that. Almost as big as your fellow.' He wiped his hand on his trousers. 'And I imagine the air will be a bit fresher, but it also means we could be spotted once in the open.'

Toryn stood and wrung the water from his jacket. 'That's a risk I'm ready to take. I only hope we don't lose any to a fever.' He glanced along the ditch. 'We number few enough already.'

Drondel nodded to the company as they woke. 'They're a tough bunch. If they can make it through this, they can make it through anything.' He scratched at the reddening skin on his neck. 'The smugglers must have made a small fortune to warrant trudging up and down this trail. Can't say I'd be willing to do it for anything less than my weight in gold.'

Cubric chewed on a chunk of dry bread. He chuckled. 'Can't think they'd have weighed much after all these creatures had fed off them.'

'Captain!' Lorek stumbled along the ditch, splashing water into their faces. 'Spiders! Three of them. Just a little way ahead. They've spun a web between a clump of trees growing over the bank. Janae is seeing if there's a way around them.'

Toryn groaned. He had hoped never to see another aralak after the ordeal at Omstrad and the nest. 'Have they seen us?'

'I don't think so. They're not moving. Just sitting on a web that's blocking the way.'

Drondel sighed. 'They'll grow big and fat on the food to be had in this place.' He stood. 'Perhaps we could make a net out of their webs.'

Toryn recalled their pincers. 'I'm afraid these beasts prefer our flesh.'

Janae returned; Toryn noticed she made no splashes or sound. She shook her head. 'There's no way around unless we climb out. But it won't be easy getting up these muddy banks. And if we do make it out, it's a long diversion to escape their attention… and there may be others.' Janae looked back over her shoulder. 'But although they're big, they look a little ragged. Perhaps they're wounded and avoid their own kind. They've been known to eat their injured.'

Toryn eyed the bank once more. 'We might be in luck. If they've resorted to eating insects, perhaps they're too weak to tackle the likes of us.'

Lorek gripped his sword. 'What about this song of yours, Toryn. Could you trick them?'

'I'm reluctant to enter it here.' Toryn lifted the *Elorsil.* 'It's the same as using this. I'd soon give away our position to the warlocks.'

Cubric scratched his chin. 'Archers? You're handy with a bow, Toryn.'

'I doubt arrows would penetrate their thick webs. We're going to have to do this the old way. Stealth and brute strength.' He turned to Drondel. 'How many spears do you have at hand?'

'A dozen. Stout chaps. Could give Broon's spearman a good contest.'

Toryn stretched his aching back. 'Then that's our best chance. But they'll have to take them down quickly, and all three at the same time. We can't risk their squeals attracting others in the region.' He looked up and down the ditch. 'This isn't the best place to defend against even a few hungry spiders.'

The company set themselves for the attack. The spears took the front, with Toryn and his best swords behind, ready to pounce and finish the job. They moved as quietly as they could through the squelchy mud. Janae held up her hand and stopped at a rock jutting out from the bank. She pointed to indicate the spiders were around the bend. The guards gripped their spears, now oblivious to the midges crawling over them.

They rounded the bend. Toryn's hand went to his sword. Three fat spiders sat inside their webs, strewn with large insects, many still struggling to escape. One of the spiders twitched, but seemed unaware of their approach. Toryn peered through the thick strands surrounding them. He shuddered as he looked straight into the eyes of the first spider. But it didn't move. Its eyes looked gray and cloudy, compared to the dark, glistening orbs that had glared at him at Omstrad. They appeared old and weak, thus hopefully presenting an easy kill.

He signaled to Drondel to get his guards in position. None were to strike until all three could be impaled. No one breathed as the spears arranged themselves beneath the flabby abdomens of the unsuspecting spiders. Drondel thrust up his thumb. Toryn winced as their sharp tips plunged deep into their soft underbellies. The spiders jerked and twisted, then sagged on the thick strands, oozing their dark blood into the mud below.

Toryn frowned. 'Something's not right. Their legs didn't twitch.'

Drondel wiped his tunic. 'But they were alive. I saw their eyes move. But I did expect them to put up more of a struggle.'

Toryn grabbed an old branch and pulled himself up. The skin on the dead spiders looked flaky and lacked the spiky hairs he had seen on others. He called down. 'These were already half-dead. They're stuck just like the flies. But if this isn't their web, it must...' The horrible truth dawned on him. Toryn cried out. 'It's a trap. Prepare for—'

The ditch darkened. The branches overhead creaked. A huge aralak scurried out of a tree and sprang. The spider landed with its hind legs on the sides of the ditch. Its forelegs shot out and snatched Elrik. Clutching him to its belly, it turned, then scampered along the bank. Cubric yelled. 'Toryn. Your sword! Blast it.'

Toryn gaped. 'I... can't. The warlocks!'

Drondel called out. 'Archers! Take it down! By the Three, take it down.' The archers let loose a volley. Most bounced off its hard shell, but two found a soft target.

Toryn drew his sword and scrambled after his friend as a second volley streaked over his head. Another arrow hit as Elrik struck a blow with his fist on the spider's skull. Stunned, the creature slipped on the soggy slope, then slid into the ditch. Toryn launched himself from the bank, raised his sword over his head, then sliced into its flaying legs from above. He landed opposite and skidded to a halt. The spider flung Elrik aside to face Toryn. It rose on its hind legs and spat. But Toryn was ready. He dropped on his back, slid beneath the beast, then thrust his blade into its soft belly. The aralak screeched. Its eyes stayed fixed on Toryn as it backed away, leaving a dark trail in the dank water. It stopped, tucked its legs under its belly, twitched and died.

Toryn climbed to his feet to see Elrik face down in the water. He grabbed his shoulders and turned him over. Elrik retched. A rip in his tunic revealed a gaping wound in his stomach. Toryn gawped at the dark fluid oozing from the torn flesh. Elrik stammered. 'I'm… cold, so… cold. It got me, Tor, it got me.'

Toryn pulled him close. 'I'm sorry… I couldn't stop it. I dared not use my sword.'

'I know. No need to…' Elrik coughed up blood.

'Hang on, my friend We'll get you sorted.' But Elrik's eyes closed as he slumped in Toryn's arms. He called back. 'Blankets. He needs to stay warm.'

Lorek brought his and wrapped it around Elrik. 'Will he… survive?'

Toryn kept his eyes on his old friend. 'Yes, if it was just the spider's poison. That keeps them alive until eaten. But… I think it clawed him once it knew it was defeated.'

Drondel slid down beside them. He called back. 'Tomis! Over here.' He laid his hand on Elrik's brow. 'Tomis has had some training with a healer. He'll know what to do.'

A young man kneeled and examined Elrik's injury. But his face paled. 'It ain't like a wound made by a spear, Cappy. Look. It's already turning an odd sort of color.' He bent forward and sniffed. 'And it don't smell right.' He shrugged. 'Sorry, I can dress it, but he needs a proper healer… and quick.'

Elrik shivered. Toryn hugged him tighter. 'Where? We can't risk finding one here. I reckon the Ruuk will have them all in chains.'

Drondel looked back. 'The best healers in these parts are back at the watchtower.'

Toryn gasped. 'But that's five days away on foot.'

'That's still two days closer than Wendale. And I can't vouch for their healers. Seransea is even farther.' Drondel thumbed over his shoulder. 'It'll have to be the watchtower.'

'Then so be it.' Toryn looked down at Elrik as his lips turned blue. 'But it means trekking back through this wretched ditch.'

The captain looked to the trees. 'We can fashion a carrier for him from the branches. And…' he grimaced, 'perhaps stretch some of that web across to make it more comfortable. Two of my lads can take him. They might get lucky and find a horse when they reach the road.'

Toryn kept Elrik warm as the stretcher was made. He looked back to the way they had come. Elrik and his bearers would face the hornrasps and their allies for a second time. But how many more stings and bites could Elrik take in his condition? But Drondel was right. Elrik would not survive the journey to Drunsberg. It had to be the watchtower at the pass.

Roold sat beside Toryn. He held out a bloodied hand. 'Would you believe it. That beast took one of my fingers. Didn't feel a thing… my hands were so numb.' He groaned. 'But it's from my sword hand.' Roold glanced to Elrik. 'But I got off lightly, eh. Poor lad. Could have been any of us. Just in the wrong place.'

Toryn's shoulders dropped. 'We grew up together. It can't imagine life without him.'

Roold patted Toryn's leg. 'He'll pull through. Certain he will. He's a tough one.' Roold chuckled. 'Must breed them strong in Midwyche.'

'But I'm not from...' Toryn stopped. 'Yes, we obviously do.'

'And I can't wait to see those Ruuk faces when you kick them out of the mines.' Roold sighed. 'I always moaned about the place, but it would be good to see it again. Ha! And what about you, eh. Last time you were there, you were Hamar's young companion. Now look at you, all the hopes—' he grasped his wrist, 'the feeling's coming back.' Roold clenched his jaw, but Toryn could see he was in pain.

'You should get Tomis to take a look at that.'

Drondel called down the line. 'Any more injured? So long as you can walk...' he glanced to Roold, 'and have at least four fingers to hold a stretcher, I've got a new duty for you.'

One of the guards limped forward. 'Can manage the fingers' — he rolled his shoulder — 'but will struggle to raise my spear until this has healed.'

Drondel nodded. 'Very well. Tomis. See to these two and make sure they can walk and carry poor Elrik.'

Roold groaned. 'Guess I'll have to wait before I see Drunny again.' He held out his good hand to Toryn. 'Good luck, my friend. I have to admit, when I swore you into the Archonian Guard in the Ruuk wagon, I didn't think we'd live to see morning.' He grinned. 'But you've certainly earned your farm on the plains by now. At the very least, one with a south-facing slope to grow the sweetest of grapes.'

'And good luck to you, Captain. Elrik is in good hands.' Toryn pointed to Roold's bloody stump, 'well mostly.'

Roold held it up and laughed. 'I hope that ruddy spider choked on my finger as it died.' And with a nod, he turned and went to seek Tomis.

While the two bearers had their wounds treated, the makeshift stretcher was finished. A blanket was placed over the webbing, and Elrik secured in place.

Toryn kneeled and whispered in his dear friend's ear. 'You're as strong as an ox, big man. You'll be back at the watchtower soon enough. And you don't even have to walk. Keep fighting, my friend. We've got our day of doing nothing to plan.' His throat tightened. 'Don't... don't you go and leave me now. Not after we've come so far.'

29. Scratching in the Dark

The cool water of Findale Lake washed away the grime, easing the inflamed skin inflicted by the Dorn Trail. Yet, it did not ease Toryn's mind. Should he have used his sword against the aralak? He could have easily killed the beast before it tore into Elrik. Toryn laid the *Elorsil* by his side. Lorek joined him as he dried beside a small fire in a sheltered spot. He read what was on Toryn's mind. 'You couldn't have risked it. I know you're feeling guilty, but we'd all have been in danger had the warlock found us.'

Toryn held his hands to the fire. 'I've known him for as long as I can remember. He always had my back when the bigger lads picked on me, but they didn't come much bigger than Elrik, even when still young.' He gathered his belongings and packed his rucksack. 'I know you're right, but if he... doesn't make it, I could never forgive myself.'

Lorek held out a hand and helped Toryn to his feet. 'We did everything we could to save him. We knew the dangers of this mission when we volunteered.' He tried to laugh. 'And we're soon to squeeze through a tunnel where even Cubric will have to duck. Then what? If the Shreek's Rage doesn't blow us to pieces, we still have the Ruuk to deal with.'

Toryn looked to the company. 'Well, after our dip, we'll at least be heading off to Evermore with clean faces.'

The old cobtroll path through the mountains, reminded Toryn of the ledge he and Hamar had taken through the Wend Gap. But to his relief, no fast-flowing river threatened to drag them to their deaths. And the miners had taken the precaution to attach a rope along the mountain wall. But most of all, Toryn was grateful the pass was clear of insects and stagnant water. The air was fresh, and the company could be forgiven for enjoying a rejuvenating stroll, had it not been for the task ahead.

At dusk, Toryn and Janae had gone ahead to check the bridge. But while the pathway had been easily negotiated, the precarious wooden bridge would likely prove a much harder challenge. It looked to be several hundred years old, judging by the state of the wood. Two thick ropes hung from posts driven into the rock. The walkway sagged into the deep crevasse, seeming to anticipate the day it would plummet into its gaping mouth. Dozens of repairs had been done over the years, but they did nothing to inspire confidence. In places, the narrow planks were either rotten or absent. It would be treacherous during daylight, but they had to cross at night… without torches.

Drondel and his guards would remain out of sight in the pass until the following evening. Then, if all had gone to plan, they would cross and take their position close to the first gate. On hearing either the Shreek's Rage ignite, or a signal from Toryn, they would rush the gate, and then hope to take the town.

Toryn and Janae returned to the waiting guards, almost bumping into them in the gloom of the pass. Toryn did not hold back. 'It's not a bridge I'd choose to cross willingly. It won't be easy, and we'll need to go one or two at a time.' He looked up to the sky. 'And it will only get harder if the weather turns. But we have no other—' The sides of the mountain glimmered to the west. Toryn used the *farsight* to determine the source of the light. 'We appear to have company.'

Cubric turned. 'Ruuk coming back from Findale, I reckon.' Harsh voices echoed along the pass. 'Sounds like they've had a skin full, mind. And they're not going to win the hearts of a fair maiden with songs like that.'

Drondel pointed to an opening. 'We found a cave in there while you were gone. Good for cooking and getting out of the chill evening air.' He rubbed his chin. 'But it ain't big enough to hide us all. We either cross the bridge now and wait farther down the pass, or... we ambush them. We're well out of earshot of the town.' Drondel laughed. 'Or perhaps they're so drunk they won't notice we're here. Or if they do, they shouldn't be too much of a handful.'

Cubric peered over the edge. 'Ambush? How? One misstep and it's over. And we can only face them one-on-one on this ledge.'

Toryn checked the progress of the Ruuk. 'There's at least thirty judging by the number of torches.' He looked back over his shoulder. 'We won't all get over that bridge safely in time. But we'll likely lose ten to twenty if we tackle them here.'

Cubric grasped Toryn's arm. 'Can you work your magic?' Toryn nodded and closed his eyes. Cubric looked to the others. 'He's gone into this song of his. He'll think of something, don't you fret.'

'There is a way.' Toryn looked back up the ravine. 'But you'll have to find somewhere to shelter. There was a ferocious storm here centuries back. The wind howled through these mountains, almost bringing down the platform at Drunsberg, before coming this way.'

Drondel frowned. 'What about that bridge? You said it's rickety at best.'

'I can bring the gale to this stretch only. And just briefly. But anyone not secured or sheltered would be blown off the path. And if the wind isn't enough to dislodge them, the ledge will briefly turn into a river with the torrent. I can direct most of it at the Ruuk, but it'll still get a little hairy up here.'

Drondel nodded to the cave. 'Half can get inside there… at a squeeze. But would that bend ahead be deep enough to protect the rest?'

Janae tapped Toryn's shoulder. 'There's another inlet at the bend, large enough for a dozen or so. The rest should be sheltered by the outcrop. But perhaps it's wise for folk to tie themselves to the rope.'

The Ruuk voices grew louder. Toryn looked at Drondel. 'Then pass a message down the line. Get all you can in this cave, the rest to head up the pass.'

The captain nodded. 'And what about you? Where do you stand?'

'Here. I'll take Janae's advice and tie myself on. I'll maintain the blast for long enough to dislodge the Ruuk.'

Those at the head filed up the pass to the bend, the rest took refuge in the cave. Toryn secured himself to the rope and waited until all were in position. He took a breath and looked down the pass. The Ruuk were no more than a hundred paces from him. Toryn bowed his head and went back through the Verses to locate the storm. Despite the rope, he shuddered at the sight of the black sky and ear-splitting howl of the wind as it forced its way through the stubborn peaks. He set his stance and unleashed the blizzard.

Toryn staggered forward as the gust hurtled through. The torches spluttered and died. The first Ruuk in the line were snatched from the ledge like dry leaves, tumbling head over heels as the gale blew them back from where they had come. Others braced but had no chance. Then the clouds burst. The last and strongest Ruuk could hold on no longer, and soon joined their brothers below.

Toryn closed the gateway. The storm departed. In the sudden stillness, the cries of the last Ruuk echoed through the valley. Toryn looked away. He took no satisfaction in their deaths, hoping their end would be quick and they did not suffer.

Lorek peered out of the cave. 'Those poor souls. I bet they didn't have the chance to think what hit them.'

Cubric emerged. 'I wouldn't feel too sorry for them. I doubt the people of Dorn will be sad to see them go.'

Toryn watched the rainwater pour from the path and down into the ravine. 'Cub's right. I imagine many have suffered under their occupation.' He turned to see Janae striding with confidence along the pathway to report all were safe. He looked up. 'Time we were moving. We need to locate the cob tunnel and be out of sight before dawn.'

Drondel clasped Toryn's forearm. 'Pity that storm couldn't be put to good use down in the mines.' He whistled. 'Imagine the damage that could do hurtling down them tunnels. That would soon flush them out.'

Toryn sighed. 'We're going to have to do this the hard way. Shreek's Rage and hard steel. But hopefully we'll have enough of the black stuff to blast their sore heads and send them running onto your swords.' His jaw bunched. 'Just be ready. There's a lot we don't know about the place. And what we do know might have changed.'

The captain patted his back. 'Then the best of luck to you and your company. And don't you worry about my lot. We'll throw ourselves at those gates. We're all eager to strike back after months of doing little more than harassing the odd scoundrel.'

'Then wait for our signal. Let's hope we can trap the Ruuk between us, or at least send them scuttling back north up the pass.'

If any of Toryn's company had yet to prove their mettle, crossing the rickety bridge over the gaping chasm, settled the matter. The walkway had swayed and creaked with every step, meaning they had to take it one at a time. With every crossing, Toryn had held his breath. The success of their mission depended on the strength remaining in the old, frayed ropes. Had just one snapped, they would have had to retrace their steps, then approached on the main road and likely met another force of Ruuk. And any who had already made the terrifying crossing, would be left stranded on the wrong side.

Thankfully, the bridge held. But it had taken longer than expected to get them all onto the main road. And now for the next challenge. With dawn fast approaching, they had to find the cob tunnel before the daylight exposed their position.

Janae led the company, all happier to be off the narrow pathway and onto a solid, wide road. Toryn peered ahead. 'The entrance is no more than half a league from the first gate, so we must be close. It's likely to be concealed, seeing as so few know of it.' But the light of the new day soon found the peaks above them, and Toryn grew impatient. Yet the task could not be rushed; if they missed it, they could find themselves stranded on the road.

'There.' Janae touched Toryn's arm. 'Could that be it?' A pile of rubble sat within a shallow inlet. They quickly cleared the stones to find a small entrance to what must be the tunnel. But many in the company struggled to squeeze through the gap, and Toryn hoped it would not get any tighter before it reached the mines. Once inside, the stones were replaced to cover their tracks. But as the pass grew lighter outside, Toryn's mood grew darker. If they were discovered, they could find themselves stuck like badgers in a trap.

Toryn crouched and lit his torch. With no room overhead, he had to hold it at arm's length, but the flames in front of his face made it difficult to see what lay ahead. Cubric whispered, sounding loud in the confined space. 'I'm afraid it's going to be tough for you bigger lads. I hope you're not afraid of tight spaces… or the dark.'

Toryn took a few paces. 'It looks small, even for the cobs.' He turned to see several anxious faces in the torchlight. He tried to ease their fear. 'According to the plan we've half a league to cover before we reach the wider tunnels in the mine. Yes, it'll be a challenge, but we've all faced worse.'

Metal scuffed against the walls as the company struggled to shoulder their shields in the cramped space. Toryn tried to make light of their situation. 'Just as well we're all friends, eh.' But few seemed amused. He nodded to Cubric. 'Lead on, Captain. And let's hope the Ruuk haven't been playing with the powder.'

Cubric set off. They stumbled on the uneven floor and scraped their skin against rough walls as the tunnel slanted down. But Toryn was happier they were descending, preferring to exit below the main halls, and avoid blundering into a band of Ruuk, drunk or sober.

After what seemed like hours, they eventually stumbled out into a wider tunnel. Toryn called for Jedrul. The miner stroked his chin. 'Can't say for sure exactly where we are. One seam looks much like the next, but I'm sure this is one of the old ones.' He kicked a rusted iron rail on the floor. 'I reckon no skips have run along these for decades.' Jedrul tilted his head. 'And no sound of digging. We must be quite deep, and some distance from the current mining.'

Toryn turned to Cubric. 'Any thoughts on where we'll find the powder?'

He shrugged. 'We'll need to go a little farther for me to get my bearings. But we might get lucky and find another stash this deep.' Cubric looked in both directions. 'I'd say we best go up. Then perhaps me or Jed can get a better idea of where we are.'

It did not take long for Jedrul to recognize his surroundings. He called back. 'Hey, Cub. Look at this.' He pointed to a wooden peg lodged in a crack. 'That's Woolber's mark. He's the poor chap who bought it at the gate when he went to help Ox. A great shame. He could swing a hammer as if it was a child's toy.'

Cubric shook his head. 'Ah yes, the big man. And just like him to help a fellow in need.'

Toryn squinted at the peg. 'And this tells you where we are?'

Jedrul nodded. 'We're in the seam I first worked as a young man… when I still had all my teeth. It was closed about a year after I started.' He looked to Cubric. 'We called it the Star Chamber, seeing as the nickel used to glisten in the black rock. Does that help you find the black stuff, Cub?'

Cubric closed his eyes and moved his hands. 'Ah. Then the powder will be a little way below us… to the south.' He wiped the sweat from his brow. 'Then I reckon our best option is to go that way. And… if I'm right, we'll join another tunnel shortly after, and then we turn left.'

Toryn stuck his torch in the crack bearing Woolber's peg. 'We'll take a brief rest here. Quench your thirsts and eat what you have left. If we're successful, we can raid the Ruuk stores, and if we're not…' he grinned, 'then it won't matter.'

Cubric soon found the tunnel where he suspected the Shreek's Rage was stored. They had gone only a few steps when he stopped. 'Can you hear that?'

Jedrul cocked his head to listen. 'That's not picks cracking rock. That's more like… scratching.'

Toryn joined them at the front. 'Rats? This far down?'

The miner's nose wrinkled. 'Yet to find a place in the realms where you won't find a rat. But that don't sound like those pests to me.'

Cubric took a few paces up the tunnel. 'It's coming

from the other direction.' He cleared his throat. 'If I could make a suggestion, Toryn. I reckon we should find out what's making that noise before we go any farther.'

Jedrul agreed. 'Me too. I wasn't expecting anything to be this deep, especially during all the Ruuk's drinking and celebrating.'

Toryn listened again. He nodded. 'That's settled then. You know the mines better than most. And we don't want anyone stumbling into us before we're ready to strike. Cubric, pass the word down the line to draw swords and stay silent.'

Cubric and Jedrul led the way. The scraping grew louder, but something else heightened Toryn's unease. He tapped Cubric's shoulder and whispered. 'Can you smell that?'

'Your nose must be... oh, wait.' He grimaced. 'By the Three. That smells like the cesspit after the lads have eaten bad meat.'

Jedrul gagged. 'This ain't right. Not down here. That's what all the hatches on the platform are for.'

Toryn's eyes watered. 'The stench is coming from the same direction as that sound.'

Janae squeezed to the front. 'Want me to go on ahead?'

Toryn lifted his torch. 'We'll both go. Wait here, Cub, but be ready to come on my call.'

Cubric grinned. 'Doubt you'll have the air in your lungs to call. I've been holding my breath these last few minutes.'

Toryn paused. 'The moment you don't have a quip, Cub, that's when I'll know we're in serious trouble.'

The captain raised an eyebrow. 'Trouble? Don't know the meaning of the word.' He stretched his back. 'These tired old bones are begging me to hurry up and claim my farm.'

'Well, I hope that's not until we've completed our mission.' Toryn winked. 'But keep your sword in hand, just in case.'

Toryn and Janae set off up the tunnel and rounded a slight bend. She held up her hand. 'Over there. There's a faint light on the wall. I'd say it's coming from a door opposite.'

Toryn held his breath. 'And the source of that sound… and the smell if I'm not mistaken.'

30. A Difficult Choice

Sea Mist was keen to remind Elodi of his prowess. He had galloped faster than Elodi had thought him capable. It seemed he was bonded with the Amayans' horses, drawing upon their strength as he sped along the banks of the River Kel. By night, the waters glistened in the moonlight to guide them, and by day, the mists spilled across their path to cool their sweating brows. By the second day, the river had widened and slowed, allowing Sea Mist to outpace its current as they neared the east coast. They had stopped briefly to drink their fill from the clear water and take their rest. And while Sea Mist fed on the rich grass, Elodi ate from her supplies spared by Bryok.

As the fourth day dawned, the early light caught the distant peaks of the Kellen Heights. Elodi drew Sea Mist to a halt, then stood in her stirrups to use the *farsight*. Keld looked at peace. No smoke rose from behind its thick, stone wall, or from between its squat, round towers. To the south, there appeared to be little activity, and certainly no sight of an army marching on the city. Had Bardon yet reached the hills? She let her eyes wander north across the flat plain that stretched all the way to the Lumreek Marsh. Her shoulders eased. A long line of wagons meandered across the grasslands, perhaps heading for the town of Breck. She could just make out a few horses galloping ahead of a column on foot. They had to be fleeing from Keld. It looked as if Nordyn had abandoned the city at the first sight of Bardon.

Encouraged, she urged on Sea Mist. Within the hour, she joined the Borrund Road as it emerged from the Kellen's foothills. Then once across the bridge, she rode the final league to the city gates. Satisfied the guards at the entrance were Archonians, she guided Sea Mist up the cobbles and under the arch. The sentries gaped, then cheered her arrival, also having assumed she was dead. Elodi smiled to herself and patted Sea Mist, proud he had outpaced the news of her return. Two guards accompanied her through the streets to take her to Bardon, now Lord Broon once more.

Word of her arrival spread quickly through Keld, reaching Bardon long before Elodi. He strode out with Gundrul, both beaming as they greeted her. Bardon stared in disbelief. 'Well, I never. When Lindell reported you'd encountered a warlock and gone missing, well... we feared the worst.'

Elodi let out a long sigh. 'Ah, that is good to hear. I feared the captain and his riders would fall foul of those scoundrels.'

Bardon scoffed. 'They're the First Horse, Elodi! They soon finished off the Nordleng in the forest. But... it pained Lindell when they couldn't find you. They came to believe you were dead and reluctantly called off their search.'

Gundrul glanced to Bardon. 'I tried to convince the old lord, and myself, that not even a warlock could defeat you, ma'am. But as the days passed... I admit I'd begun to lose faith.'

Elodi laughed, pleased to see both men once more. 'So had I. A belly full of foul aralak poison does little to maintain one's faith.'

Bardon gasped. 'A warlock and an aralak?'

Elodi grinned. 'And a rather large one at that.'

Gundrul gripped her arm as an Archonian. 'Then how they must be quaking in their rotten boots if you escaped two such terrors.'

Bardon nodded to the crowd gathering on the steps. 'Let us take this inside. We have much to talk about, and it would be better over a late breakfast.'

Keld's main hall was much like the one in Borrund but built of stone instead of wood. Bardon led them to a table beside a large fireplace, and had an ample breakfast served. The returning lord sat. 'Mercifully, Nordryn had the sense to leave before a sword was raised. Ruan's spearmen had spread the rumor of a large force,' he winked, 'four times our real number were coming north. And that, combined with the sore heads following their celebrations, was enough to convince Nordryn and his rogues to flee.' He nodded to their plates. 'And lucky for us, they left most of their food, choosing instead to fill their wagons with the contents of the treasury.'

Gundrul drained his cup. 'We considered pursuing them to take back the gold, but decided any loss of life was not worth it.'

Elodi patted Gundrul's hand. 'A wise decision, Captain. Our soldiers are worth far more than any gold at present. And Nordryn can't eat it, and I doubt there's little food to be traded once he reaches Breck.'

Bardon pushed his empty plate away. 'We'll go after him once we've consolidated our position here. I won't rest until he and his ilk are back over the border. Then he can freeze to death in the coming winter as far as I'm concerned.'

Elodi dared to ask. 'And Toryn? The Amayans were concerned his sword would attract the attention of the warlocks.'

Gundrul shook his head. 'I'm afraid we've heard nothing since he entered the pass.' Elodi's face paled. The captain moved to reassure. 'But that's nothing new. It could be days before we get news of him reaching the watchtower in the west. He may have already passed through for all we know.'

Elodi sighed. 'And I assume the same goes for Nyomae. We find ourselves spread far and wide.' She yawned. 'I shall not stay long, but I must allow Sea Mist a good rest before heading off.'

Bardon looked at Elodi. 'And you also need to recover. Your ordeal will have taken much out of you. If you're thinking of finding Toryn, you must spend at least a day or two before you leave.'

'That is my wish, but while urgency is key, you're right. I must regain my strength. It's a long ride, and I cannot rule out meeting our foe along the way.'

The door burst open. Amyndra rushed in and strode to the table. Elodi stood and embraced the Broon captain. Amyndra held back her tears. 'Ma'am! I knew it couldn't be true. It would take all the armies of Nordruuk to inflict even a scratch.' She stepped back. 'But I see you have suffered.'

'I shall recover. But I'm in no hurry to ingest any more poison.' She looked Amyndra in the eye. 'But to current matters. I imagine you'll be keen to drive out the Ruuk and free the folk of Lunn.'

'That I am. Word is coming in of my fellow captains who escaped the armies coming south. They've continued to harass the retreating Ruuk, and we'll coordinate our dispersed forces to ensure none remain inside the border.'

Elodi wavered. 'You must forgive me. Now I've eaten, I feel I must sleep for a week.'

Bardon grinned. 'I was reluctant to insist, but yes, you really should, ma'am. A room is prepared with a soft bed and a fire in the hearth.' He stood. 'I'll ensure you're not disturbed for a full day.'

'Thank you, Bardon. But I wish to be kept informed. While we've achieved much to date, I worry there are events unfolding of which we remain oblivious.'

Elodi shot up. The sheets clung to her sweaty body. At first, she thought it was due to the aralak poison, but as she came out of her deep sleep, memories of a dream surfaced. The cry echoed inside her head. Igrayne! The warlocks had captured her. She felt the angst of Eryn. Igrayne was strong, but four warlocks held her. And if they broke and turned Igrayne, the Amayans would face the dreaded task of fighting one of their own.

Elodi knew what must be done. While she desperately wished to find Toryn, that was her heart and not her head guiding her choice. Toryn had the support of able captains and guards; Nyomae was well beyond her reach far to the south. Therefore, Elodi would ride to her sisters' aid. They would seek to end Igrayne's ordeal and prevent her falling under the Ul-dalak's influence. And for the sake of the realms, they must succeed without losing another Amayan… or Amanach.

Elodi dressed and retrieved her sword. Without knowing why, she kneeled, placed the hilt upon her brow and closed her eyes. As before, she heard water. But this time she saw it. A fast-flowing river flickered with visions of her sisters and their plight. Fearing the Elda Stone was at risk, the Amayans had rushed to its aid… but had fallen into a trap. Shokresh and three warlocks awaited them. Igrayne had been separated from her sisters, bound, gagged, and taken north. Yet it was not by chance. Eryn believed Igrayne was their intended victim but was unsure why.

Elodi gasped as more of Eryn's mind was revealed. With the demise of the Amanach, the warlocks had finally discovered the location of the Crown Stone. However, the

Amayans could not yet give chase. Four Angorsil encircled the Elda Stone and had to be annulled. But the shards were most potent, forcing the Amayans to draw upon the remaining Amanach to boost its strength. It was a risk to leave it undefended, but the Crown Stone was under threat.

The waters shimmered, then cleared to show the Amayans now dashed north. Elodi's words formed in the flow. *I will come.* She would have to push Sea Mist hard. The fastest route took her around the Lumreek Marsh and through country held by Ruuk. But she had no choice: the journey had to be made in just three days. And once she joined them? Would her sword be powerless against Shokresh?

Elodi's mind raced as she strode through the stone halls of Keld. If the Amayans defeated the warlocks, or at the very least, drove them back over the border, Elodi would have to make her move on Calerdorn before the enemy looked to strengthen their position. But if the Amayans failed and the Crown Stone fell… She pushed the thought from her mind: they could not fail.

Elodi burst into Bardon's quarters. 'Apologies for waking you at this early hour, lord.'

Bardon looked all his long years as he struggled to sit. 'None needed, Elodi. I assume you have good reason.'

'Two to be precise. Our enemy target the Crown Stone. And the warlocks have captured an Amayan.'

Bardon sagged back against his pillows, abandoning his attempt to get out of bed. 'Dire news indeed.'

'I shall ride to their aid, but may I ask a favor of you?' He nodded. 'Regardless of the outcome at the Crown, Calerdorn must be taken, and taken back soon. If our enemy choose to abandon the east, they'll look to reinforce my city to consolidate the west. This would mean… well, I don't need to explain the consequences.'

'Agreed. I shall send a bird to Seransea. Whatever forces they can spare on Noor's border should be gathered at...?' Bardon climbed out of his bed and limped to his map. 'Where do you suggest?'

Elodi pointed. 'Here, just south of Dorlgoth Wood. They'll stand a good chance of avoiding enemy eyes, while being less than a day's ride from the plain. But they must not strike until they have support. Once the Ruuk are driven out of Lunn, Gundrul, Ruan and Amyndra must take as many as can be spared. But it's vital the force includes the remainder of my knights. They should be the first to ride through the gates and free my people. The Knights of Calerdorn still number forty and are a match for the best we have available.' She looked at the dark skies outside the window. 'It's a great pity Aldorman did not live to lead them back into Calerdorn.'

Bardon nodded. 'That can be arranged.' His finger moved across the map. 'The Kolossos Pass would take too long... so that leaves the treacherous route through Nordruuk and around the Crown.'

Elodi tapped the smudge depicting the Mawlgrim Mire. 'I hear the marshes are frozen over. It will be a difficult crossing, but at least they won't get bogged down. The mire is all too keen to swallow those who lose their way.'

Bardon studied the map. 'Then that shall be our plan.' He turned to Elodi. 'And then we have the small matter of overcoming the somewhat formidable defenses of your city.'

Elodi reached into her pocket. 'This plan contains directions to a secret entrance beneath the city. I have committed it to memory, so please pass this on to Gundrul, and ensure Ruan and Amyndra also learn of its contents. If I should fail to arrive, then others need to know of this. I shall endeavor to meet them at Durran, the abandoned settlement south of… what was once known locally as Wyke Wood. Both Gundrul and Ruan know of it, it's a good place to camp and will offer some shelter from the gales… and hopefully enemy scouts.' She looked up to Bardon's lined face, made all the more troubled by the candle's flickering flame. 'Please inform the captains on the strategy we discussed at Borrund. Then instruct them to commence with the attack if I don't arrive by… the crescent before the next full moon.'

She looked down to the towers of Calerdorn on the parchment. 'If I am not there by then… I will most likely not get there at all.'

Bardon took Elodi's hand. He smiled. 'I don't think our foes have the strength to achieve that, Elodi.'

'I wish that were true, Bardon.' She turned to the door. 'Now I must leave.'

Bardon released her hand. 'And may the Three ride with you, my dear friend.'

31. TOWER OF THE SUN

Nyomae cried out as the light seemed to split her head in two. Her hands went to her face, surprised to find her wrists were free of the chains. Slowly, she opened her eyes. Sunlight spilled through four windows into a sparse, circular room with a low ceiling, yet no obvious way to enter… or leave. She turned her stiff neck to take in her surroundings. The room was bare apart from a stone seat at the center. It dawned on Nyomae. She had never set foot in the place, even when holding high rank in the Order. Yet here she now stood at the top of the Sun Tower. From here, the great Archons of the day had looked out upon the lands under their rule.

Nyomae jumped. A man groaned. Behind the seat, a hunched figure sat facing the window that looked out on the north. Idraman. She crouched beside the old man and placed her hand on his shrunken shoulder. He flinched. Had no hand touched him all these years? She whispered. 'Idraman. It is I. Nyomae. Do you remember me?' He turned. Misty, gray eyes sought her face. Had the centuries robbed him of his sight? His mouth moved, but no words came. Gently, she took his cold hand. 'It is Nyomae.' She drew upon her reserves and fed him a little of her warmth.

Idraman's eyes flickered as if remembering the touch of a hand. His brow creased; his mouth tried to form words but appeared to have forgotten how. She attempted to remind him of their shared past. 'We are Imaari, Idraman. We fought the Ul-dalak on the Gormadon Plain. You reached out from the Caerwal Pass and saved me that day when all was lost.' She waited, not wishing to overwhelm him. 'Do you remember, Idraman?' Did he even remember his own name? Nyomae attempted to enter his Verse, but found it was shut. She stroked his gnarled hand. 'I have come from the north. I need your help, Idraman.' She continued to use his name hoping it would help restore his memory.

His hand warmed a little in hers. Again, his mouth opened. She leaned closer as his voice croaked, speaking barely above a whisper. 'Who… who do you say I am?'

Nyomae groaned. Had he lost his mind entirely? 'You are Idraman. An Imaari of great repute. You were once head of the Order of Echoes.'

His wrinkled brow creased. 'Imaari?' He pulled his hand free. 'No… no. Evil. I cannot be… cannot.'

Nyomae took back his hand. 'You have been deceived. It is not the Imaari you need fear.' She stroked his brow. 'Let me in, Idraman. Let me show you.'

He twisted away. 'No! I must not.' She released his hand. Idraman's head dropped, exhausted by their brief conversation. He slouched to the floor and fell into a deep sleep. Nyomae looked down at the old Imaari. She had to be patient. It would take time, but how much time did she have?

Nyomae stood and walked about the room. The Archon's quarters in Archonholm had been fashioned in the same manner. But while some comforts had been installed in the Archon's Tower, no such effort had been made here. The stone chair sat upon a wooden wheel. Nyomae assumed it would turn to face each of the four windows. She took a step towards it, but her ears popped as the air seemed to push her back. A Word of Forbidding surrounded Draegelan's Seat. But who had placed it here? And who maintained it? Nyomae had not intended to sit upon it, that did not seem fitting, but even to approach was clearly not permitted.

The tower's Verse was closed to her, so she had to imagine how Draegelan would have looked sitting upon the chair. From the tallest tower in the south, he could survey far and wide as he passed laws for the enrichment of its people. How different the region must have looked in his day. She entered the Verse of the adjacent tower. Her heart lurched as she saw the land as it had been in her days at Elmarand. The canals glistened in the sunlight as they stretched out like the lines on a leaf, taking fresh water to the farmed fields. The roads bustled with traders' carts bringing food and clothes into the city, while those leaving, carried goods ranging from pots and pans to fine jewelry. The streets below were thronged with people going about their business, fully fed and content with life in the city.

Nyomae turned away. Talamaris had fallen so far from its days of glory. The parched ground outside the new wall would have appalled Draegelan. And he could never have envisaged the use of slaves to till the fields, while condemning the people in the deserts to suffer thirst and hunger.

Idraman woke and groaned. He looked around the room seeming not to know where he sat. Nyomae noted his clean attire, combed hair, and clipped nails. Someone obviously cared for him. But when did they come? There were no doors. How did they enter? She sat beside the wall and watched Idraman. He was blind, afraid, and seemed oblivious to her presence unless she touched him. But if she had been alone for three hundred years, would she have fared any better?

Nyomae turned back to the window facing south, but to her surprise, found she now looked upon a door. Her footsteps echoed surprisingly loud for a small room as she walked towards it, but it seemed to take longer to cover the short distance than she expected. Nyomae turned the handle and was met by a welcoming cool breeze. And, as with the Archon's Tower, a narrow balcony surrounded the pinnacle. She stepped out and steadied herself to look down. The Sun Tower was easily twice the height of Archonholm's tallest structure, and although she had flown far higher on the corvraak's back, Nyomae's head spun. She grasped the iron railing and peered over the southern stretch of the old city wall.

As with the region Nyomae had journeyed through, much of the land between the city and the new outer wall was farmed. She let the *farsight* draw her closer. And to her dismay, many hundreds of slaves worked the farms to the south. But a section to the east was fenced off. Rows of huts surrounded a large, square of sand. Dust rose as lines of soldiers marched in formation. Kirol had been right. The city was raising an army. And surely it was for only one purpose: Elmarand had its eye on the neighbors. But was it those in the south? Or those in the north?

Nyomae looked beyond the outer wall, crossing many leagues of desert before seeing the first signs of greenery. But she had reached the limits of her vision and could go no farther into Armanoor.

She returned to the room perplexed. Her hand tingled as it brushed the smooth Caerwal Stone. Now she understood why and how she had been fooled. The *kruul* had taken on the semblance of an Imaari in the Song. Thus, when Nyomae had surveyed the city, she found who she took to be Idraman in the cells. And, as with the Archon's Tower at the gate, the Angorsil had been concealed beneath marble. The trap could not have been set in the Sun Tower as the shard would be rendered useless by its walls of Caerwal Stone; the same defense that concealed Idraman from her. And it seemed even a *kruul* could not enter one of the most sacred places in the realms. But why? Why had they not simply granted her access to Idraman in the tower and then entrapped her? Nyomae groaned. This was the way of the warlocks. It would have provided no sport. Warlocks took pleasure from demeaning their victims. But that only worked if the victim felt humiliated, and she was determined not to indulge them.

Nyomae's chest tightened as she recalled the warlock's name: Mosholuk. They had indeed met before. It was on the frozen plains of Nordruuk as Nyomae conducted the vain search for Sylvena. Her shoulders sagged. No matter how often she tried to justify her decisions that led to the doomed quest, her guilt did not ease. How easily she had been deceived. Uluriel had played her as if a child… and Nyomae had fallen into her trap, thus endangering the Order, and setting into play the ensuing tragic events.

Nyomae sank against the wall. The appearance of Mosholuk had stoked the embers of her shame, reviving the horrors she had tried to bury. As Nyomae and her Order had battled against the wind, she had spied a dark line through the driven snow. But what she had presumed to be the Draegelan Trench, suddenly moved. Too late did Nyomae understand the threat, and before they could flee, a dark force fell upon them. Mosholuk led a host of shrouls, Norgog and Ruuk. But that was not all. The warlock had cried out in glee as he summoned a shreek. Its howls drove their horses to madness, who bolted south, with or without their riders. Yet all was not yet lost. Nyomae and Finromir were at the height of their powers and a match for such devilry. As the shreek unleashed its fury, the Imaari brought forth a blast of air from warmer times. The Norgog thus weakened, and the resulting thaw hampered the advance of the Ruuk as they sank in the mire. Nyomae's small force held their ground and eventually Mosholuk tired, released the shreek and retreated. But the damage had been done. With the loss of the horses, they had abandoned their mission and crawled back over the border. A year later, Nyomae had faced Mosholuk once more at Gormadon… and now he promised a third meeting in the flesh.

She pushed aside the dread and went back to Idraman. He rocked as he sat staring blankly out of the window. She crouched at his side and attempted again to speak with him. 'What do you *see*, Idraman?'

'The end!' She was taken aback by the sudden force of his voice.

'Do you have sight, Idraman?' But he slumped, appearing not to hear her words. His breathing slowed and his head dropped. Nyomae sighed. This was going to take a long time. She stood and left him in peace to return to her own thoughts. She gazed out of the window looking out on the north. A sandstorm blew across the plain many leagues from Elmarand; she could only imagine the misery it would inflict upon those already struggling to survive. She turned away, ashamed she could do nothing for them at present. But what could she do to save herself?

Nyomae sat by the wall and closed her eyes. She had to clear her head, put the guilt and regrets of the past behind her, and look ahead. Taking a deep breath, she arranged the recent events into place as if pieces in a game of *Squares*. She saw them move across the board as she assessed the implications and possible outcomes of each event. It was obvious Uluriel did not know Ormoroth's Name. If she did, Nyomae would have been killed. She had been exhausted by her long, arduous journey, so a *kruul* in union with the Angorsil could have finished her. Hence, her life must have been spared for the grim task of opening the gateway to the Void. Her imprisonment would also serve to setback the efforts in the north. But what of Idraman? His part in the game did not readily reveal itself. Why had he been kept alive all these years? If the people of Elmarand believed it was to appease the dark gods, Uluriel could easily had created the illusion Idraman lived to allay their fears.

Nyomae shivered. A shadow slid up the wall to the sill of the East Window. Evening had come all too soon. Her eyes rested on the hunched figure of Idraman. He was once a tall man with broad shoulders and a straight back. Before Gormadon, Idraman was close to reaching the level of knowledge attained by Draegelan, yet the enemy had reduced him to the shell of a man that slouched before her.

Nyomae jumped as the door she believed led out to the balcony, swung open.

Lorek forced the lock and opened the door. Inside, they found dozens of prisoners cramped into a room suitable for half their number. A voice croaked. 'They're not Ruuk. We're saved.' A weak cheer went up from a few, but many appeared too weak to celebrate.'

Toryn stood aghast. 'Where… where are you all from?'

Jedrul cried out. 'Fendy! I hardly recognized you.' He turned to Toryn. 'I thought he took one in the chest at the gate. He's one of the guards… or was.'

The tragic sight of what must have been a strong Archonian, struggled to get to his feet. Jedrul went to help him but couldn't hide his horror. 'Fendrake was one of the finest swordsmen in the guard.' He steadied his friend as he wavered. 'What happened to you?'

The guard tried to stand without aid but failed. He grasped Jedrul's arm and groaned. 'They thought I was dead and left me in the hall. I woke and made my way to the entrance. When I saw you, Roold and the others being loaded into the carts, I tried to stop them. I tried my best, Jed, honest I did. But I didn't have the strength to lift my sword.' He leaned heavily against Jedrul. 'There was no room left in the wagons, so they dragged me back.' He motioned to the other prisoners. 'Some are miners, some guards like me, and others are from Findale and Greendell.' Fendrake slumped. 'Sorry, mate. I can't stand. Too weak.'

Jedrul helped him to sit. 'No need to apologize, my friend. Let's put you back by this wall, eh.' His jaw clenched as he turned to Toryn. 'We got any food to spare for these poor folk?'

The last of their supplies were collected and brought forward. Flasks were filled from the water running down the tunnel, and Tomis began to dress the worst of the wounds. Cubric drew Toryn aside. He scratched his head. 'Seems like I got my bearings wrong. This cell… it's where we found the powder.'

Toryn groaned. 'Are you certain? These tunnels all look the same.'

'For sure. I recognize the marking on the door. It means those scoundrels have got the black stuff. And we have nothing.'

'Nothing?' Toryn looked back to the makeshift prison. 'We've freed two dozen men, many of them guards and miners. Two dozen with an axe to grind with the Ruuk up there. I reckon we've got another day at least before the celebrations finish. If we can raid one of their stores, and get more food and water inside these poor folk, we've just doubled our numbers. And perhaps there'll be more such cells.'

Jedrul joined them. Cubric nodded over his shoulder. 'Toryn reckons we can use these folk seeing as we're unlikely to get our hands on the Shreek's Rage.'

Jedrul frowned. 'They're very weak. And we'll be launching our attack by… what? Tomorrow?'

Toryn looked back to the cell. 'We only need them fit for a short fight at best. The Ruuk must have fed them enough to mine the seams. If they can wield a pick against rock, they can do the same against Ruuk heads.' The moans of the injured echoed down the passage. Toryn winced. 'They'll have a few scores to settle. Perhaps the shock of the prisoners rushing at the Ruuk might just give us the edge. Then if we can drive them out of the mines, they'll have time to fully recover. And with Drondel and his force, we'll have enough to push them back to the

Drunshead Gate. If we can secure that, we'll hold the mines.'

Jedrul grinned. 'One step at a time, eh.'

Toryn grasped his forearm. 'When we took the Oath together in the wagon, we swore *not a step back*. We can take one step at a time, but it will be for nothing if we can't secure the gate.'

Jedrul nodded. 'You may have a point there, my Archonian brother. There's no point risking our necks if we only go and lose the place next month.'

Lorek strolled down the passage. 'The prisoners say no Ruuk have been down here for days.' He jabbed his nose. 'That explains the sorry state they're in. They've not had to work, but they've had no food or water in that time. They also know of two more cells with similar numbers. They're down this tunnel to the left.'

Toryn beamed. 'That would add another sixty to seventy to our ranks. If only half of them can fight, that still makes us a force to be reckoned with.' He called to Janae. 'Take six and see if you can locate the stores. We need enough food for a day for all the prisoners. You'll not likely be disturbed as they still seem to be reveling.' He turned to Jedrul. 'See if you can recover the miners' tools. They can serve as weapons until we can take some off the Ruuk.' Toryn looked back to the cell and clenched his fists; he would make the Ruuk pay for keeping these men in appalling conditions.

Janae and her companions delivered. Although of questionable quality, the Ruuk supplies were still better than what the unfortunate prisoners had eaten in months. And as Cubric pointed out, the freed prisoners would be safer to deploy than Shreek's Rage. By the following day, more than half were ready to fight. Armed with picks and hammers, they joined the company, eager to exact their revenge.

Toryn's spirits rose as they ascended. More than once, he glanced behind at the determined faces of his companions. Today they would strike back, taking the Ruuk and their masters by surprise. If all was going to plan in the east, Keld would soon be back in the control of the realms. He gripped the *Elorsil's* hilt; and Calerdorn would be next.

The first Ruuk they came across were sprawled on the floor. The two bore cuts and bruises, most likely resulting from a disagreement. Toryn was not keen to let the prisoners settle their scores on unconscious, unarmed folk; Ruuk or not. He had them bound and taken to a cell for a trial of sorts if they were successful.

'Three more here, Toryn.' Jedrul whispered. 'If we find many more in this state, we won't have to bother letting Drondel in.'

Toryn regarded them. 'Sadly, we have no idea of their numbers. But perhaps those stationed down here aren't their best fighters. I'd have those at the barricade if I was in command.'

They turned a corner to be met by a raucous sound. Jedrul grimaced. 'Not their best singers either, I'd say.' He pointed. 'We're outside the Findale Hall. Sounds daft, but they're named after lakes and forests. Sort of reminded us of what it was like to be in the land of the living. The largest is Foranfae. That hall is beyond this one, and I guess that's where we'll find most of the scoundrels.'

Janae returned. 'There's no more than thirty ahead. But half of them are asleep or out cold.'

Toryn nodded to Cubric. 'Get them ready.' He waited for the company and the prisoners to gather around as best as they could in the confined tunnel. He raised his voice unconcerned he would be heard over the singing in the hall. 'Let's make this as quick as we can. Don't let any escape to raise the alarm. Many are out cold. We'll deal with those who can raise a weapon first, then bind and gag those who can't.' He eyed his company and hoped their losses would be light. 'But remember, the Ruuk believe the more violent their end, the better the reward that awaits them. So don't give them that chance.'

Cubric positioned the fittest at the front. The least able were given ropes to deal with the slumbering Ruuk. Toryn edged forward. He nodded to Jedrul and Lorek alongside him. 'Ready, brothers?' He turned and ran. They had covered half the distance before the Ruuk saw them. But only three had weapons to hand. In moments, they had been taken down. The unarmed chose to use their fists, but after days of drinking they could barely stand and were quickly overcome, bound, and gagged. None escaped.

Cubric wiped his sword. 'We'll soon be done if the rest are as easy as this. But I can't think these fools have left the South Gate unguarded.'

Toryn checked the new prisoners were secured. He looked to the entrance. 'Onto the Foranfae.' He smiled to himself as he recalled the days he had spent in that forest, but with luck its namesake would be an easier prospect.

The largest hall housed a few more drunken Ruuk, and the result was much the same. Toryn recognized it was the hall where Porek had delivered his rousing speech; today, he hoped the outcome would be in their favor. In little time, the rest of the mine inside the mountain was back in their hands. Toryn stopped as they neared the main entrance. The last time he had stood here, a line of wagons had blockaded the way to the steps. He glanced to Lorek. 'This is where your brothers fell.' But Toryn left the details of their tragic deaths unsaid.

Lorek's jaw clenched. 'And I imagine they're now at the bottom of the ravine.'

Toryn clutched his shoulder. 'When done, we should

raise a monument to them and the brothers who died defending this place.'

He grasped his sword. 'Then let's finish what we came to do.'

Toryn and Cubric edged towards the main entrance. Outside, day would be breaking within the hour, yet the taverns in the new town were still teeming with revelers. Toryn peered down the road to the South Gate and saw six large Ruuk standing guard. He stepped back inside. 'They look sober and will offer some resistance. We'll have to risk them raising the alarm, but I can't see those in the taverns answering their call any time soon.' He glanced up to the sky. 'We'll get Drondel inside before it gets light. Then we'll tackle the town.'

Cubric eyed the Ruuk at the gate. 'I'll take ten of my lot. That should do it. Their attention is over the stockade. I reckon we can rush them, coming out of the dark and striking before they know what's hit them.'

Toryn wished Cubric luck and watched his best fighters, including Lorek, creep along the road towards the gate. The surprise attack worked. After a short scuffle, the Ruuk were dispatched, and the gate opened without a single casualty. Toryn turned back to the town. With Drondel's company, they would have more than one hundred and forty. The drunk Ruuk in the halls had presented little threat, but with greater numbers and in the confined spaces of the taverns, they would not be able to subdue them as quickly. And, as the alarm was raised, the rest would soon join the fight.

Toryn gripped his sword, impatient for Drondel and his company to arrive. The *Elorsil* warmed to his touch, but he withdrew his hand, not wishing to alert the warlocks he feared could be in the region. It had been too easy so far. If the enemy suspected an attack, why had they not prepared a better defense? Surely, they desired the metals just as much as the Five Realms. Toryn listened to the boisterous celebrations. Were the Ul-dalak pre-occupied elsewhere? Did they no longer need swords and axes to ensure a victory?

Toryn glanced nervously to the town once more. The Ruuk had tried to repair the steps where Uldrak had driven his shard into the stone. He spat as the taste of its corruption filled his mouth. The cracks were still visible where the sickening green glow had seeped through the rock and brought an end to the guards' last-ditch defense.

'They come.' Janae tapped Toryn's arm.

His shoulders relaxed as the long line of Drondel's able guards strode up the road. Toryn ran down the steps to greet them. The captain grinned. 'I hear you've swelled your ranks.' He nodded to the town. 'Now then. I say we bring an abrupt end to their celebration, eh.'

Toryn left the tactics to Drondel and Cubric, and took his position next to Lorek in the reserve line. The fresh soldiers would coordinate attacks on the four largest inns, while the reserve would take on those who tried to escape back to the mines.

Drondel gave the signal. His guards stormed the taverns. Shouts and the clash of steel soon rang out through the narrow streets. Toryn stood ready. The alarm spread. More Ruuk stumbled out of doorways, bleary eyed, and struggling to find their weapons. But they were in no shape to take on Toryn's company. Yet, despite their drunken state, they seemed determined to earn their reward. Three large Ruuk burst through and charged at Toryn and Lorek. Thankfully, two tripped over each other and crashed to the floor. But the third kept his footing and closed the gap. Something glistened in the torchlight, catching Toryn's eye. The traps! He grasped the bolt and wrenched. The hatch dropped open and the Ruuk tumbled through. Toryn stood and grabbed the rope to pull it shut.

He wondered if Hamar was right. Would their assailant die of thirst before he reached the bottom? The traps were installed to rid the town of the filth that clogged the streets. Toryn wiped his hands, satisfied it had done its job.

The sound of fighting died. Drondel strode out from the largest tavern. He called over. 'No game at all. Too far gone. But none will be suffering from a hangover come tomorrow.'

Toryn let out a long sigh and watched the vapor curl. He shivered. 'Toryn.' Janae ran towards him, pointing back to the main entrance. 'The air cools in the tunnels. The walls are covered with frost.'

He groaned. 'Norgog.' But it was not the Norgog that troubled him. His gut lurched. A warlock came.

33. A Sheek's Rage

'They come through the mines.' Janae sprinted up the steps ahead of Toryn.

'Which tunnel? Can you tell?' Toryn's mind raced. If he could bring down the ceiling, he could delay them long enough to form a worthwhile defense.

Janae reached the top. 'More than one. Possibly all three that surface here.'

'Ah. They know I can't block all three.' Toryn skidded to a halt. 'Even if I could, it would set us back weeks to clear them to start mining.' He looked to the tunnels. 'Yet if we lose the mines to the Norgog, it could be months before we can retake them… if at all.'

Jedrul staggered up the steps, gasping for breath. 'The Ruuk are finished. All either dead or tied up. Lorek and Drondel are bringing up the company. Where do you want them?'

Toryn glanced around the hall. When they had mounted a desperate defense against Uldrak, the attack came from the town. And despite being vastly outnumbered, they only had a narrow front to hold. Facing an onrush of Norgog pouring out of three tunnels, would cost them dearly… and then there was the warlock.

Toryn turned to the company running up the steps. Of the prisoners, he doubted few had the strength for another battle so soon. It would be down to the guards. But they were also fresh from a fight, and some were injured.

The air cooled rapidly. The warlock was almost upon them. Toryn had to come to a decision fast. He could retreat to the old town and make a stance there in the narrow streets. But what did the warlock hope to achieve?

If he wanted the mines, Toryn would all but hand them back to him. He clenched on his sword. Or did they want to capture him, or the *Elorsi*? Or both? Toryn looked back over his shoulder. If he retreated, the Norgog could rain down rocks from the parapet above, or worse, set the old wooden buildings ablaze. Or perhaps dislodge the supports with their great hammers to send them all tumbling down into the ravine.

Cubric clutched Toryn's shoulder. 'Any thoughts, Cappy?'

He came to a decision. 'We'll make our stand here. We can't risk getting trapped if we try to defend one of the deeper halls. And the town is nigh impossible to hold.'

Cubric shrugged. 'There's a third option.' He nodded to the road. 'It's one that goes against everything we stand for, but if we abandon the place, we live to fight another day.'

Toryn's eyes fell upon the open gate. 'It had crossed my mind. But I doubt we'd get the chance to take the mines again. Not without a force five times our size.' He shook his head. 'We've got injured to carry. It wouldn't take long for the warlock to catch up. Then I don't rate our chances on a road with that ravine below.'

The sound of the Norgog grunts filled the hall. Toryn stiffened. 'No. It has to be here. But at least the warlock makes one decision easier.' He lifted his sword. 'They know I'm here. It makes no odds now if I use it.' The handle warmed. He turned to Cubric. 'I have an idea. Get everyone up here. We'll form three deep in a square. I can't tell how many Norgog are coming, but if I can bring some heat into the hall, it will weaken them.'

Cubric and Drondel yelled out their commands, but ominously, the Norgog chants soon drowned them out. A square of shields was formed. Bristling with spears and sword tips, it resembled the huckles living in the hedgerows of Toryn's farm. But this creature could not scuttle away at the first sign of danger. They had no choice but to stand their ground.

Toryn took the center of the square beside Janae. He closed his eyes and entered the Song. Aided by the *Elorsil*, Toryn progressed far back to the time when a natural cave occupied the ground where he stood. Hamar told tales of when the north was warmer in the old days; Toryn was pleased to find they were true. He weaved his hands, forming a sphere of warm air. He called out. 'The cold will retreat, but we will not!'

Dozens of snorting Norgog burst through all three tunnels and rushed straight at the square. But their pace slowed as the hallway continued to warm. Yet, their momentum brought them slamming into the shields. Cubric yelled. 'Hold your ground!' The ranks braced, jamming their feet into the ground to shove back. Spears and swords thrust through the gaps and tore into Norgog necks until sweat dripped from the guards.

Toryn's gut churned: the warlock had entered the Song. And Toryn knew his mind. The warlock reached for the same bitter winter Toryn had used to drive the Ruuk from the mountain path the previous day. The air cooled; the Norgog stirred as the warlock's gale blasted into the hall. Toryn groaned, knowing he could not defeat his adversary in the Song.

His feet tingled; the *Elorsil* warmed. Of course! He could call upon the power of the river deep beneath the mountains. Toryn raised the sword. The water responded, flowing faster until the rock trembled. He circled his blade over the top of the shields. The air hissed as the heat from the *Elorsil* met the icy gale. Faster he swung his sword, crying out as the handle scorched his hand. The hall ignited. A wall of flame blazed around the company within, roaring as it devoured the hapless Norgog.

'Toryn! You can stop.' Janae yelled into his ear. 'They're dead. They're all dead. Please stop. It's out of control. Our shields burn.'

Toryn dropped his arm, the flames died, and he collapsed, gasping for the little air left in the hall. The guards coughed and retched on the stench of burning Norgog skin. But thankfully, a cool breeze blew in and dispatched the smoke down the tunnels. Janae wiped the tears from her eyes. She kneeled beside Toryn. 'What happened? I thought we were about to go up in flames.'

Toryn blinked as the air cleared. He stammered. 'Such power.' He looked down to his hand, half-expecting to see it seared to a crisp. 'So much power. I… I lost control.'

Lorek stumbled over, rubbing the red skin on his shield arm. He gaped. 'I bet they weren't expecting that. Or any of us for that matter.'

Toryn stared at their white eyes peering out from their blackened faces. 'I'm so sorry. I had no idea. I didn't intend to burn us alive.'

Lorek looked down at his skin. 'But you saved us. Rather a scorched arm than a crushed skull. There must have been a hundred Norgog. Maybe more. The flames shot down the tunnels. I'd say there're many who didn't even make it to the hall.'

Toryn struggled to sit. 'Any sign of the warlock?'

Cubric laughed. 'If he has any sense, he'll be a league away by now. I can't think what he—' He spun around. 'Horses? Can you hear hooves?'

Toryn grimaced. 'Sour milk. Not horses. Shrouls.' He clambered to his feet. 'Back into the square, Cub. The warlock is not done.'

Cubric showed no sign of weariness. He called out. 'Rotate the ranks. Rear to the front.' But many of the shields were still too hot to hold, leaving gaps in their line.

Toryn leaned against Lorek. 'Spears at the ready. Don't let them touch you. They may look grim, but they're easier to kill than Norgog.' But Toryn was confused. Shrouls against a few guards could present a challenge, but surely the warlock would need dozens to trouble the company. Three stooping shrouls tottered out from the tunnels. Toryn flinched as they clicked their spines to stand tall and raise their large heads.

Drondel gasped. 'By the Three. Their eyes! They look like... us.' The shrouls teetered towards them. Their sharp teeth clinked as they gnashed, ready to crunch into the guards' frozen limbs.

Cubric grunted. 'It's those you need to worry about. Them teeth will make short work of your bones. Just like crunching on a carrot.' As they neared, the front line of shields shrank back. Bony arms stretched out, and their long fingers groped, searching for a throat, arm, or leg.

Toryn spoke calmly. 'Take their legs from under them. Then go for their necks. Strike and withdraw. Don't allow them to get hold of you.' Three more creatures joined their ghoulish brothers. Now six circled the square with their ungainly strides, looking like great hounds rising on their hind legs. But while Toryn did not fear the shrouls, he grew uneasy. This had to be a distraction. While unpleasant, the experienced guards could cope with twice as many. The first snatched at a guard's sword arm. A spear thrust at its chest. It grabbed the shaft, but before it could pull, two swords took away its legs. It screamed as it fell. Another guard lunged and took off its head. The others cheered.

Jedrul bellowed as two more shrouls were taken down. 'We'll soon be done, lads. A few more, then we can have that hard-earned ale, eh.'

Lorek scoffed. 'They don't stand a chance against our—' But he spoke too soon. The hairs on Toryn's neck prickled as a gurgle echoed up through the tunnel. The sickening slap of wet skin on rock followed. A large droog wriggled through the gap like a maggot from an apple. But again, Toryn was puzzled. Why a single worm? It was vile and could result in a grim death for just one guard, but it could not possibly defeat a well-armed company of their size.

He spoke as the droog slithered towards them. 'You've heard the tales. Yes, they're… unpleasant, but it can't trouble us. Work together and we'll soon defeat it.' Toryn hoped they could. He could barely stand, let alone swing a sword. But as the worm reared, a dark shadow appeared at the back of the hall. Toryn braced as the warlock entered. In his hand, he grasped a glowing, green shard. The warlock brandished the weapon, leaving a bright streak as if he swung a flaming torch.

Toryn clutched his chest; this attack was solely meant for him. The warlock raised his free hand, extended his fingers, then curled them. Toryn gasped. He could not breathe. His heart seemed to bulge and press against his ribs. But it was not his body in danger — it was his soul. The warlock desired to wrench it free from its mortal vessel. Time slowed, the sounds of combat faded as the warlock drew Toryn into his Verse, taking pleasure in revealing his past.

His name was Shamuul. The warlock had destroyed an Elorym city close to where the ruins of Darrowyche now stood. Shamuul had built a vast army from the captured survivors corrupted by his dark arts. From there, he had razed many towns and cities west of the mountains. Toryn gaped at the slaughter. How many had fallen victim to the warlock's relentless campaign? And into these battles, Shamuul had brandished the very weapon now brought against him. And Toryn knew it to be an Angorsil, hewn from Ormoroth's vile iron pillar.

With the little strength he had left, Toryn resisted. Once more, he drew upon the power of the river. He entered what felt like a tug of war the village boys used to test their strength. The river obliged and slowly wrested Toryn's soul back from the warlock.

But Shamuul seemed untroubled. He circled his hands and formed a churning funnel between them. The warlock grinned through the shimmering air. His voice thundered into Toryn's chest. He pointed. 'I desire your sword. The rest of your rogues can go free.' Toryn's arm lifted, extending the sword as if offering it to Shamuul.

He pulled back. 'It is not mine to give.'

The warlock sneered. 'I do not ask. I will take it.' Toryn clutched the floor with his toes, imagining roots grew from his feet to connect with the river. Despite his fatigue, the sword resisted the warlock's will. Shamuul spat. 'Fool. Very well. You can all perish. Then I will take the sword.' He shot out an arm towards the entrance. Toryn's weary muscles bunched. A lightning bolt struck the steps outside.

Toryn crashed back into the present. The shrouls had all fallen, but the droog still troubled the guards. The hallway darkened. Gray smoke swirled up from the shattered stone steps. Toryn cried out. 'A shreek comes!' The guards' formation stumbled back from the entrance. At the rear, the worm struck, clamping its drooling mouth around one of Drondel's men. His companions rushed forward and drove their spears into the droog's flabby body as its victim's legs kicked, then went limp. But Toryn could not help. A dark shape took form in the smoke. Toryn recalled Elodi's account of her confrontation at Calerdorn. Yet, that was an apparition, terrible, but only a trick. Was this real?

The square retreated as the rear ranks cut open the droog to rescue the guard inside. The shreek bent its back and stepped into the hall. Toryn froze as its dull black eyes bore into him. It unfurled its wings, smothering the entrance to shut out the light. The unfortunate guard clambered out of the droog and retched; the amused warlock cackled. The shreek's mouth gaped wide. Toryn found his voice. 'Cover your ears!'

The screech hammered into them with a force greater than any worldly weapon. The front rank collapsed as every bone in their bodies shattered. Toryn desperately fought to enter the Song. But what could he find to counter a shreek? The company scrambled to the back wall, throwing up their shields in fear of a second assault.

A cry! But not from the hall. Shamuul faltered. The warlock spun about and fled down the tunnel. The shreek shuddered, threw back its head and cried out, but it had lost its force. Its forlorn cry echoed through the centuries as it was dragged back to its own age.

Slowly, Toryn's hearing returned. The hallway was filled with the gasps and sobs of the stunned company. Many lay dead, many more lay injured. Lorek stumbled over the crushed bodies of the fallen. Blood trickled from his ears. He shook his head and wiped his face. 'Has it gone? Is this finished?'

Toryn sighed. 'It is. And not a moment too soon. I saw the shreeks at Roth's Doom, but only from a distance.' He looked down to the twisted bodies of the fallen. 'But at close hand… how are we to fight them?'

Cubric picked up his shield. 'This place was hard won. We must ensure the lives lost are avenged with the new blades forged from the miners' toil.' But Toryn's attention was on the tunnel Shamuul had gone. Cubric nodded. 'You do what you have to do, Toryn. I'll take things from here. We'll tend to the wounded, and then bury our dead.'

Toryn thanked him and went to the tunnel. Why had the warlock abandoned the attempt to take the *Elorsi*? The company were on the brink of defeat, and Toryn would not have stood a chance against both a shreek and warlock. He had to know. Toryn entered the Song. A deafening screech and blast of air assailed him, expelling him from the Verse. He fell back, gasping for air, fearing another attack. But none came. In the silence, the cries from the distressed Verse echoed inside his head. A dark presence, more powerful than Shamuul, had stretched it to the point it would splinter. It had to be Uluriel. Surely, only her *kruul* could cause such a rent.

Toryn's vision blurred. A horse and rider streaked across a frozen plain. He cried out, throwing his hands across his face as they suddenly burned with a brilliant, white light. More lights blazed as if the stars had fallen from the dome. Yet they too blinded him, and he could not endure to look upon them. The vision faded as the echo died.

And Toryn understood. He had seen briefly through Uluriel's eyes within the Song. Elodi raced to join the Amayans at the Crown. Both the stone and Igrayne were in danger. But Toryn took hope. The sight alone of the Amayans had pained Uluriel, and she knew they were gathering their strength. Uluriel had commanded Shamuul to head north to meet the threat. And others answered her call. A decisive battle would soon be fought at the Crown. And as much as it pained Toryn to leave his company, he knew he must join them.

34. A Star in the North

The Ruuk still clinging onto the hope of holding their position in Lunn, quailed upon seeing Elodi. Sea Mist galloped ever faster, making easy work of the uneven ground. To the people suffering under the occupation of the Ruuk, Elodi's passage brought hope. In the dark night, she appeared as a warrior of old, perhaps even of Draegelan's reign. Word spread of the bright Amayan on her proud stallion riding fearlessly through their lands, causing the Ruuk to cower behind their shields.

As the sun rose over her shoulders on the second day since leaving Keld, the frozen Lumreek Marsh glistened to her right. But the gathering clouds soon ended the light's brief visit, inflicting a dull, gray hue on the lands already in the grip of fear. Elodi glanced towards the mire. Ice rarely formed on its dank waters, and then only in the harshest of winters. The freezing wind, so far from the Nordruuk plains, seemed to relish bringing its misery to new realms. But it could not deter Sea Mist. He did not miss a step, surging onward as if he knew the urgency of their journey, stopping only when Elodi insisted. Yet she did not sleep. Her sisters' thoughts flooded hers. Together, they shared the pain of the Amanach as the stones fought the Angorlith draining their strength.

By late afternoon, in the lengthening shadow of the Kolossos, Elodi spied torches on the Great Northeast Road. One hundred or so Ruuk marched at speed towards Dunmor. News of Nordryn's retreat had spread through Lunn, and Elodi took pleasure from their panic as they scurried north. But she knew it was only temporary. If she was in Nordryn's position, she would look to reform on the north bank of the Lind River. From there, she would wait and rebuild the ranks devastated by the defeat at Roth's Doom. But how many Norgog did the enemy hold in reserve?

Elodi urged Sea Mist on, judging she could join the road south of Dunmor before the line of torches reached the town. But then she had a difficult decision to make. Would she find a suitable point to cross the Lind River west of the main bridge? She could save many leagues if she left the road and headed for the mountains. But she doubted the fast-flowing waters, fresh from the Kolossos, would have frozen, and she could not risk drowning if overcome by the cold. The bridge was her only option, but it would be guarded.

Sea Mist sped down the slope and joined the road. He dipped his head and gained another few yards of pace. Elodi rose in the saddle. The bridge lay ahead. Guarded or not, how dare they stand in her way as she raced to her sisters' aid. Elodi glanced to the sky in the east. She would be upon the Ruuk in the darkest hour before dawn, and by the Three, she would make it an hour for them to remember.

Elodi drew Sea Mist to a halt and left the road to prepare. She dismounted and led him a little way up a slope to get a good view of the crossing. A few torches flickered on the bridge and beside three guard huts on the opposite bank. Elodi used her *farsight* to determine two dozen Ruuk stood between her and the north. Their spears and shields leaned against the stone parapet, white with frost, but they had kindly cleared the ice from the roadway. The Ruuk here would have seen little of her forces of late, but perhaps they were wary following the loss of Keld. Yet that mattered not to Elodi. Ready or not, she would gain the opposite bank.

She rubbed Sea Mist's neck. 'Right then. Let's give

them the fright of their lives, boy.' She mounted and guided him back down to the road. Overhead, the clouds thickened. Elodi smiled. They would hear her coming long before they saw her. But she would keep her blade concealed until the last moment.

Sea Mist trotted along the grassy bank to within a hundred paces of the river. Elodi checked ahead. The guards huddled around the center of the bridge, appearing to be playing a game; she would soon put a stop to that. Elodi whispered. 'Ready, Misty? We'll charge straight at them. The rogues won't know what's coming.'

Sea Mist gained speed, eating up the ground, hurtling towards the bridge. The Ruuk turned, then rushed to pick up their spears and shields. But they were too slow. Elodi drew her sword and let the Amayan Fire blaze. The blast of silver light blinded the Ruuk as if the brightest star in the night sky had come down to claim their bridge. They cried out, stumbling over each other as they covered their eyes. Some jumped over the bridge to take their chances in the icy water, others turned and fled, leaving just six to form a shield wall. But Sea Mist would not be stopped. Elodi bellowed. 'Get out of my way or die!' At the last moment, the guards wisely flung themselves clear of the charging stallion.

Elodi laughed as they reached the north bank of the river. A horn blew back at the huts, but they would never catch her. She sheathed her sword and let Sea Mist slow a little as they turned west and off the road. They followed the sound of the river to their left for another hour before stopping for a brief rest. Elodi dismounted and checked for signs of a pursuit. But none could be seen. By now, the guards at the bridge would be telling their stories to justify failing to hold their position. Elodi wondered if her charge would be attributed to the ghost of Dorlan come dawn. She hoped the tale would soon spread along the front and sow fear in their hearts.

But she could not afford to gloat. The first of the day's light found the last peaks of the Kolossos. Elodi looked on with a sense of dread. Where the mountains finished, so did the Five Realms. Never did Elodi think she would leave the lands of her ancestors. But her sisters waited. She mounted. 'To Nordruuk, Misty. We should pass—' He reared and screamed. Elodi was thrown to the ground. A dark shape swooped overhead, shutting out the few stars peering through the clouds. Elodi cried out and clutched her chest as if an icy blade pierced her heart. She jumped up to calm Sea Mist. 'It's gone. It's gone.' But her pulse throbbed in her ears as her stomach churned. She searched the skies over the mountains, but thankfully the winged beast had passed. But what was it? And where did it head?

35. THE ROOTS OF CARANACH

Toryn went alone. Lorek and Janae had protested, but the coming conflict at the head of the Kolossos would inevitably result in their deaths… and possibly Toryn's and the Amayans. Yet it had to be fought: the Crown Stone could not be lost.

Toryn sped through the tunnels, lit by the glow of the *Elorsil.* Shamuul was some way in front and surely knew Toryn followed. But the warlock's attention was fixed on what lay ahead and seemed unconcerned by what was at his back. The air pulsed through the tunnel. Toryn dipped his head and leaned forward as if striding into the eye of a silent storm. He stumbled as a scream tore through the Verses. An Amayan! It had to be Igrayne. The warlocks held her at the Crown.

Toryn's grip tightened on the *Elorsil.* The sword responded, connecting with the source of its power deep below. He stopped as the tunnel suddenly narrowed and closed in on him. The rock faded and became like glass. Toryn stared down to see the river surge far beneath his feet. He kneeled and placed the point of the sword to the ground. The six remaining Amanach made themselves known. Seven underground rivers flowed from a single point from beneath the Kolossos to the roots of the standing stones. But one ended in an open wound and trickled into the Wend Gap where Toryn and Hamar had seen the first fall.

The six stones pulsed as one, yet their power was curtailed. And Toryn saw the cause. The rivers were flecked with green. A poison tainted the pure water, thus weakening the Amanach as a tree contaminated through its roots. Toryn recalled how Calestri and Arijan had almost drowned in the pools of the Foranfae. While the Menon River had diluted the yet weak poison and carried it to the sea, the Amayans had been overcome by the foulness amassing in the still pools of the forest.

Toryn stood. He had to turn back from the Crown and head to Caranach. Deep beneath its peak was the source of the land's power. Its name echoed through the Verses: the Amanspring. The tales were wrong. Caranach did not entrap the Evil One. The mighty mountain protected the Amanspring. But now it was under threat. Through the shimmering rock, Toryn saw them. Under the command of two warlocks, dozens of Norgog had mined a deep shaft. Angorsil shards, as large as a man, were set into the rocks, spewing their wrongness to where the water gushed from the deep veins of the land. And the farther they delved and set their stones, the more vulnerable the Amanach would become to the warlocks' assault.

Toryn tore himself from Igrayne's torment. He had to stop the Norgog. But they were many, and two formidable warlocks commanded them. But he had no choice.

Toryn ran without rest, sustained by the river below. But his progress was slow. The tunnel was formed thousands of years ago by Ormoroth's slaves. But the passage was not flat or straight. It weaved, plunged, then climbed steeply, perhaps to avoid the fine Elorym halls once filled with their wonders.

Toryn sped on as if led by the hands of the gods towards his fate. He never tired. At times his hand holding the *Elorsil* tingled. And at times, the rock shimmered as if not there. Toryn could see through the mountains above, on passed the heavy clouds, up to the very dome where the stars shone, unperturbed by the old powers conspiring below. At other places, the Verses beneath opened, and his vision penetrated the bedrock, down to the wide river, and even to the world beneath. To his wonder, he saw the lower half of the dome where the sun crossed, ready to return to Toryn's world.

He ducked. A shadow swooped overhead. The Verses of the mountain peaks split at its passing, dividing from the path of a dark presence as if to preserve their existence. Toryn stopped and tried to enter the Verses to the south, but the rent had closed as the shadow departed. Nyomae! The shadow sought Nyomae. And it had to be Uluriel. Of that, he was sure. Uluriel's haste, suggested Nyomae had achieved her objective. But he could do little for her now.

Toryn pushed on… down to the foundations of the tallest mountain in the known world.

36. A Deadly Legacy

Nyomae was not surprised to see the only door in the room, now opened onto a stairway. A man strode in, despite his bent frame. He scoffed. 'I see you have recovered. It is not necessary to introduce myself, seeing as you stole my face to gain entry to the cells.' Ingollo grinned. 'But I imagine that did not work out quite as you would have hoped.'

Nyomae straightened. 'Then the same must be said of this once fine realm and city, *Varsil.*' She bit her lip, struggling to curb her anger. 'Why are you keeping Idraman here? He does not deserve this treatment.' She gestured to the windows. 'And slavery? Your ancestors would be horrified at how you've squandered their legacy.'

Ingollo took a breath as if about to explain something to a child. 'Legacy? Before you rush to judgement, *Imaari,* let me educate you on what I inherited from my ancestors. A *legacy*, as you put it, in which I believe you played a vital part.' He held up a hand as Nyomae moved to protest. 'It was your Order of Echoes' — he sneered — 'a grand name for nothing more than a rabble of conjurors and swindlers, that insisted we send our best fighters on a fool's errand. Yet you had been tricked. And then to make matters worse, you commit our full strength to meet' — he spat out his words — 'in open battle no less, the largest, deadliest force we had faced in centuries. And not satisfied by seeing our noble knights trampled into the dirt, you, and this charlatan here, then deny them the chance to retreat.' His face twisted. 'My father fought at Gormadon, Imaari. My dear mother never recovered from his loss.' He jabbed his finger at the window behind her. 'In her despair, she threw herself from the Morning Tower, a symbol of hope no less! I was but a boy. And I was by no means the only child orphaned by your actions. Just about everyone in the city mourned the loss of a loved one. Many could not bear to live with their grief, and chose the same end as my mother. And when we learned it was one of our own that obliterated our finest, are you not surprised the trust in your Order was lost?'

Nyomae met his glare. 'If you would allow me to respond, I shall—'

'You do not have that right.' The Varsil hissed. 'There is nothing you can say to justify your treason!'

'Treason! But I…' Nyomae stopped. It would be a waste of her breath to argue. She lowered her voice. 'Am I to believe I will be held here as punishment?'

Ingollo walked to the door. 'A year for every life you took.' He turned. 'I shall leave you to calculate the length of your sentence.'

Nyomae strode towards him, but he appeared farther away. 'If you won't listen to my reasons, please know this. You are being manipulated by the old enemy. A *kruul* has crossed the Caerwals, something we did not think possible.' She motioned to the South Window. 'I see you train an army. For what purpose? What have your Ul-dalak masters demanded of you?' Ingollo's eyes narrowed. Nyomae continued. 'The Ul-dalak strive to bring back Ormoroth. Surely, you're aware this would mean…' her shoulders sagged. 'Of course, you're aware. You conspire with them.'

'Conspire? You make it sound so sordid.' Ingollo smiled. 'No, Imaari. Our eyes have been opened. We await the return of the true lord.' He grasped the door handle. 'And one day you shall kneel before Ormoroth to atone for your sins.'

Nyomae woke to find breakfast laid out on a cloth upon the floor. They ate what would be considered a feast beyond the city walls. The days came and went. Nyomae marveled as the walls glowed, much like the stone in the Elorym Hall. Thankfully, Mosholuk had yet to keep his promise, leading Nyomae to suspect the Caerwal Stone could still repel servants of the Dark Verses. She grew restless, desperate for news of events in the north, but her efforts to find Toryn in the Song were fruitless. At times, the door would appear, and she could walk the balcony and take in the fresh air. But after her evening meal, she would suddenly be overwhelmed by tiredness and not wake until dawn.

Nyomae had tried another tact with Idraman. She spoke of their times together before the dark days of their quest north and the horrors of Gormadon. She recalled trivial events when not at their studies, steering clear of the significant milestones of their discoveries. By stirring memories of his past, she hoped to find a way through the fog of his mind. But the man passed in and out of sleep, perhaps exhausted by her company after three centuries of solitude. When he slept, Nyomae paced the room, looking out of the windows as she tried to make sense of her predicament. The Verses of the room were still closed to her, but she was able to find snatches of Elmarand's history by searching those of the streets below.

Ingollo was obviously under the influence of the Uldalak, but Nyomae could not tell if Mosholuk's *kruul* controlled him. Yet, if Uluriel had spread her lies immediately following the battle at Gormadon, perhaps possession was unnecessary as his indoctrination would be complete.

And Nyomae had come to understand why the Caerwal Pass was left unguarded. In the decade after Idraman sealed the route, a rudimentary defense was set with the scarce resources at hand. But as Uluriel's deception took hold, the people of the south began to fear an invasion not from the Ul-dalak, but from the Five Realms. Uluriel had convinced them, the impoverished people of the north now craved the riches of the south. Thus, the canals were drained, and the water diverted. Hence, an invading army marching on Elmarand would first have to negotiate a wide desert. It had been a challenge for Nyomae and her horse. An army making the crossing would soon weaken under the harsh conditions and leave themselves vulnerable to ambush. But the desperate measures had hurt the people in the north of Talamaris. Their livelihoods were destroyed, forcing them to either scratch out a miserable existence, or head south. Yet, those who fled the desert found the cities also suffered, and they unwittingly became at first low-paid workers, then nothing more than slaves as the new dictator took hold.

But while Nyomae came to appreciate how the south had fallen so far, she had yet to understand the real reason why Idraman had not been put to the sword. Did his befuddled mind yet conceal Ormoroth's Name? But if it did, surely it was not beyond Mosholuk to wrench it from him in his current state.

Nyomae sat in front of Idraman. His gray eyes did not see her, but he must have had moments of clarity. He had tried to warn her when, as Hope, she had heard his call when approaching Archonholm. And it must have been Idraman who had stirred Toryn's Imaari powers while he was held in the Archon's dungeon.

The old Imaari blinked. Nyomae leaned forward and touched his shoulder. 'Idraman? Do you remember Draegelan?' He lifted his head; the name still meant something to him. She tried to delve deeper. 'You and Draegelan used to walk the banks of the Menon. I saw you discussing matters you would not share with me. Do you remember?'

His brow creased. His cloudy eyes moved as if seeing the river. He went to speak, then clamped his mouth shut. Nyomae's skin crawled as the room darkened and a rush of foul air blew through the North Window. She rushed to look out, half-expecting to see the corvraak. A winged beast did indeed approach, but the creature plunging towards the city was too large for a raven, and its ragged wings ended in cruel, barbed hooks. It swooped over Elmarand, staining the white towers with its shadow. Nyomae groaned: a keshwing. It was as she feared. Not all had fallen to Draegelan's archers. Below, people cried out, covering their heads as they ran from the streets. Idraman rocked, moaning under his breath.

Nyomae shrank back, aghast at his words. 'She returns.'

37. PIT OF DESPAIR

Elmarand's streets were empty, the city silent. Night had fallen, but it was not the dark that crushed the people's spirit. Nyomae was certain Uluriel had come. Not her *kruul*, but Uluriel herself, riding upon a fearful keshwing. And according to Idraman's mutterings, it was not her first time in Elmarand. The old Imaari shook with a force belying his strength. Nyomae tried to calm him, concerned his bones would crack under the stress. But she also struggled to maintain her sanity. Unable to hold down her food since Uluriel's arrival, Nyomae felt weak, dreading the moment she would once more meet the bane of her life. She had long feared the confrontation, but still Nyomae felt unprepared. And Idraman? He was close to death. Surely, he could not survive.

The walls flickered. The light faded… then glowed anew. Nyomae held her breath, aware the ancient stone strived to counter Uluriel's presence. The door opened. Four robed figures entered. Two approached Nyomae. One held out a cloth while the other pinned Nyomae's arms behind her back. She recognized the odor of night lily on the cloth and blacked out at its touch.

The freezing floor burned Nyomae's skin. She sat and shuddered as the icy air seeped into her lungs. The dark and dank air suggested she was beneath the city, but it did not have the feel of the dungeon. Idraman moaned beside her. Nyomae reached and grasped his cold hand, but he failed to respond to her touch. She drew his shivering body close to hers but had little warmth to offer. However, it was not the cold that troubled Nyomae; they had been brought here to meet Uluriel.

Nyomae found her way into the Song and entered the Verse of the dark place. They were held in a great chamber, deep beneath the city. It had been built in the decades following the battle at Gormadon… and solely for Uluriel unable to tolerate the vibrations of the Caerwal Stone of the Sun Tower. But Nyomae could go no deeper. The Verse repelled her in the same manner as the air around Draegelan's Seat. But Nyomae would not be denied. She had to know more. Drawing on her remaining strength, she pushed back. Battling against the force resisting her presence, she suddenly broke through. Ear-splitting screams from a hundred throats assailed her. The Verse splintered. Idraman cried out as the screams burst into the present. She stared at him. He had been one of those voices. He had suffered as one of many. Their intolerable pain had shattered the Verse as if a pane of glass.

A door opened. Footsteps echoed through the hall. Torches were lit. The light revealed a high ceiling and the shallow pit in which Nyomae and Idraman sat. In front, a dark shape loomed, casting a cruel shadow with long fingers that groped at their feet. She had seen it before. At the head of the pit, sat a replica of Ormoroth's iron throne in Vortimo. Her shoulders sank as the full horror dawned on her — the chamber served the same purpose as the one in Vortimo. This was the place Uluriel had tortured and interrogated the once-proud rulers of the city, including Ingollo. Nyomae now pitied the puppet Varsil. Few could resist Uluriel… if any. And now she had to face the same trial. In their prime, perhaps she and Idraman could have met the challenge. But with Idraman weakened by the centuries of incarceration, Nyomae doubted she could endure for long.

The torchbearers departed as two more robed figures entered. They carried a slate between them, walking with great care towards the pit. An object sat beneath a cloth. Nyomae's stomach knotted: they had brought an Angorsil. The bearers lowered the slate to the floor in front of the throne. They took a sharp breath as their gloved hands lifted and placed the Angorsil on a stone slab at the head of the pit. They stood and walked away with obvious relief having completed their task.

The heavy doors swung shut and the bolts were thrown. The torches died with a hiss. The hall filled with the green hue of the Angorsil. Nyomae pitched forward. Her skull pulsed to the same vibration of the shard. She clamped her hands to her ears, and clenched her teeth, but could not prevent the dull, relentless throb jarring her bones. She clasped Idraman's hand and tried to enter the Song. But the hall's Verses were now beyond her reach.

Nyomae closed her eyes and tried to imagine the faces of Elodi and Toryn. But the Angorsil overwhelmed her, forcing its way into her Verse. Nyomae was dragged back to Gormadon... to the destructive memories she had long tried to subdue. She cowered once more as the drayloks loomed. Burning eyes from hollow skulls bore into hers; their dreadful wails ripped the hope from her chest; their flailing, barbed hair tore the flesh from her face. And then came their fire. Nyomae screamed and wrenched herself free before the flames took hold.

She lay panting on the cold floor, powerless before the Angorsil. Her hand reached out. Nyomae whispered, wary hidden ears would hear. 'Idraman? What can we do?' But he could barely return her grip.

Without knowing why, she muttered, 'Father?' His face came to her. Nyomae recalled sitting on his lap as he had consoled her. The children of the village had mocked her when she had claimed she could speak with her pet cat,

Piplo. Determined to prove it, she had sat him on her lap and revealed what he was thinking. But all the children had heard was the purring of a contented cat. They had laughed until the tears rolled down their cheeks. And when Nyomae could stand it no longer, she had fled with their taunts ringing in her ears. At home, her father spoke for the first time of the talents inherited from her dead mother. The other children could not begin to understand and would one day come to envy her powers. But her father had not suspected another would one day come to their village and take her from him.

Nyomae took some comfort from the memory of his soothing voice. But how she wished she could have lived a simple life tending to the land, oblivious to the troubles beyond her village. She sat and defied her dread to look upon the Angorsil. In a matter of days, it would sap her strength and begin to alter her Verse. Once her early years were taken from her, its corruption would proceed to the present. It was if a poison had penetrated the root, seeped through the stem, and would finally find its way into the flower.

Nyomae's hand went to her face. If she could not break free, she would return to the shadow. But this time, she would be in the thrall of the Ul-dalak, and there would be no return to the light.

38. The Monarchs of Old

Elodi pulled her furs closer against the bitter cold. The wind had dropped, and she found herself engulfed by a thick fog. Ice crystals settled on her hair and Sea Mist's mane. She cocked her head, certain she could hear the air chime as the tiny flakes danced. Had she not been on such a crucial mission, Elodi would have been tempted to stop and listen to their song. But the fog had slowed her progress. She could see no farther than a dozen paces, yet it was the silence that unnerved her. And with no mountains or features to guide her way, Elodi had lost all sense of direction. For all she knew, Sea Mist could be walking on the edge of a deep crevasse, or a host of warlocks could be on her tail.

Slowly, the fog began to lift. Elodi brought Sea Mist to a halt and lowered her hood. Ahead, the air darkened, yet it must be at least another hour before nightfall. She tipped back her head and could just see lighter skies high above. Elodi realized they must have gone farther than needed and now approached the Kolossos from the north. She stroked Sea Mist's neck. 'Good boy. You knew where we were going all along, eh. Or can you sense the Amayans' horses?'

Elodi tried once more to locate her sisters, but she had heard nothing since entering the fog. On they went. After a league, the ground became uneven, and the light began to fade. As they rode, Elodi recalled the tales of the Kolossos Crown's four peaks. Their pointed summits resembled the crowns once worn by the kings and queens of the old days. But whether they were formed by the gods from a single, vast mountain, or by the Elorym at the height of their power, or merely by the countless centuries of gales howling in from the north, no one knew.

Elodi shuddered. The silhouette now rose out of the mist as if a giant monarch stood over her, passing judgement as she dared to enter its domain. She could not remember the names of all the peaks, but the tallest, Gorgonach, featured in many a chilling tale of winged beasts that nested on its craggy summit. She patted Sea Mist. 'Don't worry, boy. Even if half true, they wouldn't bother us down here. We'd be no more than a tiny morsel. We're not worth their effort.' She glanced up, hoping she was right.

Elodi heard the howling wind far to the north as it scoured the icy plains of Nordruuk. But not satisfied with its usual haunt, the gale turned its eyes on the south. She braced as it came, thundering like a giant wave seeking to bring down the cliffs. Sea Mist steadied himself, and Elodi clung to his neck as the gust battered into them. But it carried more than just the cold from the plains. The wails filled Elodi with dread as if a warning screamed by the Maidens' hoarse throats. She cried out. 'We must find shelter! Take us there, Misty. I trust you.'

He needed no encouragement. Sea Mist trotted on, seeming as sure-footed as if on the flats of Dorn Plain. Before them, the last of the mist fled from the gale. The moon and stars shone bright in the clear skies to reveal the Kolossos Crown in its full glory. Elodi stared aghast; the tales had not done it justice.

Then, as fast as it had come, the wind departed, splitting its forces to hurtle down the east and west flanks of the mountains. Sea Mist slowed, then stopped, as if he too was taken aback. Ahead of them, a cliff rose as if a frozen wave, poised and ready to crash over them. Standing close to the cliffs, in the darkness it looked as if the giant monarch now wore a cloak. Elodi felt like a mouse that had stolen into the throne room, looking to hide under the ruler's robes. But she had more than its large feet to fear. Elodi sat taller, annoyed at herself for her childish thoughts. She was no mouse, and the mountains were just that… mountains, no matter how daunting.

But the cliff concealed something far more dangerous; the cursed ruins of the Elorym fortress. A ghostly light flickered in the deep fissure running through the mass of rock. Then Elodi sensed it. Beyond the cliff, then behind the fortress, set thousands of feet above her between the four peaks, stood the Crown Stone. But now it stood exposed, vulnerable now its age-old defenses were breached.

Elodi paused. As a child, she had been scared out of her skin by the stories of wraiths haunting the northerly tip of the Kolossos. And that child now baulked at the dread of what lay inside. She muttered to herself. 'Fool. Not now.' She had survived a ferocious storm at sea, faced thousands of Ruuk screaming for her blood, looked three Reapers in the eye, and had endured a warlock's touch. Her sisters needed her. The Crown Stone must be protected. And that was where she must go.

Elodi swallowed her childhood fears and nudged Sea Mist forward into the ravine. She shivered as the sheer walls seemed to swallow them, drawing her towards the fortress in its belly. The ghostly light was now tinged blue and flickered along the sides of the cliffs. The path dipped and led her down to a spot where the ravine widened, and then to the source of the light.

Elodi smiled. Five Amayans stood with their horses by an opening in the cliff. She dismounted and strode to meet them. They turned towards her as if expecting her arrival. No word was spoken as they formed a circle and linked arms. Elodi looked to Neeve and Madraal in wonder. Neeve was taller than her sisters, but her eyes portrayed not the centuries of wisdom and anguish of the others. Yet Neeve had an obvious physical strength her sisters lacked. Madraal appeared to share the same mother as Arijan, seeming at ease in her lithe body.

Eryn broke the silence. 'Five warlocks hold Igrayne at the stone. And Vordrak is with them.' Her fist clenched. 'And this will be his last act in these mortal realms. Amyra *will* be avenged.' She glanced over her shoulder. 'Of the others, we remember one as Shamuul before the shadow descended upon us. He came from Drunsberg.'

Elodi paled. 'The mines?'

'Do not fret. He is not in possession of the *Elorsil*. Thus, we can assume he has not defeated Toryn. I came across his company as I rode west through the pass. They were under attack.' She took Elodi's hand. 'They escaped. And I was able to reveal the sword's name to Toryn. But while he can use its power, it can still be as much as a threat to him, as it is to his enemies.'

Elodi sighed. 'But he is safe... for now.'

Eryn nodded. 'He is safe. We would know immediately if the *Elorsil* was in a warlock's hand. So yes, he still fights.' She held Elodi's gaze. 'Shokresh is also present. I'm sure you have something you wish to settle with that fiend. Yet Jehenum, the most powerful of them all, is absent. Of him, we can find no trace and have not seen him since we pursued Vordrak. He must have dark deeds to fulfil elsewhere.'

Elodi looked to each in turn. 'And Igrayne?'

'Mercifully, she is spared their torment for the moment as they prepare to strike at the Amanach. Each wields an Angorsil, and we fear it may fall soon if we cannot counter them.' She bowed her head. 'And should that happen, Igrayne will be turned and... lost.'

Calestri's jaw bunched. 'We face a formidable challenge. It has been centuries since such a force has gathered. But we must not fail. It is here we'll fight a decisive battle.'

'Then how do we fight them?'

Neeve exhaled. 'We face a dilemma. We are not yet strong enough to strike. Yet, the strength we draw from the stone will weaken its resistance against the Angorsil. But time is against us. We have discussed possible tactics. But we wish to hear from you.'

Elodi gaped. 'But your knowledge and experience are superior to mine. What could I possibly tell you that would be of help?'

Eryn tickled Sea Mist's ear. 'You have spent more time in a warlock's company than any of us of late… and lived to tell the tale. You may have learned of such things that remain hidden from us. But it's best you tell, rather than we meld our minds. I do not wish the warlocks to learn of our numbers… well, not yet.'

Elodi thought for a moment. 'If they have a weakness, it is their arrogance. I don't think they can envisage defeat. Perhaps the shadow that descended on both Imaari and Amayan following Gormadon, has convinced them we're too weak to challenge them.'

Eryn looked to the others. 'It is not without precedent. The Elorym once believed they too were unassailable. It appears to be an inherent flaw of the great races who have spent too long in power.'

Elodi recalled Nyomae's account of the Elorym's fall. 'Yet this time, the warlocks may have good reason to feel invincible. Shokresh is convinced Ormoroth's return is nigh.'

Calestri scoffed. 'They won't get any arguments from me. If their lord returns, their ultimate victory as inevitable.'

Eryn's eyes glowed. 'Then it's vital we achieve a victory here and scupper their plans.'

Arijan clasped her sword. 'Yet we face five while the power of the stones wane. And they hold our sister for a reason. They're expecting us. Taking Igrayne served to announce their intention. I believe they want us to attack.'

Elodi had a thought. 'Shokresh treated me as if they no longer regard you as worthy opponents. They see Amayans… us, as a spent force.'

Calestri frowned. 'Yet, they go to great lengths to turn us to their cause. First Tanis, then an attempt on Amyra, Cymori, and now Igrayne. Each will have delayed their preparations for Ormoroth's return.'

Elodi answered. 'I suspect that is to… as the stable hands in Calerdorn used to say, and rather crudely… rub our noses in it. I imagine they take great delight in turning sister against sister. They see themselves as the noble servants of Ormoroth, but beneath they are bitter souls, corrupted by centuries of resentment. No, I see it as nothing more than a spiteful act to possess an Amayan.' She paused, reminded of the faces of Gundrul, Cubric, and the captains onboard the *Celestra* when they had listened to her plan to take Drunsberg. That was barely six months ago, but already it seemed a decade had passed.

Eryn's eyes narrowed. 'So… aside from their dark arts, we're dealing with the likes of Nordleng.' She turned to look down the ravine. 'They'll be expecting us to rescue Igrayne, but perhaps they underestimate our strength. But… we will have to strike fast before they appreciate we are not, by any means, a spent force.'

'There's something else.' Elodi hesitated. 'I'm not sure if this is relevant. But while they don't regard us as warriors worthy of note, they do' — she shuddered, recalling the warlock's cold touch — 'desire us. Hence, they may wish to capture, rather than kill us.'

A wry smile passed across Calestri's face. 'That may give us the upper hand if they see us in that way.' The smile faded. 'But if they think we'd allow that to happen…' she drew her sword, 'they'll lose a hand before they can lay one on me.'

Elodi looked down to her hip. 'There's something else. Shokresh was the *kruul* that came to Archonholm. While in possession of the Castellan, he took my sword. I'm afraid it's now useless against him, but I don't know if his curse prevents its use against others.'

Madraal held out her hand. 'May I?' Elodi handed over the sword. She lifted the blade. 'I sense a curse of sorts. But it will still aid ours. Perhaps it's best you avoid a face-to-face confrontation with him, but its steel can still open a wound should it come to that.'

Eryn took the weapon and gave it back to Elodi. 'Thank you, sister. Your insights are most enlightening.' She clapped her hands. 'Now, if you're rested, we will attempt to penetrate the warlocks' shield and reach out to Igrayne. Shamuul seeks to sever the bond, but Igrayne has many years behind her, thus it is strong.'

Elodi nodded. 'I am ready. What do you require of me?'

'Let the Fire kindle within. Up until now, you've experienced the bond as a stream flowing through you, but with our combined strength it will be far stronger… so be prepared.'

The Amayans bowed their heads and clasped hands. Elodi's feet tingled as the ground warmed. The Fire stirred. Heat surged through her chest, into her arms, and coursed around their circle. A ball of Fire blazed at the center. Eryn called out. 'We seek Igrayne.'

Elodi swayed as a roar filled her ears. It came like a gigantic wave, breaking, then rushing up through her, stretching every sinew, urging her to places unknown.

Eryn's calm voice emerged from the torrent. *Do not resist, Elodi. Let go.* She tipped back her head. Her body seemed to rise, yet her feet stayed firmly on solid rock. Elodi's head swirled as she suddenly shot over crumbled walls and towers, through the mountain, and into the Crown beyond. She shuddered to a halt as if flying into the face of a raging storm. Eryn yelled. *Push on. The warlocks attempt to deny us.*

Back in the ravine, hands grasped hers as the ground trembled beneath her feet. The warlocks' defense screeched as the Amayans fought to enter. They broke through. In the silence, Elodi heard the gasps as her distant self struggled to breathe. Yet she was calm. And before her, stood the Amanach, clear among the air swirling about the Crown.

Igrayne was chained to the stone, surrounded by five pulsing Angorsil. Her arms were stretched back, and her head hung limp from her taut shoulders. She was weak, drained by her efforts to resist the warlocks' shards.

Eryn spoke. *Igrayne. We have come.* Igrayne tried to move, but she had not the strength to speak. Overhead, the darkness retreated as the sun rose, then quickly crossed the sky to make way once more for the night. Elodi felt as if she watched from above as the Amayans called upon the Amanach. A river flowed, glistening as if bearing a thousand stars to aid the Crown Stone. The Amayans became as one. Igrayne's head lifted.

Eryn's voice echoed. *Take heart. We will free you.* The Amayans shared the pain of the one, bringing brief respite while giving her strength. Their minds melded. But Elodi sensed doubt among them. Not since the tragedy of Gormadon had five warlocks joined forces. This was to be a crucial battle, a battle not fought by vast armies, but the powerful few of the light and dark. A bitter defeat would soon follow should the warlocks destroy the stone and turn Igrayne to the Dark Verses. But even if the Amayans prevailed, it would only delay the Ul-dalak's relentless drive to victory, unless they slew the warlocks. Yet only one had been slain since the days Draegelan wielded the *Elorsil*. But the one who had achieved that rare feat, stood with them: Neeve. And another was now in possession of the *Elorsil*.

But as the sisters began to take heart, the stone flickered green, and the air chilled. The Angorsil had penetrated Igrayne's defense. They watched helpless as the warlocks lifted the last of the shadows concealing Igrayne's recent past. And to Elodi's dismay, they found a weakness she had fought to withhold from her sisters... and herself. Igrayne screamed. The bond was severed, but not before her secret was laid bare.

Elodi fell back as their circle broke. She stared at her sisters' faces, as it dawned on them what they had just witnessed. In the aftermath of Gormadon, Igrayne, isolated and her mind lost, had wandered alone into the west. In the woodlands of Tamarand, she had met another stranded soul from the battle. In their desperation, they had clung to each other in the dark. A union had formed. Elodi now understood.

Igrayne had met Finromir: Igrayne was Toryn's mother.

But as the warlocks pursued them, they had been forced to go their separate ways. Finromir had fled north with Toryn. And Igrayne had ridden south... with Toryn's twin sister.

Elodi sat with Neeve in the opening in the cliff face. She suffered Igrayne's guilt as if her own, enduring the loss of her beloved children and Finromir. Igrayne had found refuge in the mountains east of Telamir, perhaps sensing the lingering Elorym power of the lake. But the mountains could not sustain mother and child, and Igrayne often had to venture outside for supplies. And it was on one such foray that Shamuul came across her, and then tracked her back to their shelter in a forest near Kalimir.

Igrayne had fought like no other since the height of the Amayans' strength. Her cries carried far and wide, leading the woodsmen to fear a great evil had risen in their land. They came in numbers but were too late. The woodsmen found the bodies of a dozen Nordleng, a distraught, badly wounded Amayan, but no child or warlock. They took Igrayne to the healers of Kalimir, but the shame of her failure delayed her recovery. And by the time she was able to leave, the trail was cold, and her daughter lost.

Unbeknown to Igrayne, her child had been taken to Archonholm where Uluriel was in possession of the Archon. And perhaps mercifully, she was oblivious to the horrors inflicted upon the girl to break her will. On learning all she needed, Uluriel decreed via the Archon, the child was to be executed according to the law.

Neeve sobbed. 'We did not know. We first met Igrayne in the Ravern Hills. But while we all lived under the shadow, forgetting our distant past, she wandered as if a hermit. At first, she resisted our offer of help, appearing not to recognize us. And though she eventually came to trust us, she could not, or dared not, speak of the cause of her pain. And now we understand... and the warlocks have revived the memory. They will torment her and exploit her guilt for not protecting her offspring.'

Elodi stared aghast towards the fortress. 'The last wyke hanged from the bridge must have been... ten years ago. I remember hearing the tale. At the time, I was thankful another had been removed from the realm.' Her hand went to her mouth. 'Surely, she was still only a child... and they left her to rot, dangling over the ravine. But why? If our enemy still holds Finromir captive, why would they not...?' She sighed. 'Ah, of course. Uluriel would have known the girl had Imaari and Amayan blood. She feared what she would become.'

Neeve stood. 'I cannot imagine the hurt Igrayne suffered, and now the warlocks taunt her. And she won't know Toryn survived.' She gasped. 'Wait. She met him… just before the battle at Roth's Doom. Yet the memory must be buried so deep, otherwise she would have surely known him as her son.'

Eryn returned from feeding the horses. 'It also raises another question. The *Elorsil* awoke from Toryn's touch. It was said the blade responded in Draegelan's hand as if he was an Elorym warrior. Was he also a child of such a union?'

Elodi frowned. 'And does this mean Toryn could become as powerful as Draegelan? If there was a time for such a strong ally, it is now.'

Eryn shook her head. 'It took Draegelan decades to master his skills. But we don't have decades.' She glanced down the ravine. 'It pains me to say this, but perhaps it's a blessing they concentrate their efforts on the Crown Stone. That gives Toryn a little more time to master the weapon he wields.'

But Elodi was not so sure. 'But will they tempt Toryn here? They could set a trap if they make it known Igrayne is his mother.'

Eryn's eyes glowed. 'Then let us also look upon this as a trap for them. We number six, and with Igrayne, seven. If Toryn comes, we may even hold the upper hand. Perhaps we can trap and defeat *them*.'

'Sisters!' Arijan strode towards them. 'Something stirs at the fortress. I suspect our enemy seek to raise the wraiths.'

Eryn clasped her sword. 'Then we come.' They followed Arijan down the narrow pathway leading to the ruins. Elodi's scalp prickled. Ahead, the ground flickered a faint green. It felt wrong beneath her feet.

Calestri spat. 'Their corruption spreads.'

Eryn gathered the Amayans. 'We cannot allow the warlocks to delay our approach by rousing the wraiths. We must gain the ruins and prevent them from using our ancestors against us.' She looked towards the green-tinged ruins at the end of the ravine. 'Alas, we must bring the horses. I'd rather leave them here, but speed is vital. The path through the mountains to the Crown is treacherous and steep, but they must come. They may yet play their part.'

39. The Elorym Queen

Nyomae held Idraman. She was astounded the Imaari yet lived, but surely, he could not endure for much longer. Her head ached. The Angorsil's pulse had grown until it seemed a hammer pounded the inside of her skull. Idraman no longer shook, but for no other reason that he had no strength left to respond to the torment.

Nyomae drifted into a fitful sleep. Half aware she slept, she took herself to the room at the top of the Archon's Tower, hoping to find Toryn. It was a slim hope. She had lost all sense of time. Was it night? Did Toryn sleep? But as she waited in her dream, another came. A tall woman with a kind face, took her hand and led her out of the doorway onto the balcony. A corvraak swooped out of the skies and grasped the railing. It invited them onto its back, then flew north, soaring high over the jagged ridge of the Kolossos. In no time, the peaks of the Crown came into view. The bird swooped west, down towards the Mawlgrim Mire. But no marshes smothered the land. In its place, stood a great city surrounded by acres upon acres of farm fields. And Nyomae understood. The woman had taken her back to the age of the Elorym.

Nyomae watched from afar as Ormoroth had driven icy gales to freeze the fertile plains and destroy the crop. Yet the Elorym were equal to Ormoroth's threat. They fashioned walls of ice, hundreds of feet high to deny the winds seeking to bring down their fine buildings. Pillars of stone, quarried from the Caerwals, were then set to draw upon the power of the deep rivers. Thus, behind the ice and their stone walls, the great city thrived once more and held winter's death at bay.

Yet Ormoroth was not to be denied a foothold in the south. First, he unleashed the vanguard of his vast armies to pound the city. And again, the Elorym resisted. But Ormoroth had more than armies at his call. Drawing upon the Anglorith's power, he changed the direction of the wind. Bringing warm air from the south, the Elorym's ice walls melted. As they thawed, the land flooded, and the Mawlgrim Mire was formed. Now Ormoroth sent forth his full might, razing the city to the ground, leaving the ruins to be swallowed by the marshes.

The vision did not end with the defeat. Hundreds of Elorym were taken, chained, and paraded across the mire to the glee of their victors. But many walked tall and refused to kneel before their captors. The baying hordes parted. A dark figure strode through. It stopped and removed its helm. The Elorym recognized her as one of their own kind. A queen from their legends by the name of Raanesha. She had ruled as the Elorym's power had grown. Keen to expand the empire, she had led a crusade across the seas, but was lost. Yet now the queen had returned.

Raanesha raised her hand, then scythed across the lines of the defiant Elorym. The legs of half their numbers broke. Now they kneeled before her! They were slain and left to rot in the mire — the remainder she forced to march north to Vorkirik.

The vision faded and Nyomae felt the pull of her present Verse. She groaned. Raanesha was Uluriel. She had revealed her past, and her true power. She had been an Elorym Queen. sailing far beyond the shores of the known realms… but not beyond the reach of Ormoroth. In a distant land, he had deceived, then turned her to his cause. Believing him to be a wise hermit studying the Maidens' Song, she had first listened to his teaching, then submitted to his ways. Thus, the mighty Raanesha became Uluriel, and Queen of the Ul-dalak. Ormoroth had appointed her commander of his forces, and with her knowledge of the Elorym, she had finally brought their long reign to an end.

Nyomae's shoulders dropped. Uluriel had defeated far greater powers than what the Five Realms could raise against her. Soon, all would bow before her again, whether by choice, or by force.

Nyomae woke from a restless sleep. Her dreams had been troubled, yet she preferred sleep to the harsh reality of the pit. But the morning, if it was indeed morning, did not bring hope. Her head felt ready to split as the unremitting pulse of the Angorsil forced its way into her skull.

Nyomae's stomach churned. Someone approached. The doors groaned as they were forced open to admit the warlock. For the third time in her long life, Nyomae faced Mosholuk. But on this occasion, she faced him alone. No knights or Imaari were at her side. And Idraman, the once most powerful of the Order, was but a feeble old man on the verge of death.

Mosholuk strode to the edge of the pit. He stood in his dull, black armor as if ready for battle. But he needed no weapon today. The warlock's black eyes glistened in the torchlight. His deep voice thundered in Nyomae's chest. 'I see you suffer, Imaari.' He glanced towards the Angorsil — the pulse ceased. 'There. Now you can hear what I have to say.' Mosholuk sat on the edge of the pit. 'You are eager for news in the north.' He rubbed his chin with a theatrical flourish. 'Now. Shall I tell you? Or… should I leave you guessing of the fate of your friends?' But Nyomae knew he savored the opportunity to cause her dismay. The leather of his glove creaked as he raised a finger. 'No. It would be cruel to leave you in the dark.' He smiled and waved his hand towards the torches. 'Figuratively speaking, of course. But… perhaps hearing of your friends' woes would cause you pain.' He leaned forward. 'What say you, Imaari? Do you wish to know?'

Nyomae straightened as best she could. 'Tell me, warlock. But tell me the truth. I am sick of the lies of your kind.'

He laughed as he climbed into the pit. 'Oh, you shall hear the truth, Nyomae.' He strolled towards her. 'I need not deceive you. Your predicament pleases me.' Nyomae braced as Mosholuk's hand reached out and caressed her cheek. Her jaw clenched against his cold touch. Thankfully, he withdrew, but then he turned to Idraman. He nudged the Imaari's crumbled cloak with his foot. Idraman recoiled and groaned. Mosholuk smirked. 'Did you really think this wretch could save you?' He spun around to face her. 'But I delay. What of events in the north?' He held out a hand. 'I suggest you sit. My tale may not be to your liking.'

But Nyomae had no choice. Her legs buckled and she collapsed beside Idraman. The warlock laughed. 'There. Now you can console each other. Now… I shall begin.' Mosholuk folded his arms. 'Your farm boy has not long to live. He is stranded beneath the Kolossos and will not see the light of day again.' Nyomae refused to look away. His eyes flashed. 'And as for those deluded *Sisters of the Stones*', he sneered as if taking pleasure from knowing the name they used. 'They ride into a trap. They believe they can free one we hold captive, but they will soon come to learn how the Crown of Sorrows came by such a name.' He turned to walk away, then stopped, and spun back. 'And yes, that means we know the location of the stone. But that is the least of the bad tidings in the north.' Mosholuk's eyes flickered. 'Ah yes, you are about to—'

Nyomae cried out. She clung onto Idraman as the scream of an Amanach tore through the Verses. The screech pitched ever higher, until Nyomae could feel its pain but no longer hear its cry. It stopped. Nyomae sank back, gasping for air.

A second stone had shattered. Now only five remained. She stared up to the ceiling as her hope drained away. How could they resist? The Amayans' strength waned. Toryn had yet to fully understand his powers… and she remained trapped too far away to help.

Mosholuk sighed. 'Ah. How terrible for you. I shall leave you to grieve. But you will eventually accept the inevitable. You have no choice, Imaari. You will beg for clemency before long. And… perhaps I may find it in my heart to grant it. But there will be conditions.'

As he left, he passed his hand over the Angorsil, and the pulse resumed. Nyomae closed her eyes, desperate for relief from the throbbing shard. But she could find none, and the Angorsil beat louder as if a drum pronouncing her execution.

40. Song of the Wraiths

Eryn led the Amayans to the ruined fortress that sat beneath the heavy cloud, clinging to the Crown's four peaks. Her voice echoed off the ravine's sheer cliffs. 'Stay strong. Trapped spirits of both Elorym and Ormoroth's servants will seek to delay our progress. Most are not evil, just envious of the living. But it's not beyond the guile of the warlocks to turn them against us.'

Elodi shuddered as they emerged from the ravine, but it was not the cool air trapped between the cliffs that chilled her. Ahead, the ruins of the ancient fortress appeared as if bones protruding from a shattered body.

Eryn spoke of its history. 'The Elorym quarried deep into the plateau and used the rock to construct the fortress. In its day, it housed thousands of warriors. It took decades for Ormoroth's forces to locate the stronghold, and even once known, it took decades more to finally capture it. And then it only fell once the Elorym's power had diminished.' Eryn pointed to the gap between the quarried cliffs and the crumbling fortress walls. 'But perhaps their greatest achievement was bringing the soil from the south to build farms to feed their armies. I believe they used the Crown Stone to nurture crops that otherwise would fail to grow in these climes.'

Elodi glanced up as they passed beneath the broken arch of the gatehouse. A few stones sat precariously overhead as if trying to maintain the semblance of a defense. Yet nothing remained of the huge gates that had once hung from the large, rusting hinges still set in the wall. On the far side of the fortress, three crumbling towers clung to the sides of Gorgonach, stubbornly defying the attempts of the ages to bring them down.

Arijan placed her arm around Calestri but spoke no words. This was the place, Calestri had fought a shreek. But she was just one of thousands who had suffered in the many battles of the fortress. A chill breeze blew as they entered a large square at the center. Wisps of mist weaved in and out of the ruins towards the Amayans as if to greet… or warn them away.

Elodi stared, unsure if she saw forlorn figures floating against the swirling wind. But as soon as her eyes fixed on a shape, it dispersed to form another elsewhere. But this was not the Nym. Her face tingled as the mist whispered in a strange tongue. She looked to the others. They too walked as if in a trance, gaping at the ghostly figures. Erin wandered towards a derelict hall, while Madraal stumbled, holding out her hands in front as if lost in fog. Each Amayan went their own way as if led by a host to their quarters.

They disappeared. Elodi blinked. She found herself alone in the square. But this was no ruin. Above, youthful stars shone bright, not yet dimmed by the ages. The fortress glistened as if coated by frost, despite the absence of both the moon and cold air. Ahead, the Crown appeared as polished silver, seeming taller, more splendid, more regal. This was a sacred place Elodi would lay down her life to defend.

A shadow stained the pristine wall to her right. Elodi's hand went to her sword as the shadow grew. A sickening crack of bones defiled the still air. She turned to see a cloaked figure straighten and unfurl its long limbs. A draylok! The hag's long, barbed hair hung lank from her large head. Elodi gasped; the tapestry in Archonholm had not exaggerated the horror of the demon. She backed away as the creature turned to face her. Its mouth gaped and a light flickered at the back of its throat.

But the draylok was not alone. Elodi froze as dull eyes glared from beneath an archway on the opposite side of the square. She recalled the glowering orbs of the Reapers, but this was a short, squat fiend with powerful arms. Stones dislodged as its muscular form squeezed through a gap and drew an axe from its belt. Elodi set her stance. The wraiths beseeched her to defend their sacred ground. And she accepted. She would gladly sacrifice her soul to prevent these monstrous beasts taking the fortress. She swished her sword, ready to engage, as another dark foe entered the square.

'Cease!' A cruel voice penetrated the lilting, song-like whispers of the wraiths. 'Do not heed them.'

Elodi searched for the voice that warned her. It was that of the draylok. Her grip tightened on her sword. 'Begone hag. You do not fool me.' She took a step, raising the point towards the draylok's protruding ribs.

The creature held out her hands. 'Sisters. Put away your weapons. Shut your eyes. It is I, Eryn. It is the wraiths that mislead.' Elodi did as directed and closed her eyes. The voice softened. Elodi's sword arm dropped to her side as she recognized Eryn's voice. 'Now hold out your hands.' The creatures sheathed their swords, stretched out their arms, and walked to the center. A mist swirled about them as warm hands found Elodi's, and the Amayans re-appeared.

Arijan groaned. 'The warlocks have indeed grown strong. I have never been tricked in such a way. They must—' Elodi dropped to her knees. The air burst with a crack of thunder and a blinding flash of lightning. She threw herself to the ground and clutched her ears. But just as she feared her head would splinter, the assault ceased. She rolled onto her back, gasping for air, waiting for her senses to recover.

Eryn cried out. 'It has fallen! The Elda Stone is lost.

The Crown will surely follow.'

Neeve climbed to her feet. 'And so will Igrayne if we cannot reach her.' She snatched up her spear. 'We must strike now, Eryn. Even if we're not strong enough, we must at least try.'

Madraal laid her hand upon Neeve's grasping the javelin. 'Let us not act in haste. The warlocks will know of the stone's fall. They will be waiting.'

Calestri sided with Madraal. 'The Crown Stone weakens. We cannot draw enough strength to confront both the warlocks and the Angorsil.'

Neeve lowered her spear. 'I apologize for my rash words. But we cannot wait long. If the stone fails, their malice will turn on Igrayne.'

Eryn sighed. 'You are both right. But we can neither rush headlong into a trap, nor delay much longer.' She pointed. 'The warlocks know the way through the Gorgonach Gap. We must assume they have set a trap.' Her gaze went from the peaks forming the Crown, then back to the narrow path. She drew her sword. 'But it has to be now.' She strode to Moonbeam. 'We have languished too long under the shadow. We are the Sisters of the Stones. If the Crown is lost, the rest will also fall. If that happens, we have no purpose to exist.' She sprang onto Moonbeam's back. 'We were sworn to protect the Amanach. This is where we fulfil our destiny, my sisters… or we die trying.'

The Amayans mounted. Elodi leaned forward and whispered to Sea Mist. 'You are the horse of an Amayan, Misty. You have nothing to prove. We face this trial together.'

Eryn pointed with her sword. 'The Gorgonach Gap slices through the west side like a deep wound. The steps are narrow and steep, but our horses will manage. Yes, the warlocks expect us. Now let's make them regret taking

Igrayne.'

Calestri hesitated by her horse. 'And our plan? Are we to ride blind to face five warlocks?'

Eryn kept her eyes ahead. 'Brute force. Steel yourselves, my Amayan sisters. We have not the time to plan anything more. The Crown Stone shudders, and Igrayne suffers.' She looked back to Calestri. 'And you can purge your memories of this cursed place.' Eryn's shoulders relaxed. 'We will draw as much strength from the stone as we dare, and give some back to Igrayne. Then we strike.' She turned. 'Elodi. You will free Igrayne from the stone as we engage the warlocks. I hope once free, she will be able to assist in some way. I'm sure she has scores to settle.'

Arijan drew her horse level with Calestri and linked her arm. 'Be strong, Cali. You have faced a great foe and lived. Let this be our finest hour.'

Calestri nodded. 'Then we ride.' The horses needed no cue. They set off at speed, out of the ruins, and on into the mists still clinging to the slopes.

Eryn cried out. 'It will be nightfall before we arrive at the Crown. But be prepared for a difficult journey. We ride as fast as the terrain allows, but remain wary.' She drew her sword. 'Onward, Amayans!'

Sea Mist lowered his head and galloped behind Moonbeam. But the ground soon became unsuitable for nothing more than a canter. As they neared the crest of the Crown, Elodi looked up. It loomed high above them, its pinnacle looking more like the fang of some foul beast than a mountain. The sheer face rose ahead, and Elodi wondered if any had ever managed to scale its summit. Had the Elorym seen it as a challenge and conquered the first and last mountain of the Kolossos? But she had little time to ponder the past. A dark, vertical line appeared on the west face of Gorgonach. It appeared as if a weapon wielded by the gods had splintered the rock, opening the way to the Crown. Elodi's jaw clenched as they closed in on the gap — it would be the easiest place to spring a trap. But Eryn rode on, undeterred by the menacing edifice. They had no choice but to enter the domain of the warlocks.

Eryn led Moonbeam into the gap. Neeve and Madraal followed. Calestri held out her hand allowing Elodi to go first. She and Arijan completed the company. Elodi's scalp prickled as she entered the foreboding mountain breach, barely wide enough for Sea Mist. The light from Eryn's sword flickered on its sheer sides to guide the horses. Elodi glanced up but the tiny slither of sky high above, did little to lift the gloom. They had not ridden far when Eryn held up her hand.

Elodi shivered. Ahead, the stairs were blocked by thick strands of web. Inside, a large aralak sat with its legs tucked beneath its fat body. She stared at the strange sight of black, beady eyes staring out from a stark white, frost-covered spider.

Eryn grinned and whispered. 'I think it's time we announced our arrival. We'll force the warlocks' attention away from the stone. We can then draw on its power and direct it back at them.' She bowed her head. Her sword blazed. A blade of light sliced down through the web and into the spider. The strands slackened, and the creature split, falling with a sickening thud and hiss of melting ice. Eryn directed the fading light to burn its remains. She grimaced. 'I'll spare our horses the task of trotting through its remains.'

The air tingled. Madraal drew her sword. 'If the warlocks were oblivious to our presence, they certainly know we're here now.' They rode over the smoldering corpse of the spider. The steps turned, then climbed steeply at several points, but no ambush came. But Elodi wondered if that was due to their complacent foe, or whether they had kept back their full might at the Crown Stone. She suspected the latter.

The steps came to an end as they approached the south side of the gap. The rock now gleamed with the green of the Angorsil, overpowering the blue of Eryn's blade. She stopped and turned. 'I have faith in every one of you.' She caught Elodi's eye. 'You've all stood strong in the face of terror. Igrayne needs us. We will not fail her. And if, as Elodi says, the warlocks do not fear us, then by the Three, we will make them regret their error.'

Eryn kicked Moonbeam on. No more obstacles delayed them, and the ground leveled, allowing the horses to gain speed. The gap widened a little as they approached another bend. Eryn drew them to a halt. 'We'll call upon the stone here. The warlocks know we're coming. Let them feel doubt as our strength grows.' She held out her hands. The Amayans squeezed their horses together to form a circle. But Eryn gasped. 'I cannot find the stone. It has not fallen, but... it's not there.'

Madraal gaped. 'But that can only mean...'

Eryn turned her horse and sped on. They rounded the bend. She cried out as Moonbeam came to an abrupt halt. The Amayans sat dumbfounded. Ahead, a shimmering green wall blocked the entrance to the Crown. Madraal shook her head. 'How is this possible? I thought only the most powerful Imaari could raise one.'

Elodi was reminded of the blue light above the rim of the Caerwal Gate. 'Is that...?'

Arijan slapped the rock. 'A Word of Forbidding. It would take all our strength to breakthrough... even if we could draw upon the stone. They must have waited until we...' She turned. 'Do you feel that?'

Calestri cried out. 'They've raised another at the entrance. We're trapped.' The gap darkened. Elodi looked up. The slither of sky had gone, replaced by dozens of aralaks scampering down the ravine. But that was not all. Three glistening worms slithered through the narrow gorge behind the spiders.'

Eryn groaned. 'Droogs as well. This will be unpleasant. Do not lose heart.' But Elodi could sense their spirit had gone. None welcomed the gruesome fight to come. But this was a fight of attrition. A fight that would take much of their strength. And as the Amayans tired, their chances of breaking through the Word of Forbidding would dwindle. Elodi's stomach clenched. How long could they endure?

41. Of Steel, Water & Iron

Toryn could have been running for days, or it could have been weeks or even months... he had no sense of time passing. The tunnel began to climb. He slowed. Was this the way he had come with his company? If so, it would lead up to the hall where they had found the slaves... his shoulders sagged. It would be blocked. He had brought down the ceiling with the *Elorsil*. It may have put a stop to the work, but now it delayed his efforts to reach the Amanspring.

Toryn ran the last few bends and entered the hall. To his relief, the Norgog had cleared a passage through the rubble. He smiled, admiring their work. The Norgog had done him a favor, for once finding something useful to do with the hammers. Toryn looked around the deserted cavern. The canvas covering the opening had gone and a wind chilled his bones. He could not resist a quick look and climbed up onto the rock shelf. Outside, the waning moon peeped through the clouds, and the odd star twinkled in the otherwise overcast sky. Far below, torches flickered in the windows of the watchtower. If all had gone well, Elrik would be tucked up in a warm bed and recovering from the spider's attack. But it would have been a difficult journey for the two stretcher bearers and a sick man. Had they made it to the watchtower? And if they had, was it in time to save Elrik? Toryn turned to the north. His gaze followed the dark peaks as they stretched all the way to the horizon. Where they ended, Elodi and the Amayans prepared to meet the warlocks.

Toryn's heart lurched. Had he made the right choice? His hand gripped his sword. He should be at Elodi's side.

He could not bear the thought she would soon ride into the Crown and confront Ormoroth's commanders. Toryn turned away, trying to push aside his dread. He had to focus on his own mission deep beneath Caranach. And if successful, perhaps could do far more for the realms' cause, than what he could achieve with his sword.

Toryn returned to the Norgog passage. He sat and entered the Song. Immediately, he felt the surge of the upwelling far below. But it had weakened. He passed through the Verses of the rock beneath his feet. Two dark shapes sullied the Song. The warlocks drove on the Norgog as they toiled at the base of a deep shaft, now within a few hundred feet of the spring. It was vital he disrupted their progress. But if the warlocks sensed his approach and sent the Norgog, he would surely struggle.

The *Elorsil* warmed. Toryn drew the sword, kneeled, placed its point onto the rock, and the hilt on his brow. Far below, he saw the wellspring surge and flow out to the Amanach. Suddenly, he soared up through the many Verses of Caranach's peak, then out into the night sky. A thick fog shrouded the Verses of the land, but four lights glimmered as if fires of a night watch. And Toryn knew them to be the lakes where the Elorym had raised their towers. Two had long since collapsed, yet all four lakes retained a remnant of their power.

A line formed between them. From Syris in the east, through the lake at Casteldor, then onto Telamir. The line then passed beneath the Kolossos and onto Qaamir, the tower lost at Benmuir lake in the west. As the link was made, the lakes to the east and west flared, burning ever brighter until Toryn feared they would splinter the Verses. Then, as stars falling from the sky, they streaked north to converge many leagues beyond the ice plains of Nordruuk. But the Song did not, or could not, reveal where they met.

The *Elorsil* clattered to the ground as Toryn fell back.

The vision rippled as if a surface of a pond, and it was lost. He sat, certain the *Elorsil* had revealed the existence of a fifth Elorym tower. But if Ormoroth had destroyed two, did it still stand?

The ground trembled. He had to find a way down to the shaft. Toryn snatched up his sword and ran through the Norgog passageway to the end of the hall. The tunnel beyond spiraled down steeply. Suddenly, his sword blazed green and scorched his hand. In disgust, Toryn flung it aside and sank to his knees. Another river flowed out of a gaping wound.

The Elda Stone was lost!

It had shattered, no longer able to withstand the tireless pulse of the Angorsil. Toryn sobbed, powerless to contain his grief for the loss of such beauty. He had laid his hand on the Elda Stone's dark face, and, as Hamar had promised, opened his eyes to the wonders of the land previously denied him. Toryn recalled the night he had slept beside the stone, and the dream of the woman singing softly to him. But it was not a dream. And the woman had been Nyomae, wandering the lands as Hope, still lost in the shadow of her making.

Another ancient, powerful monolith was lost. And now more precious water of the Amanspring spilled onto open ground, to be diluted by rainfall and its potency lost. How could the realms survive when even the might of the Elorym had failed?

Toryn looked up to the ceiling through his tears. His thoughts turned to Hamar. How he wished the old guard could be at his side deep beneath the mountains. He wiped his eyes, and even managed a smile. *Duty, lad, duty.* Hamar had never left him. His wisdom, his strength, and his guard's humor. Hamar was always at his side, and his voice was forever in his ears. And now he urged him to not lose hope.

The rock walls shone green. Toryn stared in horror as the blade glowed with the same sickening hue he had seen at Drunsberg... and then later as the dead had risen at the Caerwal Gate. He groaned as the awful truth dawned on him — the Angorsil had penetrated the lines of power as the Elda Stone had splintered. Thus, the *Elorsil*'s blade was now vulnerable to its distortion.

Below, the warlocks rejoiced. Their brothers had struck a blow that would be felt across the land. And they were close to inflicting a far greater wound; one the realms could not hope to heal.

Toryn spat the foul taste from his mouth and picked up the sword. His arm ached as the dull throb of the Angorsil sought to fracture the blade. He tightened his grip, determined not to lose its ancient power. Toryn entered the Verses of the *Elorsil*. He sped back through the line of Archons who had unknowingly wielded the Elorym blade. But these Verses offered nothing.

Deeper Toryn ventured until the mists cleared, and he beheld the *Elorsil* aloft in Draegelan's hand. A blinding, blue flame shot forth from the sword as he rode to the aid of Dorlan at Talaghir. This was the last time it had burned with such power... and now Toryn had to somehow revive its glory. But he was wary of the damage he had caused at Drunsberg as it had surged beyond his control. If careless, he could easily bring down the tunnel roof onto his head. But he had to try. Toryn could not hope to save the Amanspring while the Angorsil's corruption sullied his sword.

He looked down to his hands within the Song. The lines that had condemned him to death in Archonholm, had spread up to his fingers and now resembled the intricate patterns of Nyomae's. Toryn's hands tingled as he circled then over the blade. He snatched them back as if touching a flame. The *Elorsil's* power in Draegelan's hand was too much for Toryn to bear. He had an idea, recalling Nyomae's lesson on the Menon Bridge. She had demonstrated with an apple that had fallen from a cart. Perhaps a similar approach would suffice now.

Toryn used his fingers and focused on the sword's point. He moved as if plucking a cherry from a tree. A pinprick of light gleamed between his fingertips. Toryn withdrew his hand and departed from the Song. Slowly, he brought his fingers to the tip of the blade at his side. He held his breath as the sword glimmered, then turn blue as the green tinge retreated. He let out a sigh of relief; the *Elorsil* connected with the Amanach once more. But… now they numbered just five.

Toryn jumped up and sprinted down the tunnel. He could not tell if the warlocks knew of his coming, but it made no difference. Elodi and the Amayans rode to the Crown. The loss of the Elda Stone had weakened their hand. But if Toryn could break the Angorsil's influence, the Amanspring could surge once more and strengthen the five remaining stones.

Toryn slowed as harsh Ruuk voices echoed through the tunnel. Ahead, an archway led to a large cavern. Its ceiling flickered with the faint blue light, Toryn knew to be the Norgogs' Cold Fire. He edged to the opening. At the center, dozens of Ruuk worked winches that pulled large buckets of rubble up from a wide pit. Toryn marveled at the machinery that transported the buckets along an overhead rail, then tipped them into carts that ran on iron rails into another tunnel opposite.

He watched their routine, looking for an opportunity to reach the shaft unseen. From there, a narrow stairway of iron, hammered into the side of the rock, spiraled down and out of sight. A wry smile crossed his lips. The iron was likely extracted from Drunsberg; had they learned of the mines returning to its rightful owners? Whether they knew or not, if their efforts below succeeded, the metals from the mine would make little difference.

A horn blew below. The Ruuk secured the buckets, then ran to shelters in the cavern's wall. The ground shook. Toryn counted. He reached five as a boom and blast of hot air burst from the hole. It had to be Shreek's Rage! But they were deep... very deep.

This was his moment. He ran towards the pit, hoping to gain the steps before the Ruuk emerged from their shelters. Toryn approached the edge and peered down. The stairs spiraled down towards a speck of light, looking like a blue star twinkling in the night sky. But this was no jewel of the gods gifted to the people of the mortal world. This was where Toryn must go. But what would happen should another blast race up the shaft while he was on the stairs?

He had no time to consider his own safety as the doors of the shelters creaked open. Toryn dashed to the pit and flung himself onto the stairs as the Ruuk returned to their hoists. He kept his sword sheathed as he ran, taking two steps at a time. A gap appeared to his right. For a moment he feared a guard would leap out and knock him over the rail, but none appeared. Toryn stepped inside. The light from below was sufficient to reveal a large space. At the entrance a thick iron shield leaned against the rock. A shelter! As the Norgog had mined deeper more would be needed. His spirits rose. Surely, he would pass more on the way down.

Toryn returned to the stairs, and he formed a plan as he continued his descent. He sensed the two warlocks below were engrossed in their work and oblivious to his presence. Elated by the destruction of the Elda Stone, perhaps they now saw themselves invincible. But the warlocks were yet challenged, pushed to their limits as they neared the Amanspring.

The sound of hammers bounced off the walls of the shaft. Toryn glanced below. The glimmering circle appeared a little bigger, but he still had a long way to go. And how long before the warlocks spied him? Toryn figured if he could kill one before they saw him, he might stand a chance against the other. Yet the Norgog could still pose a threat. He clasped his sword and grinned: a blast of heat would surely unsettle them.

The winches above creaked as six large buckets were lowered to clear the debris from the recent blast. Toryn's hand chilled. A thin layer of ice clung to the wall but sweat poured from his brow and into his eyes. He glanced over the edge. His stomach churned as the green tinge of the Angorsil overpowered the Norgog's Cold Fire. And the lower he went, the louder the unsettling heartbeat of the Angorsil became. His ears throbbed, and his muscles ached, yet still he did not stop. The barks of the Norgog echoed alongside the chinks of their hammers. And now the sweat froze on his face, and his legs stiffened in the cold.

Toryn slowed. If he lost his step, he would tumble to his death, and gift the *Elorsil* to the warlocks. But Toryn dared not draw upon the sword to warm his bones; the later they knew of his arrival, the better.

The buckets returned slower than they had descended, laden to the brim. Toryn guessed it would not be long before another blast tore up the shaft. He looked for another shelter and found one on the opposite side a little farther down. And not a moment too soon. The hammering stopped, and the horn blared. As he approached the opening, the stairs shook. Toryn dived into the entrance but had neither the time nor the strength to heave the thick shield into place. He scrambled towards the back wall. The blast threw him from his feet; the heat scorched his back. Toryn clasped his ears and pressed his face into the rock. He cried out as the deafening roar hammered at his skull, and the heat sucked the air from his lungs. It passed. Toryn rolled onto his back, gasping as the blast careered up the shaft. He had survived… but it had been close.

Toryn shuffled outside and looked down. He was close enough now to see the Norgog hammering large spikes into the rock. Two warlocks stood by their iron shards, chanting invocations to draw upon the Angorlith far to the north. Another group of workers, possibly Ruuk, carefully rolled out a barrel of Shreek's Rage. He guessed their strategy. Once ready, the holes would be packed with the black powder, then ignited to delve a few feet deeper. It was a slow, laborious task, and judging by their progress, they must have been here for many years.

Toryn continued his descent, deciding to take refuge as soon as he found another shelter. Then perhaps he would be deep enough to execute his plan. The stench of the powder hit the back of his throat. He stopped and clasped his hand over his mouth to stifle a cough. Toryn glanced below to see the Norgog withdraw and the Ruuk open the barrel. Thankfully, the next shelter was close. He took the remaining steps, ducked inside, and crawled behind the armored screen resting against the wall. The warning from the horn sounded much closer. Toryn pressed his hands against his ears, hoping the shield would protect him from the heat if not the roar.

The boom came. The walls quaked as the blast shot up the shaft. But thankfully, the iron shield protected him from the worst. Toryn drew his sword, reassured by its glimmering blue light. He ran his hand along the warm blade. The next shelter would likely bring him too close to the warlocks — he had to strike now. But he would not use his powers within the Song. As soon as they sensed him, the warlocks might deny him entry and he could be stranded. Toryn's grip tightened as his breath quickened. He had made his decision. He would call upon the Amanspring: the next blast would come from above, not below.

The shield creaked. A crooked shadow slid across the back wall. The shield clattered to the floor. Behind, stood a warlock. His dark eyes glinted in the sickly light streaming up the shaft. The warlock clicked his fingers. Toryn froze. The commander strode forward, grabbed him by the neck and hauled Toryn to his feet.

The warlock spat. 'Fool! Do you think you can stop us.' His grip tightened. Toryn choked and gasped for air. The warlock grinned. 'But your journey has not been wasted.' He glanced to the sword. 'I see you bring a gift.'

Toryn spluttered. 'It is not mine to give, or yours to take.' The *Elorsil* warmed in his hand. The warlock stepped back and glared at the weapon. Behind, the floor shimmered. A mist rose as if from a lake on a winter's morn. Blood flowed back into Toryn's limbs.

The Nym had come!

The warlock waved his arms as if swotting at nothing more irritating than flies. He scoffed. 'Begone. Do not bother me.' Tall, thin figures formed in the haze and surrounded the commander of Ormoroth's forces who dared to trespass into their domain. The hold over Toryn fell away. He raised his sword and lunged, driving its point into the warlock's chest. He cried out and grasped the blade, striving to pull it free. But Toryn held firm, forcing the *Elorsil* deeper.

A searing light burst from the wound. Toryn was thrown against the wall. The warlock clutched his chest and staggered back. The Nym swirled about him. Long, wispy fingers reached into the gaping wound and tore it wider. The warlock sagged to his knees. For a moment his face changed. Toryn saw the proud and noble face of an

Elorym lord. He stared down to his hands as if horrified of what he had become. His eyes bulged; the hideous face of the warlock returned as it spat out a curse. The light of the Nym burst through his eyes and gaping mouth. The warlock pitched forward onto his face and perished.

Toryn stood gasping for air and blinking in the sudden dark. Cries from below found him in the shelter. They would come… and come fast. But Toryn was spent. He would not survive if the second warlock found him. He looked to the Nym. They knew his mind. His body tingled as their hands reached out and took his. Heat surged through his veins, but as Toryn's strength returned, the Nym faded, and disappeared like mist in a breeze.

The clang of buckets echoed through the shaft as they returned from collecting the rubble. Toryn heaved a sigh. The Ruuk at the top were unaware of the warlock's death, and continued their toil. The timing was perfect. Toryn stepped over the warlock's remains and left the shelter. The full buckets were not yet level. He directed the sword at the taut chains and closed his eyes.

The Amanspring answered his call. A bolt streaked from the blade and scythed through the chains as if stalks of wheat. The heavy buckets plunged. With a deafening crash, they shattered, blasting a hail of stones into the workers not crushed by the initial blow. But the shimmering green haze of the Angorsil shards had protected the warlock from the worst.

Toryn took a breath; he had the strength for one more strike. He surveyed the carnage below, recalling the horror at the Caerwal Pass. The sole survivor, the warlock, struggled to break free of the debris. But Toryn's attention was on the Angorsil. If left, the two shards would continue to weaken the Amanspring — they had to be destroyed. He set his stance and leveled the *Elorsil* at the first iron shard. The sword lurched in his hands as he called upon the waters once more. The blade came to life. The warlock waved his arms to deflect the strike, but his strength was failing. The bolt struck the Angorsil. Toryn struggled to maintain his hold as the power surged through him. He threw back his head and cried out in pain. But he held true, directing the force at the shard's dark core.

How long the battle raged, Toryn could not tell. He seemed to pass out of time, becoming a mere witness as the powers of the ancient world collided in their ceaseless conflict. But deep beneath Caranach, in the brief silence between the Verses, it was the oldest of them all that prevailed. The force repressed in the Amanspring for so long, released, penetrating the Angorsil. The shard's pulse grew as it sought to counter, but it could not match the power of the river. The iron shattered, sending splinters hurtling into the second Angorlith. Toryn cried out as the force held within the shards was ripped from their core. The blast slammed into the wall, dislodging large fragments that crushed what remained of the warlock. The Amanspring surged once more, freed from the corruption.

Toryn slumped back against the wall. As his vision blurred, and his head dropped, he hoped it was in time to aid Elodi and the Amayans at the Crown.

Shouts from the head of the shaft caught his attention. They would be coming, but Toryn had ample time to recover. And now the warlocks were defeated, he could enter the Song. He grinned as he devised his surprise for the approaching Ruuk.

42. A Long-Awaited Meeting

The doors creaked open. Nyomae struggled to sit. How long had she slept? Her throat was parched, and her head felt ready to split. Idraman lay lifeless beside her. For a moment, she thought he had finally succumbed and died, but then a wisp of breath rose from his mouth into the cold air. He lived. But Nyomae could not be certain if she felt relief or sorrow. Idraman had suffered for three centuries; he deserved peace.

Torches were lit; the flame bearers departed; the doors creaked shut. The sound of stone grinding on stone set Nyomae's teeth on edge. The ceiling glowed green. Idraman cried out and curled into a ball. Nyomae edged back, ashamed to abandon her friend, but she could not stop herself retreating from the horror that emerged behind the throne. Her back pushed against the rear wall of the pit — she could go no farther. The moment she had dreaded for years had arrived. Uluriel had her trapped.

Nyomae gaped as the torches revealed the outline of Uluriel as she stooped beneath the low ceiling. She stood as tall as Dorlan but had not his stature. Her large head hung heavy from her neck; her oversized hands twitched as if struggling to contain the malevolent spirit within. Uluriel clambered around the throne and sat heavily upon the iron seat. Her eyes blazed from the shadows and found Nyomae. She recoiled, unable to prevent her body shrinking from the glare. But part of her would not submit. The Imaari pushed against the wall and rose to her feet.

Uluriel spoke. 'Nyomae and Idraman.' Nyomae cried out. The walls quailed; her ears bled as the harsh voice forced its way into her skull. It seemed as if two voices spoke. One came from Uluriel's mortal throat. The other from the Verse forced to bear her presence.

Uluriel's head jutted forward as she peered into the pit. Her thin lips cracked. 'Ah. You are frightened. You cower before me.' Her voice thundered. 'And so you should! Kneel. Kneel before me.' A long, bony finger jabbed at Nyomae. 'Kneel and worship me, *Imaari*.' Nyomae's legs buckled. But she had not the strength to hold herself up, and she fell flat on her face. A weight pressed down on her back, forcing the air from her lungs until she felt her body would be crushed into the rock.

The pressure released. Nyomae gasped, desperate for air, no matter how foul. Uluriel cackled. 'How the tables have turned. Two powerful Imaari now grovel before me. Ah, and you mourn the loss of yet another stone. I gather Mosholuk has told you of the futile attempts of your underlings to fight back. But your brief resistance draws to an end.'

Nyomae pushed her hands into the floor and sat, determined not to yield. Her jaw clenched as she raised her head to look upon her foe. The light did not fall easy on Uluriel's haggard face. Nyomae stifled a gag. Uluriel was now more draylok than woman. Her jaw hung from an enlarged, distorted head as if about to drop to the floor. The stretched sinews struggled to keep her mouth closed, thus Uluriel drooled. But it was the eyes that sent a shudder through Nyomae. She had not the moist, black eyes of a warlock. Hers were gray, dry, and looked ready to crack as they scraped across the bony edges of their deep sockets.

But Uluriel seemed oblivious to her rotten form. She mocked. 'I expected so much more from you, Nyomae. Such a disappointment.' Her voice lowered as if her throat grappled to deliver her scorn. 'It took you longer than it should to solve Aber's Verse. But… you have done well to resist uttering our lord's name. Yet, that matters little. Time means nothing to Lord Ormoroth. I shall be his queen once more in the new age. The age of—' Uluriel faltered.

Nyomae looked up; Idraman's whimpering ceased. Uluriel's brow furrowed, shedding dead skin to the floor like ash from a dying fire. A new melody echoed through the Verses from the north. Nyomae stood, encouraged by the change. She cleared her throat. 'A warlock has fallen. It appears not all goes your way. And…' her spirits lifted. 'The *Elorsil!* It knows Toryn's hand.'

Uluriel dismissed Nyomae's optimism with a flick of her hand. 'It is but a loss of one. I have more at my disposal.' Her lids scraped over her eyes. 'Your *boy's* efforts count for nothing. He will die shortly, and my commanders will take possession of that wretched sword.' But Nyomae sensed her frustration. The bones in Uluriel's neck creaked as she lowered her head. Nyomae staggered back as her rage hurtled through the Verses to vent her displeasure at her warlocks in the north. She regained her composure and lifted her head; her thin lips stretched into a chilling grin. 'The last of the Amayans will soon fall. They walk into a trap… along with that young pretender from Calerdorn. Your interference serves only to prolong their suffering.'

Nyomae took a step, holding her nerve. 'Prolong? We strike a blow. The loss of a warlock is no trivial matter.' She tried another tact. 'You once deceived my Order, Sylvena. But now you deceive yourself.' Nyomae waited. Did a flicker of doubt cross Uluriel's taut face? 'If you succeed in bringing back Ormoroth, will he need you? Would he reward your loyalty?' Uluriel remained silent. Nyomae continued. 'If you achieve a victory, and all my people are enslaved, what use will Ormoroth have for you?' She held out her hand. 'Do you not possess a mirror, Sylvena?' She pressed her point. 'Do you think Ormoroth will share the spoils with a decaying hag? You will be no more than his servant, forced to—'

'I am his Queen!' The hall shook. Uluriel stooped; her foul breath dampened Nyomae's face. 'I shall be at his side once more.' Her anger abated. She lowered her voice until barely more than a rumble. 'And you, Nyomae… you will be *with* me. And I shall take my pleasure as I see—'

Nyomae's body warmed. Another wave flowed through the Verses. She climbed to her feet and took a step to look Uluriel in the eye. 'Ah! Another warlock falls. And…' her spirits rose, 'two Angorsil shatter. The Amanach recover. I see it now. The Amanspring! You sought to defile their source of power.' She smiled, holding down her revulsion to edge closer. 'But it appears your plan has failed.' Uluriel's mouth gaped. Her gray eyes flittered about the room. Nyomae held out her hands. 'It is not too late, Sylvena. Cease your work to bring back Ormoroth. For many years you walked among us. Do you despise our ways so much you want to destroy everything we have achieved? Does it cause you pain to look upon the beauty of the Maidens' making?'

Uluriel spat. 'Beauty? Those dull-witted daughters destroyed the beauty that is chaos. They sought to take away the suffering that is living. Theirs… and your ways weaken the spirit. I cannot tolerate the weak.' Uluriel spun away, leaving a stench in her wake as she departed the hall.

Nyomae let out a long sigh, exhausted by her defiance. She went to Idraman and cradled his shivering body. 'You felt it too. At last, a victory of sorts in the north.' Her way to the Song opened. Her strength grew as she crossed the expanse through the Verses. She held Idraman's hand. 'By the Three, Idraman. We fight back. We may yet be a thorn in Uluriel's side.'

Idraman straightened and looked at Nyomae, appearing to recognize her face for the first time. But Nyomae's joy at his apparent recovery was short lived. His mouth dropped open, and his eyes bulged as if recalling a distant memory. He whispered. 'He will return. She has found a way.' He grasped her hand so tight it hurt. 'Kill the child, Nyomae.' His voice strengthened. 'The child must die.'

'Child?' Nyomae gaped. 'Who is this child, Idraman?' But he collapsed as the Angorsil's pulse resumed, weaker, but still too much for the old Imaari to endure. His words echoed through her mind. *Kill the child?* Idraman must have discovered something of the Ul-dalak's plans. But how did a mortal child figure?

43. Conflict at the Crown

Elodi stared into the aralak's glistening eyes as it scuttled down the crevice. Mercifully, the droogs lagged behind as they wriggled and writhed, trying to squeeze their bloated bodies through the narrowing gap. The trapped Amayans thought with one mind. They could not use the Fire if they hoped to break the Word of Forbidding and confront the warlocks. But that would mean a grim fight with spider and droog to conserve their strength. But fight they must.

Elodi's grip on her sword tightened. The spider above spat. Sea Mist lurched, and the poison splashed harmlessly behind them. She glanced down the ravine. The narrow space would work in her favor, preventing the spider splaying its legs and leaping. But the aralak's burning desire to entrap its prey would not easily be doused. It clenched its legs under its body and dropped. Elodi was prepared. She thrust up her blade, impaling the plunging spider. She cried out as she drove her sword deep into its abdomen, then hurled it to the ground before its weight could drag her from Sea Mist.

Another tried the same approach, only to meet its end on Calestri's weapon. But the remainder had seen the error. One scampered ahead into a wider gap. It landed with a thud, but before it could strike, Sea Mist charged. He reared up and hammered his hooves down, cracking the small, exposed skull as the spider still had little room to raise its legs. It staggered back, cowering beneath the assault. Another blow finished it. Elodi yelled out. 'Good boy, Misty!' But she had little time to celebrate their victory as another thumped onto the ground behind.

The Amayans thrust, lunged, hacked, and slashed, thinning the aralak numbers just as the first droog squeezed into the crevice between Elodi and Neeve. It slithered towards Elodi. The worm's slathering mouth gaped. Sea Mist edged back, drawing it to a narrower part of the ravine. Its skin quivered as it prepared to vomit the foul contents of its gut at Elodi. But as the ripple slithered up its body towards its head, Neeve hurled her spear. The worm's bile splattered the walls as Neeve leaped onto its back and drove the weapon deeper. Elodi kicked on Sea Mist. Fearlessly, he slammed his hooves onto the droog's flabby head. Elodi jumped and joined Neeve as they slashed and stabbed at its glistening flesh. The worm twisted and thrashed, desperate to throw them off. But the Amayans prevailed. The droog collapsed, oozing burning juices that stung Elodi's skin.

Ahead, the last two droogs had wedged themselves between the Amayans and the warlocks' barrier. Yet more spiders dropped to the ground behind. Elodi gasped for air in the confined space, but the air, thick with the stench of the droog, stung her throat and made her eyes water. The worms writhed, leaving a sticky trail on the rocks. Elodi wiped her eyes with the back of her arm. Sea Mist snorted. Eryn spoke calmly. 'We are Amayans. We are Sisters of the Stones. These foul creatures will not defeat us. Dig deep. We are not done.'

The droogs paused. Beads of glassy slime seeped from their rippling skin as they prepared to strike. Elodi's face tingled. Eryn whispered. 'Do you feel that? The air has changed.' She tilted her head, then cried out. 'They stutter. Their Word has shattered.' Eryn's glee echoed through the ravine. 'Toryn has slain a warlock! Now, sisters. Now!' She drove Moonbeam at the droogs. He hurdled the floundering worms, quickly followed by the other horses no longer fearful of the creatures.

Elodi glanced over her shoulder. The last of the aralaks scrambled over the remains of the droogs, but their horses easily outpaced the spiders as they struggled with their legs tucked under their swollen bodies. Yet the real challenge lay ahead.

The gap widened. The Amayan horses sped on. Elodi's body ignited as the Fire stirred. As one, they raised their blazing swords. The rock walls burned white. They cried out, daring the warlocks to stand in their way. The stone would be saved, Igrayne would be rescued, and the warlocks defeated.

Elodi rode out into the Crown… alone.

Her battle cry died. Her blade glimmered no brighter than a flickering candle. Sea Mist stumbled to a halt, yet his hooves made no sound. Elodi called out into the darkness, but no voice issued from her throat. She frantically searched for Eryn and her sisters. But could see nothing beyond Sea Mist's mane. He reared, kicking up his legs as if the ground scorched at the touch. Elodi clung onto his neck, fearing she would lose him if she fell. She gagged as the wrongness beneath seeped through Sea Mist and into her back. He calmed, dropping his head as if eating from a trough. But all was not right. Sea Mist wavered as if drowsy, seeming to struggle to stay upright. Elodi tried to rouse him, but her words failed to pass her lips. Her spine ached and she too felt the strength drain from her limbs.

Elodi. She froze. Shokresh! His voice echoed as if in a cavern, vibrating through her bones, setting her teeth on edge. *Join me... or die.*

With much effort, Elodi drew back her shoulders. 'Never. I am an Amayan. I will not turn from my duty.' But her defiance sounded as a scared child lost in the dark.

'Your sisters are all dead.' She flinched as the warlock stepped out of the gloom. He grinned. 'They were slaughtered the moment they entered our domain.'

Elodi mumbled as she clung to Sea Mist's mane. 'You lie!'

Shokresh held out his hand. 'Can you *see* them? Can you *hear* them?' He sneered. 'Can you *feel* them, Elodi?' The warlock took a step closer. 'But you, Elodi, I saved for myself. The Amanach fail. Your sisters are gone… and the Five Realms will soon fall. You have no purpose now, Amayan.' He threw back his hood and smiled. 'My offer stands. You are alone. Why not join with me?'

Elodi stared into the darkness. She still had Sea Mist. Could she turn and flee? Shokresh stood before them, yet she noted her horse seemed undaunted. He appeared to read her mind. 'Ah yes, Sea Mist. Or should I call him… Misty.' He waved his hand. Sea Mist collapsed and Elodi fell from his back. The warlock loomed over her. 'Now you are truly alone.' He nudged Sea Mist with his large boot. 'A fine horse. But your mount is no use to you… dead.'

'No!' Elodi cried out. 'You will pay.' She raised her blade, but her arm dropped limp to her side.

Shokresh gestured to her sword. 'You forget, Elodi. That piece of metal is no threat to me.'

Elodi fell beside Sea Mist. She hugged him, desperate not to believe he had been taken from her. But his skin was already cold as if made of stone. Her tears soaked into his mane. Did the warlock speak the truth? Were her sisters also dead?

'Give yourself to me, Elodi, and I shall bring your beast back.' She looked up. The warlock kneeled beside Sea Mist. 'You will both ride at my side as we—' He spun around. A faint light shone in the darkness. It came from a slab jutting up from the rock. The Crown Stone! It grew brighter to reveal a green dome glimmering over Elodi and the warlock. She felt her strength return and stood. Shokresh winced as the silvery light exposed his craggy, aging face, withered by centuries of the hatred burning within.

The light of the Amanach spread. Elodi's spirit surged as she saw her sisters, confined by the same devilry. Shokresh spat out a curse. The stone blazed and shattered his defense. Sea Mist stirred. Elodi cried out with joy as he climbed to his feet, nodded his head, and tossed back his mane. Eryn called out. 'The Amanspring surges! The stones are revived.'

Elodi leaped onto Sea Mist. Without a word from her, he reared and kicked out at the warlock. The sound of steel! The Amayans fought back. The Fire kindled in Elodi's gut once more. Shokresh stared in disbelief at her blade as it flared. His spell was broken. The steel burned silver, proclaiming the warlock's fate. He circled his arms about his head, but before he could strike, Elodi hurled her Fire at him. Shokresh cried out as the bolt blasted into his chest. He staggered back, turned, and fled, leaving a churning pall of smoke in his wake.

About her, Amayan swords ignited. Elodi spun about. Eryn faced Vordrak. The warlock seemed to grow, looming over the Amayan with his dull blade ready to strike. Elodi urged on Sea Mist to her aid. But Eryn needed no help. She fought as no other had fought before. Elodi marveled at Eryn's speed as she ducked and swerved to avoid Vordrak's blows.

The warlock lumbered, looking too slow to challenge the Amayan. Eryn's blade flashed as it struck, each time finding its target as Vordrak failed to parry. His armor splintered, and the light of the Amayan blade seared deep into his flesh. Sea Mist pulled up as Eryn delivered the fatal blow. His wounds split wide open, burning with a brilliant fire as his *kruul* lost its host. Vordrak's shriek tore through the Crown to echo far and wide. The warlock's remains crumpled to the ground as a discarded cloak. Eryn thrust up her sword and cried. 'For Amyra!'

A piercing scream, followed by a gust of cold air, slammed into Elodi's back. Another warlock had fallen! Arijan rejoiced as she withdrew her sword from the chest of her assailant. Yet the warlocks were not defeated. Madraal cried out as his blade pierced her side. Elodi turned to see Madraal writhing on her back. She kicked on Sea Mist as the warlock raised his weapon. They sped towards her, but Elodi could only watch as he brought down his cruel blade. Madraal failed to roll out of its path, and the sword sliced into her leg.

Sea Mist charged him down, taking the warlock by surprise as his eyes were fixed on Madraal. Elodi wheeled, then swung at his head as he stumbled to regain his feet. Her blade sliced clean across his face. He twisted to face her, thrusting out his hand. But before he could call upon the dark arts, Elodi cut down and severed his arm. The warlock cried out, staggered back... and fell onto Madraal's sword as she thrust up from the ground.

He slumped, skewered by the Amayan blade. Light burst from the wound. His body jerked, sending out a blast of foul air that threw Elodi from her saddle. She ran to Madraal and shoved the withered body off her. He fell and crumbled to dust. Elodi gagged on the stench as she kneeled beside Madraal. But she bore two fatal wounds, inflicted by a blade forged in Ormoroth's pits. And as a last act of spite, the dark stain of the departing warlock's spirit had penetrated deep into Madraal's flesh.

Eryn rushed to her side. 'It's not too late. Get her to the stone.' Neeve came to their aid as they lifted Madraal's broken body and carried her to the Amanach. But the five Angorsil still pulsed, encircling the stone, groping at its base with their poisonous fingers. Yet still it stood: a defiant spike amid the foul roots creeping across the ground. Elodi's feet burned as they stepped onto the tainted rock.

Eryn called upon the Amanach. The Crown Stone answered her plea and glowed brighter, drawing ever more strength from the revived Amanspring. The veins of the Angorsil turned silver as the Amanach's power turned back the tide. But Igrayne was nowhere to be seen.

Arijan ran to the stone. 'What have they done with her? She was here. We saw her.'

'Igrayne is still with us.' Eryn sighed with relief. 'She is weak, but here somewhere at the Crown. Let us heal Madraal, and then we'll find her.' The Amayans gently lowered Madraal beside the Amanach. They kneeled at her side, laid on their hands, and bowed their heads. Elodi felt the warmth drain from her body as Madraal readily accepted their aid. But it was not enough. She remained motionless and cold. A mist formed above her. Eryn sobbed. 'No. Stay. Please, Madraal, don't leave us.' But Ormoroth's curse had gone deep and taken hold of her spirit — the Amayans could do nothing to save her.

Madraal's soul departed her earthly body and drifted towards the Amanach. A faint, blue mist rested briefly at its pinnacle, then slowly rose into the night sky. As it neared the peaks, it blazed, then soared up towards the dome. Elodi stared in wonder as Madraal's spirit took its place among the stars, ever more to shine upon the mortal world below.

Eryn raised her hands to the sky. 'Madraal has departed, but is not lost. She will never be forgotten. She is as one with Amyra and our sisters, all who have sacrificed their lives to serve the stones.'

Yet they had no time to lament the parting of their sister. Three warlocks had fallen, but Shamuul and Shokresh had fled. And now Igrayne had to be found. Elodi's face chilled. She turned back to the Gorgonach Gap... and groaned. The Amayans were no longer alone.

44. At Lightning Speed

Toryn had almost felt sorry for the unsuspecting Ruuk. They came in the belief there had been an accident and would be attempting a rescue. But the Ruuk had met something on their descent not to their liking. Toryn had located a rockworm in the Verses of the depths. And even with his depleted strength, he had easily brought the beast to the present time. The Ruuk would not have known what came at them. But one glimpse of its rows of gnashing teeth as it squirmed up the shaft towards them, had sent them scurrying. And to Toryn's delight, the writhing rockworm had destroyed much of the lower shaft, burying the machinery under hundreds of feet of rock.

Toryn had drawn strength from the river's returning power as he found his way back to the surface. The strip of night sky above the Kolossos Pass had twinkled with thousands of stars; did they sense the turning of the tide? But he could not afford the time to celebrate his success. Toryn sensed Elodi and the Amayans had saved the Crown Stone, but at great cost. And what of Nyomae? She remained absent from the Song. Was it the distance that shrouded her presence? Or had Uluriel found her?

The conical roof of the West Watchtower came into view. Toryn hoped Elrik had reached the post and the healers had saved him. He dearly longed to see him. But Toryn would not stay long.

'Your friend was remarkably strong.' The healer attended to a young woman who had been injured in a skirmish in the Wend Pass. 'I've seen many take weeks to recover from an aralak's poison... and many who don't.

And it was a miracle he made it here at all. The poison and the hornrasps had tried their hardest to finish him before he even got here.'

Toryn grinned to himself. 'I guess I won't hear the end of this tale for years to come.'

The healer dressed the cuts on the woman's arm. 'He was up and out of here in four days. Said he couldn't leave his fellow guards to fight without him. He left not two days ago with the fellows who brought him in. The captain was so impressed, he gave them horses.'

Toryn looked to the door. 'Then I hope he has another to spare.'

'Ah, now there you might be in luck. We've got a fine stallion in the stables that won't tolerate any rider. But from what I hear about your exploits, young man, perhaps he might take to you.'

'And who is this horse?'

The healer finished with her patient. 'I'll walk down with you. As a young woman, I used to rate myself as a rider.' She laughed. 'Well, you could say I am a healer thanks to my riding. I suffered numerous falls trying to jump hedgerows many said were impossible. My knowledge of the art grew with each fall.'

They arrived at the stables. Inside, a fine black horse knickered. The healer held out her hand for the horse to lick. 'This is Lightning. And as you can see, his name refers to his speed and not his appearance. But aptly named I'm told. One of our lads knew his rider, a scout by the name of Shelan. But she met a most unfortunate end as she tracked a large force making its way to Calerdorn. And this poor fellow must have suffered. He turned up here exhausted a few months back. Not sure where he had been and where he was heading, but he collapsed on the road outside. We took him in, fed and cared for him. He seems happy enough. But while he's friendly, he won't let any on his back.'

Toryn stroked Lightning's nose. 'He's a fine one. Reminds me of a brave horse I lost at Roth's Doom. She once carried an Amayan.' He recalled Midnight's last moments on the battlefield as she had succumbed to her many injuries.

'An Amayan's horse? And she let you ride her? Then I'm sure this fellow will oblige.' She held Toryn's gaze. 'We hear a lot of tales from travelers on the road, and the guards crossing the pass. Most are just that… tales, but from what we've heard about your exploits, Toryn, I'd say they're not too far removed from the truth.'

Toryn's face reddened. 'I imagine they'll have been exaggerated with each telling, but I can assure you the stories of Lady Harlyn and the Amayans do not do them justice. And likewise for the tales of Nyomae, the Imaari who once served under Draegelan. But…' he looked Lightning in the eye, 'sadly, the stories of our enemy's exploits also fail to tell of the full horror.' He turned to the healer. 'I'm afraid your skills will be in demand for many months to come.'

To Toryn's relief, Lightning had accepted him. And the horse lived up to his name. He sped north, reaching the Great Elda in less than a day. He had hoped to come across Elrik, but he suspected they would have abandoned their horses and taken the Dorn Trail. And it was a wise decision, despite the grim conditions in the ditches and swamps. While the realms had struck back, the Ruuk may still hold much of the territory in Dorn.

Toryn shivered in the cool air descending from the mountains. Ahead, what he initially took to be a road, glistened beneath the watery sun. Yet no routes led west until the Dorn Plain. He slowed Lightning. It was no road. He stared in horror. The River Wend had frozen. What should have been a youthful stream close to its source in the Kolossos, had turned to ice. Not until the dead of the worst winters did the great rivers freeze; and then it was only where their currents slowed as they approached the open sea. But it was still only late autumn.

Beyond the Wend, the lands were blanketed in a thick layer of new snow. In his childhood, Toryn's heart had almost burst as he awoke to find the first snows of winter had transformed their land. But today, it sank. The Uldalak must have had a hand in this. Was it the start of a new offensive? But surely, they could not have recovered so soon after Roth's Doom. His jaw clenched. Or did they intend to conduct the next stage with creatures from their unworldly ranks?

Far to the north, the skies flashed, and a dull boom tumbled down from the mountains. But Toryn knew this was no storm. A scream tore through the Verses from the Crown. Another Amayan was close to death. More cries joined the first. Toryn called upon the *Elorsil* to give strength to Lightning. He knew the warlocks would sense the sword, but he did not care. Let them know he came for them.

For three days they sped on, needing neither rest nor sustenance. To friend and foe who braved the cold night, they appeared as a warrior and steed from the old tales, galloping north to meet the threat of Ormoroth. To friends, their passing brought hope. To foe, the light pierced deep into their dark hearts, and none dared to stand in their way.

45. The Faerie in the Lake

The days in the pit had drained Nyomae. Scraps of food had been thrown in, but there was barely enough for one, and Nyomae had given most of it to Idraman. She gently rocked him, channeling all the strength she could muster to counter the Angorsil's pulse. Satisfied he could resist for the time-being, she entered the Song unchallenged. She could find no sign of Toryn and assumed he was still deep beneath the mountains. And likewise with the Amayans as a shadow concealed the Verses beyond the Kolossos Pass.

A screech pierced the Song. Nyomae drew back as Uluriel's *kruul* hurtled through the Verses to the aid of her commanders. Once passed, Nyomae looked for the Amanspring. She had known of the river beneath the Kolossos before the shadow had obscured her past. The enemy had indeed grown strong to delve so deep and attempt to defile its power. Many leagues south, the Menon River retained some of its potency, even when tempered by the many adjoining streams as it made its way through the Foranfae. And thanks to Toryn, the wellspring once more fed the deep roots of the Amanach, and flowed far and wide across the lands that provided its dwellers sustenance for the long, cold winters.

Nyomae's head snapped back. An icy grip snatched her from the Song and flung her to the floor. She gagged as she tasted the reek of rotting flesh. She opened her eyes and groaned. The Angorsil glowed anew and cast Uluriel's hideous shadow across the ceiling. She had returned.

Uluriel looked down and sneered. 'Do not take hope from your small victory, *Imaari*.'

But Nyomae sensed a change in her tone. She stood. 'Small? The surge of the Amanspring is anything but *small*. You have suffered a defeat, Sylvena. Your warlocks die at the hands of my friends. Abandon your—'

'The Elorym stones will fail!' Uluriel's ire spattered on Nyomae's face. But her flesh and bones struggled to cope with her anger, and her rasping breathe sprayed more drool into the pit. Uluriel calmed and lowered her voice. 'Our lord will return' — she licked her dry lips and grinned — 'with your assistance.'

Nyomae's skin crawled. 'I will not utter his Name.'

'You seem to think you have a choice. You do not. But fear not the consequences. I will not allow you to be expelled from this realm. I have another fate planned for you.' She pointed a long, clawed finger at Idraman and grinned. 'And his last act will be to aid my possession… of your body.'

Nyomae gaped. 'My…? Never. I will not allow it. You will—'

'Not allow it?' Uluriel's neck crunched as she threw back her head and cackled. 'Do you think you can deny me, Imaari! You are to be my vessel. Few could endure my being for long. But you will. And take that as praise, Nyomae. Then I too shall know my lord's Name. Then together we will open the gateway. And I shall grant you the honor to remain and bear witness to my becoming.'

Nyomae's jaw clenched. 'I will resist you to my last breath. I would rather let my flesh rot, than let you take me.'

'Resist if you must… but you cannot deny me. Nothing will stand in the way of Ormoroth's return.'

Nyomae held her gaze. 'Yet the Maidens' know his Name. One day they will prevail and banish him forever beyond these realms and into the Void.'

Uluriel's eyes narrowed as she grinned. 'Yet I have

outwitted those feckless daughters. On his return, our lord will no longer have a Name for them to invoke.'

'But that is not possible. All creatures they brought into the world have' — Nyomae gasped — 'unless you seek to...' her heart sank. She pleaded. 'No! Do not do this, Sylvena. You will forever change the Song, condemning these lands to—'

'Enough!' Uluriel thrust out a hand. Nyomae skidded and slammed into the wall. Uluriel reached out with her other hand to Idraman. He jolted upright. His eyes rolled up, and to Nyomae's horror, turned black. He moved stiffly as if trying desperately to resist. But Uluriel was stronger. Idraman's knees creaked as he kneeled and placed his cold fingers upon Nyomae's brow.

Nyomae sat beside the brook and dipped her hand in the cool water. Her father had told her not to stroll too far from the village as it would soon be time for supper. She watched the brightly colored fish and listened to the birds twittering as they gathered in the trees to settle for the night. Nyomae sat back. The sun reddened as it sank, and she welcomed the respite from the heat of the long summer day.

She turned to see a tall lady walking along the bank. It was rare to see a stranger in these parts, but Nyomae felt no sense of unease as the elegant woman smiled and stood before her. The stranger looked nothing like any woman she knew. She wore fine clothes that shimmered in the light of the setting sun. Her long hair was braided with gold in the way chosen by the ladies of Elmarand.

Without a word, the woman held out her hand, and Nyomae gladly accepted her invitation to join her. Supper could wait. Her father would understand why she would be late. The tall woman took her along the winding path that led to the trees. Nyomae stopped as someone called her name. Perhaps her father was searching for her, but when she tried to reply, no words came. Yet Nyomae was not troubled. She felt safe as the lady's grip on her hand tightened. She was from Elmarand, the most important city in the realms. Nyomae had nothing to fear.

Deeper and deeper, the lady led her into the woods. As they walked, the sun climbed back into the sky, the birds returned to flight, and the butterflies fluttered passed them in the warm air. Nyomae smiled at the lady; perhaps she would not be late for supper after all.

Nyomae blinked as they suddenly stepped out from under the boughs into bright sunshine. She held up her hand, dazzled by a lake glistening as if a thousand stars had settled on its surface. Nyomae kneeled, cupped her hand, and watched the sparkling water trickle through her fingers. Why had her father never brought her here? They had walked many a time in these woods; surely this would be a good place to swim? Nyomae stood and looked longingly at the tall trees surrounding the lake. She had never seen their like, and wondered if Elmarand's towers could be viewed from their tops, and perhaps even the sea.

Nyomae turned to ask if she could climb one. But the lady shook her head, then spoke for the first time. 'Do you know why I have brought you here, my dearest?' For a moment, the voice reminded Nyomae of her mother. The lady continued. 'You and I are alike, Nyomae.'

She found her voice. 'How do you know my name?'

The lady smiled. 'I know the names of all the special children, Nyomae.' She kneeled and held her hand. 'I also have powers, just like you. And I have a secret. Would you like me to share it with you?' Nyomae nodded. Perhaps the woman would come to the village and berate the children who mocked her. The woman beamed. 'I have a name no one else knows.'

Again, the voice called, echoing through the trees. But

this time Nyomae ignored it, happy to be with another like her. The lady whispered in her ear. 'My secret name is Raanesha. Do you like it?'

Nyomae nodded. 'I do. I don't know any with that name.'

'That is because it is mine alone, not to be shared with anyone.' The lady's eyes widened. 'Now I have told you mine, will you tell me yours?'

Nyomae frowned. 'But you already know mine.'

'That is your common name. Look deep into your heart, and you will find your secret name.'

The air cooled as the sun began to set for the second time that day. 'But… I don't know how.'

Raanesha smiled. 'Do try for me, Nyomae. Then I will know yours, and you will know mine. We will become sisters. Would you like that?'

'Yes, yes I would.' Raanesha's face blurred as tears filled Nyomae's eyes. 'But… where can I find it?'

Raanesha held Nyomae's hand tight. 'Only you know where it can be found. And if you really want to be my sister, you must make a wish. Only then will you discover your real and secret name. Will you do that for me, Nyomae?'

She sobbed. 'Yes. Yes, I will. I promise. I want to be your little sister.'

'Good. I shall leave you now. You can be alone and make your wish.'

Nyomae reached for Raanesha's hand. 'No, please don't go. I don't want to be here alone.'

'But you must. Your wish must not be heard by those who cannot grant it. Be brave, my little one. I promise to bring back a special gift. And when you tell me your name, you shall have it.' She stroked Nyomae's hair. 'Wait for the moon, then make your wish. Tell it to the lake and it shall be granted.' Raanesha turned and walked away, vanishing into the red, evening sunlight filtering through the trees.

Night fell. Nyomae shivered in the dark, worried her father would be furious she had stayed out so late. The moon glimmered on the still waters... and the frosty ground beneath her feet. Winter had come! She stared in wonder at the snow-laden branches, almost touching the frozen lake. A full moon rose over the treetops. It glided across the sky as its twin slid across the ice.

Nyomae did as told. She took a deep breath and spoke. 'My... my wish is to know my secret name.' She remembered her manners. 'Please.' Her words floated away like a wispy cloud, before drifting down to the ice. Where it settled, the surface darkened and began to thaw. As the lake melted, a mist rose at its center. Nyomae stood entranced as it swirled to form a funnel. She had heard stories of the water faeries; had they come to answer her wish? But it was no faerie that stepped out of the haze: it was an old man dressed in a flowing robe, whiter than the snow on the trees.

Nyomae edged back as he walked across the water towards her. He stopped a few paces from the shore and smiled. The old man had a kind face that shimmered in the moonlight. Nyomae waved — perhaps he was a faerie after all. When he spoke, Nyomae recognized his voice but could not recall where she had heard it. 'I cannot deny you your wish, but I will not speak your Maidens' Name aloud.' His brow furrowed. 'And neither must you.' The faerie began to retreat as if a force drew him back to the water. He called out. 'You are not safe here, Nyomae. You must not...' but his voice faded. His warning echoed over her head and was lost.

The moon slid behind the treetops, and Nyomae found herself alone once more in the dark. She no longer wanted to wait, caring not for the gift promised to her by the noble lady. And did she really want her as a sister? She had, after all, left her all alone in the dark wood. Nyomae gasped. The faerie had not revealed her true name. Would Raanesha be angry? But not nearly as angry as her father. Her supper would be long cold.

Nyomae searched for the way back through the trees, desperate to get back to her village before the lady returned. But she was too late. Raanesha stepped out into the moonlight. Yet this was not the elegant woman who had come to her on that warm evening. Nyomae screamed. She was a witch. Her father had spoken of such creatures in the old tales. But had they not all been driven out of the land?

Raanesha's mouth gaped in a taut, pale face. Her dark eyes bore into Nyomae. She staggered back and stepped into the icy water. The witch grabbed Nyomae's wrist and dragged her back to the shore. Her jaw clenched as if trying to contain her anger. She hissed. 'Now show me.'

Nyomae stuttered. 'Show you… what?'

'You know what I desire. The old man gave you a gift.' She bellowed. 'Show me!'

She cried. 'He… he didn't give me anything.'

Raanesha glared and pointed to Nyomae's hand. 'Then where did you get that?' Nyomae glanced down to see a scroll in her cold fingers. Her name! He would not speak it. Then he must have given it to her. But no one was allowed to know it. Nyomae shoved it behind her back. She stiffened and dared to look Raanesha in the eye. 'No… he told me I mustn't—'

'I shared a secret with you. Now you do the same.' The witch's eyes blazed. 'Give it to me!'

Nyomae! It was not her father calling. *Resist.* It was the old man's voice, but it sounded different, seeming far away, as if on the other side of the lake. With all her strength, Nyomae broke free of the witch's grip. She ran, dodging between the low-hanging branches back towards her village. Raanesha screamed for her to stop. Nyomae sped on... but not to the village. She stumbled out of the trees, back to the lake she was certain lay behind. She had nowhere to hide. The witch strode out of the trees. Her long fingers groped at the air, trying to snatch the scroll from Nyomae's hand. Her arm stiffened, then lifted as she offered the parchment to the witch.

'No!' Nyomae pulled back her arm. 'You cannot see it. It's my secret.' Nyomae spun away and hurled the scroll into the lake. But the water froze over before it could sink beneath the surface, thus it slid across the ice. She ran, skidding and slipping as she desperately tried to kick the scroll beyond the witch's grasp.

Nyomae. The voice echoed across the frozen lake. Idraman! Then she knew. She was trapped within a Verse from her youth. Nyomae stopped, then turned to face the witch as the Imaari of her present Verse. Raanesha shrieked, frustrated her ploy had been laid bare. Nyomae raised her hand. 'Begone, Uluriel! I banish you.'

Uluriel thrust out her arms. Spikes shot out from her fingers and pierced the ice. Anchored to the spot, she threw back her head and cried out. 'You cannot banish *me*, fool!'

But Nyomae was not done. 'This is my Verse.' She waved her hand across the ice. 'I do as I please.' It rippled. Uluriel tottered as it thawed. Nyomae spoke calmly. 'Begone, Raanesha! You do not belong here.' Uluriel faded as she disappeared beneath the dark waters.

Nyomae bowed her head, ready to withdraw and return to Idraman's side. But her way was closed — she was trapped in the Song! It could mean only one thing: Uluriel prepared to possess her mortal body.

46. Across the Frozen Mire

Lightning's head bobbed as he surged ever faster. Toryn's cold hands clutched the reins close to the horse's neck and, not for the first time, feared he might fall. But they could not afford to slow down. Toryn had sensed no sign of the conflict at the Crown for two days… but it was the silence that troubled him. Had the Amayans succeeded, or fallen? And Elodi…? He tucked his head behind Lightning's mane, keen to find shelter from the icy wind, trying not to think the worst. If the warriors lay dead, then so surely did the hopes of the realms. He clung onto the hope they lived, despite their absence from the Song. Yet the doubts remained; it was not beyond the skill of the warlocks to deceive and lead him into a trap.

Ahead, the Great Northwest Road began to climb as it turned to make its way through the mountains to Drunsberg. Toryn eased Lightning to a trot and sheathed his sword. The *Elorsil* had sustained them for days, but he could not draw upon the Amanach indefinitely… and he did not know when he would need its power again. He peered through the snow falling farther up the valley. It was early in spring when he and Hamar had walked up to the Drunsberg Gate. Back then, he had thought it was just a matter of reporting the sacking of Greendell, and then looking for work. But within a day, everything had changed… and Hamar had been lost.

Toryn patted Lightning's neck. 'Whoa, boy. Let's stop here. We need to find a way off this road.' The last part of the journey would take them through the Mawlgrim Mire; not a place Toryn ever thought he would find himself. The old roads built in Draegelan's day, had long since been swallowed by the marshes as they had spread east to claim the land up to the mountains. Few willingly chose to make the bleak crossing, and those who did, did so as a last resort, often failing to emerge from the other side. Even if Jedrul's stories of the bog grims were untrue, there were other creatures ready to sink their teeth, fangs, or stings into the sweet flesh of the fools trespassing into their marsh.

Toryn turned his back on the valley, trusting his company still held the mines, and Jedrul had reopened the deep seams. The road had yet to be secured before the ores could find their way to the smithies in the south, but that was a concern for others. Toryn's path lay north. He led Lightning down a steep slope towards the last stretch of the Dorn Trail that would take them to Findale Lake. Toryn smiled. He had spent the last three days cursing the unnatural winter, but now he welcomed the cold. His earlier trek along the trail had been a most unpleasant affair, but the wind and snow had driven the insects away and frozen the muddy ditches.

The ice beneath the blanket of snow cracked as Lightning made his way warily along the gulley. Toryn wondered how far the sound would travel in the still, silent evening. But that was not his only concern; a black horse against a background of snow would not easily elude enemy eyes. Having silenced the *Elorsil*, the frantic journey now caught up with him. His whole body ached, and he was in no doubt Lightning was exhausted and would struggle to canter, let alone gallop. They would be vulnerable to an attack. Both needed to rest, even if only for a short while.

The ditch widened as the trail came to an end. Lightning stumbled out into deeper snow and trudged up to the top of a nearby ridge. In the distance, the frozen lake appeared as a giant gray, slug beneath the thick clouds as the day drew to an end. A few fires dotted the lower slopes of the Findale Hills, but Toryn was hopeful the Ruuk would not be expecting company on such a grim night. He stroked Lightning's mane now clogged with ice. 'Let's find a place to rest, boy.'

At the foot of the slope, they came across the remains of a farmhouse and its outbuildings. The house had completely collapsed, but one of the barns still had part of its roof in place, and its sturdy, stone walls would at least keep the cold at bay. Toryn dismounted and led a relieved Lightning inside. He checked the wall, then smiled at his horse. 'We're in luck. See… no cracks. Let's risk a small fire and warm our bones.'

The short rest beside the fire had done them both good. Toryn set off in the early hours, hoping to reach the mire as the new day broke. Lightning's confidence grew as the frozen ground beneath the snow allowed him to gallop, and soon the hills of Findale were behind them. Yet while the wind had taken its fury elsewhere, the cold held onto its gain, and now sought to inflict its misery upon them. Toryn gritted his chattering teeth, unwilling to call upon the *Elorsil* just to ease his discomfort. But Hamar would be proud of him. He often berated Toryn when he complained about working in the heat or the cold. *What doesn't kill you makes you stronger*, he would say. Toryn managed a frozen grin. If Hamar was right, he would surely be invincible by now, following the efforts of his foes and the weather of late.

Ahead, the spikey snow-laden tops of a small wood were the only feature on an otherwise flat plain. Toryn shuddered. For a moment, he feared he had stumbled upon Wyke Wood. But that dark place lay many leagues to the west, far from the mountains rising reassuringly on his right. But despite the bleak and deserted landscape, Toryn could not shake the feeling they were being watched. Lightning's blistering pace on the road north could not have gone unnoticed — but where would the inevitable ambush come?

Toryn ducked as they passed beneath the low-hanging branches of the wood. He found the path of a stream, broke the thick ice, and filled his flask while Lightning drank. He rubbed the ice from the horse's neck. 'When we're done, I promise the most comfortable and warmest stable in the land is waiting for you, boy. But... first we must cross the Mawlgrim.' Toryn looked into Lightning's dark eyes as he looked up. 'Have you been there before? The healer at the watchtower told me of your exploits. You traveled far and wide with Shelan.' He mounted. 'I hear she was quite a rider and scout.' Toryn patted his back. 'You'll have noticed I am not the fine rider she was, but I appreciate your efforts to keep me—' A twig snapped. He spun around but could see little in the early light. 'It could be a squirrel. But let's not wait to find out, eh.'

Toryn kept one eye over his shoulder as they galloped along the edge of the wood. As they left the trees behind, the land began to drop down towards the Mawlgrim. The marshes were smothered with a thick blanket of snow, spreading as far as he could see before it disappeared into the mist. He recalled Jedrul's tale of the bog grims. But if these strange creatures existed, they would surely be cursing the cold, now that their soft mud beds had turned to ice.

Toryn rose in the saddle. 'Let's get this over with. We'll be through by nightfall.' And he dearly hoped it could be done. He had no wish to be on the mire come nightfall.

They kept as close to the foothills on their right where the terrain allowed. Toryn was wary of just how quickly he could lose his bearings in the featureless marshes, if the mist conspired to hide the mountains. But he could not resist peering across the plain. Frost-laden reeds poked up in clumps through the snow as if spears of Draegelan's armies riding north. A thousand years ago, Ormoroth's winter had packed the deep Trench with ice, opening the way for his hordes to march on the Seven Realms. And now the harsh winter from those troubling tales returned.

Toryn checked the mountains and was pleased to see they yet defied the mist. A crunch. His eyes darted left, flitting across the snow, suddenly feeling isolated and exposed. One of the reed spears moved, followed by another. But the air was still. Could it be bog grims beneath the ice? Toryn had dismissed Jedrul's stories at the time; but it had helped take his mind off his sore skin, rubbed raw by the Ruuk chains as they were taken to Wyke Wood. But now… alone, in the thickening mists, his stories did not seem so absurd. He nudged Lightning on but dared not risk more than a trot. If his horse stumbled and broke a leg, they would be at the mercy of the mire, regardless of the creatures that stalked them.

A thud. Toryn twisted both left and right, but could not tell which direction it came from. Certain it was not a shift in the ice, he drew his sword. Did a band of Norgog pursue them? Did they wait for Lightning to falter? The Norgog could easily tramp across the snow for many days in the freezing air. This was now their territory; Nordruuk had encroached far into the realms.

Lightning reared. The ground ahead rose as if a gray wave surged towards them. Frost-coated hammers burst from beneath the blanket of snow. The Norgog roared. Dozens of them charged in orderly ranks, poised to cave in his skull. 'Fly Lightning! Fly.'

Toryn had neither the time nor the strength to call upon the Amanach. He had no choice. They would have to flee into the marshes, away from the rocky outcrops where they could easily find themselves in a dead end. Lightning staggered yet managed to build speed. But Toryn was reluctant to stray too far from the Kolossos. He slowed Lightning, satisfied they had put enough distance between them and the Norgog. But what lay ahead? Were they being driven into a trap? He turned in the hope they were heading north, but he could not be certain. It began to snow. Within minutes, it came up to Lightning's knees, slowing him down to a walk.

Toryn blinked as the large snowflakes settled on his face. 'Whoa, boy. We'll soon get lost in this.' He could see no farther than a few paces, and the silence unsettled him. If the Norgog came, he doubted he would hear or see them until it was too late. But Toryn had recovered a little of his strength. He could call upon the *Elorsil* and find the river beneath the Kolossos. Then he could determine the direction he should take. But if a warlock led the Norgog, he may as well light a beacon to guide them to his position.

A cry pierced the silence. But this was not of the mire; it came through the Verses... from the Crown. The Amayans' grief pained Toryn as a spear to his gut, but it showed him the way. Norgog or not, he could not languish in the marshes a moment longer. He had to reach the Crown.

Toryn drew the *Elorsil* and summoned the power of the Amanach. Lightning surged forward, seeming to rise from the snow and glide across the mire. His vision cleared. Not far ahead, he found the Norgog... and they sensed his coming. They formed a line between two mounds, but if they thought they could prevent his passage, they were mistaken. Lightning's pace soon narrowed the gap. The *Elorsil* glowed, then grew hot, sending a beam through the heavy snow. The Norgog staggered back, shielding their eyes from the bright light.

Toryn felt the heat rise. He unleashed a bolt towards their line, melting the ice where they stood. His foes wilted in the sudden heat and floundered in the mud. Lightning jumped, passing clean over the Norgog as they scrambled to free themselves from the sucking mire. In the light, Toryn thought he saw glistening hands with long fingers grasp at the Norgogs' ankles. But he could not be sure if they were hands, or just gushing mud, freed from the layer of ice.

Toryn let the *Elorsil* fade, knowing he would need to conserve his strength for the days to come. He bowed his head and entered the Song. The present Verses of the mire revealed little, but just enough for Toryn to navigate his way towards the last peaks of the Kolossos. For the second time in his life, he passed out of the realms and into Nordruuk. He flinched as a dark shape reared suddenly up out of the gloom. But Lightning remained untroubled, and Toryn was relieved to see it was an abandoned watchtower from Draegelan's day. He steered Lightning away from its base, satisfied the Ruuk did not occupy it, perhaps not suspecting an attack by the realms.

The jagged line of the Kolossos loomed ahead as the skies darkened. Toryn let out a long, steaming sigh, thankful they had made it through before the light was lost. But they were close enough to spy the four peaks that formed the Crown. The stories never spoke well of the place, and Toryn sensed the pain its grim past had left upon the Verses.

The Mawlgrim Mire was behind him; the Kolossos Crown lay ahead.'

47. Not of the Maidens' Making

Nyomae fled through the Song, seeking a time she and Idraman were at the height of their powers. She had to break free and return to the pit in Elmarand. If she could not do so soon, she would be trapped. Nyomae had no doubt Uluriel would make good on her promise and hold her hostage in her own flesh.

Her vision cleared. She strolled with a young Idraman through the Garden of Waterfalls in Elmarand, discussing their studies of the earliest known parts of the Song. In her hand, she had not one, but two scrolls. She looked to Idraman, but before she could speak, the glistening waters darkened and the air chilled. Storm clouds smothered the sun — Uluriel had found them. The wind picked up, rustling the leaves of the trees, and silencing the birds. The wind became a gale and Uluriel burst into the Verse. Nyomae reached out to Idraman as the storm threatened to part them. He grabbed her wrist, but the gale became a tempest, snatching her from his grasp.

Nyomae tumbled back in time through the Song. She knew where Uluriel wished to take her: Ormoroth's ice fortress of Vorkirik. Her hands clutched at thin air, but she could do nothing to prevent her passage to the darkest known place in the land. Nyomae jolted to a halt, almost blacking out as she found herself in the presence of the Angorlith. Uluriel shielded her from the mighty iron pillar, not wishing to see her wither in its presence. But this was no act of kindness. Uluriel would not let her perish and thus avoid the fate she had planned. Her long fingers grabbed Nyomae's hair and snapped her head back. Uluriel pried Nyomae's mouth open and glared into her eyes.

Nyomae could not resist. She sobbed. Back in the pit beneath Elmarand, Uluriel was about to take her mortal form for herself.

But just as Nyomae feared she was lost, another entered the Verse. The walls of Vorkirik disappeared into the mist of the Song. Uluriel released her grip, confused by the change not of her making. The haze cleared. Nyomae found herself with Uluriel in a cavern beneath the Kolossos. The ground trembled. The Amanspring! Idraman stepped out of the shimmering boundary of the Verse. He circled his hands, calling upon the thundering river beneath. Uluriel cried out as a swirling wall of water rose up from the rock and engulfed her. She threw out her hands. Yet the water was potent so close to the Amanspring's source, and she could not break free.

Idraman took Nyomae's hand and spoke. *There is something you must know. I cannot hold her for long. We must hurry.* He led her through the Verses, bringing them back towards the present day… and to Vorkirik. The Song shuddered as they approached the discord of the dark fortress where Ormoroth had performed many a corrupt deed. They passed through its thick walls of ice and down into the foundations of the mountain on which it stood. The Angorlith pounded, stretching and crushing the Verse, forced to bear its corrupt pulse. The Song endured. But its pain tore at every fiber of Nyomae's being. In this Verse, a most vile act was committed; an act that threatened the very purity of the Song of Creation. But not by Ormoroth's hand… it was Uluriel.

In this deep vault, she had matched her Master's dark art of corruption. From the creatures of the Maidens' making, Ormoroth had spawned the keshwing, corvraak and shrouls. Yet, for a fleeting, terrible moment amid the silence between the echoes, Uluriel had surpassed them all… to bring forth a human child.

Nyomae recoiled as the screams of the children, imprisoned in this dark place, tore through the Song. And to her horror, hundreds had suffered as Uluriel conducted her foul rituals to seed her abomination.

Idraman retreated, taking Nyomae through the Verses that bore the Nameless Child's presence. Raised by her servants, the infant was denied a warm embrace, a loving look, and a kind word. But the child grew weak, coming close to death amid its harsh surroundings. Uluriel had force-fed her foul concoctions into the crying infant's mouth, desperate for a mother's milk. Yet even Uluriel's dark mind understood what the child lacked. It was taken south, barely surviving the journey to the fort at Draegnor. But this was not to be its home. A tower of twisted wood rose up from the mist of the Song. Nyomae watched, full of pity for the empty vessel. Then wept as the child was passed into the care of Uleva in Wyke Wood. Despite, Uleva's indifference, the infant grew, tended by an old man named Dohl. But the wood was no place for an infant, and Dohl was no substitute for a nursemaid. Then Nyomae saw it was a girl… and the full horror took hold.

As Elodi moved to rescue the prisoners in the wood, Uleva had abandoned her tower and taken the child east to the ruins of Greendell. Here, she prepared for the next stage. Uleva commanded Dohl to assume his true form as Dorlan, and then lead the people of Dorlgoth out of their homes. On the Dorn Plain, Uleva's forces had surrounded and annihilated the old and the weak. Here, she had left the young girl beneath the charred corpses to be found by Elodi. Thus, in Calerdorn, the child would be cared for properly and grow strong and healthy.

The Dorn Plain darkened. Nyomae and Idraman were wrenched back to the cave beneath the Kolossos. Uluriel fought back. She grew, filling the tunnel with a form most terrible. She called upon all the demons she had at her command — and they came. A dark wave surged towards them, forcing the Imaari to retreat from the Verse. Idraman's hold broke, and Nyomae found herself alone.

Voices screeched as if a chorus of demons performed a travesty of the Maidens' Song. Nyomae's ears bled as she was tossed about like a leaf in a storm. She cried out. The voices ceased. A light breeze blew in her face. She steadied her stance and opened her eyes. Nyomae stood at the pinnacle of the Telamir Tower. This was her Verse, but she was not in control. She tried to leave, aware of Uluriel's desire. This was the moment the Nym had revealed the last line of Aber's Verse. A dark form took shape beside her on the tower. Nyomae called out to Idraman. She sensed his efforts to pull her free, but Uluriel resisted… just long enough for the Maidens' Name of Ormoroth to be revealed. Uluriel threw back her head, thrust out her arms and cackled. In her hands, she held the scrolls the old man had given Nyomae at the lake. Her form faded. Uluriel was gone.

Nyomae fell back into Idraman's arms. His grasp was weak, but while he looked frail, his eyes shone. And when he spoke, Nyomae was relieved to hear him speak as the Imaari she had known in his prime. Idraman smiled. 'Uluriel's hold over me finally shattered when you fought back. I took you to the Amanspring to prevent her possession of you.' He sighed. 'I kept you in that Verse for as long as possible to reveal Uluriel's plans, but her demons eventually broke my hold.'

Nyomae sat. 'Where…?' Her voice croaked. 'Where is she?'

'She's gone… for now. Three warlocks have fallen in the north. But at great cost. An Amayan was slain.'

'Slain! This is a tragedy.' She tried to sit up. 'We have to—' Her head spun.

'Rest, Nyomae. You have suffered. Uluriel will return,

but I believe we have time for you to recover.' He glanced towards the edge of the pit. 'She took that infernal shard, thus abandoning her attempt to possess you. I imagine she is angry with her warlocks. She had hoped they would finish the Amayans for good at the Crown.'

Nyomae gasped, recalling the last moments in her Verse. 'She knows it, Idraman. She was with me when the Nym revealed Ormoroth's Name. She has it... and mine.' She grasped his arm. 'She knows my Name, Idraman. My time is limited.'

Idraman calmed her. 'Fear not. She has two Names, but neither are yours.'

'But... you revealed it to me at the lake. It was in the form of a scroll. She tricked me into making a wish to reveal my Name.'

He laughed. 'I may be old, but I still have a few tricks of my own.' Idraman helped Nyomae to sit. 'I guessed her strategy. The presence of two powerful forces in the Song made it easy to find you. I assumed the *role* of the faerie in the lake, knowing Uluriel would mislead the young child of your Verse.'

Nyomae frowned. 'So, what was on the scroll if not my Name?'

'Well... it *was* a Maidens' Name, just not one she was expecting.' Idraman beamed. 'It was that of your kitten. In your conversations with the little fellow you unknowingly found it. And you retain it to this day, not that you could do any harm now. I imagine he has long departed this world.'

Nyomae smiled, but it soon faded. 'That was clever of you, my old friend. But she still has Ormoroth's Name.'

He shook his head. 'Thankfully, she will not invoke it while you also know it. She needs the child to be ready. Alas, it is a most foul scheme.'

Nyomae's mind cleared. 'I assume the infant will host

his *kruul* while he grows too strong for any to resist. I had knowledge of the girl. Elodi named her Meloni.'

'Ah yes, she must have named her after the sole survivor following the sack of Kymran. I believe the young Amayan was chosen to find her. They knew that under her care, the child would grow, and one day be ready to make the journey back to Vorkirik.' He sighed. 'The poor lass will have to be strong if she's to host Ormoroth's *kruul*.'

'And when do you suspect that day will come?'

Idraman stood and stretched his back. 'All too soon. But what of Calerdorn? Can it hold out against Uluriel?'

Nyomae groaned. 'I'm afraid it has already fallen. And the child played her part in its downfall. Elodi has plans to retake it, but I don't know when she will be ready. And, of course, she will not be aware of Meloni's past.'

'This is bad news. I was not aware Calerdorn was in enemy hands. I'm afraid my mind is not what it used to be. I have spent too long under Uluriel's spell. She seeks the Name she believed I held.'

Nyomae's scalp tingled. 'And did you also bear this most terrible burden? Did you know it, Idraman? You had the opportunity to speak it when you drew upon the power beneath the Caerwals.'

'I came close… very close. But I am ashamed to say I feared the consequences… for myself. The return of the *Draedalak* took me at unawares. I did not believe they could be summoned while Ormoroth resided in the Halfway World. I dared not speak it, unsure I could banish Ormoroth for good… or enable his return. I chose instead to speak your Name.' Idraman clutched her arm. 'I am sorry, my friend. I failed. I passed the burden of responsibility of that most terrible day onto you.'

Nyomae stroked his hand. 'You have no need to apologize. It is I who should. I abused the power you bestowed upon me. I cited the Verse of Unmaking when perhaps I had other choices.'

Idraman stared at the ceiling. 'We both faced a terror we could not have imagined, driven to the very brink of madness. I cannot think of another path that was open to you in the face of those dreaded beasts. Had you not uttered those words, none would have survived.' He patted her leg. 'Let us be thankful we lived to fight another day… all be it three hundred years later.'

'Thank you, Idraman. But my guilt still sits heavily upon my shoulders.' Nyomae turned to him. 'Uluriel held you captive all this time, how have you kept Ormoroth's Name from her?'

He shrugged. 'I no longer possessed it. Thankfully, it was lost when I called upon your Name. But… had I relented and used it, it would not have been the first time Ormoroth's Name was spoken.'

Nyomae stiffened. 'The Elorym. The Nym revealed they had the knowledge, but I had not known for sure if they had invoked his Name.' She dared not breathe. 'How did it bring about their end?'

'Ormoroth anticipated their last desperate act. Following the long war, the Elorym were on their knees, and the power of the Amanach diminished. Hence, the unrestrained Angorlith gave Ormoroth the strength to summon the demons of the old days, exiled in the Halfway World. When the Elorym spoke his Name, the gateway opened… and the demons returned. While their time in the mortal realms was brief, it was sufficient to overwhelm the Elorym at Ormoroth's behest. Thus, they did not have the power to cast him into the Void.'

The pit shook. A bitter taste filled Nyomae's mouth as the torches flickered green. She waited for the ground to settle. 'You were right. It appears Uluriel is not best pleased with her warlocks.'

Idraman looked up as if seeing through Elmarand's

foundations. 'Uluriel grows weak. She may represent a threat to us, but she knows her time is limited. Her mortal vessel struggles to contain her all-consuming *kruul*. Even if she manages to possess one such as you, it would still not be long enough to achieve her ends. Uluriel is desperate to bring back Ormoroth. She knows her warlocks may yet seek to overthrow her if her powers continue to wane. They both fear and despise Uluriel. Not willingly do they serve her. If only we had the time to—'

Another tremor shook the city as Uluriel raged below. Idraman stood and walked to the center of the pit. He held out his hands and spoke under his breath. A blue light snuffed out the green hue and steadied the ground. Nyomae watched in admiration. 'Your strength of the old days returns, my friend.'

He turned. 'I have ceased my Word of Forbidding at the Caerwal Gate. That was my burden to bear all this time. I believed it necessary at the time as we did not know the extent of the danger in the north.' Idraman paced around the pit like a trapped beast. 'Demelia, the Varsil of Elmarand, initially supported my action, but I grew suspicious of her intention. At first, I could not determine why, but too late did I discover Uluriel's presence. I was taken in chains to the Sun Tower. I was still weak from my efforts at the pass, thus Uluriel overwhelmed me and then through me, maintained the Word. With the realms divided, she could more easily sow her dark seeds in the south.' Idraman walked back and sat beside Nyomae. 'We must be strong, more now than ever.'

Nyomae massaged her stiff neck. 'I'm not sure I can carry this burden for much longer. Is it wrong that I wish I had never learned of Ormoroth's Name?'

'No, my friend. It is a heavy yoke to bear. I do not blame you for wanting to be free of it.'

Nyomae turned to Idraman. 'Please. Tell me

truthfully. Do you believe we have the strength and resolve to resist?'

He stretched out his arms. 'In the years I spent in the tower, I happened upon the old Verses of this place. Uluriel came and went, freeing me from her dreadful presence, long enough for me to recover some of my strength... if not all of my mind.'

Nyomae nodded. 'Ah, that must be when you found me on the slopes overlooking the Foranfae.' She smiled. 'But I too was in a frail state. I couldn't determine if you were friend or foe.'

Idraman chuckled. 'I imagine my rants did not make much sense. Later, I found this Toryn fellow you speak of.' He looked up. 'There is reason for hope, Nyomae.' His eyebrows raised. 'And have you solved the matter of his heritage? Why would the *Elorsil* respond in his hand?' Nyomae gasped. Idraman grinned. 'He is like Draegelan. Both Imaari and Amayan blood course through his veins.'

She groaned. 'How did I not see this for myself? Even while under the shadow, I sought him. Something led me to the young man shackled in the Ruuk wagon. In all the time I spent with him, it eluded my eyes. But then, neither did the Amayans see it. No one knew.' Nyomae held out her hand. 'I had the *Elorsil* in my possession, but still failed to discover its truth.'

'Do not be hard on yourself, Nyomae. The years living under the shadow blunted your senses. Toryn's Imaari abilities grow, but the Amayan powers take longer. Only when he held the *Elorsil,* did his mother's blood stir.'

Nyomae looked to the flickering flames. 'That does bring some hope in such a dark hour. But we cannot become complacent. Toryn remains vulnerable while he has yet to master even a fraction of his powers.'

'Then we have work to do.' Idraman stood and held out his hand. 'Are you recovered from your ordeal?'

Nyomae nodded and accepted his help. He smiled and pulled her to her feet. 'Then may I suggest we make our way to the Sun Tower. There we have the best chance to thwart Uluriel's plans. She will soon summon the keshwing from the mountains in the east. She must be stopped, or at least delayed. Calerdorn must be recaptured, and as unpalatable as it sounds… the child must be killed.'

48. No More Tears to Shed

Shadows moved to Elodi's right. Shrouls! Dozens of them. The air cooled. Their cloven hooves clattered against the frozen rock as they sped towards them, surprisingly swift with their ungainly gait. Behind, the last of the aralaks and droogs scuttled and slithered from the ravine. And though free of the warlocks' command, they yet desired the flesh promised to them.

Eryn groaned. 'Once more, my sisters. Let us return this sacred place to the peace it deserves.' The warriors drew their swords and strode to meet the new threat. Elodi's Fire ignited. She raised her blade and scythed low across the first line of the shrouls. Many toppled as the strike severed their long, scrawny legs, but a dozen more took their place. Elodi set her stance. The shrouls were now close enough for Elodi to hear their teeth grating, ready to crunch Amayan bones. But Elodi's blade dulled, and to her horror, the Fire had gone and the Amayans were spent.

Neeve cried out. 'The horses! Look.' Sea Mist and the Amayan mounts charged the rear, kicking and stomping onto soft flesh and brittle bone. To Elodi's joy, the leaderless shrouls were no match for Amayan horses, and many soon fell beneath the onslaught.

Eryn rallied. 'To the fray!' They raised their swords, drew on the last of their strength, and rushed to trap their assailants. The Amayans slashed, jabbed, and stamped until they could barely stand. But the frenzied attack worked. Elodi sheathed her blade as the last spider died beneath Sea Mist's hooves. Gasping for air, she turned to the Crown Stone for sustenance. Its light shone through her sisters to project shimmering paths of blue across the ground. Yet she counted only three.

Elodi called to Eryn. 'Where's Calestri? I've not seen her since—' A scream echoed across the Crown. At the southern slope, the last three shrouls surrounded Calestri. Her red hair shone in the light of the stone as she fought the ravenous creatures, clawing at her limbs. But she was without her sword... and badly wounded.

Elodi rushed to aid her, but her tired legs moved as if running over sand. Calestri stumbled. Long claws clasped her arms and legs. She kicked out but could not break free from their ice-cold grip. Her skin glistened with frost, spreading out from beneath the shrouls' claws. Calestri gave up the fight and slumped. The shrouls howled and snatched back their skeletal arms. Elodi twisted away but could not shut out the ghastly sound of breaking bones.

Eryn and Arijan hurtled past her and felled the creatures. But they were too late. Another Amayan had fallen. Elodi could only stand and watch Calestri's soul depart. Her spirit followed Madraal's path up to the dome to settle as a star beside her fallen sister. Elodi's eyes wandered across the thousands, now twinkling in the clear night sky. Were all the stars Elorym souls?

Elodi jumped as Neeve took her arm and helped her to stand. She walked to Calestri's broken body but could not feel the ground beneath her numb feet. Eryn spoke. 'Two of us for three of them. It is too high a price to pay.' She looked to the Amayans. 'The Crown is indeed a place of sorrow. For many years the Elorym held the evil at bay from the fortress beyond, but many lost their lives. It seems we also make the same sacrifice.' She turned. 'But Igrayne yet lives. The warlocks left empty-handed. She is here... she has to be. But be wary. She may be possessed. I cannot sense the evil, but this place appears to conceal much.'

'I see her.' Neeve spat. 'Is there no end to the warlocks' cruelty. See.' She pointed to Gorgonach's peak. 'She's chained to the rockface. The shrouls must have scaled the mountain, while we fought our way through the ravine.'

Arijan's jaw clenched. 'Then so must we. She's weak. I cannot think she'll survive for long once the next storm comes.'

'But not you, Arijan.' Eryn kept her eyes on the slopes. 'A warlock's blade has left its mark. It will be days before that heals. I doubt you are fit to climb to such a height. It will take at least a day to reach her... and then she will need to be carried down.' She turned. 'Neeve is also injured. Elodi? You and I appear to be the least hurt. Will you accompany me?'

Elodi's stomach lurched as she looked up to the peak. 'I climbed the lower slopes of the Calern Mountains in my youth. But they do not compare with this.' She glanced to Arijan and Neeve, then nodded. 'But I shall accompany you. Igrayne cannot be left to die.'

Eryn linked her arm in Elodi's. 'Then we go now. We will climb in the dark and descend in tomorrow's light.' She turned to the injured Amayans. 'You must rest. Take the horses to the stone so they too can be revived. Igrayne will need all your strength on our return.'

More than once, Elodi feared she was about to plunge to her death. And even with the rekindled Fire, her cold hands had struggled to find a grip in the icy slopes. Eryn had retrieved a stretch of rope from her horse, thus, they could take it in turns to bear Igrayne back to the stone. But despite the challenge of the climb, Elodi began to dread the descent more. She had kept her eyes on the peak, desperate to reach Igrayne as her ear-splitting cries echoed across the Crown. Yet they were not a plea for help —

Igrayne beseeched the gods to take her soul and free her from her torment.

When they had finally reached their sister in the dull light of the new day, the Amayans found her in the depths of despair. Elodi was shocked to see Igrayne in such a poor state. Her ankles and wrists were black from the cold grip of the shrouls, and her skin was covered in a layer of frost. But the warlocks had not intended her to die. By their dark art, Igrayne's blood ran hot through her veins, keeping the cold at bay to prolong her agony. She writhed against the chains, desperate to throw herself from the peak and to her fate far below.

Eryn tried to console her, but Igrayne ranted and raved, screaming for death's release. With much effort, the Amayans calmed their fraught sister and lulled her into a deep sleep. But now came the challenge of the descent. Elodi looked down for the first time in the growing light. Her blood froze. Whispers carried in on the breeze, inviting her to let go. And Elodi listened. The call of the void urged her to leap into the wide, open space and leave behind the struggles of the mortal world. For a moment, she could forget her troubles as she pledged her soul to the next realm. No responsibility, no decisions to be made, and no guilt from the consequences.

Let go, Elodi. Be free. The whispers became the voices of the lost. Her father, then Wendel, followed by Dorlan. *You will feel no pain. Join us, Elodi. Be free.* She felt her numb fingers soften.

'Elodi!' Eryn grabbed her shoulder. 'Don't listen.' The voices stopped.

Her hands clenched and she sagged back against the solid rock. She stared aghast at the jagged edges jutting up from the mountain. She murmured. 'I… I came so close. I was about to…'

'It's the wraiths, Elodi.' Eryn clutched her arm. 'They

can be very persuasive. You have resisted this time, but be wary… they may come again.'

'Then I shall be ready for them.' But deep inside, Elodi was not so sure.

The wind, long absent from the Crown, suddenly picked up, sensing its chance to send them tumbling, following the failure of the wraiths. Elodi called to Eryn over the wails. 'Can we do this? Could the two of us fall to save one?'

Eryn tied the rope around Igrayne's midriff. 'We never leave a sister to die. You're an Amayan, Elodi. You are bonded to us. Thus, you have accepted the responsibility that entails.'

Elodi nodded, suddenly ashamed of her doubt. 'Then let us take her to the stone.' With one hand she clung to the iron spike bearing Igrayne. With the other, she used her sword to prize open the links of the chain. 'Be ready, Eryn. It gives.'

Eryn grunted as she bore Igrayne's weight as the link opened. She turned to the east. 'The sunrises. The clouds are thick, but we will have enough light.' She bowed her head and called upon the Fire once more. Elodi followed and let the warmth melt away her fear and doubt.

The descent was even slower than the climb, but mercifully they found shelter from the wind by taking the west side of the ridge. Night had already fallen by the time they reached the flat ground at the Crown's center. Elodi could not recall a time when her limbs had ached so much. But they had made it. Eryn and Elodi carried her to the stone where they found Neeve and Arijan, along with the horses. Sea Mist's head bobbed as they approached. He looked in fine shape, seeming to have benefited from the Amanach's power. And now Elodi felt its warmth as if a roaring hearth in Calerdorn's Great Hall.

As with Madraal, they kneeled and laid their hands on Igrayne's tormented body. Elodi flinched as her hands touched upon their sister's pain. Eryn's taut face shone in the light of the stone. 'The warlocks revealed to Igrayne what she'd tried to keep hidden all these years. It has opened many wounds, from which…' she bit her lip, 'from which she may not recover. The stone may heal her body, but… not her troubled mind. The warlocks exploited her guilt. It is her deep sorrow that ails her.' She held out her hands. 'I need your strength, my warriors. I will try to speak to her while she slumbers.' The Amayans formed a circle around their stricken sister. Eryn sighed. 'Perhaps if we can allay her shame, she may yet return.'

Neeve held back her tears. She whispered. 'I wish she could have spoken to me of her sorrow. Please, Eryn. Please bring her back to us.'

Elodi felt the Fire rise within their circle. Eryn's voice echoed as if coming from another place. 'We know of your guilt, Igrayne. We lived under a shadow. Our powers were hidden from us. You need feel no shame.'

Igrayne's lips barely moved as she spoke in her sleep. 'My beloved daughter was hanged. Finromir and my son were turned. They fight for the spawn of Ormoroth. I have no reason to live.'

Eryn continued. 'While it is true your daughter was lost, Finromir yet holds out against our foe. And your son fights with us. Your blood flows strong in his veins. He is a powerful ally in our struggle.' Igrayne's body warmed.

Neeve gasped. 'She returns.' Elodi felt her grip tighten.

Igrayne opened her eyes and blinked. 'That cannot be true.' She frowned. 'I have seen what they have become. They are beyond my help.'

Eryn broke the circle. 'Lay your hands on her. She needs our touch.'

Elodi stroked Igrayne's brow. 'You have been deceived. I know your son. He is a fine, young man with a pure heart. The warlocks have no hold over him.'

Neeve leaned closer. 'You have met him. You have met your son.' Igrayne's eyes flickered as Neeve recounted the tale. 'On the slopes overlooking Roth's Doom. He was with Eryn when we gathered to ride into battle.'

Igrayne raised her hand. 'I… I touched him.' She winced as she beheld her blackened fingers. 'His shoulder. I placed my hand on his shoulder, and… I looked him in the eye.' She sobbed. 'How did I not know him?' The tears flowed. 'I could have… held him once more… and to tell him…' She looked away. 'He does not know me.' Her back arched as she cried out.

Elodi grasped her arm. 'He will know you, Igrayne. Your son rides north. I can sense his presence. The *Elorsil* recognizes his touch. It gives him strength.'

Igrayne tried to sit. 'Can this be true?'

Eryn whispered. 'Elodi speaks the truth. He is named Toryn. Finromir took him to a village in Darrow. He grew up unaware of his heritage. But now he knows. Your son grows stronger and will one day assume Draegelan's mantle.'

Igrayne let out a long sigh. 'Deep I had driven my guilt. It has drained my spirit. Your words bring me much comfort… but alas, my time in this world draws to an end.'

Elodi held her frost-bitten hand. 'You must fight, Igrayne. Your son will be here soon. The stone will sustain and…' she glanced to Eryn, 'heal you.'

But the light in Igrayne's eyes dwindled. 'The Fire fails me… I cannot resist the call of our ancestors.' With her remaining strength she pulled herself up and clutched Elodi's arm. 'Please… tell my son that his birth brought me joy amid the shadows. Tell him how much it pained me to be parted from him and his father.' Her grip softened. 'And… tell him of his sister.' Elodi leaned closer as she could barely hear Igrayne above the gentle breeze. 'Her name was Annaya.'

Elodi held her tight. 'I shall tell him. He will know of you and his sister. And what name did you give—?' Igrayne slumped.

The Amayans bowed their heads as her spirit rose from a body, broken by years of torment. But they had no more tears to shed. Calestri, Madraal and Igrayne had fulfilled their oath taken many centuries ago. They had made a great sacrifice, living a life of hardship and pain. And now they deserved their peace.

After offering a silent word to the fallen warriors, they stood and turned to the Amanach. Eryn spoke first. 'Three new stars shine down upon us, but to where our sisters roam, we do not know. Their flesh and bone will return to dust and leave no presence in the mortal realm.' She turned to the north. 'We now number four; the stones just five. And while the strength of our enemy is unknown, we will not rest until we have secured the Amanach and rid this realm of the foul servants of Ormoroth.'

Elodi's stomach warmed. She turned as a figure emerged from the ravine, leading a fine, black horse she had seen before.

Toryn kneeled beside Igrayne's body, glowing in the light of the Amanach. Elodi stood at his side. 'She's not long… departed.'

He removed his glove and placed a hand on his mother's, crossed over her chest. Toryn bowed his head and a single tear ran down his face. 'Alas, I was delayed in Mawlgrim. If only I could have been here sooner.' His hand went to his cheek. He frowned. 'We met. I felt something. My face tingled when she touched me. Part of me must have known.' He turned to Elodi. 'Did she know me? Did she know I was her son?'

She wrapped her arm around his trembling shoulders. 'We told her of your life before she died, Toryn. We knew you came. Igrayne fought to stay. We did what we could, but the little strength she had left faded.'

'And my father? Did she know he lives?'

'The warlocks had deceived her. Igrayne was led to believe you both served the Ul-dalak. But she knew the truth before she departed. Igrayne drew comfort knowing you both yet lived and fought against the darkness.' Elodi kneeled and took his hand. 'Toryn. She spoke of a sister. Your twin sister.'

He gaped. 'I have a sister? Does she know of me?'

Elodi's jaw clenched. 'I'm afraid she's... she is dead. Her name was Annaya. She was snatched from Igrayne ten years after your father had taken you to Midwyche. The Archon... Uluriel held her at Archonholm, then... executed her.'

Toryn stared at the Amanach but saw the gorge at Archonholm. He whispered. 'The *wyke* at the bridge... the guards told me.' He looked at the Amayans, not wanting to believe his ears. 'And she was my sister. But she was only a child when they...' He groaned. 'What had she done to deserve such a fate?' He clasped Igrayne's hand. 'And my poor mother... it must have been too much to bear.'

Elodi looked down as Igrayne's glow began to fade. 'The guilt almost destroyed her. But she is free now. It is up to us to ensure her life... and those of Madraal and Calestri were not lost in vain.'

Elodi stroked Lightning's nose. 'I knew his rider. Shelan was a fine scout. And sadly, she suffered at the hands of Uldrak.' Her fist clenched. 'And he too shall pay for his atrocities.'

Eryn led them to the head of the Gorgonach Gap. 'We ride now. The warlocks have also suffered. They are weakened and will not welcome our attention.'

Elodi stroked the back of Calestri's horse. 'And what of the beasts of the fallen? Will they stay with you, Eryn?'

'No. They are free to go as they please. They will be faithful to their rider until they too depart this world.' Eryn turned back to the Amanach. 'Igrayne's horse, along with Amyra's, roam somewhere to the south. They may yet have a duty to perform, guided by our sisters in the stars.' She looked Elodi in the eye. 'I understand why you must ride to Calerdorn. Your loyalties are divided, but I believe it is vital you drive the enemy out of your city... and it is you that should lead the attack.'

Elodi held her gaze. 'I admit I am conflicted. I would dearly wish to be at your side when you confront Shokresh... but I must free my people. It pains me still that I lost the city.'

'Then we will support you where we can.' Eryn sprang onto Moonbeam's back and yelled. 'We ride, my sisters! Let us avenge our fallen. Let those who took them from us not rest while we live.'

Elodi watched with an aching heart as the three left the Crown. She clutched Toryn's hand. 'Will we see them again? How many warlocks remain?'

Toryn marveled at the speed of their horses across the difficult terrain. 'They are few, but I would be wary if I was a warlock knowing they were on my tail.'

Elodi threw her arms around Toryn. 'I can't tell you how relieved I am to see you. There were times... times when I thought you were dead.'

Toryn held her tight and breathed in the scent of her hair. 'And I too. The echoes in the Song convey so many confusing messages. I could not tell truth from lie.'

Elodi stood back and looked into his eyes. 'Nyomae

warned that this was the enemy's way. But we don't need to be deceived to know of...' She turned away.

'The loss of your sisters is a great—'

'No. Please, Toryn. Let us not speak of what happened in this place. I don't think I can bear to...' Elodi let out a long sigh. 'There is so much I want to say, but alas, another long journey lies before us. Calerdorn must be back in our hands before the snows make it impossible to reach.' She leaped onto Sea Mist. 'We have no time to waste. But this time we ride together. And what of Nyomae? Have you seen her in the Song?'

Toryn mounted. 'I lost her for weeks once she had crossed the Caerwals. But when the Amanspring surged, I saw her briefly. But... also Uluriel.'

Elodi gasped. 'She's in the south?'

'Elmarand.'

She groaned. 'The south must have suffered if Uluriel has entered that city.' She drew Sea Mist up to Lightning and grasped Toryn's arm. 'Is Nyomae safe? What would we do if we lost her?'

'She, and another Imaari I assume is Idraman, fought Uluriel. But I have not sensed their presence for days now.'

Elodi guided Sea Mist into the ravine. 'If they can defeat Uluriel, surely that would bring us victory. But if they are both lost, how do we recover from such a blow?'

Toryn gagged on the stench of rotting aralaks and droogs, fouling the air in the narrow gap. Elodi grimaced as Sea Mist's hooves squished the flabby carcass of a worm, then crunched on the bones of spiders' legs scattered across the ground. She turned back to Toryn. 'Taking Calerdorn from Uldrak will be difficult enough, but I dearly hope he doesn't command more of these abominations. I would rather face a thousand Ruuk than a dozen of these beasts.'

49. Storm Over Elmarand

Elmarand's guards were no match for Nyomae and the rejuvenated Idraman. It had been a simple task for the two most powerful Imaari of recent times, to deceive them and gain entry to the Sun Tower. But Draegelan's Seat at its pinnacle had proven a challenge. It had taken an hour to negotiate their way through the maze of Verses, serving a purpose akin to a Word of Forbidding.

Idraman gazed out across the city from the East Window. His shoulders relaxed. 'We have time to make our preparations. The keshwing will not relish the warm air, and will be slow, even at higher altitudes. Uluriel has much to do if she is to ease its passage.' He leaned against the wall. 'But I too am slow. Do not be fooled, Nyomae. My recovery will be brief. The many years of confinement have taken their toll.' He sighed. 'I am under no illusion I can defeat Uluriel. But if this is to be my last act, I wish to strike a blow she will not readily forget.'

Nyomae looked into his eyes. 'Is there anything I can do to lengthen your time in this realm?'

He shook his head. 'I have long outlived my natural years, Nyomae. Any attempt would purely serve to drain you. And if we survive the coming assault, you must race back north to aid your allies.' Idraman smiled. 'No, my friend. I thank you for the offer, but my time is coming to an end. You have many years in you yet… years the people of the Five Realms will be most grateful for.' He rubbed his hands together. 'Now, we prepare.'

Nyomae glanced to the darkening skies in the east. 'Uluriel will look to bring in a bitter winter from Elmarand's past, more to the liking of the keshwing. She will have to go back many years to find such a rare event, while our task will be easier. All we need is a scorching summer's day.' She grinned. 'One preferably ending in a storm to make these towers shudder.'

Idraman held out his hands. 'Then we will make this an event to remember. Elmarand needs to be shaken to its foundations to awaken the people to their plight. A deluge will serve both to replenish the canals, and perhaps convince the superstitious among them that their leaders have displeased the gods. We may yet turn the trickle of displeasure into a flood of rebellion.'

Nyomae gladly accepted Idraman's invitation. 'Then you shall strike your blow, my friend.' She clasped his hands and bowed her head. Idraman took a breath and led them back through the Song. As Nyomae had guessed, it took only a short passage to find a violent storm. Ten years earlier, the heat at the end of a sweltering, humid day had risen to clash with the cold air close to the dome.

Idraman spoke over the rumbles as the sky's forces assembled and made ready for the conflict. 'As Uluriel seeks to bring her winter to Elmarand, it will augment our storm. This will indeed be a battle even the gods beyond the dome will hear.'

Nyomae took strength from the Caerwal Stone of the tower, bracing herself for the coming storm. 'If the lightning does not strike Uluriel's mount, the wind and rain will surely send it hurtling down onto the towers.' Her face tingled. 'Uluriel brings forth her winter. The keshwing approaches.'

Idraman released his grip. 'Then let us unleash a storm unlike any seen in centuries.' Nyomae mirrored his movements, combining their strength to draw upon the immense power of the Song, not called upon since the fateful day at Gormadon. They circled their hands, embracing the humid summer air, ready to hurl at Uluriel's winter. The skies darkened; the air crackled as battle commenced. Day became night, night became day as lightning blazed over Elmarand's towers, casting long shadows as if hands reaching out across the plain.

Then came the thunder. The Sun Tower trembled as the front ranks clashed overhead. Nyomae's ears burst as their great shields clashed. She cowered, terrified they had cracked the dome to leave them at the mercy of the creatures beyond the Void, jealous of the order within.

Then came the deluge, streaking as a thousand falling stars, glistening as the lightning flashed to show them the way. Nyomae cried out. 'I see it.' To the east, the keshwing beat its mighty wings as it struggled to stay aloft, as first the rain, then the strengthening wind resisted its passage. But Uluriel could do nothing to counter the Imaari's storm. Nyomae sensed her anger as she fought back, but the chaos brought about by the forces of nature could not be quelled.

A jagged bolt shot from the top of the dome, striking the breast of the winged beast. Scorched feathers fell like fire arrows, before fizzling out in the rain to land harmlessly on the rooftops below. The keshwing's screech bettered even the howling gale. Its dark wings splayed, stunned by the bolt, then hung lifeless, flapping like damaged sails as the creature plummeted.

Now at the mercy of the wind, the keshwing folded its wings and accepted its fate. The gods chose to smash the insult to their eagle into the Morning Tower. Its long claws gouged the walls as it slid but found no purchase on the smooth stone as it crashed to the ground. Yet it was not finished. The keshwing had survived the arrows and swords of Draegelan's reign; it would not be killed by a lightning bolt. But it was severely wounded. It thrashed its wings and clawed at the ground, splattering Elmarand's white walls with its dark blood.

Satisfied the keshwing would not fly for many days, the Imaari departed the Song. The howling wind faded but the shriek continued... that of Uluriel's rage. But she too was exhausted, and her cries died as the storm soon abated. Nyomae listened to the distant rumbles as the last of the summer's heat dispersed.

Idraman collapsed against the wall, gasping for air. 'She will come soon enough once her strength returns. But while I'm confident the Caerwal Stone will protect the tower, I am not so sure it will prevent her entry. We have set back her plans. But she wants her revenge and will throw everything she has left against us.'

Nyomae sat beside him. 'Then perhaps we can be thankful she is driven by her rage. It may cloud her judgment.'

He sighed. 'If I were in her situation, I would concentrate all my powers on healing the keshwing and be on my way. She's aware we know her plans for the young girl in Calerdorn. But she also knows you'll struggle to inform your allies from here.'

Nyomae took his hand. 'Then it becomes a race. She has the means to send word to protect the child, but if we can get there first, I doubt Uldrak has the strength in Calerdorn to resist the two of us.'

'Us, Nyomae? No... I'm afraid I cannot make that journey.' He held up his hand as Nyomae went to protest. 'No, my friend. I will only slow you down. I doubt I would make it as far as the mountains. You must go alone. Uluriel will need time to heal the keshwing once she has exacted her revenge. She has no choice. No other living beast has the strength to bear her presence. And her *kruul* cannot leave her body now. It will be weak and vulnerable here. She knows I would find and destroy it once and for all. No, Nyomae. I must stay. I will best serve the realms by stalling her here. She'll be bent on tearing me limb from limb for defying her. If I can prolong the inevitable, I shall give you a decent head start.' His eyes flashed. 'And I shall take great pleasure in exhausting the last of my strength to defy her a little longer.'

A tear rolled down Nyomae's cheek as she clutched his hands. 'You are right, Idraman. It pains me to leave you, but yes… there are greater issues at stake.'

Idraman stood and pulled Nyomae to her feet. 'I can fool Uluriel with a semblance of your presence here, but you must be many leagues from Elmarand before she discovers you've gone. Go now, find your trusty steed.'

The keshwing's mournful cry echoed through the city. Idraman glanced to the window. 'It is time you departed. Uluriel will soon come.' He strode towards the doorway. 'I'll ensure the Verses allow your safe passage through the city. But once you're—' He pulled back. The door wavered and disappeared. Idraman circled his hands and muttered under his breath, but the wall remained blank. He raised his voice, throwing out his arms as if pleading with the Song. Nothing. Idraman turned to face Nyomae. His face paled. 'The way is shut.'

50. The Spires of Calerdorn

Sea Mist and Lightning appeared to enjoy the race to Durran. Despite the deep snow blanketing the frozen mire, both maintained a swift pace. Twice they spotted Norgog bands close by, but they tramped north and west and appeared keen to avoid a conflict. Toryn wondered if they had learned of the *Elorsil's* destructive power in his hand, or perhaps they were summoned elsewhere. They rested briefly and ate the last of their rations, but they dared not sleep as Toryn was sure he heard movement beneath the ice. But whether it was the sheets shifting under the weight of the snow, or bog grims coming to claim them, he could not tell. He shared his concerns with Elodi to find she too knew the stories of the strange creatures.

As day dawned on the second day since leaving the Crown, the dark tops of the trees of Wyke Wood appeared over the horizon. Toryn shivered. 'It seems an age since I was brought here.' He tried to grin, but his frozen face refused to comply. 'But at least we had a roaring fire to greet us.'

Elodi frowned. 'There's still mischief in those trees. We may have driven out Uleva and destroyed that awful tower, but I suspect her presence awoke the spirits of the dark days.' The horses picked up the pace as they approached the ground sheltered from the snow by the trees. Elodi called out. 'We must be close to where Uleva and her grim host assailed Aldorman.' She turned to look across the plain. 'The poor man did his best, but he was never the same following the confrontation. But little did we know what we faced back then. So much has happened since that spring.' She drew Sea Mist to a halt and turned to Toryn. 'Could we have done anything different? If I had held Calerdorn, could I have prevented the Ruuk getting a foothold in the realms? Or the slaughter at Roth's Doom?' Toryn went to answer, but Elodi rode on.

By mid-morning, they reached the outskirts of the abandoned town of Durran. Elodi looked upon its timber stockade, barely visible beneath the snow. She hoped one day its people would return to rebuild what had once been a vital part of the plain's farming community. But sadly, it would likely be many years before they could resettle the region… if at all.

Toryn spoke first. 'It appears deserted.' He turned to look behind. 'Could Gundrul and Ruan be stranded in the mire?'

'Fear not. They are here.' Elodi pointed. 'See the crossed spears beside the gate?' She let out a sigh. 'That tells me Ruan and his company are camped within. If Ruan is here, then so is Gundrul. And if it looks deserted to us, it will to our enemy.' She glanced west to the open plain. 'Now let us get inside before we're seen.'

The captains strode out to greet them as they entered the gate. They beamed, unable to contain their glee. Gundrul hugged them both. 'I couldn't be happier if the Three Maidens themselves strolled out of the fog.' He stepped back and grinned. 'I would be shaking in my rotten boots if I was Uldrak. Not even the formidable defenses of Calerdorn could keep you two at bay.' He held out his hand towards a hut. 'But first, let's thaw you two out by a warm fire.' Gundrul beamed at Ruan. 'Even the tough man of Broon is finding it a tad chilly these days.'

Toryn and Elodi stumbled forward as Ruan wrapped his big arms around them. 'And perhaps you have a few tales to tell as we eat.' He laughed. 'Gunny has plenty more now. But beware, with every punishing league of our trek, they've become so far removed from the truth, I imagine they make even Dorlan's deeds seem tame. And don't believe him when he claims to have stormed Breck and Lindmar on his own.'

'Oh, come now, Ruan.' Gundrul led them to the hut. 'Cubric also helped… a little. I can't take all the praise.' His laughter faded. 'But to be serious for a moment, ma'am. We have pushed Nordryn and his traitors back over the border. Some may yet linger in Lumreek, but they won't cause us any trouble. I can't think they'll survive long in that forsaken place.'

Elodi looked around the settlement. 'That is good to hear, Captain. But please tell me. How many did you bring?'

Ruan answered. 'We number close to three hundred here, ma'am, including many of Gunny's battle-hardened Archonians. And another five hundred from the Noor borders have gathered at Dorlgoth. It's not the largest of armies, but they're the finest. Your knights look a force to be reckoned with, and we have a few dozen First Horse led by Lindell, and then fifty or so Knights of the Archon.' Ruan folded his arms. 'Yes, ma'am, a small, but impressive force ready to take back your city.'

Gundrul smiled. 'And not forgetting Ruan's rabble with their pointy sticks. So, I reckon we've now got the strength and skill to frighten the life out of our foes.'

'And so we should.' Elodi glanced over Gundrul's shoulder. 'And Amyndra and Cubric? Are they with you?'

'They've gone out with Janae.' He patted Toryn's shoulder. 'And your friend Elrik is with them.'

'He's here?' Toryn rubbed his cold hands together. 'I look forward to seeing him again.' He peered into the gloom. 'Where have they gone?'

Gundrul pointed. 'We spied torches out on that ridge. Thought it best we take a look, just to be safe. But don't you fret, my friends. With all the spears, swords and arrows we boast in Durran, you'll sleep soundly. I promise you that. It's the least you deserve.' The captain lifted a thick blanket covering the empty doorway to reveal the welcoming glow of a fire inside. 'And what of your trials of late? I trust your arrival means you have some good news of your own?'

Elodi gladly threw off her damp cloak as they entered the warm hut. 'Some good, some… tragic.' But the strength that had sustained her for so long, suddenly failed her. 'Please, let us eat.' She collapsed into a chair beside the fire. 'We should first discuss our plans for Calerdorn before we speak of… our recent trials.'

Gundrul glanced to Ruan. 'You should know, ma'am, it appears we're not the only ones interested in Calerdorn. Our scouts have seen bands of Ruuk, Norgog, and tall, rangy creatures that sound like shrouls to me, all heading west.'

Elodi's shoulders sagged. 'Then they must know we're coming. How many more of these foul creatures do our enemy command? We don't have the numbers to sustain any more losses.' She looked at Toryn; a tear glistened in the firelight. 'Can we afford to take back Calerdorn?'

Ruan grunted as he sat on the ground. 'I don't believe they know we come, ma'am. Our scouts were leagues ahead of our ranks, and these creatures moved at quite a pace. They kept no watch. Their eyes were fixed ahead on Calerdorn, not on their rear. It's as if Ormoroth himself drove them on.'

Elodi frowned. 'Then what draws them to my city?' She looked to Gundrul. 'If you commanded the enemy, would you concentrate your forces in Calerdorn? It's a strong fortress, but would they not be wary we could lay siege by land and sea, and starve them out? It was certainly my concern when Uldrak first appeared. But at the time, I held the harbor and the service of a sea-worthy ship.'

Gundrul scratched his beard. 'It wouldn't be my choice to put all my forces in one place, ma'am. I'd be happy with what I'd got. I'd prefer to hold my gains here on the plain, and not retreat into Calerdorn.' He sighed. 'No… something else is afoot here. It appears our enemy is keen to defend more than just the city itself, or Uldrak is planning something else.'

Toryn placed a blanket around Elodi's shoulders. 'Could they be building ships? They might be gathering their forces to launch raids down the west coast.'

Elodi pulled the blanket closer, but still shivered. 'We saw Norgog in the mire. But they were heading farther north… perhaps to Draegnor. The Mawl Bay is deep enough for large ships if they break the ice. And who would be best suited for such a task?' Her eyes moved across the lined faces of her captains, suddenly looking older in the firelight. 'We don't know what transpires in Nordruuk. If they've replenished their numbers so soon, and more gather in Draegnor…' Her jaw clenched. 'And if they do have ships, they can strike anywhere they please. The south lies mainly unprotected. We cannot possibly defend our coasts against a superior force. Even if we could anticipate where and when, our horses cannot match the speed of a ship.' Her voice wavered. 'Is there to be another slaughter?'

The room sat silent as all imagined the dire consequences if that was indeed the enemy's plan. Gundrul cleared his throat. 'Ma'am? We have yet to hear of your exploits. Were the Amayans successful against the warlocks? Will they ride to our aid in the coming battles?'

'Please.' Elodi covered her face. 'Please, excuse me. I'm exhausted. I must sleep. I do not have the strength to tell my tale until rested.'

Toryn shot up. His head throbbed. Someone had

called his name, but he could not be sure if it was from outside or a dream. The frantic voice issued a warning. He blinked away the sleep and looked about the room. Elodi still slept soundly at his side; the warning must have come from Nyomae. Toryn bowed his head and recalled the dream. Reluctantly, he woke Elodi. Her eyes opened, but it took a while before she seemed to recognize her surroundings. 'Toryn? She sat. 'What troubles you?'

'It's Nyomae. I'm certain she has just spoken to me.'

She clutched his arm. 'Is she still in Elmarand? Is she safe?'

Toryn let Nyomae's words flow through his mind. 'She is with Idraman in Elmarand, but… I'm afraid she's not safe.' He shuddered. 'Another was present. I told her of our position. A shadow passed over us, then Nyomae began to fade. She spoke fast but a shriek pained my ears, and it was difficult to hear. But from what I could make out, Nyomae spoke of a child. A child in Calerdorn. She's desperate we get to the girl.'

Elodi woke fully. 'Meloni. She speaks of Meloni. She survived an attack on the Dorn Plain when all others had perished. Does she hold the key, Toryn? Nyomae must want us to save the girl.' She stood, fastened her sword belt, and gathered her firs. 'We cannot delay. Calerdorn is two days from here, possibly three with all this snow. Then we still have to find our way through the Calern Mountains to the tunnel.' She threw her cloak around her shoulders, then stood staring into the fire. 'Yes, I'm certain. She must refer to Meloni. I can think of no other child in the city that Nyomae would know. Perhaps there is something about the girl that enabled her to survive.'

Toryn tied the straps on his tunic. 'But isn't this the same child you said wounded Sea Mist?'

'While under the influence of Dorlan… who was still under Uleva's spell. But with his death, I hope the girl is now free.' Elodi sighed. 'But what has she been forced to endure in the months of Uldrak's occupation? The poor child. I do hope she hasn't suffered.' Elodi strode to the door. 'I trust Gundrul has kept his force at the ready. Word must be sent to Dorlgoth.' She pulled back the blanket covering the door to be met by a blast of snow. Elodi grimaced. 'It may slow our progress, but it may also conceal our approach.' She called out. 'Captain Gundrul! Make ready. We leave in an hour.'

The snow crunched under Elodi's feet as she walked to the edge of their camp to find Sea Mist. The riders had built a wall from blocks of ice to offer the horses shelter from the northerly breeze. But the air was now still, and their breath steamed as they chewed their fodder. Elodi stroked Sea Mist's cold neck. 'I know I made a promise to you, boy, but I'm afraid you cannot come with me today. But you shall ride with our knights and the First Horse. Do me proud, my brave Misty.'

The skies at her back grew lighter as the rising sun appeared through a rare break in the clouds. To her left, the rays found the highest peaks of the Calern Mountains. The forces gathered at Dorlgoth would join with them by mid-morning. But Elodi had decided that only Toryn, Janae, and a handful of Gundrul's best hand-to-hand fighters would accompany her through the tunnel into the city. She ran through her strategy again, but knew nothing of the enemy inside, so much would depend upon what they found.

A speck of light caught her eye against the dark sky to the west. Her heart lurched as another, then another glistened beside it. Far in the distance, the spires of Calerdorn's tallest towers rose to greet the dawn. It had been over one hundred days since Elodi had abandoned the city of her ancestors. And with every sunrise, she had vowed to return. But the shame had not eased, and now the spires twisted as she looked upon them through tears of guilt. How had those she had left behind fared?

Elodi buried her face into Sea Mist's neck as other riders arrived to prepare their horses. She did not want them to bear witness to her grief. She had to be strong; she had to lead. But so many had already been lost, so many fine and loyal fighters gone. And now her Amayan sisters numbered so few, while Nyomae faced Uluriel in the south. How much more pain would they have to endure? And would it be all for nothing?

Elodi hugged Sea Mist. 'I'm so sorry, my dear boy. I must go now.' She stood back and stroked his face. 'But I vow this is not the end. Soon, Misty, soon. We'll hear your hooves on the cobbles of our fine city again.' Elodi turned and strode through the snow back to the hut. More than once, she thought to turn and bid Sea Mist one more farewell, but she knew she would not be able to resist running back to him. Elodi had lost too many good friends in their struggle — she could not bear the thought of losing another.

Toryn stood waiting for her beside the hut. He looked up as she approached. 'Ready to take back your city?'

Elodi's hand went to her sword. 'For the last one hundred days. And I shall make them pay for every one of them they've made my people suffer.'

To be continued…

The fifth and final book in this series is due out in January 2025

You can sign up to my newsletter at

www.frontrunnerbooks.com/sign-up.html

GLOSSARY

The glossary is also available to download at
https://www.frontrunnerbooks.com/glossary.html

Aber - Imaari from before Draegelan's day who believed he had found a hidden message within the Maidens' Song.

Abernost - Seat of Learning in the ward of Holm named after the hermit, Aber.

Aldorman - Captain of the Knights of Calerdorn. Killed at the Battle of Roth's Doom.

Amanach - Set by the Elorym to counter Ormoroth's Angorlith. Also known as Singing Stones.

Amanspring - The river deep beneath the Kolossos Mountains. The source of power for the Amanach.

Amayans - Elorym warriors formed to protect the Amanach. Also known as the Sisters of the Stones.

Amman - The northern ward of Galabrant.

Amroth - Town in Darrow.

Amrul - Archonian Guard based at the East Watchtower of the Kolossos Pass.

Amyndra - Captain of Lunn loyal to Bardon, the true Lord Broon. Accompanied Elodi and fought at Roth's Doom.

Amyra - Amayan warrior captured and killed by Vordraak in the tunnels beneath the Kolososs.

Andryn - Adoptive father of Toryn.

Angorlith - The iron pillar formed by Ormoroth to corrupt the power of the land. Housed in the vaults of Vorkirik.

Angorsil - Shards of the Angorlith wielded by warlocks and Ul-dalak commanders.

Aralak - Large, vicious creatures spawned from spiders by Ormoroth.

Aralak Gorge - The fenced valley isolating the aralaks.

Arawold - Guard on duty at the Lower Gate of the

Caerwal Pass when Lord Harlyn entered the pass on the night he died.

Archon - The name for the leader of the Seven, then later, the Five Realms. See Draegelan, Malendra, Hadrul, and Mordram.

Archon's Tower - Tall tower of stone at the Caerwal Gate. Commissioned by the Archon under Uluriel's influence to convince the realms to allocate all their resources in the south to leave the north open to the Ruuk. The tower collapsed following the confrontation between Nyomae, Toryn, and Uluriel.

Archonholm - The principal city of the Five Realms at the head of the Caerwal Pass.

Archonian Guard - Foot soldiers of the Archon. Guards take an oath for twenty years' service in exchange for a promise of a farm in the Plains of Evermore if they die in battle.

Archonian Knights - The heavy mounted cavalry of the Archon.

Arijan - Amayan warrior in the same band of sisters as Eryn and Calestri. Accompanied Toryn through the Foranfae. Captured at Vortimo but escaped when Toryn's company arrived.

Armanoor - The First Realm. Farthest south with wide fertile plains. Once one of the richest of the Seven.

Ashala - The last surviving corvraak. Lived for over a thousand years and saw battle serving Ormoroth. Carried Nyomae to Archonholm, wishing to atone for her deeds and receive the Maidens' Love.

Bardon - The 44th Lord of Broon. Led the doomed Elites to sail to the Lost Realms. Survived to aid Elodi at Roth's Doom and eventually retake his seat at Keld.

Barrson - Treasurer in Archonholm. Set the task to find funds for the Archon's ambitious plans.

Behemora - Mythical whale-like creature of the Elessyn Sea separated from her mate when the world changed.

Benmuir Lake - Lake in the southwest of Darrow. Believed to be the sight of the fallen Elorym tower of

Cyloris.

Blunden - Captain of the Celestra that died in the storm that beset Elodi's journey to Calerdorn.

Bog Grim - Creatures said to live beneath Mawlgrim Mire. Believed to be a distant relation to cobtrolls.

Bonnar - Retired Archonian Guard and friend of Hamar. Lives in the Vale of Caran in the shadow of Caranach.

Borrund - Seat of Lord Ormsk. Town built entirely of wood on the banks of the Borr River. It is said it can be dismantled and moved inland if the seas rise.

Breck - Town on the coast of Lunn, and home of Ruan, captain of the Broon Spearmen.

Brock - Common name in Darrow for a badger.

Broon - The last region to be assumed into the Seven Realms. Consists of two wards; Lunn and Ormsk.

Brundell - Chief Engineer in Archonholm. Responsible for designing and building the city's weapons.

Bryok - Oldest son of Tombold. Served at the Caerwal Gate and later commanded a company of Archonians in Lunn and assisted Elodi on her escape from Shokresh.

Bulstrow (Ox) - Captain in the Archonian Guard in command at Drunsberg. Killed defending the mines against Uldrak and Ruuk invaders.

Caermund - Ship building port on the Mund coast. Isolated for many years when sea creatures washed up on its shores when the Archon altered the sea. Bardon's Elite force set sail from the port.

Caerwal Gate - The large gate sealing the Caerwal Pass. Stands at 400 feet, made from stone slabs held in place by iron girders.

Caerwal Pass - Constructed in the early days of the Seven Realms to open the way between Talamaris in the south and Farrand in the north. Later sealed by the Caerwal Gate following the tragedy at Gormadon.

Caerwal Mountains - Tall mountain range separated the first two realms from the north. Believed to have been raised by the gods, an ancient power resides in its stone.

Cafra - A town in the south of Emryst. Known for its

farming markets.

Calerdorn - Capital city of Harlyn. Built in the days of Draegelan using stone excavated from the Trench.

Calern Mountains - The mountain range south of Calerdorn forming part of the city's defense.

Calestri - An Amayan warrior in the same band of sisters as Eryn and Arijan. Suffered for many years following an encounter with a shreek.

Caranach - Tallest mountain of the Kolossos Mountains on the west side of the Kolossos Pass. Legends tell it was raised to seal the vault imprisoning the Evil One.

Casteldor - Castle built in the early days of Hadrul's rule as Archon. Situated in the Ravern Hills in Mund.

Castellan - The man in charge of the day-to-day running of the Citadel in Archonholm. His real name is not known. Possessed by a *kruul*, he died in a confrontation with Elodi.

Caster - Fortified port on the west coast of Gwelayn.

Celestra - A galleon from the days before the Age of Shadows maintained by the shipwrights of West Haven. Survived a terrible storm to take Elodi to Calerdorn. Later carried supplies along the west coast to support Dorn, Noor and Darrow during the Ruuk occupation.

Cobtroll - Small creatures living beneath the Kolossos. Believed to have descended from larger trolls, they mainly stay out of sight with no loyalty to the Realms or Ul-dalak. Do not tolerate trespassers in the mountains.

Corvraak - A large flying beast spawned by Ormoroth from the raven. They once dominated the skies and were a threat to Draegelan and his forces. Eventually wiped out by trained archers with longbows and specially made arrows by skilled fletchers. Also see Ashala.

Cubric - An Archonian Guard from Kernlow. Served at Drunsberg before becoming a drill sergeant at Archonholm. Became a captain under Gundrul and served in Lady Harlyn's forces.

Cymori - An Amayan warrior. She fought at the first Battle of Roth's Doom. Captured and turned to the Ul-dalak. Killed by Eryn, Arijan and Calestri outside Omstrad.

Darrow - The southern ward of Harlyn and home to Midwyche, Toryn's village.

Darrowyche - Once the principal city of Darrow. Destroyed in the wars leading up to Gormadon and still a ruin.

Demelia - Varsil of Talamaris, the Second Realm. She seized power from the Council of Seven following Idraman's imprisonment.

Dohl - The old man who served Uleva as jailer in Wyke Wood. Later discovered he was Dorlan.

Dorek - Archonian Guard killed at Drunsberg. He was the oldest of three brothers from Tamworth in Darrow. See Porek and Lorek.

Dorlan - Legendary knight from Dorlgoth who served Draegelan. Fought in the battles against Ormoroth and eventually defeated him at Talaghir. Enslaved by Uluriel and kept as a slave before freed by Nyomae at Roth's Doom.

Dorlgoth - A cave settlement in the ancient Dorlwood. The people rarely leave the woodlands.

Dorlwood - An ancient wood in Dorn on the edge of the Calern Mountains.

Dormarl (Uldrak) - An Imaari who rode with Nyomae on the doomed mission to find Sylvena. Fell under the influence of the Ul-dalak at Gormadon and became Uldrak.

Dorn - The northerly ward of Harlyn. The farms on the Dorn Plain, sandwiched between the Calern Mountains to the west and Findale Hills in the east, provide most of the meat for Harlyn.

Dornan Mountains - Mountain range north of Calerdorn.

Dornan Pass - The single route through the Dornan Mountains. Also see Tunduska's Gorge.

Draedalak - Also known as Drayloks, the Draedalak are believed to have been spawned in mockery of the Three Maidens by the Evil One. Resembling tall hags with barbed hair, they fought in the battles of old, also brought back briefly by Uluriel to fight at Roth's Doom.

Draegelan - The greatest and longest living Archon of the Seven Realms. Along with Dorlan, he drove Ormoroth out of the realms.

Draegelan Trench - A deep trench separating the far north from the Seven Realms. Named after the Archon of the time. Eventually breached when Ormoroth brought down the gales from the top of the world and packed the trench with ice.

Draegnor - The most northerly fort in the Five Realms situated on the Nordruuk border close to the mouth of the Mawl River.

Draego - Dorlan's mighty stead who rode with him into all his battles. Died at Talaghir as Ormoroth invoked the Verse of Unmaking. The fort at Draegnor is named in his honor.

Drakelow - Marshal of Midwyche, Toryn's home village.

Dravic - A builder of the Archon's Tower at the Caerwal Gate. He, along with the other builders, were thrown into the dungeons as the work was complete. Dravic was in the neighboring cell to Toryn, who later secured his release. Then worked on Kernlow's wooden tower at the gate.

Drayloks - The common name for the Draedalak.

Drondel - Captain in the Archonian Guard who assisted Toryn's company to retake the Drunsberg Mines.

Droog - Large, distended worms spawned by Ormoroth. While slow, they are feared by the guards due to the extremely unpleasant and drawn-out death if swallowed by a droog.

Drunsberg - The deep mines in the north of the Kolossos Mountains. The ores extracted were vital to the Five Realms for forging armor and weapons.

Durran Wood - A small wood in the north of Dorn. The locals renamed it Wyke Wood following Uleva's occupation.

Edwald - Youngest son of Tombold, injured on the false flag attack at the Caerwal Gate.

Eldamouth - Fortified port in Darrow at the mouth of

the Great Elda River.

Eleni - Amayan warrior and mother of Elodi. Died shortly after giving birth after sustaining injuries in Nordruuk as the Amayans fought to free Tanis from the Ul-dalak.

Elessyn Sea - Wide sea off the west coast of the Five Realms.

Elmarand - The capital city of Talamaris and the Seven Realms at the height of its power.

Elodi - Daughter of Eleni, an Amayan, and Lord Harlyn. Took on the leadership of Harlyn following the death of her father. Became commander of the forces of the Five Realms to achieve a victory at Roth's Doom.

Elorsil - Elorym sword gifted to Draegelan by the Amayans.

Elorym - An ancient and powerful race who inhabited the land many years before the coming of humans. Fought many battles against Ormoroth. Eventually defeated but the Amanach still stand and counter the Angorlith.

Elrik - Blacksmith of Midwyche and friend of Toryn. Joined the Archonian Guard and accompanied Toryn on the mission to find the Amayans, and later fought against the aralaks at Omstrad.

Elsaya (Uleva) - Young Imaari who fell at the Battle of Gormadon Plain. Became possessed by the Ul-dalak and named Uleva.

Elwold - Retired Archonian Guard who became a cook at the Drunsberg. Died in the defense of the mines alongside Hamar.

Emryst - Southern ward of Galabrant. Known for its abundance of precious gems.

Eryn - Amayan warrior who found Toryn on the edge of the Foranfae Forest. Took the leadership of their band following the death of Amyra. Fought in many battles over the years, including both at Roth's Doom.

Evil One - An old god from the legends who despised the Three Maidens' creation. The tales tell of his deceit to capture and torment the Maidens, thus forcing them to sing a song to corrupt their creation. He is said to be imprisoned to this day in a vault beneath Caranach.

Faerl - The name for the Nym in Broon.

Farrand - The southern realm of the Five Realms and home to Archonholm.

Fidric - Archonian Guard. Died at the Caerwal Gate when the Ul-dalak raised the dead.

Findale - Town at the eastern edge of Dorn Plain in the Findale Hills situated by a lake.

Findale Lake - Large lake bordered by the Findale Hills in Dorn.

Finromir - Imaari who first served under the Archon, Malendra. Became a powerful mage in the Order of Echoes. Fought at Gormadon. Father of Toryn.

First Horse - Formed by the warrior Archon, Malendra, the First Horse are highly skilled riders, sword masters, and archers.

Flint - The settlement on the coast of Lunn on the *Bony Witch's Finger*. One of the bleakest places in the realms owing to the bitterly easterly winds coming from the Karajan Sea.

Foranfae Forest - The largest forest in the realms. Believed to have been seeded by the Nym to heal the hurt of Gormadon Plain after Nyomae had recited the Verse of Unmaking.

Galabrant - One of the Five Realms. Situated on the east of the Kolossos Mountains.

Galafan River - River running through Amman to the Karajan Sea at Galant Estuary.

Galan Hills - Range of hills in the east of Amman.

Galant - Town in Amman situated on the Galant Estuary.

Garamond - Fortified port on the east coast of Mund.

Gildorul - Known as Gildorul of Keld, the legendary knight of Broon was said to have fought alongside Dorlan, but little written history records his exploits.

Glambul - Lord Ormsk holding court at Borrund.

Golesh - The race believed by the Five Realms to have invaded the south. However, with the lifting of the shadow, the Golesh were found to be a deception spread by Uluriel to keep the realms divided.

Gormadon Plain - The location of the battle that led to the fall of the Seven Realms. Fought between the might of the Ul-dalak and the Order of Echoes and the Elites of the realms.

Gorgonach - The mountain that forms the crest of the Kolossos Crown

Gorgonach Gap - The treacherous ravine that leads to the Crown Stone.

Great Elda - The longest river in the Five Realms. Springs from high in the Kolossos Range and dissects Noor and Darrow to meet the sea at Eldamouth.

Grebb - Ruuk warrior involved in the taking of Drunsberg. Toryn holds him responsible for the death of Hamar. Also serves under Uleva at Wyke Wood.

Greendell - The remote settlement at the head of the Wend Gap, destroyed by the Ul-dalak.

Gregor - Archonian guard serving in Drunsberg when Toryn and Hamar arrived.

Gundrul - Captain in the Archonian Guard. Headed the small company of young guards assigned to Elodi. Continued to serve under Elodi and fought in both battles of Calerdorn and then Roth's Doom.

Gwelayn - The wine-growing region of Kernlow.

Gwend - Small fishing port in Ormsk.

Gwend Bay - Large bay on the Ormsk coast contained three islands, believed to have been formed when the Karajan Sea rose and flooded much of the region, destroying the city of Borrusk.

Hadrin - Settlement situated in woodlands in Amman.

Hadrul - Archon who succeeded Malendra. A knight of great skill, he led the armies of the Seven Realms to Gormadon. Killed by the Draedalak.

Hallows Night - The longest night in winter when it is said the dead can return to visit their loved ones.

Hamar - Retired Archonian Guard who worked on Toryn's family farm. Accompanied Toryn to Greendell. Died with a sword in his hand at Drunsberg.

Harlyn - Realm on the west side of the Kolossos Mountains that borders Nordruuk. Capital city of Calerdorn.

Harruld - Experienced Archonian Guard serving in Archonholm. Arrested Toryn on his arrival at Archonholm. Fought alongside Toryn and Odrun when the Ul-dalak raised the dead guards at the Caerwal Gate.

Holm - The central ward of Farrand. Much of Holm is covered by the Foranfae Forest, but is home to Archonholm, the most fertile plains in the Five Realms, and Abernost, a Seat of Learning.

Hope - Nyomae when living under the shadow following Gormadon. Name was given to her by Toryn following his rescue from the Uleva and the Ruuk.

Horace - Helmsman onboard the Celestra. Was previously a fisherman in West Haven, but became captain of the Celestra when Blunden died in a storm as they sailed to Calerdorn.

Hornrasp - Nasty insect that frequents marshlands. Multiple stings can result in death.

Huckle - Common name in Darrow for a hedgehog.

Idraman - Powerful Imaari who first joined the Order of Echoes under Draegelan. Long-serving Imaari who sealed the Caerwal Pass following the loss at Gormadon. Held prisoner in Elmarand by Uluriel.

Igrayne - Amayan warrior who joined with Eryn to fight at the Battle of Gormadon.

Imaari - Mages in the Order of Echoes. Have the ability to enter the Song and access the Verses of individuals.

Ingollo - A Varsil of Elmarand at the time Nyomae arrived at the city. Under the influence of the Ul-dalak.

Inverdorn Bay - Deep bay to the north of Calerdorn.

Jacken - Retired Archonian Guard and friend of Hamar. Was killed by the Ul-dalak in Greendell.

Janae - Tracker from Galabrant. Accompanied Toryn on the mission to find the Amayans, and also to Drunsberg. A brave and accomplished fighter.

Jedrul - Miner at Drunsberg. Captured and taken to Wyke

Wood. Took the Archonian Oath along with Toryn. Part of Toryn's company that drove the Ruuk out of Drunsberg.

Jehenum - The most powerful warlock. Took little part in the battles against the realms. Rarely leaves Vorkirik where he plots for Ormoroth's return with Uluriel.

Jerrum - Young man who worked with Toryn on the family farm in Midwyche.

Jorim - Taken prisoner from Greendell to work in Caranach to build a weapon platform to attack the West Watchtower. Freed by Toryn and his company.

Kalamir - Beautiful city of towers on the coast of Emryst on the banks of the River Mir.

Karajan Sea - The sea to the east of the Five Realms.

Karrock - The twin-towered city on the Amman coast and banks of the Vynmar.

Keld - The seat of the Lord of Broon. A city built of stone on the Lunn coast where the River Kel meets the sea.

Kernlow - Realm on the west side of the Kolossos Mountains.

Kernlow's Tower - The wooden structure commissioned by Lord Kernlow when serving as Steward of Archonholm. Originally planned so he could look into the Lost Realms, the building was abandoned when priority was given to the outer defensive wall of Archonholm. The tower was never completed.

Kernrim - Principal city of Perran, a ward of Kernlow.

Keshwing - Large flying beast spawned by Ormoroth from the eagle.

Kinderach - Mountain bordering Caranach.

Kirik - Principal city of Gwelayn, a ward of Kernlow.

Kirol - Young man who assisted Nyomae escape from the hunters in the Talamaris desert.

Kolossos - The huge, towering mountain range that dissects four of the five realms. Believed to have been formed by the old gods to prevent the Evil One bringing down the sky to crush the land.

Kolossos Crown - Formation of four mountains at the

northern tip of the Kolossos.

Kolossos Pass - Pass formed in the days of Draegelan through the Kolossos Mountains to promote trade between the realms.

Kragan - Old general serving the Archon. Died at sea when the Elite's mission to the Lost Realms was sank by Uluriel.

Kruul - The spirit of a servant of the Dark Verses. In this form they can leave their body and possess the mind of another.

Leaflaps - Moth-like insects that live in woodlands and forests of the warmer regions.

Lena - Accomplished rider and messenger in Harlyn. She rode to Midwyche to investigate Toryn's heritage. Later crossed Ruuk-occupied to Tunduska to warn Ruan of the fall of Calerdorn.

Lightning - One of the fastest horses in the Five Realms. Was once ridden by Shelan, a tracker who served Harlyn.

Lind River - River on the border of Lunn and Nordruuk. The river is frozen for all but the summer months.

Lindell - Captain of the First Horse.

Lindmar - Ancient Lunn fort on the Nordruuk border and Lind River. Damaged by both the Ruuk and extreme weather, remains in a state of disrepair.

Little Folk - Name given to the Nym by the people of Darrow.

Lord Kernlow - Old lord who assumed the role of Steward of Archonholm following Mordram's death.

Lorek - Brother of Dorek and Porek who died defending Drunsberg. Took part in the defense of Tunduska with Elodi. Accompanies Toryn on the Amayan mission.

Loromar - Principal city on the south coast of Tamarand. Built in the latter days of Draegelan's reign, its unique tower straddles the River Lor.

Lumreek Marsh - Large marsh in the north of Lunn. Mainly uninhabited aside from a few settlements on its border. Occasionally freezes over in the coldest winters.

Lugnach - Mountain bordering Caranach in the Kolossos

Range.

Lunn - The northern ward of Broon that borders Nordruuk.

Madraal - An Amayan warrior who fought at both battles at Roth's Doom.

Malendra - The Archon succeeding Draegelan. She was the first knight to take on the role. She fought alongside Draegelan and Dorlan in the battles with Ormoroth.

Marafan - Settlement on the banks of the Marafan River in Amman.

Marrick - Retired Archonian Guard from Loromar. Became Advisor to the Council of Tamarand before moving to Archonholm and gained the trust of Elodi.

Mawl Bay - Deep bay to the north of Calerdorn.

Mawl Bay Bridge - Ancient bridge built in the days of Draegelan across the Mawl River to connect Dorn with Draegnor Fort.

Mawlgrim Mire - Large marshland in the north of Dorn. The roads built in Draegelan's reign have long since been swallowed by the mire and few people willingly cross. Creatures known as Bog Grims are said to live under the mud.

Meloni - Name given to the young girl Elodi found among the charred remains of the people of Dorlgoth who followed Dohl/Dorlan across the Dorn Plain. Meloni was taken back to Calerdorn but injured Sea Mist and remained in the city after its fall.

Menon Bridge - Long, wide stone bridge outside Archonholm that spans the Menon River.

Menon River - Long river said to contain mystical powers. Flows from the southern tip of the Kolossos, through the Foranfae Forest, then across Farrand to the Elessyn Sea at West Haven.

Midnight - Amyra's horse that bore Toryn on her death. She died from her many wounds sustained at Roth's Doom.

Midwyche - Village in the ward of Darrow on the River Tam. Toryn's home.

Miram - Toryn's adoptive mother.

Moonbeam - Eryn's faithful horse.

Moran - Messenger from Lunn who brings news of Nordryn's treachery to Archonholm

Mordram - Imaari who served under Sylvena before she went north. Fought at Gormadon, but was possessed by Uluriel when he fell. Assumed role of Archon but under the influence of Uluriel.

Mosholuk - Warlock who led the attack against Nyomae and the Order in Nordruuk when they searched for Sylvena.

Muldrin - Mason from Darrow who answered the call for workers needed in the south. Possessed by a kruul before entering Archonholm, he murdered three guards before the Castellan killed him.

Mund - Eastern ward of Farrand.

Mundrake Isle - Island off the Mund coast in the Karajan Sea. Also known as Plague Isle following the mass exportation of plague sufferers. Island where ships from Bardon's mission washed ashore.

Nander - Archonian Guard serving at Drunsberg. Captured by the Ruuk and taken to Wyke Wood. Not seen since Elodi took back the wood. Believed to have died while in captivity.

Ned - Workhorse on Toryn's family farm.

Neeve - Amayan warrior known for her skill with a spear. Joined Eryn before the battle of Roth's Doom. Last known Amayan to kill a warlock before the Age of Shadows.

Neverdor - Seat of Learning in the ward of Tamarand.

Noor - The middle ward of Harlyn.

Nordleng - Race living on the Nordruuk border. Skilled, but cruel fighters who take the gold of Ul-dalak to spread fear. Usually fight in small bands to raid farms and villagers. Rarely fight in open battle.

Nordruuk - Region north of the Five Realms. Consists of mainly frozen plains and mountains. Home to the Ruuk clans.

Nordryn - Bardon's controversial successor as Lord Broon.

Norgog - Squat troll-like creatures from north of the Draegelan Trench. Very difficult to kill owing to their thick skin. Hammer is their favored weapon. Carry torches of Cold Fire. Also known as Hammerskulls due to the shape of their heads.

North Forest - Forest in Ormsk known for the hardy trees used for shipbuilding. Was once a large forest joined with the South Forest. Chosen by the aralaks to build their nest.

Nym - Faery-like spirits from the ancient days. The Nym reside in either the mountains, rivers or woodlands.

Nyomae - Powerful Imaari. Discovered by Sylvena/Uluriel and taken to Elmarand in the last days of Draegelan. Studied the earliest known parts of the Song. Led the fated mission to locate Sylvena. Invoked the Verse of Unmaking at Gormadon. Lived as a nomad in the Age of Shadows before rescuing Toryn and recovering her memory to serve the Five Realms once more.

Odrun - Old Archonian Guard serving in Archonholm in his later years. Was one of the guards who arrested Toryn on his arrival at Archonholm. Died in the Caerwal Pass when the Ul-dalak raised the dead from the guards crushed by the Archon's betrayal at the gate.

Omstrad - Logging town on the edge of the South Forest in Ormsk. Successfully defended by the realms against a mass aralak attack.

Orlo - The name given to a horse loaned to Nyomae.

Ormoroth - The dark lord served by the Ul-dalak. Little is known of his origins but believed to have been a spirit corrupted by the Evil One and give form in the mortal lands.

Ormsk - The southern ward of Broon.

Orstrad - Logging town in the middle of the South Forest.

Palace Guard - Guards under the command of the Castellan in the Citadel at Archonholm. Responsible for the safety of the Archon.

Perdew - Member of Council of Harlyn.

Perran - Northern ward of Kernlow.

Perran Hills - Range of hills in the center of Perran, ward of Kernlow.

Piplo - The young Nyomae's pet cat.

Plains of Evermore – Archonian Guards taking the Oath at the start of their service are promised a farm in the other world if they die with their swords in their hands.

Porek - Archonian Guard killed at Drunsberg. He was the second oldest of three brothers from Tamworth in Darrow. See Dorek and Lorek.

Rand - Settlement in Lunn situation on the Great Northeast Road on the Lunn southern border.

Ravern Hills - Range of hills in Mund between the Foranfae Forest and the coast.

Reapers - Tall creature of the Underworld. Can be summoned only by those with great power to instill dread in their foes.

Rhydor - Old town on the coast of Perran. Once famed for its soldiers of the Phalanxes of Rhydor. But town fell into decline in the wars leading up to Gormadon.

River Kel - River running through Lunn to meet the sea at Keld. Formed the front when the Ruuk occupied Lunn under Nordryn.

River Mawl - Formed by the water from the Mawlgrim Mire. Runs into Mawl Bay in the north of Dorn.

River Tam - River from the Kolossos Mountains that flows through Darrow to Tamforth on the coast. Runs through Toryn's village of Midwyche.

River Wend - Flows from the Kolossos Mountains through the Wend Gap and Noor to the coast at Seransea.

Rockworm - Large worm-like creature from the old days. Origins are uncertain but exploited by Ormoroth to tunnel beneath the Kolossos Mountains. No longer thought to exist in the Five Realms.

Roold - Archonian Guard serving at Drunsberg. Captured and taken to Wyke Wood. Escaped and continued his service, fighting at Roth's Doom.

Roth's Doom - Deep crevasse in Ormsk close to the Kolossos Pass. Legends tell it was formed when Ormoroth tried to free the Evil One from the vaults beneath Caranach. But his giant axe shattered and injured Ormoroth. But few believe this to be true.

Ruan - Retired Archonian Guard chosen by Bardon to train and lead the renowned Broon Spearman. Went to the aid of Calerdorn and served in every major battle since. Instrumental in defeating the Ul-dalak's right flank at Roth's Doom.

Ruuk - The race living in Nordruuk. Consists of many clans who often are in conflict with each over. United by the Ul-dalak to form a formidable force to first mount raids in the Five Realms, and then head a full invasion.

Saphrir - City on the east coast of Emryst. Considered one of the most beautiful cities in the Seven Realms. Built with the wealth from the jewels mined in the region. Birthplace of Finromir, Toryn's father.

Sea Mist - Elodi's faithful horse.

Searith - Small fishing village on the coast of Tamarand. Birthplace of Mordram.

Seldric - Mason from Darrow who accompanied Muldrin to Archonholm. Assisted Elodi to discover what had happened to Muldrin who murdered three guards.

Seran River - River in Noor that is joined by the River Wend before meeting the sea at the port of Seransea.

Seransea - Ancient port, older than Calerdorn, in Noor. Elodi fled to the town when evacuating Calerdorn. Became new seat of the Council of Harlyn.

Shamuul - Warlock who led Ormoroth's armies in the wars against the Elorym.

Shelan - Scout who tracked Uldrak's army coming through the Dornan Mountains. Captured and beheaded on the Dorn Plain as Uleva and Uldrak led the second attack on Calerdorn. Also see Lightning.

Shepra - Sheep dog of a family killed by the Nordleng in Cafra. Joined Toryn and his company and saved him from an aralak at Borrund. Also accompanied Toryn to Roth's

Doom.

Shokresh - Warlock whose Kruul infiltrated Archonholm to possess the Castellan and tempted Elodi in the Great Hall. Fought alongside Ormoroth and sailed with his master to lands beyond the Karajan Sea.

Shreek - Creature from the old world. Three times the height of a man, their weapon is a dreadful shriek than can rip limb from limb. Can be brought through the Song to present day by a powerful Ul-dalak.

Shroul - Originally hardy people of the north who stood against Ormoroth. He punished them through torture, then turned them into bone-eating creatures who roam the frozen lands. A favored weapon of fear by the Ul-dalak.

Singing Stones - Also known as the Amanach. These stones were set by the Elorym to channel the power from the Amanspring, the river deep beneath the Kolossos.

Starwings - Large butterfly with delicate wings that glisten like stars at night. They live for just a few days in summer. Quite rare, preferring the shelter of old woodlands.

South Forest - Situated in Ormsk, known for its hardy wood used for shipbuilding. Location of an Amanach.

Sylvena - The Imaari who discovered Nyomae and brought her into the Order of Echoes. But she was Uluriel of the Ul-dalak, deceiving Nyomae and the Order. Returned to the north, leading the Order to believe she was lost. The mission to rescue her was ambushed, and the Seven Realms had no choice but to commit its full strength to meet the new threat. Following the defeat at Gormadon, Uluriel possessed Mordram and assumed the role of Archon.

Syris - Mysterious Elorym Lake Tower in the east of Mund. No mortal can enter. The Order of Echoes believe the Elorym raised them to channel the power beneath the land.

Talaghir - Also known as Talaghir Plain. A frozen region north of the Draegelan Trench in Nordruuk. The site of Ormoroth's last battle as Dorlan at the height of his powers. It was said Ormoroth invoked the Verse of

Unmaking in the face of defeat.

Talamaris - The Second Realm south of the Caerwal Mountains. Its name means Land of the Sun in the old tongue.

Tallabar - City within a wide, tall tower on the banks of the Vynmar in Emryst.

Tamarand - Western ward of Farrand. Known for its wheat and barley fields, rolling hills and rivers.

Tamforth - Small fishing port at the mouth of the River Tam in Darrow.

Telamir - Elorym Lake Tower standing east of the Kolossos Mountains in Emryst. Believed to have been built by the Elorym race to channel the powers beneath the land. The tower was visited by Draegelan and latterly Nyomae to solve the mystery of Aber's Verse.

Tempest - Horse of the rider, Lena. One of the fastest horses in Harlyn.

The Lost Realms - Name given to the two realms south of the Caerwal Mountains. Said to be 'lost' after the closing of the Caerwal Gate when the people to the north believed the south had been invaded by the Golesh.

Three Maidens - The daughters of the gods who came to the mortal lands believing their fathers had created a paradise for them. Disappointed to see the chaotic state of the land, the Maidens took it upon themselves to sing the Song of Creation. Deceived and tormented by the Evil One before the gods returned and imprisoned him. Ashamed by their defilement, the Maidens hid beneath the ice in the north.

Tombold - Retired Archonian Guard and friend of Hamar. Served as an aide to both Lord Harlyn and Elodi in Archonholm. The Castellan banished him from Archonholm on hearing he had spoken to Elodi about his doubts of the account of Lord Harlyn's death. Returned to his vineyard in Gwelayn.

Torm - Small settlement on the Keld Road and banks of the River Kel. Became of strategic importance when the Five Realms initially held the south bank of the Kel against the marauding Ruuk.

Toryn - Son of the Imaari, Finromir. Taken by his father to Midwyche when fleeing from the Ul-dalak. Brought up by Andryn and Miriam on the family farm. Headed north with Hamar when his family believed he would be persecuted as a wyke if he went to Archonholm and join the Archonian Guard.

Tunduska's Gorge - Deep ravine in the Dornan Mountains said to have been formed by the giant axe of Tunduska, the Old God of the North.

Ul-dalak - The servants of the Dark Verses.

Uldrak - Commander of the Ul-dalak. Took the Drunsberg Mines from the Five Realms. Later led the two attacks on Calerdorn, taking control of the city on the second strike with Uleva. He was once an Imaari - see Dormarl.

Uleva - Commander of the Ul-dalak. Resided in Wyke Wood, formerly known as Durran Wood, was also known as the Lady of the Wood. Took control over Dorlan (as Dohl), and kept him in his crippled state until the Ul-dalak were ready to unleash their forces against the Five Realms. Killed by Dorlan at the Battle of Roth's Doom.

Uluriel – Fell under the influence of Ormoroth overseas. Returned to the Seven Realms and took on the guise of Sylvena to be invested into the Order of Echoes. Quickly rose to become the head of the Order and deceive the Imaari into committing all their strength to save her, and thus divided the Seven Realms.

Umnavarek - A port on the east coast of Talamaris, the Second Realm.

Verse of Unmaking - Part of the Song that is the antithesis of the Maidens' Song of Creation. Believed to have been planted by the Evil One.

Vice-Archon - Woman who served under Mordram as Archon. Unaware he was under the influence of Uluriel, she became afraid of him and failed to question his authority. She jumped from the Caerwal Bridge to her death on learning of the Archon's treacherous act at the gate.

Vinlayn - Town at the center of Gwelayn, the wine-growing region of Kernlow.

Vordrak - Once an Elorym warrior captured and corrupted by Ormoroth. As a warlock, he fought in many battles in Draegelan's day, including Talaghir. In recent times, he captured and killed the Amayan, Amyra, in the tunnels beneath the Kolossos.

Vorkirik - Ormoroth's ice fortress in the far north. Built on the top of a hollowed mountain, its single tower stands taller than any other structure in the known world. From here, Ormoroth mined deep in the roots of the land and forged the Angorlith.

Vortimo - Ormoroth's mountain fortress in the south in the ward of Amman. Fashioned out of the mountains, Vortimo was considered impregnable until Draegelan led a large host to eventually wrest it from Ormoroth. Many died, and to this day, the spirits of the fallen are believed to haunt its halls.

Vymarl - Small settlement on the Great Northeast Road. Has the misfortune to be close to the cursed valley that leads to Vortimo. Both Toryn and Elodi took shelter in the village on their missions north.

Vynmar - River running the width of Emryst out the Karrock on the coast. Known as 'The Vynmar' it means *winding river* in the old tongue of the region.

Waldryn - Captain at the East Watchtower at the Kolossos Pass. Held out against an aralak attack to keep the pass open.

Warlock - Ormoroth's commanders. Once great Elorym warriors, they were captured and turned to the Dark Verses

Warrior - Fast and loyal horse ridden by Amyndra.

Watchers - Spirits who exist only in the Song. Believed to be a creation of Ormoroth to watch over those entering the Verses.

Wend Gap - Ravine running from Greendell to the Noor flats. Toryn and Hamar took the route on the way to

Greendell.

Wendel - Harlyn's Chief Advisor serving under both Lord Harlyn and Elodi. Saved the vital information on the secret entrance to Calerdorn when the city fell. Died onboard the Celestra at Seransea.

West Haven - Port in Tamarand at the mouth of the Menon River.

Wyke - The common term for the Imaari. In the Age of Shadows following the battle at Gormadon Plain, they were believed to be mischievous wizards and witches.

Wyke Wood - Also known as Durran Wood. Locals named it Wyke Wood after Uleva inhabited the woodlands and built a dark tower.

Made in the USA
Monee, IL
10 August 2024